G000075646

DUALITY

DUALITY

A Sean Colbeth Mystery

CHRISTOPHER H. JANSMANN

Ephram Cotte & Company, Publishing

Books by this Author

SEAN COLBETH INVESTIGATES

Blindsided

Outsider

Downhill

Duality

Bewitched

VASILY KORSOKOVACH INVESTIGATES

Pariah

Peril

Ditched

Bygones

Focus

Contents

For Paula:

Always and forever yours.

ISBN: 979-8-9858668-4-1 (Kindle Edition)
ISBN: 979-8-9858668-6-5 (Paperback)
ISBN: 979-8-9858668-5-8 (Hardcover)

Library of Congress Control Number: 2022921057

Printed in the United States of America

First Printing, 2022

One

"I t might be nothing."

"The very fact that you've reached out tells me you think it's *something*."

The Deputy Chief of Police for Rancho Linda, California, smiled slightly; had he not also been my best friend of nearly two decades, it would have been easy to have missed the subtle traces of stress on his otherwise youthful face. When I'd last seen him over the Christmas holidays little less than a month earlier, Vasily Korsokovach had looked far more at ease than the image I was now observing on my laptop. "I could never hide much from you, could I?"

"No," I agreed with a slight shake of my head. "A simple social welfare check doesn't require an interagency MOU," I added. "Who, *exactly*, is this Don Davies I'm going after?"

Whatever facade Vasily had been maintaining finally crumbled as he sighed loudly and wearily ran his hands through the wildly out-of-control mop of blond hair that was his current style. "I'm sorry," Vasily replied. "I'm juggling a few cases right now, and the stress is starting to get to me."

"It happens to the best of us," I said.

"Not to *you*," he pointed out. "In my decade by your side, I never saw you as anything but calm, cool and collected."

I smiled. "I just hid it better. And did double workouts at the pool to blow off some steam."

The crooked smile I always loved to see on my friend appeared, telling me I'd managed to break the tension for him — at least, for the moment. "I guess that was another habit I picked up from you, though it doesn't seem to be working this time around."

That made me frown. "This Davies person must be important?"

"Yeah," Vasily nodded. "I didn't realize that when his daughter, Gennifer, first reached out to our department." He looked away. "I don't get many missing person cases here in Rancho Linda, but when I do, normally the individual in question is a teenager skipping out on class or a senior that managed to evade security at the retirement home. Normal stuff, such as it is. But in this case, Davies isn't even a resident of Rancho Linda — or California, for that matter. I wasn't entirely sure what I could do for her."

"He's not?"

"No," Vas continued. "Turns out, he's *the* top-rated talk radio host in the South/Central Maine market."

I felt my eyebrows go up. "You know, his name *did* seem vaguely familiar. My tastes stray more to live sports, but I feel like I heard a promo for his show during a Red Sox game."

"You probably did," Vasily nodded. "Davies was syndicated nationally, but his home station was WWWD 1460AM in Portland. To make a long story short, he was supposed fly out this past Monday to spend a few weeks with his daughter and her kids. When he didn't turn up as planned, she called the airline and discovered he never boarded his flight in Portland."

"Wasn't Monday a holiday?" I asked, brow furrowing.

"Martin Luther King, Jr., day," Vasily nodded.

"No text? No phone calls?"

"No *nothing*. The last she heard from him was ten days ago, finalizing minor details of the trip. Flight numbers, arrival times and the like."

"And you think he's here in Windeport?"

Vasily nodded. "My ears are ringing with how much time I've spent on the phone with this woman. I deal with all sorts of personalities in this gig, but dude, she is the definition of a helicopter parent. I feel bad for her kids. Anyway, when I finally connected with the station manager in Portland, they told me Davies had signed off at the end of his Friday drive-time show with the intent to spend the weekend skiing up your way before flying to California on Monday. The station didn't realize he was missing because, well, he was technically not due to be back on the air until mid-February."

I rolled my eyes. "Of all the hills to choose. Snowden Notch isn't *exactly* the cream of the crop; he would have done better over to Sunday River or driving out to North Conway."

"True, except that his daughter says he owns a small cabin up there. Something he purchased thirty years ago when he first hit the big time, I guess." Vasily smiled tiredly. "You well know how true-blue Mainers never let anything go to waste. Even if it means an extra few hours in the car."

"So, drive he did," I nodded. "All right, text me the address and I'll head over now."

"Don't you want to sign the MOU first?" Vasily asked.

I glanced over my shoulder and out of the massive window behind my desk. "I've only got an hour of daylight left, maybe ninety minutes at most, so the paperwork can wait," I said. "Besides, I'm not certain you aren't sending me on a milk run. No reason for you to pay for my time if I'm just checking in on a citizen."

"I know it's an inconvenience—" Vasily started.

I waved at him and interrupted. "Nonsense. You're saving me from staring at my unforgiving budget for another few hours. I could use some time away from the desk."

"Are you sure?"

"Yes, and that's final," I smiled. "I'll call once I know this is just some sort of crossed wires between the daughter and father." I paused. "You're certain there isn't anything going on with them? Some sort of spat we don't know about?"

"Other than Davies potentially trying to get out of visiting his over-bearing daughter?" He shook his head. "None that I can detect, no."

"Okay. Talk to you in a bit."

Vasily nodded and looked a bit relieved. "I appreciate this, Sean. First round is on me when you come out for the convention."

I arched an eyebrow. "My rates are a bit more than that," I deadpanned.

"Are they?" Vasily laughed. "I hadn't noticed."

"The *hell* you hadn't," I replied as I waved and shut down the FaceTime session.

I stood from my desk and grabbed my heavy jacket from the coatrack and wondered if I should bring coffee with me; staring at my Keurig, I figured another cup could keep me warm on an otherwise chilly late January evening. It was helpful to ignore that it would probably be my eighth of the day, something that my girlfriend would likely have frowned upon. Dr. Suzanne Kellerman, M.D., assured me she had only my best interests in mind by recommending at the very least I switch to decaf after lunch; so far, I'd taken her suggestion under advisement, which was another way to say I'd blithely continued to feed my caffeine addiction well into the evening most days.

While I waited for the thermal mug to fill with the dark liquid, Vasily's text came in and I found myself frowning. Having lived in Windeport for most of my life, I knew just about every square mile, and that particular location was about as far from what passed for a ski resort in our county as you could get and still be within the village limits. Still, I supposed even a fifteen-minute drive would be little to pay if, as I suspected, this specific cottage had as nice a view of the ocean as it probably did. I was in the process of punching up the address on my map app just to confirm my inkling when I heard a gentle knock at my door.

"Sean?"

I turned with a smile to find Suzanne standing just inside my office; my smile grew wider when I watched her eyes drift to the steaming mug still sitting in the Keurig. "I was just thinking about you," I said.

"I'm sure you were," she replied, arching an eyebrow. "How many is that today?"

"I've lost count," I lied. "Would you like one?"

"No, thank you," she answered as she came over and gave me a quick kiss before backing away slightly. "Your heart rate is elevated," she clucked.

"Can you blame me?" I asked with a grin. "Whenever I see you, my pulse races."

Suzanne smiled slightly. "Is that so?"

"Most definitely."

I could tell Suzanne wasn't buying what I was selling, but she decided to let it go when her eyes caught my jacket slung over the back of one of my visitor chairs. "You look as though you're about to head out."

"I am," I nodded. "Doing a welfare check on someone — a special favor for Vasily, as a matter of fact."

"For Vas? Really?" she asked. "Wouldn't you have to fly to Rancho Linda for that?"

"As it turns out," I replied as I capped my mug and pulled the jacket from the chair, "the person in question is a Maine resident, ostensibly skiing up here in Windeport. His daughter is worried about him because he was *supposed* to be in California this week."

Suzanne frowned. "This has bad written all over it."

I shrugged. "Or not. Either way, it's a quick trip to check it out."

She frowned deeper. "I'll come with you," she said firmly. "I'm done for the day, anyway. I walked down from the office to see if you wanted to catch happy hour at Hotel Desrosier."

"I'd love to," I answered. "This won't take long. We'll be sipping fine wine before you know it."

Suzanne looked as though she wanted to say something, but thought better of it; instead, she looped her arm in mine as the two of us made our way out through the small cubicle farm that was my squad room. Between the budget cuts I'd been enduring for the past few years and the hour, the space was deserted, and felt all the more desolate with half of the lights turned out. We found Caitlyn Romero in her usual spot, seated behind the semi-circular intake desk that served as the nerve center for my department.

"Heading out early, Chief?" she asked with a smile.

"Despite appearances, not entirely," I laughed. "Vasily of all people has sent me on what I think will be a wild goose chase. But after *that*, I'm off for the night."

"Good," Caitlyn replied before looking to Suzanne. "He works too much."

"I know," she sighed. "Sean is a work in progress."

"I am?"

"You are. Come on, my wine is waiting."

The snow crunched under our boots as we crossed the parking lot to my departmental SUV, reminding me that we were still in the thick of the winter season. Part of me was a tad jealous of the mild weather Vasily was experiencing out in California, making me look forward all the more to our trip in a few weeks. Thinking about warmer weather made me also consider my father, now living out his retirement along the West Coast of Florida. We'd had something of a family break-through during the holidays, a slight melting of the icy détente that had lingered since he'd booted me from the apartment over the pharmacy. I spoke to him at least twice a week now, a small step in a much longer process that might finally restore our formally close relationship. Everything had fractured after the death of my mother, with recriminations and lingering anger still a palpable undercurrent between us. I knew there was much hurt to be dealt with, but I took solace in the fact I was at least able to hear his warm baritone every now and again. For now, it would have to be enough.

Pulling out onto Main Street, I handed Suzanne my phone. "I'm reasonably sure I know where this is, but just in case, you can be my navigator."

"All right," she said. "How far out is this?"

"It's at the very edge of town," I replied as we moved through the light traffic. We were about a week away from another cruise ship docking, and I found myself relishing the relative quiet between tourist invasions. "You remember that case with the murdered developer last year?"

"Brad Donohue? How could I forget?"

I nodded. I'd caught the case the summer Vasily had been recuperating with us from his near-death experience in California; worried at how slow he'd been to regain his sense of self, I'd made an ill-advised attempt to use the case as a way to draw him back into his life as an investigator long before he'd been ready. It had led to hard feelings and his second abrupt departure from Maine. After months of not talking, my cousin had wisely plied me with large quantities of alcohol before ganging up with Suzanne to insist I invite him for Christmas. To my surprise, he'd accepted, and we'd managed to finally patch up nearly a years' worth of angst in the process. I still missed seeing my friend every day, but we talked with enough regularity that the ache of his absence had significantly receded.

"Donohue had a smaller development at the north end of Windeport, running right along the shoreline," I explained. "It was one of his first forays into real estate and nominally successful. This address is within that little grouping."

"Small world," Suzanne observed.

"Small *village*," I chuckled. "Unlike my little bungalow, if memory serves most of the places up there are very petite cottages. Mostly one- or two-bedroom."

"Vacation-oriented, then?"

"Probably," I agreed as we passed Calista's Bakery and the spires of St. Catherine's-By-The-Sea.

Coming around the curve, the lighted sign for the Colonial appeared in the distance; I'd not had the occasion to go up to the grand hotel in the month since we'd dined there with Vasily and his significant other, Alejandro. While the food was certainly good, the tourist-level prices left quite a bit to be desired, leading Suzanne and I to favor the more wallet-friendly *Millie's On the Wharf* whenever either of us didn't feel motivated to cook. Passing the sign put us into an area of Windeport where the single-family homes gave way to large farms and wide fields; a few miles further, and the forest crowded in along the road, the dense trunks of white pine making it nearly impossible to see any hint of the coastline we were roughly paralleling.

"If I am reading this right, your turn is coming up," Suzanne warned me.

I nodded, spying the small gash in the forest that represented where a side road had been carved out. Slowing, I turned onto the petite lane and found the forest thick enough at that point we'd been plunged into semi-darkness — enough that the automatic headlights on my SUV popped on, the light dancing across the ice crystals of the snow along the road. It took a moment for me to appreciate the road had been plowed, for it was not a village-maintained one; I wondered if each of the small homes we passed had to chip in something toward keeping the road clear.

As was custom in that part of the state, each cottage had a small street number posted on a wooden sign beside the even smaller drive-way leading away from the main drag; none were plowed, though, forcing me to reevaluate who might have paid for the service. In the end, I didn't need to hear Siri announce we were getting close, for the plowed road ended just a few feet beyond the only open driveway we'd come across; slowing, I turned in and drove a few hundred yards further before we entered a clearing that revealed the vacation hideaway Don Davies had apparently retreated to.

Cottage appeared to be a misnomer, for the whitewashed clapboard sheathed two-story structure in front of us was closer to a mid-sized home than a cozy spot along the shore. Lights were on behind traditional multi-paned windows along the first floor, though the interior appeared to be hidden behind a diffusing curtain; squinting, I was reasonably sure a light was on in a room on the second floor, too. A dark brown Lexus was parked beside the stone steps that led up to a small porch and the stately front door beyond; a browning Christmas wreath hung upon it, a reminder that the season had been long over. Most remarkable, though, was the unobstructed view of Windeport harbor, a clear indicator that the plot had been purchased prior to current zoning ordinances preventing such clearcutting along the shoreline.

"Wow," was all I could think to say. "I guess I've not been up this far in a while."

"Some place," Suzanne said appreciably. "Who is this person? They must be loaded."

"A very successful talk radio host based in Portland," I said as I put the SUV into park. "Clearly the salaries are better than public service."

"Or he was a smart investor," she countered.

"That too." My finger hovered over the on/off button for the SUV. "I'm sorry to drag you all the way out here. This won't take long; you want me to keep it running?"

"Yes, thanks."

I leaned over and kissed her, then quickly slipped out of the driver's side of the SUV. The cold of the late afternoon made my breath billow as I walked over to the Lexus and peered as best as I could through the frost-encrusted windows. That made me pause, for the layer of ice on the windshield alone spoke to the vehicle not having been used in a good long while. Bracing my hand on the hood, I knelt beside the front wheel and nodded, for the slight ridge of ice along the tire confirmed the car had been parked in one spot long enough that the daytime melting from the sun was refreezing around the rubber each night. Standing, I felt the first vestiges of unease beginning in the back of my brain.

Vasily said he was supposed to be in California Monday, I thought. *It's now Wednesday. If he was supposed to get here late Friday... could that be five days of ice? Damn! I should have pulled his vehicle registration before I came up...*

Suzanne had apparently seen me pausing and popped out of the SUV. "What's wrong?"

"I'm not sure," I replied as I moved toward the steps. "Stay in the truck, if you don't mind."

"Okay," she said.

The passenger door to the SUV clunked shut as I made my way to the front door; that unease bloomed into full-on concern when I saw the front door was ajar, allowing a tiny spill of light to cascade across the shoveled porch. As I grew closer, I could feel a slight wisp of warm air as it escaped from the interior. Not one to be overly dramatic, I nonetheless found myself placing a hand on my service weapon at my hip before I knocked three times against the wood of the door frame.

"Mister Davies? Windeport Police. Are you in need of assistance?"

I paused for a moment, listening intently for anything and only hearing the occasional crash of the waves on the shoreline below the home. Waiting a moment longer, I tried again.

"Mister Davies? Your daughter asked us to check on you when you didn't return her calls. Are you okay?"

The silence lingered, laden, I feared, with secrets I was only then beginning to realize would need to be unearthed. Pulling the screen door with my free hand, I pulled my Glock out with the other and held it low, then leaned my shoulder into the open door to gently push it open. As expensive as it looked, it was equally as well balanced and easily swung into the small hallway just off the entrance. Bringing my gun up, I scanned the space, taking in the staircase along one wall leading to the second floor, and the doorway at the end; turning, I could see there was some sort of dining room area to the right, and a library/study room to the left with several bookcases full of hardcovers along one wall. Both had lights on and neither appeared to be holding Don Davies.

Slowly, I called out again as I moved down the hallway; a small kitchen turned out to be at the end, and there I found the first evidence that Davies might have been living there. A pot of coffee, long cold, sat beside a plate of white china, upon which was a very moldy sunny-side-up pair of eggs, a mound of moldy breakfast potatoes, and two slices of bacon; a smaller plate of wheat toast sat beside it, the green of the penicillin made it hard to tell whether butter or some sort of jam had been spread across the grain. The small pan the eggs had been fried in was sitting inside a country sink, along with several other cooking implements; a quick check of the cabinets and fridge proved there were enough provisions to last at least a week.

Backing up, I slowly made my way toward the staircase, and then up, calling for Davies as I moved; the higher I went, though, the less hopeful I was becoming that there would be a positive ending to my wellness check. At first glance, there appeared to be four rooms on the second floor; one had its door slightly ajar, and the light on. Pushing it open a bit more, I could see it was a small bathroom with a walk-in shower; a towel had been placed over the clear door, and a quick sniff brought with it the sense that it had been hung wet some days earlier. Returning to the landing, I eyed the three remaining doors and wondered: did I really have a one-in-three chance of determining the fate of the successful radio personality?

I randomly chose the door to a room that presumably overlooked the shoreline first; pushing it open allowed the eye-watering stench of decomposition to hit me full-force, and I nearly stumbled backwards as I pressed a gloved hand to my mouth and nose. Eyes watering, I steeled myself and moved into the space, idly noting that my luck with Powerball tickets wasn't nearly as good.

The room ran the length of the back of the home, with tall windows providing unparalleled views of the ocean; a small door to one side gave access to a second-floor patio, which in good weather likely housed chairs and tables, and maybe even a telescope. A long couch and two small recliners filled the space, all facing a massive flatscreen television that was tuned to some sort of round-the-clock news channel; I'd not noticed it earlier, for it appeared to be muted. There was a tablet face down beside the recliner that held the remains of Don Davies; at least, I assumed it was him, for I'd not thought to pull his driver's license photo before heading up, either.

An eye-popping amount of blood had pooled beneath the recliner, turning the dark color it often did when it had been exposed to air for a significant period. Gingerly stepping closer, my eyes scanned the corpse until I caught the gashes on one wrist as it hung over the armrest. It only took a moment longer to locate the old-fashioned razor blade that had been dropped to the hardwood floor, stained with use.

Well, shit.

Kneeling next to the tablet, I fished a pen out of my pocket and gently turned it over; the large screen had the telltale spiderwebbing where it had cracked when it had fallen, but the screen still lit up when I tapped the home button with the pen. The white background of a word processing app appeared, displaying just a single line of black text.

I'm sorry. Please forgive me.

Sitting back on my haunches, I sighed deeply before retrieving my iPhone. *So much for happy hour,* I thought as I dialed my friend.

"Hey," Vasily answered brightly. "That was fast."

"We're all about customer service here in Windeport," I said, trying for humor but not feeling it. "It seems I have bad news and worse news," I continued. "Which would you like first?"

"Better give me the bad news," he replied.

"I... found Don Davies," I said.

"You did? That's not necessarily *bad* news," Vasily said. "What's the worse news?"

"Davies will definitely not be seeing his grandchildren anytime soon."

There was a long pause from the other end of the line. "Oh... *fuck,*" he finally said.

"I couldn't agree more."

Two

Ever the trooper, Suzanne insisted on hanging around instead of allowing me to drive her back to town so she could still catch some part of happy hour. Quite honestly, I was glad for the company while I made the usual calls to get the ball rolling. While it appeared to be a case of suicide, I'd done the job long enough to know it was important to go by the book; in less than six minutes after my first call, the EMTs had arrived and officially pronounced Don Davies dead; in twenty, my two officers were combing the exterior of the house for anything that might look like a clue, while I began a more thorough perusal of the interior. I'd barely made it through the second row of books in the small library by the time the recognizable shape of the Medical Examiner's van rumbled into view beside my SUV, followed closely by two sedans carrying the crime scene nerds.

I met Heather Graham on the front porch. "Sorry to haul you all the way to the coast on a weeknight," I said as I shook her hand. "I've already made arrangements for you and your crew to be our guests overnight at Hotel Desrosier."

"No problem at all," she smiled as she followed me in. "Especially if it means we can still get lobster rolls at *Millie's on the Wharf*."

"I have it on good authority they have plenty on hand."

"Good." She quickly scanned the space much as I had initially and nodded to herself before turning back to me. "Depending on what we have here, one of us might have to run the body back to the morgue."

"I can call in another favor at UEM," I replied, referring to how that past December, we'd been forced to borrow a deep freezer at the university just outside of Windeport to temporarily store a murder victim.

"Lou would prefer that we not send another human popsicle to her exam table," Heather reminded me. "And you don't want to get on the bad side of the Chief Medical Examiner for the state, now do you?"

"Probably not," I nodded.

"What have you got?"

"Dead body up on the second floor," I replied, inclining my head toward the staircase. "Seems to have been the only person here. Dr. Kellerman is up there now; she's been making some preliminary observations that we'll pass on to the M.E. Aside from the EMTs, no one has touched anything."

"All right," she nodded.

"I've started poking through the items in what appears to be a library; I'd like the entire house gone over, please. Photos, fingerprints, the whole deal."

Heather arched an eyebrow. "Is this a suspicious death?"

"I just want to cover my bases," I hedged. "The victim appears to be Don Davies."

Her eyes widened. "Oh, *shit*."

"I've been hearing that a lot today," I smiled slightly.

"What is it with you and high-profile deaths?"

"I have no idea," I sighed. "Believe me, I'm not looking forward to my next conversation with the Chair of the Village Council. Honestly, I'm just a simple police chief; I'd prefer to be handing out traffic tickets to our lovely tourists."

"I'll bet. Okay, standard package then; hand off whatever you've found in the library to my techs, and we'll take it from here. I saw Lydia and Mark going over the grounds outside."

"They'll stick around and assist your team," I said. "And other than the victim's apparent fascination with the American Civil War, there wasn't much in the library."

Heather smiled slightly. "We'll go through it again all the same."

"Sounds good. Come on, I'll take you to the body."

Heather picked up her bag and followed me up to the second floor; we found Suzanne bending over the body, her half-moon cheaters propped on the bridge of her nose. She looked up as we entered. "Come take a look at this," she said without preamble.

"Hello to you too, Suzanne," Heather chuckled as we walked over.

"Sorry," Suzanne replied sheepishly. "That came out as more of an order than I'd intended. Good to see you again, Heather."

"Same," the lead crime scene tech replied. "What did you find?"

Pointing to the side of the recliner Davies was still sitting in, Suzanne asked: "Does this look sticky to you?"

Heather put her bag down and unzipped it, then pulled out a small magnifying lens that had a built-in light. Snapping on the device, she leaned down and peered through the glass. "Maybe," she replied.

"And how about here?" Suzanne asked, pointing to a spot on what looked like a relatively expensive brown cardigan.

Heather moved to the second spot, then carefully followed a linear path across the chest of Davies and over to the other side of the chair. "Maybe," she murmured as she stood slightly, moved around to the rear of the seat, then began examining the back. After a moment, she beckoned us toward her. "Not bad Suzanne," she said appreciably as she stood back but held the light over a spot about three-quarters of the way up the back. "Take a look."

I leaned down and had to squint, but I thought I could see a slight speckle of silver. Moving out of the way for Suzanne to take a look, I turned to Heather. "Tape?" I guessed.

"I'll take it back to the lab to confirm," she nodded, "but I believe so." She pointed to the spot. "The angle would be consistent with restraining the victim just above the elbow; I'll test the rest of the chair for residual adhesive, but it's a solid bet there will be more."

I moved back to the front of the recliner, somewhat amazed that I'd gotten used to the odor of decomposition, and tried to visualize one or more strips of something essentially like duct tape fastening the victim to the leather of the chair. Davies appeared to have lived well, as suggested by the healthy roll of fat around his abdomen; it wouldn't have taken much to lash him down and allow his own girth to work against him. Eyeing the trail of blood from the one exposed wrist, I tried to visualize a different explanation for how the radio host might have died and frowned.

"So much for suicide," I said, looking to Heather.

"We'll treat it as suspicious for now," she nodded. "Once we get everything back to the lab, I'll have the team go over the body with a fine-tooth comb for trace to confirm our theory."

"I guess someone will be making the drive back to Augusta," I sighed. "Sorry."

"All part of the job," she smiled. "Frank won't mind, actually. He's got a new dog and wanted to get back home tonight anyway."

"All right," I nodded. "I'll be at the station for a bit getting the paperwork started. Touch base before you quit for the night?"

"Will do," Heather nodded. "Suzanne."

"Heather."

Suzanne followed me out of the room and down the steps. "I take it happy hour is out?" she asked, a tiny note of teasing in her voice.

"Maybe at the hotel," I replied as we reached the foyer. "Doesn't mean we can't celebrate your catch with our own toast at home this evening."

"I don't quite know how I saw it," she said as we exited the house and paused on the porch. "The light from the lamp hit something just right as I was circling the chair."

"That's kind of how it works," I shrugged as I pulled off my exam gloves and watched as she did the same. "You just keep looking and looking until something suddenly pops out at you." As we stepped down toward the SUV, I paused. "What do you make of the body?"

Suzanne looked at me for a moment. "I don't want to get ahead of Heather or the Medical Examiner," she hedged. "Or prejudice your view of this in any way."

"I appreciate that," I smiled slightly. "But I'm a grown-up police officer and can make my own judgement calls. Tell me your thoughts."

My girlfriend sighed. "I'll allow that, from all appearances, it looks like suicide, but a few things trouble me. I've never dealt with one in my practice, but have read about them in the literature; usually people driven to something this extreme have some sort of underlying psychological issues that have been simmering for a while and finally come to a head. But you said there was breakfast in the kitchen, right?"

"Yes."

She shook her head. "That seems odd to me that he'd have gone to the trouble of making a meal, then carefully went upstairs to kill himself."

"I thought the same thing."

"The sticky substance stands out, too, but..." she paused, and I could see she was thinking through what to say. "Did you notice the watch?"

"No," I replied after a moment of thought. "I didn't think he was wearing one."

"He wasn't," she nodded. "It was on the side table by the remote."

I looked at her. "I'm not sure what you're getting at."

"The table was on the *left*," she replied. "I think he was left-handed; most people favor the side closest to their dominant hand. I know I do."

I felt myself start. "The slashed wrist was the left one, wasn't it?"

"Yes. And the gashes were clean cuts, done with a quick stroke."

"Is that possible from a non-dominant hand?" I asked, starting to see where she was going.

"Only if he was ambidextrous. And only," she added a bit quieter, "if he were similarly well versed in biology. Those cuts were designed to maximize the... bleeding."

"Yeah," I sighed as we continued to the SUV and got inside. "That was my first impression, actually."

Suzanne put her hand on my arm. "I don't think he committed suicide," she said softly.

"I don't either," I nodded. "I'm afraid it's going to be a long night, my love."

"I figured. But we're still having cocktails."

"Absolutely. I'll have to speak with his daughter; Vasily was going to do the initial outreach for me." I sighed again as I backed up slightly and then drove down the driveway to the small road. "I'm not looking forward to the call, though."

"What are you going to tell her?" Suzanne asked.

"What I can," I replied. "Other than her father being dead, not much else at this point."

"She'll be looking for answers."

"I'm sure."

The drive out of the forest and back to Route One was quiet; I knew I was processing what I had seen at the house, and presumed Suzanne was doing something similar. The darkness of night always seemed to be oppressive at that part of the season, compounding the feeling of despair that I always dealt with when a life had been extinguished on my watch. There had been far too many of them as of late in Windeport, a data point I knew my boss on the Village Council would likely be quick to point out to me. I was well aware that such things were not always preventable, no matter how competent the public safety department might have been, but explaining that to the Council as a whole had always been problematic. They were of the opinion I could somehow erect a magic wall around our fair village, one that could prevent any and all woes of modern society from entering; it was a foolish, unrealistic desire, but one I continually had to deal with.

As I turned back onto Route One, Suzanne broke the silence. "I think I'll have you drop me back at the apartment, if you don't mind," she said, referring to the old building that had housed both the pharmacy my family had run for generations and the apartment above it I had once shared with Vasily. Suzanne had become the new owner the prior year and built out a sizable medical practice instead. "If you want to stay there tonight instead of the bungalow, I'll take some of Charlie's chili out of the freezer and warm it up. I might have one of those cornbread mixes to add to the kitty."

"That sounds like a wonderful plan," I replied. "I don't know how late I will be, though."

"Then I'll bring the chili over to you."

"You don't have to do that," I said.

"Nonsense. It's just down the block, anyway."

"I won't say no," I chuckled. "Thanks."

"You never think of yourself," she reminded me. "At least one of us does."

"True, that," I laughed harder.

A few minutes later, I'd left her with a goodbye kiss and continued onward to my parking space at the front of the monument to Brutalist architecture that was the Public Safety Building. The small lot was pretty much empty, a testament that just about everyone I had was either out on their nightly patrol route or up to the Davies' house assisting the State Crime Lab techs with their search. As I entered the reception foyer, I was somewhat thankful we were in that lull between cruise ships and could devote some extra attention to the early stages of the case. I wasn't entirely sure what else they might find that would help explain the circumstances of the death, but I didn't rule out a surprise or two, either.

My night operator, Emily Wilson, had taken up position at the semi-circular desk and waved at me as I passed on my way to the security door barring access to the bullpen; the fact she had replaced Caitlyn brought home how late it had become, and did nothing to improve my gloomy mood at how many hours of work I still had ahead of me that evening. The cubicle farm was empty, the lights still only half on, exactly as I had left the space some hours earlier; I made a beeline for my office and prospect of a caffeine hit to get through what had to be done.

I wisely put my steaming mug of coffee just off to the side of my laptop when I finally settled in at my desk to call Vasily; with the time change, I knew it was likely to be outside of his normal shift and smiled slightly to see the framed artwork of the Disneyland Castle over his shoulder in confirmation. "Am I catching you at a bad time?" I asked. "I don't want to interrupt anything you have planned with Alejandro."

"No," he replied, shaking his head. "Alex has practice tonight, so I was catching up on my other cases. What's the latest?"

"Things have become complicated," I said before quickly sketching in the details of what we had found once Heather had arrived. He asked a few clarifying questions here and there, but otherwise mostly nodded as I spoke. "So," I finished up, "it looks pretty much like you handed me a murder. One that I'm not sure my MOU template was designed to cover."

Vasily smiled slightly sheepishly. "I'm sorry this has happened, but I can't imagine it landing in better hands. If you need any help, I'm happy to fly out."

"I appreciate that," I said. "And I'll keep it on the back burner. Let's see how this develops — that'll help me decide when it's time to call in the calvary."

"Sounds good."

"Can you tell me any more about the daughter and her relationship?"

"Not really," he replied, then smiled sheepishly again. "You'll be able to ask her yourself, though. She's booked the first flight she could to Boston and expects to be in Windeport by the end of the day tomorrow."

"Thanks for the warning," I sighed. "That's the last thing I need — a concerned family member under foot."

"Better you than me," he smiled. "I was seriously beginning to lose my cool with her."

"I might yet drag you here," I warned.

"Don't make promises you won't keep," he chuckled. "Let me know how it goes."

"Will do."

The image of my friend faded from the laptop's screen, allowing me to groan — loudly — at the kettle of fish I now seemed to be floundering around in. Being forewarned that Gennifer Davies-Benson was inbound would lessen the shock value of her appearance at the station, but I wasn't wrong in worrying about her hovering around the periphery of the investigation. Sighing again, I swapped screens and created a new case file in our system then began to fill in the details of what had transpired so far. It was sufficiently mindless work transcribing the notes I had made on my phone over the past several hours that it took Suzanne sliding the steaming bowl of chili across my massive desk for me to realize she had entered my office.

Looking up at her bemused expression, I glanced at the clock and then immediately apologized. "Damn. Time got away from me again."

She leaned across my desk and I rose to meet her for a kiss. "I know," she replied. "I hope it's still warm."

"Smells like it," I nodded as I accepted the spoon from her and took a small sample from the bowl. The spice of the seasoning had the usual punch to it that only my cousin could add, partially gentled by the flavorful ground beef. Closing my eyes in appreciation, I sighed. "I'm not sure I ever had lunch."

"That's quite the admission from an athlete," Suzanne chuckled as she settled in on one of my visitor chairs and munched on what looked like a cupcake. "Shouldn't you be eating regular amounts of calories?"

"I should," I nodded. "This has been a bad day for sticking to my schedule."

"Happens to the best of us." She leaned down and pulled a bottle of red wine from the handbag at her feet. "Are you allowed to drink in your office?"

"Probably not," I said, "but I have it on good authority the guy in charge will look the other way just this once."

"Good."

I slid my bowl to the other side of the desk and came around the behemoth piece of furniture that was a carryover from a time long forgotten, then sat in the visitor chair opposite my girlfriend. I wasn't the least bit surprised she had brought two wineglasses and had pre-opened the bottle; setting the glassware on my desk, Suzanne expertly decanted two servings before handing me one.

"To unexpected deaths," she said softly. "May it never happen to anyone else."

I clinked my glass to hers. "Hear, hear."

I had less than a moment to savor the flavor of the wine before my iPhone sang out; putting down the wineglass, I moved back to the other side of my desk and saw it was Heather. I tapped the button to answer. "Heather, what's the good word?"

"We're wrapping up for tonight but will want to be here again tomorrow," she said. "Often we can pick up more details in the light of day. I don't expect to be here past lunch though, so don't worry about accommodations for tomorrow."

"All right. Can you give me the rundown?"

"Yes and no," she replied. "We've uploaded what we'd done so far to the State system, and it should be available to your database a bit later this evening. I'll also swing by with what we've bagged and tagged so you can put it into the evidence locker before I turn in for the night. If it's possible, though, I'd prefer to walk through the scene with you tomorrow morning. Say, about ten?"

"Sure," I replied, frowning. "Can you at least give me a hint as to time of death?"

"Only a ballpark," she replied. "Maybe a week? Ten days? I'm not sure I can be more specific based on the tools I have access to; you might get more at the PM, but honestly, at this point anything would be an educated guess."

Thinking about the moldy eggs, I found myself asking: "Can you narrow it down with that breakfast we found in the kitchen? It feels to me like the victim might have been in the middle of preparing it when whatever went down, went down."

Heather smiled at me. "Maybe? Fungi aren't my specialty, though, so I'll have to take a sample back to the lab."

"Makes me wish I'd paid more attention in college," I smiled. "Well, you've given me a window to work with at least. And one that sort of aligns with when the victim went missing."

"If it helps, the morgue van has already left for Augusta; I spoke with Lou, though, and the earliest she could do the postmortem is late tomorrow afternoon. I assumed you'd want to be there; the scheduling office will call with something more definitive in the morning."

"I appreciate that — and thanks for working so late."

"Don't thank me," she laughed. "Thank the taxpayers of the State of Maine. I'm in golden overtime thanks to this case."

"Ouch," I replied. "I'm glad you don't back charge small, broke departments such as mine for your services."

"Don't think we've not talked about it," she chuckled. "I'm off to bed. See you in the morning."

Three

The massive aquatics center on campus at the University of Eastern Maine had long been a sanctuary for me, dating back to when my age had been measured in single digits and I was just getting used to wearing a Speedo. While the space had undergone some significant renovations over the years, the basics had pretty much remained the same with a twenty-five yard by fifty-meter pool[1] on one side and a twenty-five meter by twenty-five meter square diving well that doubled as the practice space for the water polo team on the other. As with most weekday mornings, both spaces were busy at the eye-popping hour of five A.M., filled comfortably with a combination of older swimmers who may had once competed in the sport (or in my case, *still* were), and others simply enjoying a different kind of whole-body workout. The coach for the Masters Swimming group I belonged to had been there long enough to easily handle the disparate levels of ability and assign workouts accordingly; since I was a former Olympian, he often set aside a special lane for me and anyone else who cared to experience the appropriately grueling workout that came with the privilege.

That morning I had the lane to myself, which turned out to be a godsend, for I knew I would be swimming well above my normal pace. After dinner with Suzanne, I'd stayed at the station until close to two, carefully logging the mass of items Heather had dropped off from the Davies house before storing them away to review in more detail later. It had been quite the cornucopia, ranging from the rather sizable designer suitcase Davies had been living out of to the moldy food from the kitchen that I'd had to squeeze into the small evidence fridge. A ton of fingerprints had been collected as well, but those I'd left with my overnight operator to process against the national databases we had access to. It felt like I had barely cuddled in next to Suzanne in her comfy oversized bed before my alarm had quietly sounded; for a long moment, I'd contemplated skipping practice, but I also knew the physical activity would center me, providing a counterpoint to what I knew would be another long, trying day.

As I suspected, it took the first third of the workout for me to get into the zone, but when I did, I focused on my technique and the slow, deliberate breathing that came with it. There were times when I could check out from the workout and let my brain churn through something else, but that particular morning, it felt like a better tactic to simply give myself over to the physical exertion. Once I did and managed to achieve that peculiar Zen watching the tiles slide by below you can bring, I lost complete track of time and had to be pulled out of the water by the coach so the pool cool be reset for the college team due to practice directly after us.

One shower, shave and change of clothes later, I was back in the department SUV and on my way to breakfast at Calista's Bakery, my usual after practice hangout. Most mornings for nearly fifteen years, Vasily and I had cornered a small table in one of the French windows facing Route One; in the year since he had left, Suzanne had become my intermittent dining companion, her attendance dependent on how early her day had to start at her medical practice or whether it was her week to be on duty down at Maine Medical. As I pulled into the small and nearly full parking lot beside the red brick of the bakery building, I could see Suzanne's form in our usual spot, and waved at her as I stepped out of my vehicle.

The warmth of the bakery as I entered was welcome against the chill of the early morning, and the air was fragrant with the scent of fresh bread baking in the brick ovens at the rear of the space. I made my way through the crowd lined up even at that hour for the various tasty delicacies on offer that day in the glass display case and pulled out the chair across from my girlfriend.

"Hey," I smiled as I sat down and then leaned across the small two-top table for a kiss.

"How was practice?"

"Better than I expected, given how little sleep I got last night."

Suzanne smiled impishly. "And this time, it wasn't my fault."

"No," I nodded. "Though I wouldn't have minded."

"I'll keep that in mind."

"Did you already order?"

"Just coffee," she replied.

My eyes fell upon the small ceramic mug sitting between her hands, the tiny wisps of steam curling up and away from the surface of the hot liquid. "Always a good start to the morning, that."

I didn't need to look up to see the arched eyebrow from my girlfriend. "As long as it's done in moderation, naturally."

"Naturally," I nodded.

Running her finger along the rim, Suzanne eyed me closely. "How many cups did you have yesterday?"

Unused to getting interrogated, I shifted a bit uneasily in my chair. "A couple?" I replied.

Her eyes narrowed. "Give me a number. Two? Five?"

I felt my face heat up slightly and couldn't help but glance out the window, a clear tell.

"Dear Lord. Was it more than *eight*?"

"In my defense, it was a very long day," I said, turning back to Suzanne.

Shaking her head sadly, she taunted me slightly by taking a sip of her steaming beverage. "You're *beyond* addicted, my love," she sighed. "We're going to have to figure out a way to get you down to safer levels of caffeine."

The waitress chose that inopportune moment to arrive and plunk down my own mug — and a thermal carafe alongside it; I was a frequent enough visitor to the bakery that the staff were well aware of my love for the organic suspension and were unwittingly enabling me. I smiled sheepishly as I gingerly took a sip from my mug. What could I say? She'd caught me red handed, as it were. "Is that strictly necessary?" I asked.

"Yes," she replied firmly. "I'll come up with a plan and we'll talk it over."

"Yes, Doctor," I sighed.

Wondering if the good times were coming to an end, I opted for the short stack of chocolate pancakes with a side of sausage, eliciting a second arched eyebrow from Suzanne; fortunately, given my athletic predilections, my other numbers were well within the normal ranges across the board. Almost as a counterpoint, she selected the egg white omelet and bowl of fresh fruit; when the orders finally arrived, it looked like we were in open warfare with conflicting aspects of the food pyramid squaring off across the small table. I waited until she had eaten a bit of her dish before changing our topic.

"That was quite a catch yesterday at the house."

"Total accident," she replied, waving her fork in the air. "My phone had beeped with a message from my service, and I'd crossed to the nearest light to read it. That happened to also be the perfect angle to see the remnants of what the tape had left behind when it was peeled away."

"I imagine the fabric of the cardigan made it difficult to get it off cleanly."

"Agreed. Or the tape was on the cheap end of the scale. I had some truly awful stuff I picked up once at the dollar store; it sure is true when they say you get what you pay for."

"You had enough time to look at those wounds," I said, lowering my voice slightly. Talking about murder in a busy breakfast joint wasn't exactly the most polite thing to do. "I know what you said last night about not wanting to get ahead of the medical examiner, but what is your first impression? Medically speaking."

Suzanne chewed thoughtfully on a pineapple she'd speared from the dish. "It's funny you should ask. I thought about it more last night while you were finishing up at the station. I'm still inclined to think your victim didn't do it, at least, not without help. And the angle is nearly *perfect*," she added very quietly — almost as a whisper. "Almost as if someone had done research into what would lead to the speediest way to get to the finish line. So to speak."

"Is that all that unusual, in this age of the interwebs?" I asked equally as softly. "There are videos about cooking paella; maybe there's something... equivalent... for folks looking to exit this mortal coil prematurely."

Suzanne smiled. "How do you know about *paella*?"

"I did some digging around on that Google thing after Alejandro confessed his mother's recipe for enchiladas actually came from some celebrity chef. I had no idea people were willing to share almost any kind of recipe."

My girlfriend slowly shook her head in amazement. "How can you be such a premier investigator and not know about such things?"

I shrugged. "If it's never come up in a case, a class, or a competition, it's outside of my scope. Simple as that."

Suzanne chuckled as she reached across to my hand to pat it affectionately. "My poor, poor sheltered soul. We're going to have to take a tour of everything the internet can provide. Thank God you know about Netflix."

"I blame that on Vasily."

"Undoubtedly. Did you say the postmortem is this afternoon?"

"Yes," I nodded as I finished my last piece of bacon. "I might be late for our makeup happy hour."

"I might be, too," she replied. "One of my regular medical device sales agents emailed me last night; she's in the area and wants to talk about the latest in automated blood pressure cuffs. I'm booked solid to five, so that's the soonest I can fit her in."

"Sounds less than exciting."

"You have no idea. Especially since I just bought a bunch of last year's model when I opened my doors. Not likely I'm gonna need anything new for a bit."

As I looked at my girlfriend, I noticed for the first time the subtle hint of gray that had appeared in her otherwise raven hair, and the tiny set of worry lines around her eyes. Being the sole physician for practically the entire county was weighing on her more than I had realized, and I berated myself for not picking up on it sooner. Setting aside my concern — for the moment — I smiled. "Well, either way, first drink is on me. I need to congratulate you for helping to complicate my case."

"Anything I can do to keep it interesting," she chuckled.

I reached over and put my hand on top of hers, then gently squeezed it. "I might be able to grab a quick lunch before heading to Augusta. Want me to bring you a sandwich or something?"

"I would never say no to my handsome kitty rescuing his princess for a bit," she smiled, using the nickname she'd given me after the first time she'd seen me in my Chat Noir costume. "Though given how booked I am today, it might literally not be more than a few minutes in between patients."

"I'll take what I can get," I replied, squeezing her hand again before flagging down the waitress for our bill.

After a lingering kiss in the parking lot that promised to develop into something far more interesting later that evening, we parted ways, destined, it seemed, to begin our day on opposite sides of Windeport. The day had dawned cloudy, portending the distinct possibility of snow by noon; it continued to be bitterly cold, enough that the seat warmers in the SUV were more aspirational than useful. I could never get used to how the damndest things would start to squeak in my vehicle when the thermometer flirted with negative temperatures; as I turned out onto Route One, headed back toward the Davies cottage, the steering wheel sounded as though it required the loving attention of an oil can.

The small lane leading to the shore was no less foreboding than it had been the day prior, and for some reason, I felt a small sense of relief that I'd not be alone when I saw the crowd of vehicles from the State Crime Lab in front of the two-story structure. Pulling up beside the truck I assumed belonged to Heather, I turned the SUV off, clapped my gloved hands twice to try and restore some feeling to them, then exited for the house. The bite of the icy cold air was more than bracing, and I could feel my exposed cheeks tingling as I pulled open the screen door, then pushed into the warm embrace of the interior.

Heather happened to be coming down the steps from the second floor as I closed the front door behind me. "You're early, Chief," she said, pausing three steps from the floor. "I distinctly remember telling you ten."

I shrugged. "I'm an early riser, and something told me you'd want to be on the road as soon as you were done."

She nodded. "Those instincts of yours are as good as always. We picked up a case in Wiscasset; I'm headed over there as soon as we're done here."

"And you're done now?"

"For now, yes," she nodded again. "Come on, let me walk you through what we found, and then tell you about some of our informed guesses."

"Okay," I nodded. "Lead away."

Heather turned and was just about to head up the steps to the second story when my iPhone sang out; I paused at the bottom step and dug it out of my khakis and was surprised to see my cousin's number. I looked up at Heather. "I'm sorry," I apologized. "Head on up and I'll join you in a moment."

"Of course."

I smiled and then answered the call. "Charlie? Is everything all right?"

"Yes and no," she replied. "And it pretty much depends on whether you are free tonight."

I cocked my head slightly. "Well, it's not the *best* time for me — I picked up a case yesterday. But I can work around it; what do you need?"

"Oh!" Charlie said. "I didn't realize. I've not gotten to the library yet."

I smiled wider, for I knew in her role as the Director of the Windeport Public Library, Charlotte O'Connor was information central — in more ways than one. Often it was extremely conducive to swing by the WPL's massive circulation desk a few times a week to get the general pulse of the Village. Glancing at my watch, I felt the smile shift to a frown. "It's nearly eight-thirty," I observed. "Don't you open at—"

"Eight-thirty, don't remind me," she sighed. "I had the most improbable phone call from Paris, of all places. It's thrown me for a complete loop."

"Paris? Did somebody need to renew a book they took on vacation?"

"No," she chuckled. "I've been invited to speak at a conference taking place there next summer. Apparently, someone actually *read* that paper I wrote last year on children's literature; it's quite the gig. Travel and accommodations are included."

"That's... quite a phone call," I said. "But you're not going to Paris tonight...?"

"I wish," she sighed. I could hear the muted sound of the wind whisking past Charlie's car, softened somewhat by the Bluetooth connection. "No, I need to ask a favor. Can you pick up the girls from school tonight and feed them dinner? I've got to drive to Bangor for a statewide meeting this afternoon and won't be home before ten. Mom would normally do it for me, but she had to go to Fort Fairfield unexpectedly. I think a classmate of hers passed suddenly and the funeral is tomorrow."

"Of course," I said immediately. "When do they get out?"

"Three-thirty."

"I might have to see if Suzanne can spring them, then," I said thoughtfully. "I have a postmortem in Augusta to attend and won't be back until close to five. Assuming you don't mind them hanging around a doctor's office for a bit?"

"Not at all," she said. "They might actually enjoy that, so long as Suzanne is willing to keep half an eye on them until you get there."

"I'll call her right now but assume we're on the job. Even if I have to send a police cruiser after them."

"Jesus, Cousin," Charlie breathed. "That's the *last* thing you should do!"

"Even if I let them use the lights and sirens?"

"*Especially* that," she replied. "Text me when everything is confirmed?"

"Will do."

I hung up with Charlotte and immediately tapped out a quick message to Suzanne, knowing she was probably already in her first appointment of the day. To my surprise, she answered back immediately in the affirmative — the school was only a block or two from her practice, anyway; we agreed to hammer out the finer details over lunch. I sent a quick text to Charlie letting her know we had her covered and then took the steps two at a time, cognizant of the fact I'd kept Heather waiting.

She was standing just inside the door of the room where we'd found Davies, and looked a bit concerned. "Everything okay?"

"Oh yeah," I smiled, waving my hands in the air. "Emergency childcare, that's all. I get to spoil Charlie's kids tonight while she's at a meeting."

Heather visibly shuddered. "Kids. How do you do it?"

"It's easy," I replied. "I give them everything they want."

She cocked her head at me and arched an eyebrow. "Seriously?"

"No," I laughed. "Charlie would kill me. But I've known the twins since they were born. They're not quite to the teenage stage of questioning everything; in fact, they still think I'm pretty cool. I'm going to ride that to the bitter end."

"I don't envy you the fall from that pedestal."

"Me, either. Sorry to hold things up."

"No worries," she smiled before leading me over to the recliner. "I know you're heading in for the postmortem later; fortunately for you, our decision to drive the body back last night had the side benefit of allowing the lab to go over it for trace before Dr. Hamilton starts the autopsy."

"What are you hoping they'll find?"

"Other than the adhesive residue Suzanne detected? You never know, really," she replied. "Bodies tend to hide the damndest things. Whatever we do find will help paint in a better picture." Heather frowned. "And we could use the help, for this one is seriously muddled."

I nodded. "The breakfast downstairs, for example?"

"Exactly. I've worked a number of suicides and I have to say, this one is very atypical." She held up her hand and started ticking things off with her fingers as she spoke. "The breakfast tells us it started off as an ordinary morning, confirmed by a small load of laundry in the washing machine that had yet to be put in the dryer. There's a master suite on the other end of this floor, and the bed has been fully made up, with a fully-packed suitcase sitting on top of it."

I felt my eyebrows go up. "He was getting ready to leave?" I asked.

"That's what it looks like. Not what I would expect from someone planning on ending their life."

"Definitely not."

"Then we have the actual scene itself," she continued. "If we ignore having found the tape residue, you could be forgiven for assuming the victim just picked the most comfortable chair in the house and literally gave up. It's not the first time I've found someone who'd slashed their wrists outside of the bathroom, but again, it's also unusual. Most choose a tub or a pool, partly to speed up the process and partly to contain the mess. I mean, doing it this way is pretty brutal, with plenty of time to have second thoughts long after they would be able to save themselves."

"And factoring in the possibility he was restrained?"

"I have two theories on that," she said. "The first is unlikely, for we didn't find a roll of tape. However, it's within the realm of possibility that the victim slashed his wrist and then lashed himself to the chair to prevent the ability to act on those second thoughts. Blood spatter patterns don't really support this theory, though, and like I said, even after scouring the entire house, we haven't come up with the roll of tape in question."

"All right. What is your second theory?"

"We're looking at a murder," she replied instantly.

"Is there any evidence someone else was in the house?" I asked.

"Nothing obvious, but we've printed everything we could find and will run them through the system back at the lab," Heather said. "Just eyeballing them, I think we have at least one print — a thumb, would be my guess — that doesn't appear to belong to the victim."

"Where did you find it?"

"Zipper on the suitcase," she replied. "I suspect they were searching for something."

"Or placing something," I mused.

"True." She beckoned me around to the front of the recliner, then pointed at the hardwood where there was still a significant puddle of blood. I felt for whomever would be hired to attempt to scrub that out of the grain. "I'm not sure this recliner is supposed to be at this angle," she continued. "In daylight, we noted how there was a darker shade to the flooring right there; the blood is sort of masking the discoloration, but it's clear that exposure from these windows has done a number on the wood not covered by furniture."

"Evidence of a struggle?" I asked softly.

"Maybe? It's hard to know the position of *anything* in this room before we appeared on the scene; given his girth, it's just as likely your victim might have stumbled into it one night and never got around to fixing it."

I knelt to ponder the sliver of flooring Heather had indicated, then looked back at the heavy bulk of the recliner. I found myself agreeing somewhat with Heather's observation, for I wasn't entirely sure Davies had the musculature to move the chair on his own once seated. Then again, it wasn't unheard of for victims to have an unusual burst of adrenaline when it appeared that the end was near. "Two solid explanations that both fit the evidence," I sighed.

"Exactly. And then we come to the curious case of the tablet."

"I noted it was in our inventory to review," I replied, passing on my chance to comment on her paraphrasing of classic Sherlock Homes. "Looked like a pretty standard model."

"It's the latest iPad," she nodded. "And when we tapped the screen, it was unlocked and down to about six percent on the battery. More than enough for us to read the suicide note."

My eyebrows went up. "That's very modern. And also flies in the face of the evidence you've presented so far."

"Maybe not," she replied. "It had been wiped clean of prints."

I smiled slightly. "That's awfully considerate of our victim."

"And probably not high on his list of things to do as his life literally trickled away from him."

"No," I sighed. "Probably not. Anything else?"

"Just two more things," she said. "We never located a phone, nor did we find any personal documents. No wallet, driver's license, credit cards or anything remotely looking like a government-issued identification."

Something buzzed at the back of my brain. "Where were the keys to the car?"

"In the car," Heather replied.

I knew Heather well enough to trust that when she said her team had searched the entire house from stem to stern and not located anything, there was nothing there to find. I nodded thoughtfully. "That's damn peculiar. I can't believe he drove all the way from Portland without stopping for gas, at least."

"Agreed."

"The phone troubles me a bit more," I mused. "Although it offers a partial explanation for why he didn't reply to his daughter's outreach. If he had an iPad, maybe he also had an iPhone," I started.

"You'd be able to use the 'find my device' feature, then."

"Assuming it's on and somewhere close by."

"Hope springs eternal," Heather laughed.

"Doesn't it?" I replied. "Half of my job is hope, and the rest is dumb luck."

She cocked her head at me. "That can't be completely accurate."

"True," I smiled as I headed for the stairs. "It's actually *shitty* dumb luck. Thanks, as always for your efforts."

"Our pleasure," she replied as she followed me down. "The final report will be in the system tonight."

"A little light reading while I'm babysitting," I sighed. "Life doesn't get any better than that."

"You need to get a life, Chief," Heather chuckled.

"Suzanne tells me that constantly," I replied. "I'm starting to think she's right..."

Four

I spent the balance of the morning back at the Public Safety Building, first pawing through the sizable quantity of evidence boxes that had arrived just ahead of me, adding to those that had been dropped off the prior evening. Since everything had already been entered into the system by the techs, it was more of a perusal than the normal inventory process I would do. Nothing jumped out at me as overtly unusual as I reviewed inordinately mundane leftover debris of a person I assumed had led something of an interesting life, but then again, at that point in the investigation, it was hard to know what *should* be jumping out at me. It still bothered me that the team hadn't come up with a wallet or a cell phone; in this day and age, even people who had lived as long as Don Davies tended to not leave home without either in their possession.

Chewing that over as I pushed the final box onto a shelf, I made my way back to my office and another cup of coffee before settling in behind my battleship of a desk to review the electronic version of the evidence Heather and her team had collected. As promised, they had ensured everything entered into the state system had synched up with the Windeport database, and I soon lost track of time flipping through photos from the scene and the commentary each tech had added to them as metadata. If I ignored for a moment that the cottage was far more ostentatious than anything Windeport would normally see, it was otherwise a pretty ordinary single-family dwelling of a kind I'd encountered in more suburban parts of the state. The appliances, for example, were as old as the house itself, which according to the property records, was close to twenty-five years; I'd wracked my brain trying to think why I had no recollection of its construction in the first place, given how notorious it must have been, and presumed I'd been far too young to have understood why the adults around me might have been all atwitter about it. Then, like most things in Windeport, it had become part of the rich tapestry of the Village and blended into the background, much like the massive vacation homes the wealthy from Boston had once lived in that loomed along the Sea Road between Route One and the shore.

Flipping to a photo of the Lexus, I glanced at my watch and realized I had just enough time to sneak down to Millie's on the Wharf to retrieve lunch and meet Suzanne at our agreed-upon time. I closed my laptop and stuffed it into my backpack, yanked on my winter coat and made for the parking lot as quickly as I could, nodding to Caitlyn at reception as I pushed through into the still-bitter cold of the noon hour. Given Millie's was just half a block from the station, I eschewed the SUV and instead waited for a break in the much-slower than normal traffic along Main Street before crossing diagonally to the old cannery disguised beneath all sorts of tacky plastic shellfish and antique lobster traps, hurried along the short sidewalk to the main door. Reaching for one of the handles, I smiled slightly at how they were shaped like a crustacean who had already met their demise in a vat of boiling water; pulling the door open to gain entrance, I found myself musing on how terrible those final moments must be for lobsters on their way to that incredibly bright red coloring. I didn't know what it meant that it had never stopped me from continuing to eat them.

As quiet as the parking lot had looked, the muted hubbub within bespoke the normally hopping lunch hour Millie's was known for year-round; during tourist season, locals hardly ever were able to get in, though it had far more to do with the massive markup the menu sported than, perhaps, having to deal with the crush of out-of-towners. During the long, cold months of winter, though, we owned the place, and the lower menu prices reflected that understanding. I smiled slightly when I approached the host stand, recalling from my conversation with Charlie earlier that the restaurant's namesake would not be at her usual post that noontime. My aunt was quite the firecracker, capable of handling the wide spectrum of guests she hosted with her unique blend of Downeast humor and dry wit. The young woman holding the menus was a student from UEM, and she nodded when she saw me.

"Chief," she smiled. "One second while I bus a table for you."

"No need, Ginger," I waved her off. "I'm doing take out today."

"Okay," she said as she whipped out one of those small, white order pads, ubiquitous at any Maine restaurant. "Two specials?"

"How did you know I was ordering for two?" I asked, cocking my head slightly.

"Dr. Kellerman isn't with you," she answered with a shrug. "I assumed you were taking the takeout to her."

"This town seems to know me better than I know myself," I chuckled. "Yes, two specials, hold the mayo on one and add extra butter to the other — on the side."

"Okay," she nodded. "Chips or fries?"

"Homemade chips, of course."

"Coffee?"

"One coffee, one diet."

"Okay," she nodded as she ripped off the order from her pad and put it and her pencil back into the small pocket of the apron she was wearing. "Let me run this to the kitchen. Should be less than five minutes."

"I'll be here," I replied as I watched her turn and disappear into the main dining room.

I waited a beat before starting to move over to one of the long benches covered in what I was starting to think of boiled-lobster-red cushions that ran the length of the entrance foyer and became something of a standby queue for the summer visitors, intent on spending the time reviewing email on my iPhone while I waited; halfway there, though, I heard a discordantly familiar chuckle from the main dining room and paused for a beat. The laugh came again, and with it, the cold shiver of recognition that squeezed my heart with gloves made of ice. Unable to stop myself, I moved back to the host stand, and then around it, seeking out the voice I thought I'd never hear again.

Her brilliantly red hair was cut far shorter than the last time I'd seen her, but the deep green eyes that turned toward me at my approach were just as I remembered them; the half smile, part humor, part regret, was also something I recalled from our many years together. Even dressed in a very professional pantsuit, her form still had all of the curves from her own decades spent both in the pool and out, pursuing triathlons in places far and near. I'd managed to master two of the three disciplines – running and swimming -- but had never found the time to seriously tackle cycling, one of many regrets I thought I had finally put behind me in the year-plus since Deidre had left me.

Maybe *left* wasn't entirely accurate.

A year of being with Suzanne had unlocked my ability to listen to my inner emotions; a year of introspection had concluded I was as much to blame for Deidre's seemingly spontaneous departure and the subsequent fracturing of our engagement. After the death of my mother, I'd withdrawn into a world where nothing outside of work or the pool existed; despite living with her at the time, Deidre had found herself frozen out, and while she may have attempted to pull me back into reality, nothing broke through until I found myself standing in the lobby of the Boston Harbor Hotel, alone, and with the dawning realization she'd emptied far more from her closet in our apartment than what would have been strictly necessary for a weekend trip to Massachusetts. Being more self-aware also meant that running across her at Millie's bubbled up all sorts of feelings I wasn't entirely prepared to deal with at that moment, including far, *far* more anger than I realized I had over what had transpired. But as she struggled to push herself out of the small booth, that anger turned to something else entirely when her very pregnant form became fully apparent.

"Sean," Deidre said with a warmth I wasn't feeling. "It's good to see you."

"De," I replied with a slight nod. A stubborn streak I didn't know

I had kept me from accepting the embrace her half-raised arms were hinting at, and after a moment, she gracefully let them drop to her sides. "What brings you to Windeport?" I asked, registering in my periphery that the Village's last remaining lawyer, Frank Smithwick, was sitting on the other side of the small booth and taking in our little reunion with that classic used-car salesman smile he featured on his business cards.

"Tying up some loose ends, it seems," she sighed, unconsciously rubbing at her enlarged belly. "There was some sort of reporting snafu from my last handful of quarterly tax filings for the IGA while I was still owner. I came up to help sort through the mess and put it to rest."

I managed to keep something of a customer-service smile going as I replied. "It must be more than just a snafu to bring you all the way up from Atlanta."

Deidre smiled slightly. "I didn't realize you knew where I'd wound up."

"Not initially," I said. Thinking that I might be coming off as something of a stalker, I shrugged and continued. "When I missed you in Boston, Vasily took it upon himself to connect some dots I'd been refusing to even see." I glanced meaningfully at her abdomen. "It looks like the change is agreeing with you."

"She's due in February," Deidre said, before pausing for a moment. "Pregnancies for women over forty can be a bit riskier for the baby — and the mother — so it was important for Thom and me to get started sooner than later." She rubbed her stomach again. "We're hoping for three altogether."

Despite my attempt at composure, I knew my face betrayed me at the mention of Thomas Feldman, the one-time starting quarterback for UEM and NFL benchwarmer Deidre had married not long after she'd left Windeport; the subtle twin digs about my age — which, like her, was still *well* south of forty — and my lack of desire to have children made it a struggle not to respond with some pithy sarcasm that would have been wholly inappropriate. Both underscored just how poor our interpersonal communication skills had been while we'd been a couple, for I'd not realized how desperately she'd wanted to become a mother until it had been pointed out to me by, of all people, Vasily. I couldn't deny that the flicker of anger I was feeling made clear there were still a few unresolved issues that I'd simply buried.

It was a bold attack, though; she'd known she'd run into me at some point and had come armed and prepared. And why shouldn't she? From Deidre's perspective, she'd finally gotten everything she wanted; whatever had been between us was long gone, nothing more now than the occasional pleasant memory here or there. Slowly, I nodded, realizing I had become just a page or two for her in a yearbook that she would likely never open again once she returned to Georgia; the half-smile that appeared on her face when she saw me adjust to my new status confirmed that we were on the same wavelength.

Finally.

"Including the two from his ex?" I asked, trying for a similarly pleasant expression while fighting the urge to remind her how we once had *both* been of the opinion Feldman was a womanizing jerk.

Something flashed in her eyes for a moment. "We share custody of his older sons," she shrugged. "But we hope to have three of our own."

"That will make for cozy family holidays," I replied evenly. "How long will you be in town?"

Deidre twisted her head slightly. "Do you ask all of the tourists that? Or just a select few?"

Recognizing I'd perhaps come across a bit too much like an investigator, I realized I wasn't in the best frame of mind to attempt a civil conversation with my former fiancé. The hurt was suddenly too fresh; the desire to do something with my anger nearly too tempting to ignore. Neither of us were in a place to simply talk as we once had; there would be no tying up of loose emotions that day. What surprised me, though, was the intrinsic understanding that maybe we would – we *could* – get there.

Eventually.

Changing tacts, I smiled widely and shrugged with my best *aw-shucks* look. "We're a full-service village," I replied. "Catering to all." I nodded to Frank. "I'll let you get back to your power lunch. I hope all goes well with the Revenue Service."

"The who?" she asked.

"Your tax issues?" I reminded her.

"Oh — right," she nodded. "Sorry, we call that agency something different in Georgia."

"You've only been gone a year," I teased. "How quickly they forget."

"It seems more like a lifetime ago," she countered quickly. "And then some."

While the dagger might have been small, it plunged just as easily into my heart all the same. Fortunately, Ginger arrived with two plastic bags and rescued me. "Chief?" she said genially. "Want it on your tab?"

"Please," I nodded, before turning back to Deidre. "I have a lunch date, and I don't want to make her wait," I found myself saying, unsure of why it was important to me to tell her I, too, had moved on.

Her eyes flicked to the bags, and then back to mine. "No," she said softly, almost with a slight trace of sadness. "No, you probably don't."

We stared at each other for a long, awkward moment before I smiled a final time, then fled the restaurant.

The freshening icy breeze from the harbor did little to distract me from the turmoil of my thoughts and the matching roil of emotion in my stomach; clutching the takeaway bags a bit tighter, I bent slightly against not just the wind as I made my way back up Main Street before crossing at the intersection beside the old brick pharmacy building. Normally my spirits would lift each time I approached the tall display windows that had once featured hand-lettered banners announcing the weekly specials, or during holiday times, little tableaus of product my mother would craft to help make the season merry; Suzanne had left the glass pretty much intact with her renovation, allowing the cheery lights and comfortable furniture of her waiting room that fronted Route One to be equally as welcoming. Stepping into the angled alcove that protected the glass double-doors of the main entrance, I pulled one open and stepped into the warm interior, thankful for the sudden respite from the biting cold while wondering if it could do anything about the chill to my soul.

My timing was close to impeccable, for the waiting room was empty given it was Suzanne's normal lunch hour; no one was at the small antique reception desk that sported a somewhat incongruent flat screen computer, so I slipped around it to the small corridor beyond to make my way down to my girlfriend's private office. I passed several open doors that led into small exam rooms and one closed one; pausing beside it, I heard the beautiful tones of Suzanne's voice, her calmness a counterpoint to the somewhat anxious voice that seemed to be pressing her about something. Bowing away so as not to overhear anything I shouldn't, I quickly made my way to her office at the end of the hall and closed the door behind me, smiling slightly as I did so; across the hall was the small therapeutic spa Suzanne often used for her arthritic patients, something that had had come in rather handy when we'd needed to thaw out Vasily after his near drowning in Windeport harbor over Christmas. I could still see in my mind's eye the roiling rough seas I'd insisted we'd risk in order to run down a lead on the case we'd been working — and the split second when my best friend had slipped on the slick deck of the small boat we'd been on and gone over into the icy water. My fingers tingled at the memory of grabbing his boots at the last moment and the subsequent struggle to pull him back onto the boat; it wasn't hard to recall the ache of performing CPR, along my panicked fear I might have well killed my best friend in my zeal to catch a murderer.

Sloughing off my jacket and laying it across one of the guest chairs, I slumped into the remaining one and realized I was in something of a foul state of mind. Waves of guilt washed over me, for between Deidre and Vasily I had certainly quite a bit to atone for. Despondently pulling off my knit cap, I reflected on just how close I had been to losing Vasily, as well as the future with Deidre I had sacrificed while *not* dealing with my grief over my mother's passing. The latter was still a work in progress, one that had been helped along immensely through the patient efforts of Suzanne; the former, fortunately, hadn't come to pass, but the nearness of it had reminded both Vasily and I just how important we were to each other. Our relationship would never be what it once was, of course, not with him in California; still, much like any restoration project, I *was* starting to see the familiar outlines of what we'd had. And it was enough for me to want to keep going.

Deidre was an unexpected wildcard, though, and her sudden re-appearance in my life was not entirely welcome. That I was introspective enough to understand that made me somewhat hopeful that I might get through the event a bit more maturely, however much I wanted to slink off to my bungalow, climb into bed and pull the comforter over my head until I knew she'd left the village once more.

Yep, I sighed. *Still a work in progress.*

I heard a door in the hallway open, followed by muted conversation; a moment later, footsteps grew louder until Suzanne pushed into her office wearing a smile. "Hey, Kitty," she said softly as she moved down to my slumped position and planted a kiss on the top of my head. "I hope you've not been waiting long. My last appointment went long."

"They *all* go long," I said, my tone a bit more sullen than I'd intended.

Suzanne stood back and reappraised me for a long moment before her eyes narrowed. "What happened?" she asked without preamble.

I looked into her deep blue eyes and then felt my vision waver; blinking, I cleared my throat before turning to the takeaway bag in the chair next to me. "I got the special," I said, trying to keep my voice sounding normal. "I hope that's—"

Suzanne put a gentle hand to my shoulder and carefully turned me back toward her. I saw she'd knelt beside the chair so she could be close to eye level, and her concerned look gave me pause. "Sean."

Sighing again, I glanced away once more as I tried to sort through my emotions. "Deidre," I said simply. "I ran into her at Millie's." Looking back at Suzanne, I smiled thinly. "It appears I was not emotionally ready for her to suddenly appear."

Reaching up to brush a curl or two of my dirty blond hair away from an eye, she then placed her hand against my cheek. "Who would be?" Suzanne replied quietly. "I'm not sure any of us are *ever* ready to encounter an ex. More so when you are on home turf."

"Yeah."

"Do you want to talk about it?"

"Not particularly," I replied.

"Sean—"

"I know I probably should," I continued. Closing my eyes, I leaned into her touch and sighed. "Somehow, it feels wrong talking to my current girlfriend about my last relationship, though. Besides, you're on your lunch hour," I added as I opened my eyes and looked into her concerned expression. "I don't want to spoil this brief respite of your hectic day. You see enough troubles during the day; let's save my existential angst for tonight."

"All right," Suzanne nodded after a long second, then smiled a bit impishly. "A glass of wine might make it go easier, too."

"I'm not sure that's entirely necessary," I replied. "Welcome, of course, but honestly, I've never had much trouble telling you my deepest secrets, Suze."

My eyes wandered from Suzanne's face to the window of her office that looked out on the side street running past the old pharmacy building; for a brief moment, I thought of my years growing up along Route One, and later, the significant part of my life spent with Deidre in the apartment above that very space. Our time together had been perfect right up until it wasn't; that I had missed every sign the relationship had been crumbling around us continued to be a bitter pill to swallow, given my vocation. As I sat there with the woman who had carefully and lovingly repaired the gaping hole that had been blown through my heart, I realized my connection with Suzanne was entirely different from what I'd experienced with Deidre. Turning back toward her, I felt my efforts to blink back the cascade of emotions blurring my vision begin to fail; I hurriedly tried to wipe away the tears representing the depth of my despair at what I had lost.

Then again, when I thought about just how much joy had entered my life as a result, maybe those weren't *solely* tears of sadness.

"Sean?" Suzanne asked softly.

"I don't think I say it enough," I replied as I leaned over to her desk to grab a tissue for my now running nose. "Having you in my life has made me... made me a better person. One who truly understands the value of love." Wiping at my face, I knew I looked anything but the cool, collected Police Chief everyone expected — and that something inside of me had finally shifted, allowing that shell to dissipate and expose my true self. "One who I feel perfectly at ease baring my soul to."

"Oh, you do," Suzanne replied softly, leaning forward to put her forehead against mine. "In ways little and big every day." Kissing me gently, she pulled back and eyed me for another long moment before nodding slightly. "We'll get through this. And," she smiled wryly, "I'll try not to kill her in a way that will lead you back to me."

"Don't even joke about that!" I frowned, but her humor had broken the moment perfectly.

Glancing at the clock over her desk, Suzanne looked back to the bags I'd started to empty and reached into the one closer to her. "How was the walk through with Heather?"

"Interesting, to say the least," I replied as I pulled out my meal and then quickly ran down the bullet points, happy for a change of topic, even if it *was* murder. Suzanne nodded and asked a few clarifying questions as I went through my precis. "There are a few troubling things that I've not been able to reconcile," I added as a conclusion. "For example, the breakfast in the kitchen seems to be at odds with Davies calmly going upstairs to kill himself."

"Well, I'm not entirely surprised," Suzanne said as she munched on the slice of dill pickle that had come with her baked haddock sandwich. "The tape pretty much telegraphed it was murder."

I plucked a house-made chip fry from my stash. "We don't know for sure that it was tape quite yet, Suze."

Arching a sculpted eyebrow, Suzanne looked at me, hard. "I'm not wrong."

"I don't doubt it," I chuckled, "but I need to wait for the forensics to come back before I run with it. For the record, though, Heather agrees with you completely."

"Smart woman."

"Another oddity were the car keys," I continued thoughtfully. "That, and we didn't locate his wallet."

"This is Maine," Suzanne countered. "And we're in the middle of nowhere. Most people leave their keys in the ignition around here."

"True," I nodded. "But Davies is from the big city. I doubt he would have done that down there."

"Good point," she replied. "I wonder where his wallet wound up? How on earth did he pay for gas on the trip up?"

"I said something similar to Heather," I chuckled.

"They didn't find it anywhere at the house?"

"Nope."

"Weird." Glancing to the clock once more, Suzanne sighed deeply. "To be continued, Kitty," she said before tossing her napkin into the small aluminum takeaway container. "Duty calls."

"Same here," I replied.

"Off to Augusta, then?"

"Yeah. If everything goes well, though, I should be back to rescue you from Charlie's kids. Thank you for keeping an eye on them for me."

"Of course," she smiled.

After a lingering goodbye kiss, I packed up the remains of our two lunches and tossed them in the small dumpster behind the pharmacy; it was a short walk across the street and down the sidewalk to the Public Safety building and my waiting SUV. Driving to Augusta was never a favorite pastime of mine, but as a Police Chief for a small municipality, there always seemed to be a reason for my presence to be needed in the capital city every few weeks. The worst part of the trip was the cross-country portion, heading inland from the coast to catch the Interstate for the final leg. Given it was winter and the dearth of tourist traffic that implied, I figured I'd be able to make the sojourn along Route 203 with few interruptions.

The SUV took an extra second to start up in the bitter cold of the early afternoon; cranking the heater for the main cabin, I turned out onto Main Street and tucked in behind a small pickup truck pulling a trailer piled high with empty lobster pots. It was an unusual thing to see, given how winter had yet to give up its hold on the landscape, and made me wonder if we had lost yet another family business, one finally forced into a final liquidation of assets. Caitlyn had given me a list not long ago of the remaining — viable — lobstering families in Windeport, one short enough it could be counted on one hand. I shook my head at the far cry that sorry state of affairs was, even from the days of my teenage years, but the sea was a fickle mistress — not to mention the industries that relied upon her beneficence.

Turning onto Route 203, I briefly considered pausing at Calista's Bakery for a fresh cup of coffee before deciding to press on... and then made a quick U-turn less than a quarter of a mile later. Despite having just eaten lunch, fresh croissants were just coming out of the oven as I entered; by the time I'd returned to my waiting SUV, two of the divine flaky creations were stashed on the passenger seat in a small brown bag bearing the logo of the bakery. The combined smell of freshly brewed coffee and buttery pastries filled the cabin and put me into a comfortable frame of mind.

That introspective mindset deepened as I passed the sprawling campus of UEM, which led to thoughts of Vasily. After doing a bit of mental temporal calculations, I figured he wasn't quite at lunch yet and punched up his number on my iPhone, making the assumption he'd appreciate something of an update.

He picked up on the first ring. "Hey, Sean," he said brightly, though he sounded a bit winded. "Is it snowing up there yet?"

"It *always* snows here," I chuckled. "But nothing quite yet today. I've not looked at the forecast to see if we're expecting some for the weekend."

"From what I saw over Christmas, the skiing must still be pretty good."

"It is. Given how deep the base is at Snowden Notch, I expect the season might last to Memorial Day."

"That would be extraordinary."

"I didn't catch you at a bad time, did I?"

"No," he replied, his breathing sounding a bit more regular, "not at all. I left a bit early for my lunchtime run."

I felt an eyebrow arch. "Knowing you as well as I do, that tells me you're trying to work out a thorny problem."

"Or three," he laughed. "It's been one hell of a week."

"I got that impression when you called initially."

"So cheer me up a bit," Vasily said. "Tell me you've solved the case I inadvertently handed off to you."

"No such luck. I'm headed down to Augusta now for the autopsy; Heather's team finished going over the scene this morning. I managed to catalog most of the evidence she handed off to me last night, but I still have a ton to go through when I get back."

"Damn."

"It's not all bad news," I continued. "I'm reasonably comfortable saying it's not suicide, based on what we found so far. We think we have signs of a struggle, at least, and the fatal wounds were on his dominant hand."

"Interesting."

"We'll use the daughter's DNA to positively identify him when she gets here," I continued. "We weren't able to locate his photo ID, and the cottage didn't have any framed family photos — which seems odd to me — but Louise will be able to pull the digital image from the DMV during the postmortem."

"Wait — *what*? You're not *sure* it's Davies?"

"You know me," I chuckled. "I'm not a fan of getting ahead of the evidence, as much as I would like to presume it's him based on where we found the body. If it helps your sanity, though, the car registration came back to Davies when Caitlyn pulled it for me this morning."

"I'll breathe easier once you have," Vasily said. "Doubly so since with the daughter is on her way to you. The last thing I need is her blaming me for an unnecessary cross-country trip."

"The odds that an interloper drove up from Portland in Davies' car just to expire in Davies' cabin are pretty low," I pointed out. "I'll know for sure in a few hours. Hang tight."

"I'm not worried," Vasily replied, but I could hear in his voice just a tinge of concern. I had no reason to think it wasn't Don Davies on ice in the morgue down in Augusta, but for the first time a tiny bit of doubt entered my thoughts. For once, I was looking forward to the closure the postmortem would bring. "No wallet, though? That's as odd as the missing family photos."

"It is. I'll call later tonight with the results — no, scratch that, I'll have to call tomorrow. Charlie has me watching the twins tonight, so there won't be a lot of free time."

"Lucky you. I know how you *love* to babysit."

"I'm getting better at it," I replied. There might have been a tiny bit of defensiveness in my tone.

"Still giving in to anything they ask, then?" Vasily chuckled.

"Why mess with a winning formula? Talk tomorrow."

Five

The interior of the state morgue was every bit as chilly as the crisp day outside, or at least *felt* that way when I entered; for a long moment, I wondered whether I wanted to risk wearing my heavy winter jacket into the exam room and chance getting it impregnated by the unsavory panoply of odors endemic to the space. In the end, common sense won out and I quickly changed into a pair of scrubs provided in the visitor locker room before joining Dr. Louise Hamilton in her domain. As the Chief Medical Examiner for the state, it was rare to for her perform a post, but the two of us had been friends more than a decade, dating back to the first case I'd worked on when I was fresh out of the Justice Academy and partnered with Mike Gilbert. Lou had herself been a rookie in the Coroner's Office at the time, and I'd been so impressed with her professionalism, I'd tried to steer any exams to her queue in the years after. Once I'd become Chief, she'd made a point of personally handling my postmortems — though, thankfully, they had tended to be few and far between.

Excepting, of course, the unexpected run of murders in Windeport over the past year.

Dr. Hamilton turned as I pushed through the swinging metal doors to Exam Seven, attired in her trademark purple scrubs, color-coordinated face mask and matching hair cap. "Sean! You made good time."

"Traffic was better than I expected," I replied as I finished tying my own mask behind my head. For the millionth time I wondered what the point was, since it neither stopped the smell nor was the victim likely to catch any bugs I happened to be carrying. Looking down at the table, I nodded. "You didn't start without me, did you?"

"I might have done a few preliminary observations," she chuckled. "Height, weight, and the like. My lab geeks finished pulling trace from the body about thirty minutes ago; we were a bit backed up this morning, so everything got delayed slightly."

"No worries. Did they find anything interesting?"

"You'll have to ask them."

Louise looked down at the naked body lying on the aluminum exam table, drawing my attention to the lifeless form. It was a stark reminder that it didn't matter if you believed in a concept of an afterlife, for at the end of the day we were all going have every vestige of our humanity ripped away, leaving nothing more than an inanimate mass of skin and bones that would wind up being someone else's problem to deal with. I'd seen more than my fair share of people in such a state of affairs, a sobering reminder of just how transitory our existence could be.

"My geeks took fingerprints and drew what they could for other screening tests; we had to get creative with the DNA for, as you are well aware, there wasn't much actual blood left in your victim. It'll take longer for us to spin it down from a tissue sample, but it's completely viable." Lou looked back up at me. "We'll run both the prints and the DNA through the usual databases, of course, but Heather had already put a note on the file that you identified the victim as the famed Don Davies?"

"We found the body in his cottage out on the fringes of Windeport," I demurred.

"Damn," she sighed, missing my equivocation entirely. "Must be nice to have a vacation home."

"I wouldn't know," I smiled, though the most Louise could see was the crinkling around my eyes. "I never caught more than a few minutes of his show. You?"

She shrugged. "Every now and then when I'm looking for brainless background noise. Talk radio isn't really my thing."

"Yeah. About that identification," I continued somewhat sheepishly, "we actually haven't officially matched him to the photo on his DMV record. All I did was run the plates on his Lexus; I assumed you guys would."

Dr. Hamilton rolled her eyes. "On any other day, that would be my first order of business," she sighed, glancing at the computer workstation perched at the head of the exam table. "But you managed to bring in Mister Davies on a day when the damn system is down."

"The *entire* system?" Both eyebrows went up. "When did that happen?"

"Early this morning. The IT group was running some sort of update to an unrelated software package overnight and somehow managed to take out everything. I've heard through the grapevine there have been more than a few angry patrons at the various DMV branches across the state today."

"Yikes. Did they even send out an email about it? I don't think we were even notified."

"Probably not," she sighed again. "They seem incapable of any sort of timely communications, that department. Anyway, once it's back up I'll do the confirmation and let you know formally."

"Sounds good."

Stepping closer to the table, Lou picked up the slashed wrist. "Heather's observations were accurate as always. These wounds were made by someone comfortable using an extremely sharp edge to slice; very professional, clean lines. Not at all what I would expect from someone who was taking their life."

I nodded. "Most suicides have evidence of that hesitation just before they pull the trigger, so to speak."

"Exactly. I know the blade was recovered at the scene, so we'll see if we can't match it to the wound. Regardless, I'm already leaning toward this not being suicide."

"Oh?" I smiled. "And here I thought you always waited for the body to whisper it's secrets to you before you made any rulings."

"Mr. Davies here has been speaking rather loudly," she replied as she turned the wrist over. "For example, note the slight dimple here?"

"Yes," I nodded, peering a bit closer. "Wasn't he wearing a smart watch or something on that hand?"

"He was. We took it off during the trace part of the fun, but this confirms just how tightly his arms had been taped to the sides of the chair — tight enough to drive the back of the dial into the skin and leave a mark."

I found myself nodding a bit more. "We know about the band of tape across the chest from what Suzanne had located; you found more?"

"Yes, but I'll get to that in a moment." Lou put the wrist down gently and walked around to the other side of the body, then raised the right hand slightly, turning the back of the wrist to me. "What do you see?"

I squinted a bit. Despite the bright overhead exam light, my contacts weren't all that great at close examination any longer, though I was loathe to leave the room to get my cheaters from my jacket. Squinting harder, I felt my eyebrows go up. "That looks like the same sort of indentation."

"It is. Heather had a note in the file that you thought Davies was left-handed; there's some slight confirmation for you. I think he typically wore his watch on his right hand, but I'll need to do a bit of fancy skin microscopy to confirm whether there is actually long-term skin irritation."

Unconsciously rubbing my own smart watch beneath the glove, I asked: "You can see that sort of thing?"

"Science is amazing," she laughed as she gently put the arm back beside the body. "I'm not sure what this means, exactly, but it *could* be evidence that the killer needed us to think the victim was right-handed."

"I have no idea why they would," I sighed. "Other than trying to cover up the fact they slashed the wrong wrist. Another oddity for the list."

"Now, about the tape." Dr. Hamilton pointed to a several spots of skin discoloration along the arm she was closest to. "Clear indications that something tight had been wrapped at these points, with matching antemortem marks on the chest and other arm. Whatever was used had been cinched quite snuggly."

"Enough to prevent Davies from struggling when the wrist was cut?"

"Likely, yes," she said. "Also explaining why the lines are so smooth."

"He might have also been drugged," I mused, thinking back to the scene before shaking my head. "Though it seems a bit unlikely. Breakfast was in progress in the kitchen, which tells me Davies was interrupted by someone and either took them or was forced up to the room where we found him."

"We'll run the toxicology panel just in case," Lou said before pointing to the face. "But there is also some irritation around the mouth and jaw, possible indicators that he'd been gagged by the same tape." She looked up at me. "Whoever did this to your victim likely wanted him aware of what was going on; that would kind of preclude any sort of drug angle."

I looked down on the slack face of the radio personality. "Davies' cottage was quite distant from his neighbors; and, given the time of year, I'm not certain there would have been anyone around to hear any screams for help." Looking back at Lou, I felt a frown forming beneath my mask. "The killer *wanted* him to feel helpless."

"That would be my read on it," she said.

Looking back at Davies, that frown of mine deepened a bit. "This feels personal. Visceral, even."

"Very." Lou replied. "I can't help the impression someone was settling a score here."

"I imagine as a radio personality, he likely had his share of detractors," I thought out loud. "What I *can't* imagine is he said anything that would have led a listener to try and fake his suicide, though. Kill him, maybe, but make it seem like Davies took his own life?" I shook my head. "Something's not quite right here."

"And you're frustrated you can't figure it out," Lou observed.

"Yeah."

I slowly walked the edge of the exam table, running my gloved finger along the cool aluminum as I looked over the body anew. While

I'd already come to the conclusion that suicide was out, I also knew I had very little background on my victim — so little, in fact, it was hard to formulate any sort of theory of why he ended up dead in his cottage, if not downright impossible. Digging through the data sources I had access to would only get me so far; in order to move beyond the high-level sketch that would provide, there was no way around having to travel to Portland and dig into Davies' life the old-fashioned way: knocking on doors and asking questions of anyone and everyone that had so much as a tangential connection to the victim. With enough persistence — and no small amount of luck — I might be able to dislodge some sort of tidbit that would connect enough dots they would lead to an explanation that made sense.

"Hair is natural," Dr. Hamilton continued after a moment, respecting my moment of rumination. "And I don't see any evidence of plastic surgery. Based on his BMI, I would venture to guess we'll find Davies was borderline diabetic, but the bloodwork will fill in more details from that end."

I nodded. "Sitting behind a microphone doesn't appear to have aided in his fitness."

"Not everyone can continue to swim as an Olympian," Lou laughed.

"I spend a fair amount of time hunched over my laptop at the kitchen table," I admitted. "Though the swimming does help. And running."

"And weightlifting?"

"Only when I have to," I sighed. "Which, as it turns out, seems to be three to four times a week."

"I hadn't noticed," Lou deadpanned. "Nor had any of my staff."

"Right," I rolled my eyes. "Anything else?"

"Just one more thing," Lou said. Moving to stand beside me at the end of the table, she pointed with a gloved finger to the feet. "The discoloration is a bit hard to pick out owing to how dehydrated this body is, but I'm reasonably sure this person had a fairly advanced case of peripheral arterial disease."

"Peripheral *what?*"

Turning a leg slightly, she indicated a slight bumpiness along the calf muscle. "In simpler language, varicose veins," she explained. "Oddly, I wouldn't expect to see them on someone with a sedentary lifestyle; people who stand for a living — and have other circulatory issues — tend to sport these beauties. They appear when there is a weak lining to the blood vessel, or plaque buildup that forces blood to back up in the damndest places."

I looked again at the slightly extended midsection. "Or are obese?"

"Yeah," Lou nodded. "That's another risk factor. Still, unless Davies did his radio show from a standing desk every day, it seems odd that he would have developed them. It might mean there is some sort of genetic issue that runs in the family."

"Good to know," I said.

"That's about it, save for reviewing the internal organs. Time to crack him open."

"Ah," I replied. "Lovely. I think I will leave you to it, then."

"And read about it in the report?" Dr. Hamilton asked as she moved over to her table and plucked some tools from the surface. "You'll miss all of the fun."

"Somehow, I doubt it," I chuckled as I began to pull off my gloves. "You'll update the file when you are done?"

"Of course," she replied before glancing to the clock on the wall. "It's late enough, I might not get it fully transcribed until tomorrow morning. The good news there is your lab results might come in at the same time."

"I'm disappointed," I teased. "I was looking forward to some light reading at bedtime."

"Sorry to crush your hopes," she chuckled.

"It's okay," I continued. "I'm probably headed to Portland in the morning anyway. I won't have much time to read it until I get back. But you'll text me if something extraordinary comes up?"

"As always."

"Then I am off to rescue my girlfriend," I said as I started toward the door. "She's watching my cousin's kids until I get back to Windeport. No telling what sort of trouble the three of them are getting into."

"You? *Babysitting*?" Lou asked, the incredulousness clearly visible in her voice. "I never thought I would see the day."

"People change," I replied simply. "Lord knows, I have."

"Not as much as you might think," Lou observed. "In fact," she added softly, "maybe you're just realizing latent talents you never knew you had."

I paused at the door. "You sound like my girlfriend."

Lou laughed as she picked up her thoracic saw. "One smart woman, that."

Six

The trip back from Augusta took longer than I expected, proof positive that Newton's Third Law could be applied to travel. For it was clear that the universe was paying me back for having arrived early for the autopsy by throwing one semi-truck after another into my path, especially along the long, windy two-lane stretch of Route 203 between the interstate and Windeport. On the one hand, it was nice to know that some sort of commerce was still taking place along that portion of the Maine Coast; on the other, this particular late afternoon, I found myself seriously wishing far more of it had been routed via the railroad tracks that paralleled the county highway, for that had always seemed to me a far more sensible use of resources on a ton-by-ton basis. Adding insult to injury, about twenty miles outside of Windeport the overcast day made good on its threat of snow, appearing first as gently descending waves of lazy flakes, but quickly degenerating into a full-on thick veil of white. Conditions worsened from there, making it impossible for me to safely get around the logging truck I found myself trailing.

Wanting someone to complain to, I asked Siri to dial Suzanne. My heart did its normal flutter when her warm voice filled the cabin of my SUV. "Hello Milady," I sighed. "How are you holding up?"

"Funny you should ask," she chuckled. "How far out are you?"

"The snow's picked up a bit; I'm not far from UEM, so maybe forty-five minutes?"

"Good," Suzanne replied. "Something's come up, and I need you to make a side trip for me."

"Of course," I said. "What do you need?"

"Well, Kitty," she said, lowering her voice slightly, "it seems the twins are doing a little make-believe and have managed to 'steal' Ladybug's Miraculous. They are anxiously awaiting Chat Noir's arrival to save her."

"Seriously?" I asked, rolling my eyes. "I thought they were into *Star Wars* now — it's been ages since I've seen them playing characters from *Miraculous* over at Charlie's house."

"They are."

I frowned at my reflection in the rear-view mirror. "I'm confused."

"I'm not surprised," she laughed. "But kids will be kids. At any rate, it would be most helpful if you were to arrive in, uh, character."

My eyebrows went up. "You... you want me to come wearing the *costume?*"

"Yes," she confirmed, before lowering her voice further. "I'll make it worth your while, Kitty."

Before I had a chance to respond, memories of the last time the two of us had been attired in our costumes flashed into my brain, as well as how difficult it had been to get the eye makeup I used beneath the domino mask off the sheets of her bed. It seemed like a small sacrifice to make, so I smiled as I replied. "As you wish, Milady. I'll need to zip past the bungalow to change."

"I figured. I think I can keep them distracted until you get here; dinner will be ready by then, too."

"Oh? What's on the menu?"

"Fried tribbles, blue milk, dark matter fingers with a side of space cucumbers."

"Tribbles? Blue milk? What the hell am I getting into?"

"More than you can know," Suzanne chuckled. "See you soon."

Sighing as the call beeped to a conclusion, I focused on the road conditions and ignored, for the moment, that I would soon be wearing form-fitting spandex from head to toe all because of my love for Suzanne. As I slowed further to more easily navigate the slushy buildup beneath my wheels, it occurred to me Deidre and I would never have romped around Windeport in coordinating superhero costumes at Halloween charity events, nor could I picture the two of us working the halls of the Children's Hospital Critical Care Ward much as I did with Suzanne on a monthly basis. My life had changed significantly in the year since my fiancé departed, though it was almost as if I were just *now* coming to understand just *how* significantly.

The snow was falling thickly enough that only mere glimpses of the UEM campus were visible when at long last I finally passed it by; one of the massive plows from Public Works met me at the corner of Route 203 and Main Street, with another close on its heels. Route One appeared to have recently been cleared, with the dark pavement glinting icily beneath the light of cute-but-nearly-useless carriage lamps that had replaced the streetlights through what we euphemistically thought of as the downtown area. A few blocks later, my headlamps raked over the first of multiple stately homes that had once upon a time been summer getaways for the wealthy of Boston or points further south as I turned onto the Sea Road; Ocean View Avenue appeared lifeless as was appropriate for that portion of the season, save for the twin sprites of illumination emanating from my bungalow — one sconce to either side of the carport, recently wired into a light sensor so they would be on from dusk to dawn. I smiled slightly at the beacons in the night as I pulled into the driveway and then beneath the shelter of the overhang, a pleasant reminder that I had arrived home.

And home it had become; when I'd first moved into it, I hadn't been so sure, but over time — and with lots of help from Suzanne — I had carefully crafted something that was uniquely my own. Slipping out of the SUV and hurrying through the cold to the door, I thought about how the bungalow had in its own way managed to push aside my tortured memories of the final months I'd spent in the apartment: all of the angst over Deidre's departure and my father evicting me had gradually been replaced by happier thoughts of evenings curled up with Suzanne, watching the fire flicker in my living room, or the months we'd hosted Vasily as he'd recuperated from his assault. As I stood just inside the kitchen and looked out at the living room and the tall windows facing the ocean beyond, I realized my fondest memories (so far) surrounded the four of us celebrating Christmas together, despite the Nor'easter (and a murder).

What a long way I'd come, I thought with a trace of satisfaction. *What a long way* all *of us have come.*

Dropping my keys on the dish atop the table beside the door, I shrugged out of my jacket and hung it on a peg before kicking off my boots; pulling off my sweater as I moved down the hallway to the master bedroom, it took me a moment to find the unrelieved black fabric of the Chat Noir costume in my closet, along with the small box of accessories that completed the outfit. Having worn it so often in the year-plus since Charlie had given it to me, I had become something of an old hand at squeezing myself in the fabric that seemed preternaturally capable of revealing every ripple of every muscle, leaving very little to the imagination. Despite being a swimmer who regularly revealed even *more* on the deck of the pool, I always felt more than a little exposed while wearing the outfit – a feeling that somewhat ironically abated the further I got into costume. Less than twenty minutes later, I was staring at my superhero alter ego in the mirror of the master bath, fully decked out in black from head to toe with a matching domino mask, blond wig with two feline ears and a pair of boots that Charlie had somehow managed to craft with a paw-print logo on the sole.

Grabbing the overly long leather belt from the counter that served as my "tail," I buckled it behind me and adjusted it so I could press the small metallic baton into the hidden Velcro that held it at the small of my back. A recent upgrade from Charlie had allowed me to stash my actual iPhone inside the device, along with my wallet and keys — especially helpful since the two visible pockets on the front of my costume were more or less useless. Nodding once more at my reflection, I smiled at how just a little makeup and a change of clothing could so completely alter one's perspective; while I didn't know the character as well as either Suzanne or Vasily, I knew *enough* that I could always feel a part of me shift into a somewhat wilier frame of mind, a looser, freer version of myself that I only seemed capable of showing when hiding beneath the mask and wig.

Returning to the door for the carport, I grabbed my keys for the SUV from the dish by the door and then hurried back out into the storm only to be reminded immediately of how thin the fabric of the costume was when the bitter cold air sliced directly through it. Sliding behind the wheel of the vehicle, it took a moment for me to arrange my tail so I wasn't tangled in the pedals before I started it up and began to back out of my driveway. For a fleeting moment, I wondered if I should have packed an overnight bag with a change of clothes; since Suzanne had more-or-less moved in with me at the bungalow, we tended to only overnight in the pharmacy on the occasions when my girlfriend was on-call and needed ready access to her office. I saw my masked face frown in the rear-view mirror as I tried to recall what might still be left in the emergency stash I kept at Suzanne's apartment.

I'd just reached the corner of Ocean View Avenue and the Sea Road when my iPhone sang out; triggering the Bluetooth function on the SUV, I smiled as I answered. "Cat calling again, Milady?"

"Most definitely," Suzanne answered. "Have you left yet?"

"Just turning onto the Sea Road."

"Great. Can you swing by the IGA? It seems I need some more bubble solution."

I felt my heart sink. "You need me to go to the store? Tonight?" I asked, nearly choking.

"Yeah. Don't ask me why, but the twins seem to need bubbles in order to subdue Chat Noir. I think they are misremembering an episode where Marinette *and* Chat were trapped by the villain in giant soap bubbles, but I am loathe to correct them. That, and I need more wine."

"Uh..." I started, glancing quickly from the road down to my black-spandex-cladded chest. "How badly do you need either item?"

There was a long pause as I slowly drove down the snow-covered road. "You're wearing the costume without anything over it, aren't you?" Suzanne finally asked.

"I... am..."

"Well now, that's a bit of a predicament. Not that anyone in the IGA hasn't already *seen* you in said outfit. If I recall correctly, you had a half-page photo in the paper from this past Halloween."

"Don't remind me. I am *never* going to live that down."

"No, you aren't," Suzanne laughed. "I feel like something sweet, so can you get a blend?"

I blinked as I realized I had already lost the higher ground. "Of course, Milady," I sighed, defeated. "You know I'll do anything for you."

"I promise to only use my powers for good. See you in a bit."

Trying to steel my nerves, I turned away from the old pharmacy building when I reached Route One and instead made my way south toward the small grocery store that had once been owned by my ex-fiancé, Deidre. I felt slightly better when I saw the parking lot was nearly empty and pulled into a spot a few down from the double doors of the main entrance. After taking a moment to slowly pound my blond wigged head against the steering wheel, I locked up the SUV and entered the IGA, trying to make it seem completely ordinary that the Chief of Police would appear attired as I was in such a public space.

Ignoring the slack-jawed expression from the sole cashier on duty, I waved a claw-tipped glove in her direction as I plucked a basket from the container by the door and then quickly made my way first to the small liquor aisle. I breathed a bit easier when I saw it was deserted, and moved down to the red wine section in order to grab the brand I knew Suzanne enjoyed; thinking it might be a long night, I snagged a second one to help salve my wounded feline dignity (damn, now I was *thinking* like Chat) before tacking around to the toy aisle in search of bubble solution. My prey was on the bottom shelf between bouncy balls and Crayons, forcing me to kneel on the cold industrial tile in order to determine if there was a significant difference between the various colors of containers.

"Sean?"

Freezing at the familiar voice, I slowly turned and looked up at the astonished expression on Deidre's face from where she stood at one end of the aisle. For once, I was happy that the domino mask covered as much of my face as it did, hiding the deepening flush of my embarrassment. "Hey, De," I smiled, trying to sound far more nonchalant than I felt. "Do you know which one of these is better?" I asked holding up two different bottles. "This one says the bubbles are long lasting, but I fear they are lying."

Trying — and failing — to suppress a smirk, Deidre moved over to me; aware once more of her pregnancy, I stood so she'd not have to dip toward my level. "I've never bought either," she replied, eyeing me again. "And I can't imagine what has transpired that would make you want to buy some."

My masked eyes narrowed as I found myself compelled to respond with a healthy dose of snark. "You seem surprised to see this side of me, Deidre. Ironic, given how long we were together; it was always here."

Deidre seemed taken aback by my reply. "You buried your inner child from me, Sean. I can only assume it was related to your stance on having a family."

The power of the costume I was wearing unexpectedly gave me the courage of conviction. "The two are not related, my dear. And of the two of us, I think you were far more opaque with your desire to have children."

"You made it quite clear that you hated the idea of having kids of your own," she replied, the plastic canister of bubbles in her hand forgotten for the moment. "It seemed like an argument not worth pursuing. Which is why it's all the more incredulous to me you are standing here in a *child's* costume, buying toys. It makes me wonder if you were lying when you said you hated children."

"Oh, Deidre," I smiled sadly. "I never said that."

"You—"

"I remember that conversation," I continued. "Rather clearly, since it was the day you told me you weren't ready to get married. I believe my exact words were something like 'I'm not sure I'll *ever* be ready to be a father.' A sentiment, I believe, many men often feel when they first consider the implications of starting a family. You, on the other hand, were apparently far more ready than you let on."

"I don't see the distinction."

"I'm sure you don't," I said, shrugging. "But you also clearly hadn't paid attention to how I doted on Charlie's kids while we were together. The number of weekends I romped through the woods with them, fighting imaginary dragons or having tea with the Queen of Hearts." I smiled a bit more. "I'm not sure I could blame you for not seeing it, for it wasn't until after you left me that I saw it myself. Then again," I paused, reaching over and putting a claw tip to her chin, "communication doesn't seem to have been our strong suit, either."

Deidre looked at me. "You want kids now, don't you?"

"No," I replied easily as my hand dropped. "But that doesn't mean I don't now understand that I *could* have become a great father. That, though, is a career I will never have. My calling is elsewhere."

Slowly, Deidre nodded. "You're not the same man I left."

"I am, actually," I replied, cocking my head as Chat did in the show. "You're just finally seeing the *true* me for the first time."

A genuine smile appeared at the edge of her lips. "I suppose so. And I'm glad I had the chance."

"Me, too," I replied after a moment.

"All of those years together," Deidre continued. "We kind of screwed it up, didn't we?"

"Maybe. Maybe not," I shrugged again. "Tell me this: are you truly happy with what's-his-name?"

"Thomas? Yes," she answered.

"Then *that* is all that matters at the end of the day," I replied. "What we had, for a long time, was the most perfect love I had ever experienced to that point, and I thank you for that. I'm sorry I wasn't who you wanted me to be, but that doesn't detract from the fact we were happy. For a while."

Deidre half smiled. "To that point?"

"Well," I smiled slyly, "I shouldn't tell tales out of school, but this feline's heart has been captured completely by another."

That brought a chuckle. "You really do get into character with that outfit, don't you?"

"It's magical fabric," I corrected with mock seriousness. "It's hard not to."

"This one, I think," Deidre said as she handed me the bubble solution she'd been holding. "I presume this is for your nieces; I think they'll appreciate the unicorns on the side."

"They will," I nodded as I slipped the bottle between the two of wine. Pausing for a moment, I added, quietly: "I'm glad I ran into you."

"Me, too," Deidre replied after a moment. "Take care of yourself, Sean."

"Same for you and your new family," I smiled.

We looked at each other for a long moment, and briefly, the connection we had once shared burst into being; I put down my basket and drew her into a quick hug before we parted ways. The clerk still appeared to be speechless as I checked out, though I did manage to get a slight smile from her when I twirled my tail as I waited for her to process my order. Halfway out the door to the SUV, though, my iPhone buzzed within the baton, and I shifted the bags in my hands to grab it and free the device long enough to answer.

"Chief Colbeth."

"Chief, it's Caitlyn. Are you back in Windeport?"

"I am," I replied as I leaned the phone on my shoulder so I could unlock the SUV.

"Then would you mind swinging through the station? There's a woman here claiming to be the daughter of the victim we found yesterday."

"Lovely. I imagine she wants an update."

"And more," Caitlyn replied, sounding a bit exasperated. "She won't leave until she's talked to you."

Looking at the bag on the passenger seat, I sighed. "I had dinner plans."

"The sooner you get here, the sooner we can all go home," she pleaded.

"Fine," I sighed again. "Let me call Suzanne and break the news."

"Bless you, Chief."

I hung up with Caitlyn and immediately dialed Suzanne; being the long-suffering girlfriend of a Police Chief meant she was well aware my plans could change on a dime, so she graciously allowed that she would save a plate of fried tribble for me in the oven — though she was less inclined to say that Ladybug would be able to hold out for Chat Noir's rescue.

"Things are getting dire," she finished with deep seriousness. "You'd better hurry."

"I'll do my best," I laughed grimly as I hung up and started the SUV.

The snow accumulation along Route One had become significant, making the otherwise short drive between the IGA at one end to the Public Safety building at the other something of a trial. Several passes from the snowplows had left a sizable bank in front of the station, making me thankful I had a four-wheel option on the SUV; clambering over the hurdle, I pulled into my designated spot and paused, taking in the reflection of my masked visage in the small rear-view mirror. While it wasn't the first time I'd been at the station in full cosplay mode, it *would* be the first time I'd be talking to a relative of a victim in a case I was working clad in something other than professional attire. Sighing deeply, I turned off the SUV and pushed out into the snow, suppressing a shudder as the frigid wind sliced once more through the thin fabric of my costume.

The things I do for family, I thought to myself.

Pulling open the outer door for the police portion of the building, I stomped the snow out of my boots and tried to act as normal as possible as I entered the outer reception area. To her credit, Caitlyn barely arched an eyebrow when she saw me from her perch behind the semi-circular intake desk; a short, brown-haired woman was leaning on the transaction counter to her right and also turned at my entrance. Assuming she was my prey—er, guest, I smiled my warmest smile and reached out a claw-tipped glove.

"Ms. Davies?" I asked. "I'm Chief Colbeth. Deputy Chief Korsoko-vach let me know you were planning on stopping by."

"Chief..." she said, her eyes slowing traveling from my feline ear-topped blond wig to the domino mask to the long belt tail that I'd let drag along the floor. Returning her gaze to mine, she finally took my hand. "It's Davies-Benson, actually."

"My apologies," I replied. Now that she wasn't leaning against the counter, I could see she was a bit taller than I'd initially suspected, enhanced a bit by boots that seemed to have a significant heel to them. Knowing that she had flown out from California made it unsurprising that she was clad in light fabric — some sort of denim cut specifically for the type of boots she had on, a blouse of matching fabric and an anorak of contrasting color. The entire ensemble made her look more as though she'd been shopping at one of the gargantuan malls I knew dotted Southern California like palm trees instead of hopping on a plane to cross the country on the hope we'd found her father.

I wasn't looking forward to the rest of the conversation.

"No need to," she said after she shook and dropped her hand. "I probably should have changed it after the death of my husband, but for one reason or another, never got around to it." She looked at me again. "Do you greet all strangers to Windeport this way, or were you on your way to a costume party?"

"Babysitting, actually," I replied. "My nieces have a rather active imagination; my cousin encourages their creativity, so by extension, I do as well."

Gennifer smiled slightly, which took some of the tiredness away from her smooth features. "Kids can do that to you. Thanks for inter-rupting your evening to speak with me."

"Of course," I tilted my head toward her in assent. Catching her try to prevent a shiver, and knowing I was feeling just as frosty myself, I inclined my feline ears toward the locked door that led to our inner sanctum. "Come back to my office and we'll talk over a cup of coffee."

"That sounds divine," she replied.

Having left my badge in the SUV, I had Caitlyn buzz us through the door, and I led Gennifer down the short passage past the framed photos of all the chiefs that had come before me and into the squad room. Though the lights were on, the cubicles were mostly empty save for one of my newest hires; Danielle was fresh from the Justice Academy and therefore had drawn the short straw for the overnight shift. I nodded at her as we passed, though the look on her face made me wonder if she thought the Chat Noir costume was some sort of weird hazing the senior staff hadn't clued her in about.

"Small department," Gennifer said as we navigated the cubicle farm toward my office in the corner.

"We are," I replied. "Smaller now than ever, given how Windeport is pretty much a village in decline."

"I'm sorry to hear that," she said. "Vasily — I mean, Deputy Chief Korsokovach, speaks highly of you."

I smiled as I opened the door to my office and turned the lights on. "Vasily and I go way back. And please, call me Sean."

"All right," she nodded.

Waving to the guest chairs in front of my battleship-sized desk, I moved to my cherished Keurig and turned it on. "I can offer regular or decaf; I might even have a K-cup of hot cocoa if I root around a bit."

"Regular is fine," she said as she settled into the left chair.

"Cream? Sugar?"

"Black, please," she replied.

I put the first K-cup into the device and turned to lean on the counter as it started to chug into life. "How was your flight?"

"Better than I expected. It was so last minute, my only option was something into Manchester; it's been years since I've been back to visit Dad at his cottage and had misjudged how much of a drive it is from that part of New Hampshire."

"Boston isn't a whole lot closer," I observed. "And I'm sure you probably wouldn't have found anything into Portland."

"Not that wouldn't have required a second mortgage," she said wryly.

"Thank you," she added gratefully as I handed her a steaming mug. "Though I have to admit, this is the first time I've ever had coffee with a human-sized cat."

"Windeport is a unique spot," I smiled.

"I remember that much," she nodded as she blew across the surface of her coffee.

"When was the last time you were here?" I asked as I repeated my operation for my own cup of joy.

"Senior year of high school," Gennifer replied. "I spent the summer here before going to UCLA."

"You never came back?"

"No," she said. "I fell in love with the weather in Southern Cal and stayed. Besides, I work in the film industry; not much of that in Portland."

"Oh? Are you an actor?"

"Hardly. I'm a makeup artist on staff at Paramount Pictures."

"I feel like I should know that name," I said as I took my own mug from the Keurig and moved behind my desk.

"It's one of the older studios in Hollywood," she explained. "They've made some of the best known movies over the years. *Rocky. The Godfather. Titanic.*" Gennifer paused when she saw my blank expression. "Or maybe not – you act like you don't recognize those pictures. They do still have movie theaters in Maine, right?"

"The last one in Windeport closed about a decade ago," I replied. "We have to drive to Augusta if we want to take in a show."

"Wow. This *is* a small town."

"We do have cable," I replied, "and Internet. But in my defense, it's only through the efforts of my girlfriend that I feel like I have any sort of grasp on popular culture, tenuous though it is." I waved at my costume. "I'd not even heard of *Miraculous* before dressing the part of Chat Noir at our village Halloween party more than a year ago."

Gennifer smiled slightly. "The costume suits you, oddly."

"So I've heard."

The conversation lapsed comfortably as we mutually sipped our respective coffees; then, Gennifer cleared her throat. "Did you find my father?"

Putting my mug down on the surface of the desk, I frowned. "We did find someone at the cottage, yes, but I'm still awaiting an official identification."

"But it was him?" she pressed.

I nodded slowly. "Based on the circumstances, I believe so, yes. I am so sorry to be the one to tell you."

"I think... I think I knew he was gone. When he didn't return my calls and never showed," she said. I noticed that she was gripping the mug with two hands, tight enough that her knuckles were white.

"You were close?"

Gennifer nodded. "Despite the distance, we spoke every day and he generally came to California on most major holidays. After my husband died — damn, I guess it was ten years ago next month — Dad spent three months in California, helping me get our life back together." She smiled slightly. "He had the station ship him equipment so he could broadcast from a small conference room at the hotel where he was staying."

"Wow."

"Yeah," she nodded. "My kids grew up with him in their lives. They're teens now, but it's still going to be hard on them."

"And you," I observed quietly.

"Yeah. Me, too." Sipping from her mug, she considered me for a moment. "What can you tell me? And how can I help with the identification?"

"It's still pretty early for our investigation," I replied. "So other than telling you we found your father, I can't provide too many details quite yet. Are you planning on staying in Windeport?"

"I can't," she shook her head. "I'm working on a show right now and need to be back; my return flight leaves tomorrow morning. I need to head back to Manchester tonight so I can catch the flight."

"Then that partially answers your second question. Normally, I would ask you to come with me to the morgue, but given your tight turnaround, with your permission we'll do a DNA swab and use it to confirm the identity of your father."

"I can do that."

I looked at Gennifer. "You flew a long way just to spend a few minutes with me," I observed. "Why?"

The woman's face flushed slightly. "I... expected to find Dad here," she replied after a moment. "When I landed, I drove straight to the cottage. My original plan was to yank him from whatever he thought was more important up here and drag him back to Los Angeles with me." She put her own mug down on the far side of my desk; the way the mugs were aligned made them look like they were opposing football players on an empty field. "That kinda went out the window when I found the crime scene tape on the front door."

"You bought *two* return tickets? Last minute?"

"I did," she said. "My credit card balance is pretty ugly. Now I'm out that too, I suppose."

"I wish I'd had better news for you," I apologized again. "If you wouldn't mind providing me your contact information, I'll keep you in the loop — unless you want me to use Chief Korsokovach as a go-between."

"No, contact me directly," she said.

Pulling open a drawer, I retrieved a notepad and pen, then slid them across to Gennifer. "Let me get the DNA swab and consent form, then we'll get you on your way back to Manchester."

"Thank you," she nodded as she began scribbling on the paper.

Slipping out from behind my desk, I moved out into the main space of the station and over to the small supply closet we had next to the evidence room. Sorting through the shelves, I came up with a standard DNA kit, then went to a small filing cabinet beside it that held paper versions of our legal forms. Normally I would have her fill out something on one of our tablets so it could become an immediate part of our case system, but I figured the old-fashioned route would get her out a bit faster; besides, I could scan it into the system in the morning.

Returning to my office, I handed her the form and pointed to where she could sign. "This will authorize us to run your sample through the State of Maine's testing systems in order to match the sample we took from your father," I explained. "If you have done anything illegal over the past two decades, you might want to tell me now, though."

Gennifer sat back, pen in midair. "Why?"

"The system runs the sample against all other samples in the database," I said. "So if you broke into a house in Sheboygan and left some trace behind, we might connect you to that case."

She looked at me for a long moment. "Are you trying to be funny?"

"Kind of," I replied, before smiling slightly. "Just my poor attempt to lighten the mood a bit."

"Thanks — I think, though it's a bit scary there is such a database in existence."

"I agree," I nodded as she signed and then turned toward me.

It took just a moment to swab her cheek and then pack up the sample, and a moment more to walk Gennifer back toward the entrance. "You'll let me know once the results are back?" she asked as we paused by Caitlyn's desk.

"Absolutely," I nodded. I could feel the feline ears shift as I did so and wondered at how seriously she'd been taking me. "Safe travels back to New Hampshire."

"Thank you," she replied as she shook my gloved hand once more.

"A pleasure meeting you. Again, I'm sorry it was under less than ideal circumstances."

Looking at me again for another long moment, she nodded. "I think I'm in good hands," Gennifer said before pushing through the door and disappearing into the night.

Turning back to Caitlyn, I held up the small sample package. "I need this taken to Augusta immediately," I said. "Think Danielle is up to the task?"

"What recent recruit wouldn't want the challenge of driving to Augusta in middle of a snowstorm?" she replied with her own question. "She might think we're punishing her."

"It'll build character," I laughed.

"Sure it will," she replied as she took the package from me. "I'll enter it into the case system for you and then dispatch her right away."

"Thanks," I nodded. "And now, I am off to rescue Suzanne."

"Looking like that," Caitlyn replied, a smile playing on her lips, "the situation must be pretty dire."

Moving to the door myself, I paused with a claw-tipped glove on the handle. "I'm *paw*sitive I'm the *purr*fect feline for the job."

Caitlyn snorted. "I don't doubt it. Have a pleasant evening, Chief."

"I have a *feline* it will be," I smirked as I pushed through the door.

Seven

As I'd predicted, I wound up spending the night at Suzanne's apartment; Charlie had arrived far later than she'd anticipated, having run into the same challenges as I had with the deepening snow. That didn't seem to have mattered to my girlfriend, though, for mere moments after my cousin departed with her two sleeping kids close to midnight, Suzanne grabbed me by the belt tail and tugged me into the master suite. It didn't take a rocket scientist to figure out what her plans for me were, especially when she began to slowly pull the bell-tipped zipper on the front of my costume down. I was well aware of how Suzanne's stress levels surrounding running her practice had been inching ever upward; as the sole family practice for miles in any direction, she had a huge book of business and very little backup to support it. Our upcoming vacation to the comic book convention in Anaheim was one of the few times during the year when she could get coverage and, at least for a while, let her hair down. In the interim, I had made it my mission to relax her as best as I could (and as frequently as I could) in whatever manner suited her best. Some days, it was a lazy dinner watching the tide change from the back porch of my cottage; other nights, it was allowing her to have her way with a feline-themed superhero, right down to the mask and faux ears.

My internal alarm clock woke me a few minutes past four, my usual time in order to change and make it to morning practice at the UEM Aquatics Center. Lying against a particularly wide pillow on Suzanne's bed, her warm body curled into mine beneath the only comforter pulled just to her chin, I debated the wisdom of leaving the cocoon of warmth we had created, but my overwhelming guilt at possibly missing even *one* session had me carefully sliding out from beneath Suzanne and padding across the cold floor to the master bath. Gently closing the door, I snapped on the light and immediately hoped the road to UEM had not been plowed, for my image in the mirror confirmed I was still wearing the domino mask, though every *other* piece of the Chat Noir costume appeared to have been removed. Sighing, I opened the medicine cabinet and hunted for the makeup remover Suzanne kept on hand, as well as the small bottle of Westmore adhesive remover; by the time I'd pried off the mask to reveal my raccoon eyes, I was resigned to the fact that getting to the pool on time wasn't going to happen and reset my workout expectations accordingly. Fortunately, Suzanne had a treadmill down in the office below us, one that she used for stress tests with her cardiac patients; though not my first choice, running to no-where seemed more agreeable than trying to locate my crampons and working my way through the snowy streets of Windeport.

Wiping away the eye black from first one eye, and then the other, I quickly scrubbed my face with soap and then dried off before stealthily sneaking back into the master bedroom to search for a set of workout gear from my side of her closet. I smiled slightly as I groped around in what had once been Deidre's portion of the space, another reminder of how my situation had flipped since Suzanne had appeared in my life; as my fingers latched onto the technical fabric of my running tights, I wondered for a moment just how much of my gear was spread out between our two places, and then realized true love – at least for me – meant *home* was wherever Suzanne happened to be. I was equally as happy sitting by the fireplace with her in my bungalow as I was curled up beside her in the bed of her apartment. Tugging on a muscle tank top in the dark, I successfully managed to pull on the compression leggings without tumbling to the floor and waking my still-slumbering girlfriend; not long after, I was tiptoeing down the back staircase to the rear entrance of the medical practice, then let myself in using the spare key Suzanne had provided. Closing the door behind me, I slipped the key into the small pocket in my tights before snapping on one bank of lights in the hallway I'd entered, then crossed to the room holding the treadmill.

As it happens, it was the same space that the therapy jacuzzi occupied; opening the door, the comfortable smell of chlorine hit my nose, though it wasn't nearly as pronounced as what I experienced at the UEM pool. The treadmill was up against the wall and had been turned to face the door, so I stepped around the control panel and up onto the belt, then clicked through some of the options on the presets before landing on an easy five mile run with a two percent grade. After three initial warning beeps, the belt began to move then quickly came up to speed so I could begin my journey to nowhere.

The first mile was usually the one where I focused the most on the workout; by the second, the fitness part of my brain generally went on autopilot, allowing me to shift my thoughts to something else entirely. That morning, I began to chart out how I wanted to spend my day while trying hard not to analyze what little evidence I'd reviewed so far. I'd already decided that I needed to get to Portland and talk to people who knew Don Davies; that seemed like a higher priority to me that combing through the boxes Heather had left in the wake of her crime scene review. While the majority of the items had already been cataloged and were accessible in the case system, I always felt like personally reviewing the evidence could lead to interesting discoveries; still, the fact they had been digitized meant if I had to stay down south for a day or two, I'd be able to paw through the data in my hotel room.

Will I need more than a day? I wondered. *Maybe. I've got to talk to his bosses at the radio station, and there's no question I'd like to take a peek at his house. I need to know more about this guy before I can start to understand why someone wanted to kill him — and make it look like a suicide.*

While I'd been working under the theory that the killer hadn't known Davies was left-handed, I knew I needed hard evidence to confirm what I'd seen anecdotally at the cottage. With my luck, he'd wind up being ambidextrous. Still, I'd worked with Vasily long enough to appreciate some of the quirkiness that came up when someone was left-handed;

he'd always tended to place his phone to one side when we were at a table together, and had preferred sitting on the end of the couch in our apartment closer to a particular end table he preferred. That, and he invariably folded the towels in a way that always seemed backwards to me, but he found perfectly natural. There was some humor in using a bath towel to help support a theory, though it wouldn't be the first time something so mundane had broken a case wide open.

The treadmill had just chirped the beginning of my final mile when the door to the room opened; Suzanne appeared wearing a bathrobe and holding a steaming mug of coffee. Smiling, she moved to stand in front of the workout machine. "You missed a spot," she said, smiling wider.

Knowing she meant I likely had a dark smudge of black eye makeup still around one orbit, I rolled my eyes. "Lovely," I breathed, trying not to sound winded. "I'll need some help getting it off before I leave."

"I'm all for that," she smiled wider. "You're up early."

"I was going to go to practice before I realized I still had the mask on."

"That was the *only* thing you had on for most of last night," she reminded me.

"So it seems," I replied, trying not to laugh. "I've got to go to Portland, so I'm probably going to get out of here before breakfast."

"I figured. How long?"

"A day, maybe two. I'd ask you to come, but I know you can't."

"Sadly, no. If it were next weekend, I could since it's my turn on the Children's Ward."

"I understand. Hopefully I won't *still* be there when your weekend rolls around."

"Jesus," she replied, eyes wide. "What exactly are you expecting to dig through?"

"I've no idea, Suze. I have a victim without a motive for his death and know next to nothing about his background to help paint in the details. There are people to talk to," I breathed, trying not to gasp as the treadmill kicked into a higher speed for my final sprint. "And places I need to see."

"I hope it goes well, then," she said. "And efficiently."

"Same," I replied.

"I'm going to go upstairs and shower now," Suzanne said as she moved back to the door. Pausing with one hand on the knob, she smiled impishly. "If you hurry, I might still be there when you arrive," she added before disappearing into the hallway.

Appropriately motivated, I finished out the final quarter mile of the workout with a personal best and joined Suzanne beneath the delightfully hot water pouring out of her upgraded showerhead. We seemed to sense it might be a few days before we'd be able to repeat the sensuous events of the prior evening, so by unspoken agreement, we eschewed removing the final vestiges of my eye makeup in favor of holding each other close under the deluge; slowly, deliberately, I used every technique I had learned from our time together to remind her how much she meant to me. Gasping together with her back pressed against the tile warmed by the steam billowing around us, she shuddered with sweet release a fraction of a moment before I felt myself tumble over the edge of no return. Coming back to my senses took longer than I expected, helped not in the least by how Suzanne appeared fixated on, shall we say, getting a second rise out of me.

That she turned out to be successful delayed my departure long enough that I decided to pick up breakfast on my way to Portland; despite having to dash to my bungalow to gather enough clothes for a few days on the road as well as pick up my laptop backpack, I still managed to sail past the campus of the University of Eastern Maine just a hair before six. Looking longingly at the pool and the workout I had missed, I put it aside with a promise to try and do a double workout when I returned; if I wound up in Portland longer than a day, I knew I had a standing invitation to work out with at least one of the Masters clubs there. I hoped it wouldn't come to that – especially since I'd not packed any swim gear – but was pragmatic enough to know investigations never proceeded in a linear fashion; it didn't help that as the UEM campus receded in my rearview mirror, I could already feel my body longing to return to Suzanne's side.

Route 203 had been plowed to the dark asphalt, the snowfall having stopped some hours earlier. Traffic at that early hour was relatively sparse, allowing me to make great time to the Interstate; as I turned south toward the big city, one glance at the clock on the dashboard of the SUV told me Caitlyn was likely back on duty at the station. Hitting the speed dial button for the intake desk, I waited as the call rang through.

"Chief," came Caitlyn's cheery voice. "Can I assume since you're not here yet, you've decided to go to Portland this morning?"

"You could," I laughed. "I need to talk to a few people down there, and possibly get into the victim's house. Can you pave the way for me with the radio station where Davies worked?"

"I'll reach out right away," she replied. "And as you've correctly divined, it will go easier if they know you're on your way already."

"That was part of my evil plan."

"I figured. If I can also tease out the address of his home from the station, I'll make some additional calls to see what jurisdiction it's in."

"Brilliant as always," I said. "And—"

"Yes, I'll book you into the Marriott. How long?"

"Two nights to start," I replied. "I hope to God it won't be longer."

"Sounds good. Oh — Danielle checked in as I was coming on shift. She made the round-trip to the crime lab in record time, and says the results should be available later today."

"Good. Ping me when you see them?"

"Of course. Good luck down there."

"Thanks," I replied.

Hanging up with Caitlyn, I found myself wishing the SUV had the same satellite radio Vasily had installed in his Camaro; having done that very drive with him on more than one occasion in the candy apple-red sports car, I had come to enjoy listening to the same station for the duration of the trip. Given the budget woes of my tiny village, the best they'd been able to afford in my replacement SUV had been a standard FM radio, which I snapped on and began to fiddle with the tuner. About the only station I was able to get was the statewide public radio channel, and though it was one I often listened to at home, for some reason hearing the day's news delivered with the deliberate thoughtfulness that was a hallmark of NPR was something I was not in the mood for that morning.

Casting about the dial, I landed on the soft rock station Suzanne used as her background music at the practice, frowned, and turned it off, opting for the whooshing of the wind past the vehicle as my soundtrack of the day. The miles slipped by far slower than I would have liked, underscoring my unusual anxiousness to reach my destination expeditiously. Augusta finally appeared on the horizon, and I ducked off the interstate long enough to hit a Dunkin' Donuts drive through, retrieving an extra-large coffee and two sesame seed bagels; I'd demolished both and had drunk enough of the coffee that a quick pitstop at the Gray Rest Stop was in order before continuing on to Portland.

Morning rush hour caught me as I passed the Falmouth exit; turning off, I sailed through the toll booth and then entered the fray that was I-295 as I headed ever closer to the city. At that point, Siri burst into life, beginning the countdown to the exit I needed for the radio station where Davies had been employed. The location of the station had been something easily located on the internet; details about *who* I needed to talk to, not so much. I was on the cusp of calling Caitlyn back to inquire as to her success when my phone started to ring.

"Chief Colbeth," I answered as I rounded a corner of the Interstate and the city of Portland was revealed to me.

"Chief, I'm sending you the address to Don Davies' house. The station manager — Wendy Hackett — is willing to talk with you, but she's doing the morning show in the while Davies is on vacation and won't be free until 11."

"Lovely," I replied. "I'm almost there, too."

"I figured as much," she replied, "so I went ahead and contacted the LEO where the house is located. Norman Thomas of the South Windham Police Department will meet you there at nine."

"How far away am I?" I asked as I scanned the signs for the next exit, assuming I'd need to shift my trajectory.

"Look for the offramp to Route 302 and head west," she replied. "Apparently, his house is about fifteen miles or so from the radio station." There was a pause as I heard her tapping on her computer. "I'm pulling up the map now; it appears he's got a nice little place on a small lake. Guy seems to have a thing for water."

"Must have been a swimmer in a past life," I mused. "Okay, I see the exit. Let Thomas know I'm on the way."

"Will do."

The phone triple-beeped the conclusion of the call just as I exited I-295; deciding it would be prudent to gas up, I pulled into the first station I found to top off my tank. While I was waiting for the pump to do its magic, I entered the address Caitlyn had provided into Apple Maps, then triggered the updated routing after paying for my fuel and returning to the main drag. That portion of the road appeared to slice through an interesting mix of apartment complexes, small single-family homes and a healthy dose of commercial buildings in all shapes and sizes. The four-lane road expanded to include left-turn lanes at the major intersections before finally dwindling back to a pretty standard two-lane rural highway not dissimilar from what we had up in Windeport. Portland's urban vibe gave way to a more rural feel as I put distance between me and the coast; soon, rolling farmland dominated the landscape, though given how much snow the area seemed to have accumulated, there was no way to determine what sort of animals might have normally grazed in those spaces. As with most places in Maine I had travelled, I marveled yet again at how quickly the contours shifted; per the odometer on the SUV, I knew I was little more than eight miles from where I had exited the Interstate, and yet, the emptiness around me made it seem as though I was a world away from the big city. It was easy to see why Davies might have decided to live out that way, though as cities went, Portland was pretty modest.

I sailed through a large traffic circle that evoked the ones I despised in Augusta, then continued onward until evidence of civilization began to pile up once more. Slowing to more sedate speeds as befitting the town I was entering, I started paying closer attention to the cross streets while keeping half an ear on Siri's pronouncements. Slowing even further, I turned at the entrance to a small subdivision with a subdued monument announcing its name; the road was wide, and moved into a thick area of trees before thinning out to expose one large single family home after another. Given how large the yards appeared to be, it wasn't a stretch to assume each had some version of a well-manicured front lawn from spring to late fall, resplendent with even mowing lines reminiscent of a golf course. Though not quite on the order of the massive McMansions I had seen in other parts of the state, the homes were definitely on the generous side, but more in line with those who wanted an understated elegance.

Rounding a corner of the street, I slowed down when I saw a traditional public safety sedan parked at the base of a plowed-in driveway; bearing the logo for the South Windham Police Department, I slid in behind it and parked the SUV. Pulling on my knit cap, I shrugged into my heavy jacket as I exited the vehicle and walked over to the stocky man wearing a standard issue duty officer overcoat who'd taken up position on the bumper of the sedan.

"Chief Colbeth?" he asked as he extended his hand. "Officer Norman Thomas, part of the day shift and one of the handful of Police Officers we have in this tiny little berg."

Laughing as I accepted his firm grip, I countered: "I suspect Windeport is even *smaller*. Call me Sean."

"A pleasure," he smiled. "And yes, I think you have the edge on us, if what I read about your village is accurate."

"You did *background* on me?" I felt an eyebrow arch. "That's a lot of work in a short period of time, Officer. Are you always so thorough with your visitors?"

"Please, I go by Norm," he said, looking a bit sheepish. "And it's not every day we get celebrities around here."

"I wouldn't go that far," I said, rolling my eyes. "I've solved a case or two, to be sure. Nothing spectacular."

"Don't sell yourself short," he chuckled. "I had to fight off the Chief herself in order to meet you today." Norm paused. "You don't remember me, do you?

The question caught me off guard. "I guess I don't," I said slowly. "Have we met before?"

"Multiple times," Norm chuckled. "But in your defense, you probably don't recognize me without goggles and a Power Rangers swim cap."

I tilted my head as a memory burst into life of a skinny ten-year-old on the deck at UEM. "Dear *Lord*. You were at the Olympian Swim Camp?" I asked. "That was, like, fifteen years ago! You were the kid that kept asking me tough questions about butterfly. I think Vasily and I even wound up swimming a sprint with you, too."

"I still have the photos," he said proudly, "though my swim career, sadly, didn't go as well as yours."

"You didn't swim in college?"

"I did — University of New Hampshire, Portsmouth. It paid the bills, but not much else."

"Every little bit helps," I replied.

"I hung up my goggles professionally after that."

I smiled. "Do we ever *truly* hang up our goggles?"

"No," he laughed. "I still swim with a Masters group, but I did retire the Power Rangers swim cap."

"That's a true crime right there," I chuckled. "Thanks a ton for meeting me."

Norm nodded toward the house. "So, you found Don Davies up in Windeport?"

"Yeah, though I'm still waiting on confirmation of the identity; honestly, I think I'd have enough probable cause to enter the house, were it in my jurisdiction, but since we're in your backyard, I'll defer to you."

Norm looked at me. "How certain are you that Davies died in Windeport?"

"I hate to get ahead of the evidence," I sighed, realizing for the first time that deep down I wasn't as sure as I thought I *should* be. There wasn't any one reason why, though: just a bunch of tiny things nibbling around the edges of my certainty. "Without confirmation, it's likely a judge would pass on my warrant."

For some reason, that brought a smile to Norm's face. "Well," he said after a moment, "good thing I came armed with a backup plan."

"You did?" I asked, eyebrows going up. "And what would that be?"

The young officer unzipped a pocket of his winter jacket and retrieved a folded piece of paper, which he handed to me. "You're not the only thing I researched this morning," he said, a trace of pride in his voice. "I pulled the property records and discovered this house happens to be on the market."

Unfolding the paper, I took a moment to scan the printout of the listing Norm had made from the online real estate service all agents used; my eyes fell on the date, causing them to immediately snap back to Norm. "It's been up for less than a week?"

"Yes," he nodded.

"That would be quite a trick," I frowned. "Considering Don Davies has likely been dead about that long."

"Good point," Norm said as he pulled out his phone. "As it happens, I know the listing agent," he added with a slightly cheeky grin. "How interested are you in purchasing a little piece of Southern Maine, Chief?"

"More than most," I laughed.

Eight

❦

While it was quite clear that gaining access to Don Davies' house under the guise of a private showing from a real estate agent was unlikely to hold up in court, I was more concerned with trying to make sense of what was feeling more and more like a senseless death; there wasn't a better place to start than the abode the famed broadcaster had apparently called home for close to three decades. My guide turned out to be Officer Thomas' boyfriend, Daniel, a clear conflict of interest that would be the final dagger into using any evidence I might find in my perusal of the two-story structure. For whatever reason, it didn't seem to trouble me like it once might have, making me wonder if my years of investigations had finally begun to erode my normally rock-solid adherence to proper procedure.

Daniel unlocked the front door for us after we trudged up the plowed driveway. "I'm sorry nothing has been shoveled," he apologized as he moved his lanky frame away from the door after pushing it open for me. "The agency wasn't aware that Mr. Davies had gone on vacation, otherwise we would have called in the service we normally use to keep properties pristine while owners are away."

"Is it true this place has only been listed for a week?" I asked.

"About ten days, yes," Daniel nodded. "It's been in the works a lot longer than that, of course," he added, possibly as a result of seeing my arched eyebrow.

"Oh?" I asked. "I've only ever been on the purchasing side of the equation, which went rather quickly for me."

"If the financing is worked out, that's normally the case for the buyer," Daniel replied. "For the seller, there are hundreds of tiny things that need to be reviewed before a home goes on the market. I don't think we had the final paperwork completed until late December, actually; with the Christmas holiday and New Year's, we decided to push the listing date to mid-January."

"Makes sense. Have you had a lot of interest in the property?" I asked as we entered a small foyer.

"Yes," Daniel replied as he pulled off his hat, releasing a mop of unruly brown hair. Shaking it out slightly, he unzipped his jacket to expose an understated sweater over a coordinating turtleneck; it took me a moment to realize he looked a bit like a younger version of a certain technology entrepreneur. "Real estate in general has been crazy for a few years now, especially anything within easy driving distance of Boston. This house has relatively direct access to the interstate, and as a bonus, frontage on Lake Catherine."

I nodded as I took in the foyer and unzipped my own heavy jacket. The warmth of the interior defrosted me slightly, and also told me the house was staged to be ready in a moment's notice when a prospective buyer happened upon it. Most normal New Englanders tended to set the thermostat to something far lower than the temperature I was feeling, given how expensive heating oil was during the winter; more so when they knew they were going to be away for an extended period. Mainers were especially pragmatic in not wanting to heat a space no one was going to occupy for a while.

It was clear the house had once held a family, for photos lined the wall behind the stairwell leading to the second story; a small mirror was just inside the door, with a full umbrella rack beside it. Boots were carefully lined up on a waterproof mat beneath a coatrack that was presently empty; the hardwood floors looked to have been recently refinished, or exceedingly well taken care of. Off to my right was an archway leading to a traditional sitting room; on my left, a mirrored version of the archway that guarded what appeared to be a formal dining area, replete with a small chandelier. A beautiful china closet made from dark wood graced the far wall of the dining room and was tastefully showcasing pieces from a collection I knew was well outside of my own budget.

"The house is four bedrooms, total," Daniel was saying as he led us into the living room, clearly trying to keep up the pretext of a showing for all involved. "What's unusual for a house of this age is that each bedroom has its own bath, and there is a half bath here on the first floor just for good measure."

"Perfect for guests," I murmured as I examined the couch and the wall-sized bookcase beyond. "Did Mr. Davies tell you why he was selling?"

"Downsizing," Daniel replied. "A one-bedroom condo along the water in Old Orchard Beach." Holding a hand toward the back of the house, Daniel tried to continue our showing. "Through here is a recently renovated kitchen—"

"One moment," I said, moving toward the bookcase. "Are these photos of Davies' family?"

"Yes," Daniel replied. "Everything here is from the owner, actually; we didn't have to bring in anything to stage the house at all."

"Indeed." I leaned down to look at a small, framed photo of a man standing in front of a castle, with a tiny five- or six-year-old girl just in front of him. Judging from the balloon sporting mouse ears, it wasn't hard to recognize one of the vacation kingdoms run by Disney. Leaning closer, I thought I could see something of a resemblance to the young woman I'd met the prior evening, but the face of the man was partially obscured in the sunlight; still, from the way he was holding the hands of the small girl, it wasn't hard to imagine they were related.

"That's one of the few photos of Don in the house," Daniel remarked as he came over to see what I'd been looking at. "He's quite a talented photographer, so he's usually the one behind the camera."

"It's hard to tell if it's him," I observed.

Daniel leaned down beside me, close enough that I was able to smell his cologne. "Huh. Now that you say that, I wonder if that's his brother."

I turned to look at the agent. "He has a sibling?"

"Yes," Daniel replied. "A twin, actually. Frank is his name; I don't know much about him other than I *think* he's an investment manager with an office in Portland. Mr. Davies listed him as the backup contact if we had trouble getting ahold of him for a showing."

That knot of unease that had been festering just behind my breastbone tightened. "What sort of twin?"

"I've not met Frank in person, but the way Don described him to me as his 'mirror.' I took that to mean he was identical."

"Indeed," I breathed, leaning down again and trying to divine any sort of detail from the photo that might tell me if I was looking at my victim, but the sunburst continued to frustrate any sort of ability to do so.

Standing, I turned thoughtfully and walked back out into the foyer, ignoring for the moment Norm and Daniel as they trailed a few steps behind. I'd seen the framed photographs when I'd entered the space, of course, but hadn't really *looked* at them; now, as I worked my way up the steps, I could see clearly the resemblance of my victim to the man who seemed to move from his mid-to-late twenties at the bottom step to somewhere closer to grandfather at the top. Still, the smooth lines of the face, the color of the hair and eyes — every aspect, especially in the final photo — matched my memory of the victim as we had found him in Windeport.

Reaching for the last of the framed photos, I asked over my shoulder: "Would it be possible to borrow this photo for a bit?"

"I guess," Daniel replied. "I need to find something to replace it with so there's not an empty nail at the top of the staircase, but there are tons of family photos in this place."

"Thanks," I said as I carefully removed the eight-by-ten from the hook it was on. "Did Davies live here alone?"

"That's my impression," Daniel answered. "I never met a wife, or," he added, shooting a glance at Norm, "significant other. The deed appears to be in his name based on the title search we performed."

I turned toward him. "Had it been changed? It wasn't joint tenant?"

"Not that I recall from the file," Daniel said. "I can look it up if it would help."

"It would," I replied thoughtfully. "Bedrooms are up here?"

"Yes," Daniel said, pointing as he spoke. "Master is to the left, two guest rooms on the right and one on along the back. That last one seems to have been converted into something of a den."

I moved up the final step and crossed the hardwood floor to the room in question; like any house staged for showing, the door was already open, exposing the wide surface of a cherry desk, behind which was a pretty standard bookcase filled comfortably with books of every size, shape and type. An all-in-one computer was sitting on the desk proper, with an unusually large screen; a fairly expensive-looking microphone had been clamped to the side of the desk, with an extensible arm that reached to about where the chair was at the center of the tableau. Moving around to the chair, I smiled to see the small set of framed photos just beside the computer, angled so whomever was using the machine (and the microphone) would be able to see them. The largest of the set had a handsome looking woman who appeared to be in her late forties, smiling and hugging a younger version of Gennifer; I wasn't an expert at dating people in photos, but was reasonably certain it had been taken some time ago. Two smaller frames seemed to focus on Davies' grandchildren, and had been carefully arranged around the larger photo. One focused on a young boy who appeared to be rushing across the deep green of a soccer field, the white-and-black ball a few feet ahead of him. The snapshot appeared to have been taken at a night game, though the clarity of the image spoke to how good a photographer Don Davies appeared to have been.

The second smaller frame held a smiling teenaged girl, standing beside a pool in her one-piece competitive swimsuit with a glass-and-bronze award of some sort in her hands; based on cut of the suit — and the fact that it went down to her knees — it looked to me like the young woman had been participating in either a regional or national level swim meet. I knew from experience that those suits were incredibly expensive *and* only intended to be worn when shaving milliseconds from your time meant the difference between coming in first and not making the finals at all. I'd come up through the ranks at the tail end of the full-body versions and recalled just how much of a struggle it was to get in and out of them without damaging the fabric; smiling wryly, I could still remember vividly how upset my father had been when I'd accidentally put a toe through the leg of a suit and had needed to purchase another. Looking at the strikingly dark-haired teenager in the photo more closely, I figured I'd not been much older than she was when it had happened — and that I'd never truly gotten over the sting of embarrassment at needing a last-minute suit replacement. Setting aside a sudden burst of teenaged angst, I tapped at the keyboard of the computer to see if it would wake and was greeted by the login window for the operating system.

"He must have done remote broadcasts from here," I mused. "How is the broadband in this neighborhood?"

"Excellent," Daniel replied. "It's one of only a handful in this part of town that has access to the fiber backbone that runs directly to Portland."

"This is a fairly old neighborhood," I observed, smiling wryly. "Don't take this the wrong way, but you're not exactly on the main drag out here. I can't believe the local telephone company just *happened* to redo their infrastructure with the most current tech available."

"You're not wrong," Daniel chuckled. "Partly it's by luck: from what I understand, the statewide 9-1-1 dispatch center system is just down the road, so it's continually being upgraded to the latest and greatest in telecommunications."

"That's not exactly open to the public," I replied, arching an eyebrow.

"No," Daniel agreed. "But there was enough excess capacity that when someone like Don Davies approached the carrier about high-speed internet..."

"Ah," I nodded. "I'm sure he had to pay for it, too."

"Quite likely, yes."

"Well, however he managed to do it," I said as I moved to the window on the far wall, "I'm sure it came in handy on those snowy days when getting to the studio in Portland was less than desirable."

"I would imagine."

The windows for the house had seemed larger than normal when we'd approached from the street; standing in front of one made them seem even *bigger*, since it stretched nearly from the floor to the ceiling. I was used to seeing walls of glass in homes along the coast or with mountain views, but as I stared down into the rather pedestrian back yard of Don Davies, I found myself wondering what he'd been taking from the vista provided. Setting aside the irony of the in-ground pool that was *maybe* fifty yards from the sizable lake the home backed up against, there really wasn't much to see; unlike his cottage up in Windeport, the trees had been allowed to crowd the shoreline, making the small pier jutting out into the frozen water barely visible. In fact, aside from the wide openness of the front yard, the forest surrounding the house made it seem a bit claustrophobic.

I caught Daniel glancing at his watch out of the corner of my eye and realized he probably had other places to be; he was, after all, doing a favor for his boyfriend, and like anyone on commission, acutely aware that a conversion was nowhere near imminent from the strange visitor he was hosting. Turning, I smiled at both Norm and Daniel. "Thanks. I think I've seen what I need."

"Are you sure?" Daniel asked. There was enough genuineness to the question that I almost believed he meant it.

Looking at Norm, I smiled slightly. "Well, to be honest, I wouldn't mind a glance at the kitchen, but I can do that on my own. That is, if you don't mind — I can lock up when I leave."

Daniel turned to Norm. "I'm not sure," he hesitated. "It's against protocol."

Norm nodded toward me. "Chief Colbeth is pretty well known in my circle, babe," he said softly. "You can trust him. But if it makes you feel better, I'll hang out with him."

Daniel hesitated further before nodding. "Okay," he said, looking at both of us. "Please try not to disturb anything beyond that photo you've borrowed."

"I won't," I smiled.

With one last glance at Norm, Daniel proceeded us out of the miniature recording studio and trotted down the steps two at a time; I paused at the head of the stairs and waited for the door to click shut before looking at Norm. "How much time do I have?" I asked. "I don't want to keep you from something."

"Are you kidding?" he smiled. "I've read all about you and want to see you in action. Take as much time as you need."

I rolled my eyes again. "You make me sound like some sort of institution. And you can't believe everything you read online."

The young officer smiled. "Are you impugning the integrity of the *Bangor Daily News* or *The Portland Press Herald?* Or how about those journalists at Maine Public Radio—"

"All right, all *right,*" I sighed. "Maybe you can believe *some* of them." I nodded toward the closed front door. "I might have undersold how much digging around I want to do."

"I thought as much. If you tell me what you're looking for, we can split the house up."

"That's the problem, Norm," I sighed. "I'll know it when I see it."

"Then I'll stay close."

Moving down to the master bedroom, I found the door open just as it had been for the small den. The space was one long rectangle, with a nicely-sized queen bed at one end and small sitting area at the other. Two doors on the interior wall led to a walk-in closet and the master bath, respectively; poking my head into the closet first, I realized it was one of those fancy California ones, with built in drawers and enough storage slots for three dozen sets of sneakers. It was evident Davies had been flying solo, for barely half of the space had been taken up by items as varied as a leisure suit from the late seventies to multiple tuxedos with tails; one of the only full drawers had ties so ugly, I wasn't surprised they were tucked away from sight.

"Have you two been together long?" I asked as I re-entered the bedroom proper. The walls were rather bereft of any sort of... well, *anything*, which struck me as unusual in a house where Davies had presumably lived for more than three decades.

"A couple of years," Norm said from where he was standing by another of the large windows. "We met soon after I started."

With the closet as tricked out as it was, there were no other dressers in the main space; moving to the bed, the nightstands were just as bare, save for a small notepad and pen next to an honest-to-goodness telephone. Holding up the pad, it was clear there were no faint scribbles on the paper, eliminating any possible clues from prior scribbles; the pen, however, proved to be a bit more interesting. Twisting it in my hands, I realized it bore the same logo as the notepad, proving both items had been purloined from the Hilton Orange County. A second look at the notepad revealed the address of the hotel had been printed in a small block below the logo; it took me a moment to register the location was firmly within the boundaries of Rancho Linda, causing me to arch an eyebrow.

Given how his daughter lived in Los Angeles, it seemed unlikely he would book a room more than thirty minutes' drive from his grandkids when visiting the West Coast. I supposed there was always the possibility he'd traveled there for a conference of some kind, but that seemed a long way to go for business travel; then again, it was just as likely he'd snagged pen and paper from a coworker at the station, too. Still, as I put the pen and pad back down on the nightstand, I felt a frown forming.

That, and the knot in my stomach had become something far more queasy.

Coincidences didn't exist in my line of work; finding something in Davies' house that tangentially connected him to Vasily's home turf seemed more like the clue I'd been hunting for all morning, albeit one that didn't appear on the face of it to make any sense. I'd have felt better if there had been contemporary photos spread around the house showing a recent visit to Disneyland, for even *that* would have provided a reasonable explanation of the notepad and pen given Rancho Linda's proximity to the park. Pulling out my phone, I took a quick set of photos of the nightstand with the pen and notepad in place, then turned to Norm.

"Do you have evidence bags?" I asked.

"Yeah — out in the sedan. What did you find?"

"It's probably nothing," I said, pointing to the notepad. "But this seems out of place to me."

Norm raised an eyebrow. "I doubt you'll find prints or anything on the pad," he replied. "Not with how many people have likely been through this house for a showing."

"Agreed," I nodded. "Still, I'd like to take it back and compare it to the materials we found in the cottage. While I'm not connecting any dots right now, it might tie to something we inadvertently collected a few days ago."

"All right," he replied. "I'll go get my kit."

"I'll be here in the bathroom."

The young officer moved from the room as if his life depended on it, making me smile a bit at how a few more years in the trenches were likely to sand that level of anxiousness down. Pausing at the door to the bathroom, I realized he reminded me of another eager young man I'd taken on a decade ago; it was hard to believe how quickly time had passed, and I smiled to think that Vasily had ultimately turned out pretty good, despite my best efforts. I'd always considered him a peer, so it was nice that he finally had the rank to go with it — even if it was a few thousand miles away.

I found the master bath to be in line with the rest of the house: comfortably sized with a touch of class, but not ostentatious by any stretch. A dual vanity sat beneath one of the few sets of small windows, looking out into the back yard much as the den had; medicine cabinets were on either side, allowing equal storage for the married couple. The toilet was inside a small room of its own, and it, too, sported a landline hanging just beside the toilet paper roll. I'd only ever seen that in homes of the significantly wealthy and wondered just how comfortable I would be holding a conversation in such a space.

A small linen closet was beside the toilet room, and rounding out the space was a walk-in shower, tiled in earth tones. Poking my head into the actual stall, I could see one of those magnificent waterfall-type shower heads had been mounted in the ceiling, with several sets of what looked like satellite jets on the walls below it. I couldn't help but picture just how much like a carwash the setup seemed to be; it was clear that without turning at all, every square inch of one's body would be inundated with water.

Set into a small, tiled alcove was a bottle of shampoo I'd seen on the shelves of the IGA, partnered with a well-used bar of soap. Sniffing, the scent of the soap seemed vaguely familiar to me but was not a brand I recognized. Stepping back out of the shower, I returned to the dual vanity and randomly opened the medicine cabinet on the left; save for a single forlorn toothbrush, it was completely empty, leading me to assume it had belonged to Davies' presumably late wife — a stark reminder that I didn't really have a full background on my victim yet. The drawers between the two sinks had the usual bric-a-brac I'd found in most bathrooms, from Band Aids to spare tubes of toothpaste to cough drops that had expired the year prior. The ordinary effects of daily life, more poignant now that their owner would no longer be searching through them looking for the comb they'd misplaced.

Opening the remaining medicine cabinet, I found myself stepping back slightly; every shelf was full, though the items had been arranged neatly enough that locating something would have been fairly straightforward. The bottom shelf held multiple pharmacy bottles of various sizes; I didn't recognize the names of the drugs on any of them, so I snapped a photo of each one to research later. Of more interest, though, was the injector of epinephrine that had been carefully placed atop the bottles; a high school friend of mine had been allergic to bee stings and had carted around an earlier incarnation of the device wherever he went. At the time, I'd been more intrigued with how the gizmo worked rather than what it was designed to treat; despite having a pharmacist for a father, it wasn't until I was in college and saw someone experiencing anaphylaxis during an outdoor swim meet that I'd finally understood the full horror it represented.

Looking at the pill bottles again, I wondered what it was that Don Davies was so allergic to, and if any of the prescriptions were preventative in nature. Save for taking the occasional antihistamine, I'd never been worried about any sort of allergies myself.

The rest of the cabinet was pretty mundane, so I closed the mirrored door and turned to lean on the vanity, arms crossed. Staring out into the space without really seeing it, I realized something else had been troubling me subconsciously, and had become more pronounced with the discovery of the empty cabinet. Slowly moving out into the master bedroom, I nodded at Norm just as he zipped the pen into an evidence bag, then stood in the center of the space and did a slow turn, then another.

No photos, I thought to myself. *I would have expected at least one of the late wife — but then again, I'm presuming they were separated by death; if they divorced, then it makes sense not to keep a reminder of what went wrong close at hand. But why not replace them with snapshots of the kids or grandkids? Odd.*

Norm moved to my side. "What are you thinking?"

"That love can be a fickle thing," I smiled. "One last stop if you don't mind."

Norm nodded and followed me out of the master bedroom, then down the steps to the first floor. The layout of the house was simple enough that Daniel hadn't needed to point out the kitchen, for it was just down the small hallway beside the stairs. Passing beneath a small archway, I found myself within an extremely modern space; stainless steel appliances appeared to be the order of the day, nestled into enough counter space several generations could have prepared Thanksgiving dinner without bumping into each other. A wide island sat in the middle of the room, with a hanging rack of pots and pans just above; glass-fronted cabinets easily showcased the everyday china, cookware, or kitchen gadgets every chef seemed to need. There was an unusual bow window at one end, creating some sort of breakfast nook where a small table was ensconced; I could easily visualize children sitting around the small table while feasting upon their frosted corn flakes. A door led into the dining room from one side, and another door lead out into the garage; every square inch of the space was spotless, owing more perhaps to the fact the house was on the market than a reflection of Don Davies' general housekeeping skills.

There was a page torn from a coloring book on the front of a French door fridge, held in place by four magnets shaped like small potatoes; the garish colors and inattention to that inviolable rule to remain within the lines made me smile, and pegged the artwork as something from Davies' grandchildren. Stepping closer, I could see — barely — that there was a superhero character hiding beneath the layers of color, though not one I recognized. On a whim, I reached for the handle and pulled open one side, curious to see what the famed radio broadcaster might have had on offer. I wasn't surprised at how empty it was, given how Davies was ostensibly travelling. Pulling open the other door, I started to paw through what *was* present and discovered just about everything left had expiration dates well into the following month — again, completely in line with someone who knew they were going to be away for a while and didn't want to come home to a gallon of spoiled milk. I ran my fingers along the various cartons and containers, idly noting that Davies appeared to favor the store brand of a supermarket I'd seen advertised as being more wholesome and natural than its rivals; the prices on the flyers seemed to indicate there was a steep tax for the privilege of eating better. Popping open the butter compartment confirmed that pattern.

Leaning down, I slid the freezer drawer open and found it similarly half full, with the inventory containing several tubs of ice cream, including one that appeared to have only recently been opened, given how little frost was within it. Sliding the freezer closed, I paused before reopening the fridge and confirming what my subconscious had been telling me was missing.

Eggs, I mused. *Where are the eggs? He's got everything else — but not eggs.*

Closing the fridge doors once more, I felt myself sighing. *It's probably nothing. I'll bet those were going to spoil before he got back... and yet...*

I took another look at the expiration date on the milk; in keeping with how expensive it had to have been, it wasn't slated to go sour until sometime in mid-March. The cream was even *later* into the following month, making me frown over the missing eggs; as I closed the fridge doors again, I wondered if I was so desperate for a clue of *any* kind, I was seeing one where none existed. It began to worry me I might not recognize a real one should I stumble across it.

Looking at my watch, I started when I realized I'd taken more time than I'd intended. "I need to get going," I said as we moved toward the front door. "Thanks for your help."

"Absolutely," Norm said as he handed me the two evidence bags. I put them on top of the framed photo I'd been carrying around. "I slipped my card into one of the bags," he continued. "If you need anything else, just shoot me a text."

"Thanks. I just might," I replied as we stepped back into the brisk morning. Zipping up my jacket, I turned to watch Norm as he locked the door behind us. "I never really know where these cases will lead me."

"That seems pretty true about life in general."

"Yeah," I smiled as I started back toward my SUV. "That it does."

Nine

Late morning traffic on U.S. Route 302 was fairly light, allowing me to make up enough time that I felt capable of swinging through the first Dunkin' Donuts I passed for a much-needed second hit of caffeine. Suzanne wasn't wrong; the amount of coffee I ingested on a daily basis was far, *far* above the levels even a swamped college student might consider, though any attempt I had made to try and dial it back had ultimately fizzled. As I gratefully accepted the extra-large takeaway cup from the drive thru, I thought I could understand how someone similarly addicted to nicotine never truly felt at ease until the next cigarette was between their fingers. Sipping gingerly at the scalding hot nectar of life, I was loathe to admit I felt slightly naked without a cup of coffee in my hand.

Feeling the burst of energy flow through my system, I glanced to the two evidence bags on the passenger seat and wondered how I'd be able to connect Don Davies to Rancho Linda — or if it was even necessary in the first place. With the time difference to California, I hadn't yet called Vasily to get his thoughts on the anomaly, having assumed he was only just starting his day at the office after what had likely been a massive workout at the pool. I'd never been a fan of walking through the door and immediately getting hit with something, so I figured I'd spare him the same and reach out after my visit to the radio station.

It wasn't like Davies was going anywhere, anyway.

On the fringes of Portland, the landscape shifted back to something more urban and the traffic, predictably, began to fill in and slow down as a consequence. The day seemed to be unsure of whether it would commit to being partly cloudy or partly sunny, a typical circumstance for that time of year that had me constantly pushing my sunglasses up to my hair or just as quickly reversing the process to protect against the glare. It was one such changeover that led to my missing the turn Siri had been suggesting I take; sighing, I continued onward while I waited for my iPhone to recalculate the route. Portland wasn't exactly an unknown city to me, for I often had business that took me either to a State agency that had an office in Maine's largest city or one of the many consulting labs based there that could do specialized forensics the Crime Lab just didn't have the budget — or technology — to perform. Still, I didn't know it as well as other places, such as Bangor or Augusta, and tended to rely on my navigation software to find my way around.

Fortunately, missing my turn meant that I exited Route 302 back onto southbound I-295 just below the old B&M Baked Beans factory, which, based purely on the luxuriously rich smell that suddenly filled the cabin of my SUV, seemed to still be operating at full capacity. Making a mental note that it had been way too long since the last time I'd had beans and brown bread, I merged into the flow of traffic and began the short transit around Back Bay and into the heart of the city. Siri chirped to life once more, encouraging me to turn back off 295 at the Forest Avenue exit just a moment later; I didn't truly need any further advice, for the tall transmission tower for the radio station was apparent from the highway, guiding me like a beacon to a small, squat and otherwise nondescript office building surrounded by an equally as slight parking lot. Space appeared to be at a premium, given how the snow had simply been pushed to a far corner of the lot and left to melt on its own. It took me a few moments to wedge the SUV into what *might* have been a legal spot, or then again, it might have been the access for the dumpster, too.

Locking the SUV as I exited, the intense bite of the salty ocean air hit me immediately, a different sort of tang than what we experienced in Windeport. The station was about two blocks from Back Bay, which was fed from a small inlet that led to Portland Harbor and the Gulf of Maine beyond. Still, despite the ocean proper being a good handful of miles from where I stood, the brisk breeze felt like it was coming directly off the Gulf and contained enough moisture to make me guess that partly cloudy was likely to turn into full on snowstorm in the coming hours. It wasn't much of a stretch to think I'd be spending the night in the city simply to avoid driving home in bad weather.

I made my way through the sun-warmed slush of the parking lot to the small shoveled-out sidewalk leading to the main entrance. Posters promoting some artist or another hung in giant windows to either side of the door, which seemed odd for what I'd assumed had been a talk-radio station; I was disabused of that notion further when I came into the main foyer and saw four sets of call letters hanging on the wall behind the reception desk, only one of which looked to be the one for whom Don Davies had broadcast. Gone, apparently, were the days when a given radio station was just that: a single station. Like every other industry, commercial radio seemed to have undergone some consolidation, too.

There was a borderline senior citizen behind the reception desk who smiled at me but held up a finger as he continued to speak into the headset he was wearing. "I'll have to put you through to our advertising department, ma'am. They are the ones who would know how to get ahold of the vendor. Please hold." He pressed a button on a phone console that seemed to have three dozen flashing lights on it before returning his attention to me. "How may I help you?"

"Chief Sean Colbeth," I replied. "I have an appointment with the General Manager?"

"Ah, yes," the gentleman said, looking down for a moment. "I'll let her know you're here; if you'll have a seat, please? They still have about ten minutes before the show ends and I can get her out of the studio."

"Thanks," I said as I moved over to a small area that held two couches perpendicular to each other.

Shrugging out of my heavy winter jacket, I placed it on the seat beside mine and pulled out my iPhone; Suzanne had texted me at some point during my travel back from South Windham with a note that I call when I was free. Taking a chance that she'd be on an early lunch, I punched up her number.

"Hey," she said, picking up on the first ring. "How goes your investigation in the big city?"

"Early days," I sighed. "But not uninteresting. I have a few prescriptions I'd like to run past you, if I can; I'm wondering what sorts of ailments afflicted my victim."

"Absolutely," she replied. "What are they?"

"I'll send you the photos I took. Not sure I can type out what I was reading; they don't make the names easy to pronounce, do they?"

"Welcome to my world," she chuckled. "I'm a firm believer that they get paid by the syllable."

I caught a note of something in the way she laughed — a hint of fatigue. "But enough about me," I continued cautiously. "What's going on at your end?"

"All sorts of excitement," she replied. "Deidre's gone into premature labor."

My blood ran cold. "She... *what?*"

"I have her here at the office now, in my maternity exam room," Suzanne continued. "I'm not sure it's safe to move her, so I've called Yasmine for an extra set of hands."

Still processing what she was saying, I heard myself ask: "How... how serious is this?"

"If she delivers, it will be about four weeks early," Suzanne replied. "Nothing we can't handle. It would be easier in a full birthing ward, of course, but we'll make do."

"Suzanne..." I started, then paused, unsure of what I wanted to say. Myriad emotions were warring for supremacy, a few of which I didn't think I still had when it came to my former fiancé.

"I've got this," she replied, answering my unspoken question. "And both she and her child will be fine. I debated whether to call you in the first place, but Deidre insisted that I would."

"I'll leave right away—" I started.

"You'll just be in the way," Suzanne reminded me. "And that was pretty much why Deidre wanted me to call — to let you know that she'll be fine and not to come rushing back here."

"She... she *told* you that?"

"Yes," Suzanne replied softly. "She seems to know you as well as I do."

"I guess she does," I said after a moment, before realizing it might come off wrong. "Suze—"

"I know where we stand with each other," she said. "I also am not blind to how long the two of you were together. It would be wrong if you *weren't* concerned."

It took a moment for what she was saying to sink in, and I felt myself nodding slightly. "I love you, Milady," I said softly, squeezing the phone in my hand. "More than you can ever know."

"I think I have a pretty good sense of it, actually," she laughed. "I'll touch base in a bit."

The phone chirped the ending of the call, and I managed to slide it back into my pocket just as a striking woman woman appeared from the hallway to my left. "Chief Colbeth?"

Standing, I grabbed my jacket with one hand while stretching out the other to greet her. "That's me," I smiled as we shook. "Call me Sean."

"I'm Wendy Hackett, General Manager. Sorry to make you wait; with Don on vacation, I've had to juggle the station talent and fill in the gaps myself when I was lacking coverage." Smiling wryly, she continued. "Thankfully, I came up through the ranks behind the microphone, so it's not unfamiliar territory; but I'd forgotten how much it takes out of me to be on air that long."

I nodded toward the wall and the different call letters. "This isn't just WWWD?"

Wendy chuckled. "Originally, this building was *only* for The Dub, but that was before an out-of-state firm bought us and those other three stations. I suppose I should be thankful; WWWD is the only locally originated, live station left out of the four; the rest are just rebroadcasting national programs."

"Ah," I said. "Downsized a bit, then?"

"We had to let a lot of good people go," she sighed. "Radio is a pretty competitive business with tiny margins; without Don's program on The Dub, I'm not sure we'd still be afloat."

"'The Dub?'" I asked, perplexed.

"You must not be a listener," Wendy laughed.

"Guilty as charged."

"'The Dub' is shorthand for WWWD," she explained. "I think we stole it from the internet."

Feeling more confused, I lamely asked: "The internet?"

"Yeah," she replied. "You know – *w w w* dot *something*? Most people use *dub dub dub* as shorthand, and it kind of just stuck due to our call letters. Hence, 'The Dub.'"

"Ah," I nodded sagely, unsure if I truly understood what she was saying. I filed it away to ask Suzanne at some future point.

Wendy looked at me for a moment. "Your office said you needed to talk to me about Don?"

"Yes," I confirmed. "Is there a place where we can chat privately?"

"Come on back to my glamorous office," she chuckled.

I followed her down the hallway and past a wall of glass that looked in on a recording studio; based on the bustle of activity, I didn't need to see the red *on air* light to know they were in the moment with their audience. A small cubicle farm replete with multiple ringing phones appeared, followed quickly by what must have been the executive suite; each door had a plaque where the occupant's name was posted, though only two seemed to be in use. Conveniently, Don Davies appeared to be right next door to the much larger office for Wendy.

Waving me into one of two guest chairs, she shut the door behind us and immediately apologized. "Sorry for the mess," she said as she slid a bunch of paperwork off the desk and onto the floor behind her. "With Don out, I'm behind on paperwork — hell, behind on *everything*."

"I know the feeling," I smiled.

"So," Wendy said as she settled into her chair behind the desk, "what do you want to know about Don? Is this some sort of background check for a segment?"

"I *am* doing background for a case I'm working," I hedged.

"What sort of case?"

"There was a break-in at his cottage in Windeport," I replied honestly. "We've been unable to reach him to confirm if anything of value was missing. I'd hoped to talk to him personally but didn't realize he wasn't here."

"He's on vacation for a few weeks," Wendy confirmed. "He generally tries to visit his daughter in California every January, just long enough to get away from the worst of our Maine winter. Don kind of goes radio silent for the duration, and we usually respect his well-deserved time off, but he is reachable if needed."

"Does he usually stay with her?"

"Gennifer?" she asked. "Yes, save for a few days set aside to attend the National Radio Personality Conference. It's always in Southern California, which is another reason he takes time off at this point in the calendar."

Something clicked in my brain, and I found myself nodding. "Don does talk radio?" I asked.

"Four hours five days a week," Wendy nodded. "Number one rated show during evening drive time here in Southern Maine; as a syndicated show, nationally, we're in the top twenty."

"Wow," I said. "Politics? Sports? News?"

Wendy smiled. "A little bit of everything," she answered. "He's always called it a show about potpourri since anything and everything can come up. And often does. Don has some amazingly loyal listeners, too."

"Really?"

"Yeah. He's been on the air close to thirty years now, and his ratings have never been higher. That's despite some pretty healthy competition from younger hosts that are, shall we say, somewhat more provocative. Don's gentle manner and easy connection to his audience makes him come across like a genial uncle you always look forward to seeing at a family dinner."

"You must live in fear of his retirement."

Wendy did the sign of the cross. "Do I ever. I've got nothing in the pipeline to replace him."

I nodded again, not wanting to be the one to tell her she was going to need to start looking. "He must be well liked by the staff, then?"

"He is," she replied before looking at me again. "You're not vetting him for another station, are you?"

"Not in my job description," I replied. "I just was curious about the kind of person he was."

"Irreplaceable on multiple fronts," Wendy said. "But if you really want to know more about him, you should talk to his twin brother, Frank. Those two are inseparable, and, in many ways, also two sides of the same coin. In fact, he might be able to tell you about the cottage if you need immediate answers."

"Oh?"

"Yes," she nodded. "Don often spent time up there with Frank. Don's kid is grown, and Frank never had any, so they've kind of fallen into spending their downtime together. More so after Don's wife died."

I nodded again. "How long ago was that?"

"Oh, shoot, maybe fifteen years?" she replied. "Breast cancer, second round. It was tragic — and led to Don starting a new foundation to fund research. Frank helped him set it up and manages the grant awards for him."

"Interesting," I said. "Do you have the address of his office? I might swing over and visit him before I head back up state."

"How well do you know Portland?"

"Fairly well."

"His office is in One City Center, eleventh floor. Can't miss it."

"Perfect." I stood and reached for her hand. "Thank you for your time," I said. "I'll let you get back to it."

She laughed. "Thanks — I think. I have about twenty minutes of lunch left before I must get back into the studio. I can't *wait* for Don to get back."

"I can imagine," I replied. "I'll see myself out."

Wandering back out into the hallway, I peered briefly into Davies' office but didn't linger; I hesitated to draw any further attention to his absence and my questions about him than I already had, and instead made my way out to reception. Shrugging into my jacket, I braced for the inevitable gust of cold air as I exited into the winter day, then paused on the sidewalk. I felt like I had a thread of a connection to the Hilton Orange County now, as well as a possible explanation for why Davies might have stayed there. I also realized it had been many, many hours since I'd grabbed breakfast, and decided it might be wise to satisfy my now rumbling stomach.

Sliding into the frigid interior of the SUV, I started it up and began to pull out of the spot I'd carved for myself when my iPhone sang out. When I saw who had called, I pulled back into the spot and tapped answer. "Vas," I replied warmly. "I was just about to call you."

Vasily didn't mince words. "How the *fuck* did Gennifer's DNA match a cadaver here in Rancho Linda?"

Ten

"*S* ay *what?*"

Vasily sighed, and I could easily visualize him running a hand through his shorter hair. "Sorry," he replied. "It's been a very, *very* long morning out here. Let me back up a bit."

"I'd appreciate that."

"Remember when I told you I was juggling more than a few cases?"

"Yes."

"Well, I caught a new one the day before I spoke with you about Davies; a dead body turned up in a dumpster behind one of our malls, devoid of any identification. M.E. did the post and ran prints and DNA through all of the usual databases; nothing matched until we got a flag this morning."

"From Gennifer?"

"Yeah," he sighed. "I called Lou immediately when I saw the location tag on the sample. It was a familial match, which means my victim is either a parent or—"

"An uncle?"

"Exactly. What the *fuck* is going on out there?"

"That is a good question," I replied. "Especially since Gennifer's sample was *supposed* to match my victim."

"You might want to call Lou," he replied. "Because it did."

I found myself nodding. "I will, as soon as we get done. But Vas, I think we might have a larger problem."

"Fuck. *Fuck,*" he swore. "Why did I *know* you were going to say that?"

"Because you know me," I laughed bleakly. "Let me make some calls and I'll get back to you."

"All right," he sighed. "Don't leave me hanging."

"I won't."

Ending my call with Vas, I scrolled through my contacts until I came to the main number for the Coroner's Office and dialed; it took a few minutes for the operator to track down Dr. Hamilton. When she finally came onto the line, I could hear a bit of frustration in her voice. "Hey, Sean. I imagine you've talked to Vasily by now."

"Oh yes," I replied, chuckling despite myself. "At the risk of sounding like Vas — what the *fuck* is going on?"

That got a laugh. "You two are a matched set. So, yeah, like I told you during the Post, we ran the samples we took from your victim through all of the standard databases. We didn't get a hit until the lab ran Gennifer's swab, and then it was like Christmas."

"Okay," I said. "So she matched both my victim *and* a case in California?"

"Yeah. We'd need to do a more comprehensive test but suffice it to say she is a familial match to *both* your victim and the one Vasily found in Rancho Linda. Which is damn confusing."

"Not especially," I sighed. "Turns out, Don Davies — my victim — has a twin brother."

There was a long pause at the other end, and then Lou swore. "Shit. That muddles up everything."

"It does," I concurred. "I only just found out, Lou. And if my hunch is correct, regardless of who I have in your morgue, I think his opposite number is on ice out on the West Coast."

"I'll reach out to the medical examiner there," Lou said. "There are some other tests that we can run to try and confirm that the two victims are brothers. That might help a bit in the identification, though you'll probably need a bit more to know who is who."

"Would a simple paternity test narrow anything down?"

"It might," Lou replied thoughtfully. "It does get a bit tricky with twins, though."

"I'll reach out to Gennifer and see if there were any sort of identifying marks or, well, anything that would help her to keep the two straight. And even if they *were* identical, there must have been some sort of slight difference between the two."

"There can be," Lou confirmed. "Sometimes it's as simple as one twin being a mirror of the other."

I blinked. "Mirror? In what way?"

"Oh, something like Don parted his hair in one direction, and his brother, the opposite."

My pulse kicked up a notch. "Could one be right-handed? And the other, left?"

"Sure," Lou replied. "I've seen that quite a bit. It has its basis in genetics and the way the DNA strands replicated during gestation, so often the individual has no choice."

"How far could the opposites go?" I asked. "Would their personalities be wildly opposing? Food preferences?"

"Now we're getting out of my comfort zone," Lou said. "You'd need to talk to a geneticist and maybe a psychologist for those sorts of answers. There's a fine line between nature and nurture and some of your questions cross between the two."

"Good point," I said. "If you have a suggestion for who I should talk to, send me their contact info."

"I might have one or two."

"One last thing," I added, sensing that Lou needed to get off the line. "Why didn't you match my victim to the one in California sooner? If I understood Vasily correctly, his victim had already been sent to the morgue by the time we were doing our postmortem."

"That's an easy answer," Dr. Hamilton sighed. "The data didn't appear in the national databases until this morning; that's why it was a hit with Gennifer first."

"They must be backlogged out there."

"Maybe. I've got to run, but if we get more info, I'll reach out."

"Sounds good. And thanks, Lou."

"Always."

Tapping my phone against my chin, I realized I had a number of new problems, not the least of which was my still-rumbling stomach. Restarting the SUV, I backed out of my slot a second time and pulled out onto the street, trying to remember if I had passed anything vaguely like a fast-food spot on my way into the station. At the intersection with Forest Avenue, the tall Glickman Library building for the University of Southern Maine caught my eye; the coffee shop on the top floor suddenly seemed like a good choice, especially since my status as an alumni with the system would grant me free access to the high-speed Wi-Fi. Crossing the intersection, I turned down the first side street I could find, hunting for an open parking meter while knowing just how unlikely that would be in the middle of the day with school in session.

Oddly, I rounded a slight curve on the street just as a small, beat-up sedan pulled away from where the curb would have been, had the snowbank not been masking it. Flicking on my blinker, I wedged the SUV into the spot as best as I could; it took a few minutes for me to figure out how to pay for an hour of parking using my phone, but once that task was complete, I grabbed my laptop from the rear seat, locked up, and made my way down to the main entrance of the library. I'd been in the Glickman a few times over the years for one meeting or another; housed in what had once been a bakery, the building now boasted multiple floors of books, team rooms for the students and a handful of seminar rooms. The coffee shop had been one of the final additions, and from what I could see as I stepped off the elevator, remained an extremely popular destination. I was never sure if the main draw happened to be the food and drink, or whether it was instead the magnificent view across the city the tall windows provided; both had always appealed to me, so I supposed I was the wrong person to judge.

Snagging a small table in a far corner of the space, I returned to the counter and ordered the soup and half-sandwich special, then in a weak moment, an extra-large cup of coffee. Hoping that Suzanne hadn't somehow tapped into my Apple Watch and was therefore monitoring my caffeine-heightened blood pressure, I took my wares back to the table and settled in; a spoonful of the rich tomato bisque told me it needed to cool for a bit, so I retrieved my laptop from the backpack, then scrounged further to locate my ear buds. A few moments of fiddling with the Wi-Fi settings on my MacBook ultimately begat the tired but nonetheless smiling visage of my best friend.

"That looks good," Vasily said, his eyes firmly on the small tub of soup and the chicken sandwich beside it. "Lunch?"

"As much as I can squeeze in at the moment, yeah," I replied. "Do you have time for a quick chat?"

"Sure," he said. "You spoke with Lou?"

"Yeah," I nodded. I glanced around me to ensure I was more or less out of earshot of my nearest neighbor; with Vasily's audio only in my ears, I figured anyone hearing just my side of the conversation might still be rather intrigued by the content, so I lowered my voice a bit more. "She confirmed what we both suspected already — Gennifer is related to both victims. We'll need to essentially run a full-on paternity test but even that might not be completely conclusive."

"Paternity?" Vasily asked. "That's an unusual way to connect the next of kin to a victim."

I smiled wryly. "That comes from the added complication I mentioned earlier. It seems, my dear friend, that Don Davies had an identical twin brother."

"Shit," Vasily swore. "So the guy out here could be Gennifer's uncle... *or* her father?"

"Exactly."

Vasily looked at me. "It can't be a coincidence both Davies siblings die within a week of each other," he said thoughtfully. "And Don was *supposed* to be here visiting Gennifer. You must have found the brother."

"That's kind of where my thoughts are going," I nodded, smiling a bit wider. "You catch on fast."

"I had a good mentor," Vasily smiled tiredly. "So Davies *did* get here? Then why was his brother—"

"Frank," I supplied helpfully.

"—Frank at the cottage in Windeport? And I thought Gennifer told us the airline had confirmed to her Don never got on his flight?"

"She did," I nodded, and couldn't help the smile.

Vas rolled his eyes. "That Cheshire Cat grin tells me I've missed something."

"Just context," I continued. "There are two possibilities. Either Gennifer is lying to us, and she both picked up and then ultimately dispatched her father, or she had the wrong set of flights. You've dealt with her as much as I have at this point, do you think she's leading us on?"

"If she is, it was a pretty bold move flying out there," Vasily replied. "Wouldn't Davies have told her about the flight changes?"

"Only if they happened in advance," I pointed out. "I've travelled enough to know that things can happen; maybe he didn't have a chance to call her when they did, or maybe he had always intended for his arrival to be a surprise and never expected her to follow up."

Vasily looked at me. "Why would he do that?" he asked.

"That is an excellent question. And honestly, I don't have any way to answer it — but Vas," I added softly, "my gut tells me that's what happened. Don Davies had some need to be in California for a few days incognito; I'm starting to think his 'appearance' in Windeport was to cover that."

"He used his brother as a stand in?" Vas whistled. "That ended badly for Frank."

"And, apparently, Don," I reminded him before taking a spoonful of my soup. "Unfortunately, this is all conjecture. I have zero evidence to support any of it."

"Maybe," Vasily replied. "But I'll take your conjecture as a starting point any day. I'll dig through the arrival manifests for both LAX and John Wayne for the ten days on either side of when Don was supposed to appear; maybe I'll get lucky."

I nodded. "I don't think I have enough yet to get a warrant for his computer or other financials," I warned him. "We need to identify one of our victims before I can go any further."

"Gennifer was on her way back here, right?" Vas asked. "I'll snag a blood sample from her to run the paternity test. That might jump start things."

"Cool."

"What's our next move?"

"I'm off to see if I can confirm Frank's movements are as I suspect; after that, well, I'm not entirely sure."

"We know both of our victims were murdered," Vasily pointed out. "I'm pretty much out of luck in terms of what was at my crime scene, but you must have come up with *something*."

"All Heather snagged me was a fingerprint that didn't match the victim," I said. "I've not checked the case system today, but I imagine since my phone isn't ringing off the hook the print didn't match anything on file here in Maine or nationally."

"*Fuuuuuuck*," Vasily breathed, putting his head into his hands. "Just once, would it be too much to ask that the clues just popped up when we needed them?"

"Oh, you know it's more fun this way."

"Sadist," he said though his hands.

"Not really my style," I replied. "Though if I recall correctly, *you* were the one with the leather outfits."

Vasily looked over his hands at me, a slight flame to his cheeks. "That's, uh, never been my scene," he said softly. "Though I do like the occasional roleplay."

"I had no idea," I deadpanned.

The flame darkened on his cheeks.

"Anyway," I continued, trying to put my friend out his misery, "I'm planning on staying in Portland overnight. I'll touch base after I've finished scouring the city for any sign that we're on to something."

"Sounds good."

I waved at my best friend as the screen went dark, then focused on my food for a few minutes. The soup was as delicious as ever, though the sandwich proved to be a bit dry. Sipping at my coffee, I logged into the case system and quickly confirmed what I had told Vasily: the single print we had found at the cottage in Windeport hadn't been matched to anything, anywhere. While not exactly a dead end, it was also less than helpful; sighing, I opened a new tab in the system and did a quick brain dump of my morning adventures in South Windham in an attempt to feel as though I were making progress. By the time I had transcribed my notes from the conversation with the General Manager at WWWD, the cafe had emptied out completely, and the sun looked to be rather low on the horizon.

Startled that I had let so much of the afternoon slip past me, I hurriedly punched up the address for One City Center, then packed up my laptop so I could return to my SUV. Unsurprisingly, there was a small parking ticket safely tucked beneath my windshield wiper, a gentle reminder that the streets around the university were patrolled with regularity. The amount of the fine made my eyebrows go up, but it was appropriate penance for underestimating my time.

Crossing Portland at that hour turned out to be a bit of a trial, not that the city had a *bona fide* rush hour like Boston; still, I lost twenty minutes between getting to Congress Street and the subsequent search for yet another parking spot close to my destination. Unwilling perhaps to risk a second ticket, I opted for using a garage after three orbits around the block had netted me absolutely nothing, though squeezing the SUV into a slot proved even trickier than parking in the snowbank at WWWD. Trotting down the icy sidewalk a few minutes later, One City Center was an easy landmark to identify; entering at the street level, I found myself within a multiple story atrium that at its lowest level seemed to house a food court. I could see irregularly-spaced doors on the levels above, hinting at entrances to professional offices. Despite having eaten lunch, the smells of fast food wafting up at me nearly distracted me from my main purpose, though I nearly lost the battle when the hint of freshly brewed coffee appeared in the air. Circling until I found the building directory, I located the suite number for Davies Financials on the eleventh floor, then took another moment to figure out where the elevators for the building happened to be. Why the directory was not close to the elevators was beyond me.

When the doors opened on the eleventh floor, I realized that all office building interiors seemed to be similar. In this iteration, a small plaque on the wall opposite the elevator indicated which direction the suite numbers went; below it, a small half-table hosted a fake potted plant and a phone to presumably call someone in order to get the leaves dusted. Following the sign, I wandered down the hallway, passing multiple glass doors that had been frosted to prevent one from deducing the space had not been leased. I figured the ruse would have worked had there not also been a *For Lease* placard taped prominently to the portal as well. Davies Financials appeared to have a corner suite at the end of the hallway, a prime location somewhat mitigated by being right next to the restrooms and the emergency stairwell.

The lights were on in the space beyond the glass, so I pulled the door open and entered a modestly sized reception area. There was an older woman situated behind a half-wall of a reception desk backed up against the tall windows looking out over Portland; she smiled as I passed the comfortable looking couches to stop at the counter. "May I help you?"

"Yes," I smiled. "My name is Sean Colbeth, and I'm looking for Frank Davies. Is he in?"

"Are you a client?" she asked.

"No," I replied. "I'm the Chief of Police for Windeport, Maine, and I need to ask Mr. Davies a few questions."

The woman's eyes went wide. "Is Frank in trouble?"

There's no easy way to answer that, I thought, so instead, I smiled slightly. "It's about his brother, actually."

"Don?"

"Yes," I nodded. "He was supposed to be in California but never arrived; his daughter is pretty worried. I'm working with a colleague from out there to try and trace Don and wondered if Frank might have had any information on Don's whereabouts."

"Don's missing? Holy *hell*," she breathed. "I'm afraid I'm not going to be much help. Frank went on vacation about a week ago; he doesn't usually check in when he's out of the office."

"Where was he vacationing?"

She smiled slightly. "Honestly, I don't know. He truly didn't like to be contacted when he was taking time off."

"Ah," I smiled again. "I can understand that. He does investments, right?"

"Yes," the woman nodded. "He's also an adjunct faculty member at the University of Southern Maine."

I nodded, wondering if I'd backed into evidence of who was on ice up in Augusta as I pictured Frank Davies pacing at the front of a lecture hall. "He's a teacher?"

She nodded again. "Nearly thirty years, though he's down to just one lecture a semester now."

"I'm impressed he managed to balance both vocations. I can barely keep up with one."

"Well, it helps we're not as large as the commercial brokerages, of course; still, our returns are fairly steady for our clients. Frank specializes in conservative to modest growth portfolios, and that appeals to a certain segment."

"I can imagine. Does Frank have any family?"

"Just his brother," she replied, though for a moment, I thought I could see in her eyes she had once hoped to be on the shortlist to create one with Frank. "He's pretty much married to his job."

"When will he be back?" I asked, knowing already the answer.

"Three weeks," she replied promptly. "If you'd like, I can take your contact info. Should he call in, I'll pass it on to him."

"I'd appreciate that, thanks."

She shuffled some paper on her desk and then paused before placing a yellow-line pad in front of me. "I'd nearly forgotten, you're the second person who's come in asking about Frank."

I started. "Someone *else* was here recently?"

"Yeah," she replied, pointing to the scribbling on the paper she'd handed me. "This guy. About ten days ago, I think."

Looking down, read what had been written in blue ink.

D. Houston - (626) 555-5555

I looked back at the receptionist. "What was this visitor hoping to speak to Frank about?"

"He told me he was from Augusta, actually," she replied after a moment. "One agency or another, I'm not certain now; I assumed it was one dealing with regulating investing offices such as ours. Maybe about an audit? Or paperwork? I honestly don't recall — whatever it was, the guy said it could wait until Frank was back from vacation."

"Can you describe this individual?" I asked.

She smiled and pointed over her shoulder to the small camera mounted on the ceiling; I'd not noticed it earlier. "I can do better. Given the business we are in, Frank always felt like we should have a record of our interactions with clients," she explained. "All of his conversations with clients are similarly recorded in an effort to better protect all involved."

"I imagine it cuts down a bit on the 'you never told me it would be risky' accusations," I mused.

"You have no idea. Hang on while I call the gal that does our technical support," she added as she picked up her phone. "She can get a screen grab in less time than it takes for me to log into my computer. If it would help."

Thinking that I might have an actual break, finally, I nodded. "It will indeed..."

Eleven

"There's a Daniel Houston on a flight from Boston," Vasily said. "Arrived a few days after Don Davies did — and a few days *before* we found the body."

I nodded at my friend's image on my laptop as I munched on the last of the chef's salad I had ordered from room service; I'd checked into my favorite Marriott close to the Jetport after my visit to One City Center and subsequently set up a small remote office on the desk and table the room had provided. Halfway through my dinner, Vasily had texted he'd found something in the passenger manifests. Popping a crouton into my mouth, I wondered if we had hit that part of the investigation when the trickle of facts threatened to become a flood.

"They both left from Boston?"

"Yes," Vas nodded. "Davies was on a different airline than the one Gennifer was anticipating; it fits your theory that something changed at the last minute." He looked at me. "You think this Houston person is the one that killed your victim?"

"He's definitely a person of interest," I replied.

"That's pretty bold to put your name down on a piece of paper," Vasily observed. "Not a professional hit, then?"

"No," I shook my head. "It's personal. And it fits the scene I had at my end: whoever wanted to kill Davies had a very, *very* personal score to be settled. I'm not sure our suspect cares one way or the other about being caught — or is righteous enough to think the law will never catch up with him."

"That would make him quite dangerous."

"Yes," I nodded. "Personal also makes me think it's not something Davies might have said on-air; this doesn't feel to me like a fan gone rogue. Houston's actions seem more consistent with someone trying to balance the scales of Justice on his own."

Vas blinked at me. "Over what?"

"I don't know yet," I sighed. "I'll run his name through our systems here, and you do the same. Maybe something will come up."

"All right," he replied. "I'll put a BOLO out on Houston. His last known address is here in California."

"Why am I not surprised?" I asked rhetorically. "Wasn't that phone number using a California area code?"

"Yes," Vas nodded. "Pasadena, which matches the address."

"Listen, do you know anything about the Hilton?"

Vasily smiled. "There are a number of Hiltons in California, Sean. You're gonna have to be more specific."

"I found a pad and pen from the Hilton Orange County in Don Davies' bedroom," I explained. "At the time, I thought it was a non-sequitur worth following up. Now I'm wondering what the actual connection might be."

"Well, that particular hotel is one of two in Rancho Linda with something of a conference center. I've never been inside it, but I hear the restaurant is pretty good."

"Conference?" I sat up. "Hang on—"

"I've seen that look before," Vasily said slowly. "What is it?"

Shifting screens, I flipped through the case file while silently cursing how slow the hotel Wi-Fi was; it took longer than I thought before I was able to pull up my notes from speaking with Wendy Hackett. "Here it is — Don attended something called the National Radio Personality Conference in Southern Cal every year." I flipped back to Vasily. "How much do you want to bet it was at the Hilton?"

"I can check into it," he offered. "The hotel isn't far from the station."

"Thanks."

I eyed him for a moment, wondering how best to broach the next subject. Despite the mountain of evidence we had collected from the cottage in Windeport, and what else we might yet discover in Don Davies' home in South Windham should I be able to score a search warrant, the nagging feeling that the answers I truly needed lay elsewhere had grown significantly in the hours since I'd left Frank Davies' office at One City Center. Finding out my first solid person of interest seemed to have a connection to Southern California had shoved that nagging feeling into something far more urgent — a sense that if I didn't move quickly, I might let my best chance to solve the case slip through my fingers. Looking at Vasily, though, I hesitated another few heartbeats, for it felt awkward inserting myself into what by rights was now *his* investigation; if I'd any sense at all, I'd simply pass on whatever else I uncovered in Maine to my friend, and assist him as best as I could from afar.

And yet, it felt like the wrong move. Somehow, I knew I needed to get out there.

Swallowing hard, and feeling unusually tentative, I decided to take the plunge. "Look, don't take this the wrong way—"

"You're coming out," he smiled. "How soon can you get here?"

My eyebrows went up. "How on earth—?"

"Easy," he laughed. "I used to work with you, remember? I'm pretty sure you were already thinking the answers to both murders might be here in California. Houston's arrival just put you over the top."

"It's only a hunch," I hedged, slightly taken aback that my one-time mentee had read my thoughts so easily.

"Probably a pretty good one," Vasily nodded. "I'll make up the couch for you; send me your flights once you're booked."

"As long as you don't think I'm horning in on your turf," I said. "With our person of interest in California, it's pretty much your case now."

"I told you before, I could really use the help on this one," he replied. "Even if I originally thought it was a wild goose chase I was reluctant to send my best friend on. Besides, it will be good to see you."

"You were *just* here," I reminded him. "And Suzanne and I are crashing with you in less than three weeks."

"Really?" he looked at me with mock seriousness. "Seems like it was a lifetime ago."

"Maybe it was," I smiled back. "Murder tends to age people."

"Does it ever," he replied ruefully. "I'm going to keep bleaching my hair to make sure the grey never sees the light of day."

"What grey?" I asked, perplexed; looking over his bed-head style didn't reveal any streaks that hadn't been artificially induced by his hairdresser.

"Exactly," he laughed. "Let me make some calls to get the ball rolling here; have Caitlyn update the Interagency MOU you sent me earlier to include ten days of travel to the West Coast."

"Ten *days*?" I choked. "This better not take that long — Suzanne will kill me if we miss the convention."

"You won't," he smiled.

It took me a moment to understand. "Oh," I smiled. "Well, if we *do* solve this quickly, I wouldn't be opposed to a few quiet days on the sand."

"I didn't think you would," Vasily chuckled. "Call me once your flights are booked."

"Will do."

Closing the FaceTime call, I swapped back over to the case system and waited for the virtual table of contents to load. Fishing out the final pieces of lettuce from my salad, I chewed thoughtfully while the system rather deliberately painted in the data for me. I needed some way to establish a connection between one or both of the Davies brothers to Houston, or barring that, Southern California; the fact that Don had attended a conference that *might* have taken place in Rancho Linda some time over the past decade helped, but something a bit more contemporary was in order. I decided since the victim had landed in my backyard, I at the very least had the legal authority to dig around in his emails or review his phone records. Shifting to my contact application, I scrolled down to a judge I worked with frequently, checked the time, and then punched the number into my iPhone.

Judge Stephanie Rayo picked up on the third ring. "Sean Colbeth," she said. "If you are calling me this late, it can't be good."

"Sorry, Judge," I smiled, easily picturing her reading glasses perched on top of her short-cropped salt-and-pepper hair; if I wasn't mistaken, a tumbler with her favorite whisky was rattling around in one hand. Through a strange quirk in the politically-drawn judicial boundaries, her court had jurisdiction over Windeport — despite the fact she was based out of Bangor. "I've got a bit of a conundrum with a case."

"It's never easy with you," Rayo chuckled. "Tell me what's going on."

"The short version is we found a body in Don Davies' cottage in Windeport," I started.

"Don Davies? The radio guy?"

"One and the same. I got a call a few days ago from my old partner, Vasily Korsokovach, to do a wellness check on Davies — he was supposed to be in California, visiting his daughter and her kids, but never showed."

"Ouch. I take it you found him, then."

"That's where this gets complicated," I replied. "The DNA on my victim was a familial match to the daughter — she flew out here to confirm it was her father, so we were able to get a sample — but when the State Crime Lab entered the results into all of the usual databases, it also came back as a match to a body that turned up in Rancho Linda."

"It... *what?*"

"Turns out, Don Davies has an identical twin brother. Without a few more tests, we're not sure whether I found Don, or his brother, Frank, in Windeport. Same goes for our colleagues in California."

"I think I see where this is going," Judge Rayo murmured. "You want a search warrant, but don't know who to put on it?"

"Pretty much," I concurred. "I'd like to get access to the phone records, emails and bank records for both Frank and Don; we've identified a person of interest who happened to visit Frank's office before returning to California, but I don't have enough to go after him, yet. Unless I can prove a connection between one of the brothers and the suspect." I decided to leave out the fact that we thought Don had flown to California for the moment, correctly guessing it might make matters even more complicated.

"Do you have an identity for this 'person of interest?'"

"Yes. We pulled a screen grab from the security camera and matched it to a DMV photo. Vasily is running that down in California as we speak."

"You think this is the guy that murdered Don Davies? Or whomever you found?"

"I'm not sure," I replied honestly. "The fact that he openly gave his name when he travelled seems odd, but like I said, until I have more, I can't paw through this guy's finances."

There was a long pause as Judge Rayo considered what I had told her; the ice clinking in her tumbler as she swirled it punctuated her thought process. "All you have is a possible DNA match to your victim? And you don't even know if it's Don?"

"Or Frank, right."

The silence stretched for a moment, then another; the clinking of the ice in her glass became more pronounced before she finally spoke. "This is a bit of a chicken-and-egg problem. You don't have quite enough to prove to me the person you want to dig into is who you purport them to be; but you also have a good chance of determining that if I allow the warrant."

"That's pretty much it," I sighed. "Never have I had so much evidence and no way to use it effectively."

The ice clinked again in the glass. "Write it up and send it to me," Rayo said. "I'm not promising anything, but I'll review all of what you have to this point and see if there is enough of a *smidgen* of probable cause to get you something."

"Will do," I said, letting out the breath I didn't know I'd been holding. "You'll have it in an hour or so."

"Good night, Chief."

I put my iPhone down on the small desk I was seated behind and then stood, stretching a kink in my back. Despite the Marriott advertising their rooms as being friendly to business travelers, I'd never found them terribly accommodating to people such as myself who were over six feet tall. Still, I could appreciate the effort it had taken to ensure there were power plugs easily at hand, and enough desk space to spread out a file or two (had I still been using paper). Moving to the window, I pushed back the curtain to look at the lighted parking lot below me, and the Maine Mall in the distance beyond. The chill of the evening was palpable through the glass of the window, and if I wasn't mistaken, snowflakes had slowly begun to drift into the pools of light from the lamps. After the innumerable storms we'd suffered through this winter, I was beginning to have a very negative reaction to seeing the ice crystals thicken outside my window; as much as I enjoyed the seasons in the state where I had been born, I found myself giving serious consideration to taking a position in a warmer climate. Not for the first time did I think that perhaps Vasily had been on to something with his relocation to California.

Sighing, I knew my life was pretty much tied to Maine, and Windeport in particular; back a year ago, when it appeared my career in law enforcement might have ended sooner than I had anticipated, I'd entertained the thought of going private — and going wherever that took me. Now, a year later, there was absolutely no way I would ever leave Suzanne, nor would I ask her to put her own career on hold to follow mine. We were both realists, though, aware that she might have about a decade before there wouldn't be enough clients left in Windeport to make her practice profitable; she'd either have to merge with one of the massive statewide medical organizations or hang up her stethoscope altogether. As committed a physician as I knew her to be, the former seemed more likely despite how she detested the bureaucracy that came with someone else calling the shots. Then again, with the arrival of the cruise industry the prior fall, Windeport had seen a small but significant bump in the local economy. Who knew what might happen if my village finally realized its dream of becoming a Downeast version of Kennebunkport...?

Thinking of Suzanne reminded me of our earlier phone conversation; letting the curtain fall back into place, I reached for my iPhone and dialed the number I knew by heart. "Hey Suze," I said when she picked up. "How's the patient?"

My girlfriend sounded tired. "She and her new daughter are doing just fine," she replied. "I delivered a healthy five pounder about three hours ago; the kid's sleeping in my makeshift crib right now."

"And Deidre?"

"Exhausted, as you can imagine, but perfectly fine. She's been sleeping as well; Yasmine and I have been trading off checking on her or the baby but so far, everything is fine. When Deidre wakes, we'll decide whether she wants to go to the maternity ward just in case, or stick it out here until she's ready to leave."

"Does she need to go to the hospital?"

"Not necessarily, but they have a few more technical gizmos that can ensure she's not off on her electrolytes or some such thing. Depends on whether Deidre wants that sort of peace of mind."

I felt an eyebrow arch. "I've seen your office, Suze. You have quite a few of those magic gizmos."

Suzanne chuckled. "I do, but nothing for premature births, I assure you. My tech skews more toward the older demographic I tend to treat."

"Maybe it's time for an investment."

"Wash your mouth out," she chuckled again. "And hope to God my equipment saleswoman isn't eavesdropping. How's the case going?"

"Interesting," I replied before quickly sketching in my day's activities. Somehow, they didn't seem quite as exciting in the retelling as having participated in a live birth. "I've got to work on my warrant request for Judge Rayo," I finished. "But it also looks like I'm headed to California."

"I thought that might be in the cards once you told me about your suspect," she said thoughtfully. "Twins? That's insane."

"It makes it insanely complicated, that's for sure."

"Vas must be excited to have you visit early."

"He knew I was coming before I did," I sighed. "I think that kid misses me."

"I wouldn't doubt it. The connection between the two of you is pretty strong."

"Yeah," I nodded. "Any chance you can come with me?"

"I'd love to," she replied. "But Deidre's likely got another day here with me if she doesn't go to the hospital; on top of that, Yasmine's got her monthly rotation starting tomorrow. She moved it up so she could cover during my vacation."

"I had to ask," I said sadly. "I will probably hang out there until the convention," I continued.

"Don't worry, I'll pack for the two of us. You're not getting out of wearing that sexy feline costume that easily, Sean."

"I would never—"

"Like *hell*," she chuckled. "When do you leave?"

"Caitlyn is my next call," I replied. "As soon as she can get me booked."

"All right. Call before you leave?"

"Absolutely." I waited for a brief heartbeat. "Suze — I love you."

"I know," she replied softly. "And the feeling is mutual."

I waited for the triple chirps to tell me the call had ended before I pulled up the number for the station; given the hour, I was actually surprised when Caitlyn answered. "Why are you there?" I asked.

"Scheduling snafu," she replied. "I'm covering as a result."

"You worked this morning, too," I observed. "How much is this costing me?"

"I don't hit double time until — oh, ten minutes from now," she laughed.

"I thought your boss had to authorize overtime?"

"He does," she replied sagely. "And I'm sure he will sign the form that's been sitting in his email inbox since noontime."

I flipped to my email and frowned. "That he will," I said, chagrined. "Sorry I missed it."

"I know you're good for it," she chuckled.

"Now that I know you're there," I continued. "I need you to work your magic with the travel system and get me on a flight to Los Angeles."

"How soon do you need to leave?"

"Yesterday," I said. "And while you're at it, update the MOU we crafted for Rancho Linda and add ten days travel to it. Vasily is expecting it."

"Got it," she replied. "Break in the case?"

"Possibly," I confirmed. "Our only person of interest appears to have fled to LA."

There was a long pause at the other end of the phone. "Chief... I don't normally question these things, but... does Vas really need your help on this?"

"It's a fair point," I allowed. "This case with Don Davies has gotten kind of complicated, though. I think we are both in agreement that two sets of eyes on it could be beneficial."

"All right," she said. "Let me see what I can come up with."

"Thanks," I said before she hung up.

Putting aside my phone, I sat back down at the small desk and punched up the standard template for a warrant request, then buried myself in completing it with as much detail as I could provide from the various artifacts in the case system. Oddly, such activities tended to provide a bit of clarity to me, especially when I had to spell out what I was looking *for* as a result of what it was I already *had*. This time proved no different, for it allowed me to expand on my cursory review of the items Heather had dropped off at the Public Safety building. Flipping through the images I had, and the associated commentary from Heather or one of her techs, the picture resolved into a scene of someone who had been planning a quiet long weekend alone. The fridge had been comfortably full of supplies, as were the cabinets that were acting as a pantry; the suitcase in the master suite had only a handful of outfits. Both hinted strongly that my long weekend hunch was more than probable.

I paused for a long moment on the photo of the moldy eggs and breakfast potatoes when it appeared on my screen, though. There was a cross-linked note from Heather that my guess on the growth of the mold had indeed supported the estimated time of death they had come up with — about a week prior to when we found the body. Flattered that my college-level biology had indeed come into play, something else struck me about the eggs. Flipping back to the photos of the contents of the fridge, I found myself tracing the products one-by-one with a finger.

Milk. Orange Juice. Cream. Eggs. And all of them are name brand items. That feels... off? But why—

Startled into insight, I opened a new tab in the case system and pulled down my notes from the quasi-search we had done in Don Davies' home. Halfway through the page, I found my observation about the contents of that stainless steel appliance.

Milk. Orange Juice. Cream. All are store brands from that wholesome food place. And there are no eggs. Where are the eggs?

Sitting back in the very uncomfortable desk chair, I laced my hands behind my head and stared at the screen. It felt like I had stumbled onto something; shifting forward, I changed the screen on my laptop so I could see both sets of notes side-by-side.

If I didn't know better, I'd say two different people went shopping—

I sat bolt upright.

Shit. Two different people did *go shopping. Don Davies wasn't the one at the cottage. It was* Frank.

I thought about that for a moment, and then felt more pieces falling into place.

Somehow, Houston must have found out about the cottage. Maybe he assumed that was where Don had retreated to when he couldn't find him Portland, but it's actually irrelevant, I thought. The important part is Houston thought he had finally caught up with Don Davies. That explains the way we found the body — he had to shift the watch to the hand Don would have worn it, to try and throw us? Houston must have realized too late that he was killing the wrong person; and with Frank gagged —

My stomach roiled as I realized Frank had had no way to tell Houston he had the wrong guy; or, if he did, Houston hadn't believed him and gagged him to keep him quiet. Those last few minutes must have been excruciating for Frank, but in the end, somehow Houston had come around — and at the same time had figured out where Don had *actually* gone. Too late to save Frank, of course, though I was starting to think killing the wrong person probably had been viewed as karma.

Fingers flying over the keyboard of my laptop, I returned to my warrant request and modified some of what I had put into the form, then added my epiphany. While I still lacked a few critical pieces to the entire puzzle, I felt like at least one side of it was complete; I'd also become convinced that reasons for Houston's actions — assuming, of course, he was my guy — existed in California, not in Maine. Something had happened out there, something that intersected with Don Davies and Daniel Houston in such a way that led to Davies' ultimate demise.

Reviewing the warrant one final time, I'd just hit the *send* button when my iPhone rang. Rubbing at my dry eyes before picking it up, I marveled at how several hours had passed in the blink of an eye. "Caitlyn," I answered. "Now you must be into Golden Time."

"I am," she laughed. "Since you didn't give me a limit on what to spend, I booked you on the first flight of the day to Atlanta; you've got a bit of a wait for the connection to LAX, though, and won't get in until the late afternoon."

"I'll take what I can get," I said.

"Good," she replied. "Tickets have been forwarded to your phone. Happy hunting."

"Thank you," I said. "Hold down the fort while I'm gone?"

"Chief, one of these days you are going to have to hire a number two."

"Someday," I allowed, thinking at how unsuccessful I'd continued to be at replacing Vasily. "I'll check in when I get to the West Coast."

"Sounds good."

Putting my phone down again, I stood and stretched once more, then looked at the paltry duffle bag I'd packed when I'd assumed I'd just be spending a day or two in Portland. While I had one set of running gear in there, I'd left my swimming items behind; Vasily was going to have a field day with loaning me some of his more... vibrant... briefs, should I take him up on the inevitable offer to hit the pool with his team. Sighing again, I put the bag on the small counter beside the television and started to change for bed just as my laptop *pinged*, announcing an incoming email.

Assuming it was my itinerary from Caitlyn, I instead found it was an approved search warrant for both Frank and Don Davies; reading the notes from the judge, I discovered my last-minute addition to the request had proven to be what put it over the top. Rubbing my tired eyes, I settled back in behind the MacBook to begin firing off my requests to the various organizations the warrant covered; feeling like I had *finally* begun to get somewhere, I knew sleep would have to wait just a bit longer.

Twelve

There was a favorite song of Suzanne's that played fairly regularly on the soft rock radio station she used for background music at her medical practice, and while I didn't particularly feel like I was an expert in such matters, as I stepped out of the double doors of Baggage Claim for Los Angeles International Airport, I was reasonably certain it did, indeed, rain in Southern California. I'd had time during my layover in Atlanta to check the ten-day weather forecast and been dismayed to learn that I'd be leaving behind unseasonably cold and dreary weather in Maine for... unseasonably cold and dreary weather in Southern California. About the only redeeming quality lay in the degree differential, for the lows over the next few nights back in Windeport were expected in to be in negative territory; in Anaheim, I was reasonably certain I'd be able to suffer through the mid-sixties being predicted. My winter jacket seemed a bit like overkill against the quasi-warm gusting breeze, though it did remind me how my father used to break his shorts out when the thermometer hit fifty each spring; the winter running gear I'd packed for Portland would now be similarly out of step with the actual weather. It seemed I'd be needing to borrow more than just swimming briefs from Vasily, should I wish to work out while I was there, though I worried about what he might loan me on that front, too. Much like his eclectic color choices for the pool, his running tights tended to stand out a bit more than I would be comfortable with.

Assuming, of course, we had time for such personal luxuries.

It took me a few minutes to find a spot on the curb that was both not upwind of a designated smoking spot and still within shouting distance of the door to baggage claim for my airline; I'd no sooner taken up position before my iPhone buzzed in my pocket. Fishing it out, I smiled to see the number of my best friend and current Deputy Chief of Police for Rancho Linda, California. Tapping the icon to answer, I started to look for his candy-apple red Camaro among the stream of vehicles jockeying for a spot along the Arrivals sidewalk.

"This city feels like it's gotten busier since I was here last," I said.

Vasily Korsokovach chuckled in my ear. "It's *always* this busy. You country folk never seem to appreciate that."

"I hesitate to point out how long you lived in said country."

"I have no idea what you're talking about," he laughed harder, choosing to ignore the plain fact that he'd moved to Windeport as a college freshman at the University of Eastern Maine and had only recently relocated *back* to California some fifteen years later. "I seem to have missed you on my first lap around this crazy speedway. What door did you say you're in front of again?"

"Memory is the first thing to go after thirty," I teased, knowing full well my best friend was a tad sensitive about his recent birthday.

"That's just mean, dude. Mean."

"Sorry — I couldn't resist. It looks like I'm outside of the second doorway for Delta."

"*That's* why I was having trouble," he replied. "You normally don't fly them."

"No," I agreed. "They were the best option given the last-minute nature of my trip."

"I'm coming around the loop now," he said. "What are you wearing?"

"I suspect you won't be able to miss me," I answered before deciding to needle him a bit more. "Assuming your vision hasn't gone, too."

"It's gonna be like that, is it?" he sighed dramatically. "All right. Game *on*."

I laughed as the line went dead, and went back to scanning the passing cars. Maybe a minute later, the very recognizable profile of Vasily's sports car appeared, and I watched as it dodged around slower vehicles before smoothly slipping into the space just in front of where I was standing. Making my way to the trunk, it popped open just as I alighted by the bumper, allowing me to slip my duffle and smaller laptop bag inside. Cognizant of the flow around us, I quickly moved to the passenger door and slipped inside the cabin.

Vasily smiled at me before turning his attention back to the traffic. "You were right," he said as I buckled in. "There was only one tall Greek god standing on the curb."

Shaking my head, I sighed. Some things never change. "I was referring to the winter jacket," I replied, pointing to the embroidered L. L. Bean logo on the chest. "Considering everyone else out here is wearing shorts and a t-shirt, I thought it would be obvious."

"That, too," he laughed as he swiftly accelerated into a gap between vehicles I'd thought too small to squeeze into.

It had only been the better part of a month since I'd seen my friend; through some serious Christmas Miracle action, he'd agreed to spend the holiday with me back in Windeport despite the snow. He'd been far more relaxed — and far more comfortable with where he was in life — than ever before, which I was certain had helped the two of us patch up things over his abrupt exit from Maine the prior summer. I smiled a bit to see the same unusual haircut in person again, one that featured short sides as an accent to an out-of-control top that appeared as though he'd simply rolled out of bed with no further thought. While I missed his original ponytail look, I had to admit his new style complimented him immensely — though I also was aware of the inordinate amount of time it took for him to make it appear as though it had taken no time at all. I'd never been much for contemporary styles myself — how could I? With the curly body I'd inherited from my mother, there was very little I could do with my own hair save gel it into some sort of submission.

Shifting lanes as naturally as any California native would, Vasily glanced at me for a moment. "Thanks for coming out. The deeper I get into what I have on this side of the country, the more I appreciate having a second set of eyes." He glanced at me again, with a trace of a smile. "Especially when they are *your* eyes."

"I sort of invited myself along," I reminded him, finding myself bracing a hand against the door. The way he was constantly darting between lanes to gain some sort of advantage reminded me that living in California had affected Vasily's driving habits; while like him, I was trained in typical law enforcement driving techniques, I'd never thought of applying them to my daily commute. It was clear he *had*. "I looked over what little you were able to send me before I boarded the flight. There wasn't much there, frankly."

My friend groaned. "I'm so sorry about that. With our ongoing budget woes, the department shifted to a shared I.T. infrastructure with Orange County last summer; according to Chief Gilbert, I apparently missed the fun of the transition. The latest fiasco resulted from the central I.T. nerds down in Santa Ana running an unscheduled upgrade on the case system a few weeks ago and it's been *hell* ever since. Transferring data between agencies has been an especially troublesome issue." He nodded toward the backseat. "I've got an iPad for you with direct access to our servers. You're welcome to it for the duration, but I'll warn you, it won't be easy going. We've resorted to printing everything off and going back to three ring binders — that's how unstable the system has become."

"*Paper?*" I chuckled. "What is this, the dark ages?"

"I know, right?" he laughed.

"That also explains why it took so long for Gennifer's DNA to get flagged," I added after a moment.

"Yeah," Vasily replied. "*Everything* is slower right now."

"Just one more thing for us to work through."

"I'd prefer if we could skip that particular hurdle."

"Paper. Jesus. You're going to make me pine away for that huge desk of mine," I replied. "Or someplace large enough to spread out the files."

"I think we've got that covered," he chuckled.

"Oh?"

"There's a conference room at the office I think you'll like. We have so few people these days anyway that it hardly gets any use; you can have the space as your home away from home while you're working the case."

"Nice."

Despite all his efforts, it took quite a bit of time for the Camaro to finally exit the covered area for the Arrivals sidewalk; when it did, the car was shaken severely by an immediate broadside from the storm. Vasily had to increase the tempo of the wipers just to get some fraction of visibility. Reluctantly, he and the drivers around him were forced by the deluge of rain to slow down, resulting in a sea of red taillights winking on and off in front of us at irregular intervals. Stop and go traffic always seemed to ratchet up my blood pressure for some reason; more so in Maine, when the options for getting anywhere were so much more limited.

"This weather is something," I observed, trying to distract myself from the mess ahead of us.

Vasily shrugged. "You should have been out here this fall. We had so much rain, half of Rancho Linda was flooded out." He paused for a moment as he successfully managed to creep the Camaro into a turning lane. "There was a period there when I thought I'd be able to swim from my condo to work each day."

"Brings a whole new definition to 'open water swimming,'" I replied. "Though I'd probably be reluctant to immerse myself in flood water."

"I fear I regularly swim through *worse* when I'm surfing. At any rate, this should clear out by the weekend."

"Thank *God*. We've not seen the sun in *months* back home; I'd appreciate a clear day or two. And a bit of warmth."

Vas pointedly twisted the dial on his heater up a few notches. "A little thin-blooded in your old age, aren't you?"

"Like hell."

He chuckled as he finally merged into the flow, turned out of the airport and down into a tunnel; I knew just enough of the overwhelmingly confusing geography for the Greater Los Angeles area to be happy that someone else was driving. "Want me to round out what little you *were* able to download about my victim?"

"I'd appreciate that," I replied. "Not that I don't love a good mystery."

"I'm sure you don't," he nodded. Vasily paused long enough to merge onto a four-lane highway before continuing. "Damn," he sighed as we both saw the slow-moving lines of cars. "I hope you can hold out longer for dinner; drivers in Southern Cal always freak out with any kind of weather and tie the freeways up in knots as a result."

Thinking back to the outrageously expensive snack box I'd purchased on the final leg of my flight — and how far from satisfying it had been — I smiled wryly. "I won't waste away, if that's what you're asking."

"Good," he replied. "Alex did a pot roast in the slow cooker; despite how short a time he's lived here, my boyfriend seems to have correctly gauged how late we'd be."

"Clearly he's been paying attention."

The warm smile that lit his face spoke volumes about their relationship; I couldn't be happier that he'd finally found someone to fill the gap in his heart where his affection for me had once resided. "He certainly has."

I paused for a long moment, unsure of exactly how to broach the nagging guilt that had been dogging me since I'd essentially invited myself into his case. "Look, I just want to say again that I'm worried about stepping on your toes while I'm here. I know I sort of pushed you into—"

"You did *nothing* of the kind." Vas glanced at me, that trace of a smile on his face. "Our cases are connected," he continued. "It makes perfect sense that you'd at the very least want to personally take a look at what I've got here. Only you can tell me how it relates to what you found back in Windeport."

"You could get that from my file," I pointed out.

"I could. I'd rather get it directly from you." Vasily looked at me for a long moment. "This case... I'm not afraid to admit it might be more than I can handle. It's certainly more high profile than anything I've ever worked before — as a lead," he quickly added. "I know the Pelletier case was pretty big, but it never had the potential for national exposure."

"National?" I replied quizzically. "What do you mean by that?"

"You already know Don Davies was syndicated," Vas replied. "I forget how many markets, but the important part is that he's just as well-known as Oprah was in her day. When his disappearance finally becomes public, I'm going to have every major news outlet breathing down my neck."

"*We* will," I corrected. "I'm right there with you, all the way."

"I won't lie," he continued. "This could get pretty messy. We need to have our ducks lined up *completely*, for we're likely to have an entire fanbase questioning every bit of evidence we collect."

"When have we done otherwise?" I asked. "It's what we do. It's why you're now Deputy Chief."

"I appreciate the vote of confidence." Vas cursed suddenly and swerved, barely avoiding a motorcycle that appeared to have been riding the line between lanes. "I *hate* it when they do that," he said after a moment. "Especially in this kind of weather. It's already hard to see them!"

"Is that maneuver legal?" I asked.

"Here in California, yes," he replied. "Not sure I'd try it myself, though."

"No kidding." I felt my foot squash a non-existent brake pedal as Vasily came up fast on another car. "I don't truly understand this syndication thing, actually."

❖

"How much do you know about radio in general?"

"The technology or the physical device?" I asked.

"*So* like you to be literal," Vasily chuckled. "I was referring to the industry."

I rolled my eyes at the dig, but then again, he wasn't far off. "Not much," I admitted. "Only a handful of stations reach Windeport, given our geography. Of the ones we *do* get, I happen to prefer the jazz station UEM hosts, if you're asking about music; for sports, I can usually get something out of Augusta to hear Red Sox games. Suzanne seems to enjoy a soft rock station that, frankly, drives me a little batty."

"I seem to remember there wasn't much in the way of talk radio."

"Maybe one station," I reminded him. "On AM only. If the weather is just right."

"Oh, I forgot about that. Anyway," he continued, "out here there are a *ton* of talk stations, both on AM and FM. They run the gamut from sports to politics to just general chit-chit; while several of the shows airing on them are produced locally for our Southern California market, a significant portion are syndicated nationally, shows that would air on small stations like the one you can get back in Windeport. Davies essentially did that from Portland."

"How popular is that format?" I asked.

"That's hard to answer without going deeply into the data I've been reviewing," he replied. "And believe me, you don't want me to do that. At least not without a good glass of red in your hand."

"You're scaring me."

"Then I'll give you the shorter Vasily read on it. Much depends on the topicality of the show and how dynamic the host is. The most successful stations have at least one show that manages to balance both aspects; there are outliers, of course, but that seems to be the winning formula."

"Timeliness I get, but what do you mean by *dynamic?*"

"Probably about what you are *thinking* it means. A host who has complete command of the topic in question, or, barring that, one willing to push the envelope in order to keep the audience engaged." He paused for a moment just as the traffic started to break up a bit and increase in speed; maneuvering around the several lanes of irregularly moving cars, he managed to slide in behind a pickup truck loaded with furniture barely protected from the downpour by a poorly tied down blue tarp. "That's partly where our case comes in."

I felt myself nodding. "The General Manager at WWWD told me Davies easily engaged his audience, and had been doing so for years."

"Exactly. Don Davies happens to have been the latter; he hosted a show that aired during what would have been the drive time slot back East, but landed mid-day here. He's had an extraordinary multiple decade run at the top of the ratings in just about every market where he airs, including the Greater Los Angeles region. From what I've read, people thought of him as that—"

"Genial relative who could tell good stories?" I replied, thinking to what Wendy Hackett had said.

"Exactly. But the more amazing thing is that he connected to *everyone* almost *everywhere* the show was broadcast. Quite a feat in radio."

"Ah," I replied. "I'm starting to see where your 'national' fear is coming from."

"Exactly." There was another pause as Vasily deftly switched lanes again to hit an off-ramp at a speed far faster than I would have been comfortable with, given the conditions; I didn't need to look down to see my knuckles were white where I was holding onto the door for dear life. "I feel like there is a 'rest of the story' part of this tale coming," I said once it looked like we were again on a freeway and at speed.

"You clearly know more about radio than you are letting on," he teased.

"I might have done some internet searches on the flight out based on what little I'd gleaned from the files," I replied. "Paul Harvey seems to have been pretty popular for a while there."

"That he was." Shifting lanes once more, Vasily shook his head. "But in all honesty, I can't seem to get to a second page, let alone a viable reason why anyone would want to kill him — at least, not one that has come up in the work I've done from this side."

I shook my head as well. "Same for me. I managed to get a warrant served for his electronic records — emails, phone records, finances — but nothing had come in before I left Portland. I'm hoping something there tells us why someone wanted him dead. Certainly not his station; from what the General Manager told me, Davies' show was the only thing keeping the lights on. Killing the golden goose would be a terrible business plan."

"We'll have to go off your system to review that data," Vas murmured. "If you try to send it to me, it could be days before it appears in our case database."

"I do think you have Don in the morgue," I said.

Vasily nearly drove into the car next to us. "How the *hell* do you know that?"

"Conjecture," I explained. "There was a disparity between the types of food I found at Don's home in South Windham, and what was in the cottage. I think Frank happened to favor name brand products, and Don, the versions found at that high-end wholesome foods supermarket. And," I added, "Don seems to not like eggs. At all."

Vas glanced at me. "That's pretty thin."

"It was enough to get the warrants," I smiled.

"Shit."

I shrugged. "Like I said, once I get more records, I'll be able to piece it together further."

"May fortune favor the researcher," Vasily prayed.

"Amen to that." I tried not to grimace as Vasily slammed on the brakes to avoid hitting a car that swerved in front of us. I wondered if the bruising from the seatbelt would be visible in the morning.

"You know the rest. About ten days ago, our intrepid host was last seen taking off his headphones and leaving the studio after wrapping his Friday evening show, with a weekend of skiing in mind; just about a week later, I apparently found his body in a dumpster behind the Rancho Linda Mall."

"Isn't that the place with the coffee shop?" I asked.

"*The Alternative Way*? Yes. In fact, the dumpster in question was only a few spaces away from where we established Chase Cromwell had been killed."

"That's an odd coincidence," I replied.

"Maybe not. The mall is right off the 57, one of the busier freeways in that part of Orange County. Someone wanting to dispose a body could easily swing through Rancho Linda and be on their way in mere minutes."

"All right," I nodded. "But why dump a body there? Aren't there better places where it might not be found?"

"Of course there are," he agreed. "I feel like I've seen most of them in my brief time working for Rancho Linda, to be honest. However, I'm reasonably certain we were meant to find the body."

"Really? What makes you say that?"

Vasily looked at me for a moment. "There wasn't a drop of blood in the body when we found it," he said.

I frowned slightly. "That's not all that unusual," I reminded him. "If the body had been there for a while, and he'd sustained injuries—"

"There was no blood *in* the dumpster," Vasily interrupted.

Something in the way he'd emphasized *in* gave me pause. "Where, exactly, did you find blood?" I asked.

"In a series of glass containers," he replied quietly. "Placed neatly *in front* of the dumpster."

"You're shitting me," I said after I let what he'd said sink in.

"I'm not," Vasily said. "Forensics confirmed that Davies had been, literally, drained. The volume in the glass jars equaled what an average human being would have pumping through their veins; I was hesitant to accept it myself until the DNA test came back as a match."

"Well, the good news is the murderer isn't a vampire," I replied with a hint of gallows humor. "Not if all of the blood was accounted for."

"True," Vasily sighed. "Though it might have been far, far simpler had that been the case."

Again, something in my friend's voice gave me pause. "There's more, isn't there?"

"Yeah," he said, and for a moment I thought he looked nauseated — though it was hard to tell given the dim light. "His... genitals... had been... disconnected, shall we say, and relocated to his throat." He glanced at me again. "The Medical Examiner ruled that he died from asphyxia."

I felt my eyes widen, and unconsciously placed a hand over my crotch. "He was alive...?"

"Yes," he said simply.

"And... *then* his blood was drained?"

"We'll go over the forensics in more detail, but the scarring indicates it was postmortem."

I blinked. "Shit, Vasily. That's an insane escalation from the staged suicide I had on my hands."

"I agree," he replied. "I didn't understand it initially, but now that I know there were twins, and there was a chance that our suspect killed the wrong one first..."

"Double the anger," I nodded slowly. "God*damn*. And I thought the *suicide* was crazy brutal." I paused for a moment. "What the *hell* did you pull me into?"

"Damned if I know," he sighed again. "Definitely not just a missing persons case, though."

"I hear you there," I replied. "Shit," I said again.

"You didn't think I'd bring you in for something ordinary, did you?" Vas teased.

"A guy can hope. I think I might need one of those strong margaritas your boyfriend makes just to try and make sense of what you've told me."

The white of Vasily's teeth flashed momentarily as we went beneath a streetlight. "The pitcher has already been made," he laughed.

Thirteen

"How did you sleep?"

I smiled at the beautiful face looking up at me from my iPhone; we'd been together long enough for me to have correctly guessed that without me to distract her, Suzanne would sneak to her office well before dawn to try and get ahead of the never-ending paperwork that threatened to drown even the most successful medical practice. With the time difference between the coasts, it also meant that getting up early enough to join Vasily at the pool for his team's five-thirty practice would also conveniently allow me a few moments to catch the love of my life before she faced her first appointment of the day. As I started to answer her, though, I could see the lines of worry around her eyes and deduced it had been a long night watching over Deidre and her new baby. I smiled and tried to counter that slightly.

"Terrible," I answered.

Suzanne frowned with concern. "Really? What's wrong?"

"This couch pulls out to a nice queen, but it's way too big for one," I said with all of the seriousness I could muster. "I just couldn't get comfortable without having someone to cuddle up against."

The frown turned into a slight smile as Suzanne brushed back a lock of her gorgeous raven hair that had managed to slip free from the professional bun she sometimes wore. "I see."

Patting the mattress beside me, I smiled a bit wolfishly. "It also appears to be of sufficient size for all sorts of carousing. Something I'd be able to do if my significant other had managed to accompany me."

"Carousing, you say?" she smirked slightly. "Didn't you get enough of that *before* you left, Kitty?"

"One can *never* get enough carousing."

"I can recommend a few activities that would take the edge off," Suzanne smirked.

"Do any of them involve you getting on the next flight out here?" I asked hopefully.

She sighed. "Sadly, that part hasn't changed — but Deidre should be leaving my care later today. Her husband is scheduled to arrive this morning and will be taking her back to Atlanta this afternoon."

"I take it everything is going well, then?" I asked carefully.

"More or less," she nodded.

I looked at her carefully. "What is it?"

"If it were anyone else other than you, I'd clam up right now," Suzanne sighed before continuing. "I'm not an obstetrician by training, though I obviously know the basics around delivering a healthy child while keeping the mother safe. But unless I miss my mark, I think Deidre is suffering from some sort of postpartum depression. I've been having trouble getting her to take the baby; Yasmine and I have been feeding it, of course, but I worry a bit about what might happen after they leave our care."

"Can you reach out to her normal doctor?"

"That's the only reason I'm letting her out of my sight," she replied. "Deidre has a follow-up as soon as she gets to Atlanta."

"Good." Shifting slightly on the thin mattress, it wasn't hard for me to look concerned. "You've done what you can. And it wasn't my intent to make you feel bad for not being here."

"Sure it was," she chuckled.

I smiled slightly. "Okay, maybe a *tiny* bit," I replied sheepishly. "My life has changed incredibly since you came into it. I miss you when you're not around. Horribly."

"I feel the same way," she smiled. "And it's only two weeks. If you are lucky, maybe the case will break your way and you'll be able to spend the balance of your time living the surfer life you've always dreamed of pursuing."

"That's more Vasily's dream than mine," I laughed quietly. "Though given how tough these past few months have been, I won't deny a few days of sun and sand wouldn't be appreciated."

"Carve out some time," Suzanne replied. "It would do you good." She smiled a bit slyly. "Wear your briefs when you do and surprise me with one of those amazing California tans."

"I didn't think to pack any for my trip to Portland."

"Perfect," she replied impishly. "I'm sure Vasily can loan you a super tiny pair instead."

"And here I thought you loved me for my personality," I teased.

"That, too. But your physical assets are just as appealing."

"Madam," I deadpanned, "I am more than just muscle."

"I'll confirm that when I arrive," she chuckled. "Again."

"I look forward to the exam, Doctor."

"Indeed," she laughed. "Anyway, tell me what you found out about Vasily's side of the case. You didn't know much before you left."

"Yeah, Vasily apologized about that. Their computer nerds ran an update on the case system, which is why I had so little information to go on."

"I feel their pain," she sighed. "Computer trouble is the worst."

"Agreed."

I took a few moments to quickly sketch in what Vasily had told me on the drive down from LAX, and layered in more information from the quick perusal I'd made of the three-ring binder Vasily had left for me on the couch. Since becoming a couple, Suzanne had often lent an ear to my musings on one case or another, and in more than a few, had even acted as an unofficial scientific consultant. With our two immersive careers, it had been impossible from the start not to bring work home at the end of the day; it had helped me immensely to talk through thorny issues with her, and in turn, I often acted as her confidential sounding board when she faced a difficult decision regarding a patient's treatment plan.

As I wrapped up my quick precis, I saw Suzanne frown. "Don Davies?" she said slowly. "It's still hard for me to believe that someone wanted to kill him."

"You listened to him?" I asked, slightly shocked. "From the way both Vas and the General Manager described Davies to me, I wouldn't have expected him to be your cup of tea, aurally speaking."

"He wasn't," she replied. "I never went out of my way to listen; when I was just starting out in New Hampshire, though, there were only a few radio stations I could get while driving around the valley making house calls. Invariably, *The Don Davies Show* always seemed to be on when I was driving." Suzanne smiled. "Thank *God* my next car had satellite."

"I didn't know you made house calls."

"Best way to reach rural patients," she said. "And I was young enough — and foolish enough — to agree to do it."

"Happens to the best of us," I smiled.

Suzanne looked thoughtful. "Did you say *all* of the blood had been removed from the body."

"Save for a few milliliters," I nodded. "The coroner joked that even a *vampire* would have left more behind."

"Movies notwithstanding," she said. "Nothing replaced it?"

"Replaced—?" I asked. "What, the blood?"

"Yes," she nodded.

"No," I replied. "Why do you ask?"

"Well, when a body is embalmed, typically a fluid is pumped *in* so the blood can be pumped *out*," she explained. "This sounds more like something you'd see in a slaughterhouse."

A sudden image of a human body hung upside-down on a meat hook flashed in my brain, and I grimaced. "That's a picture I didn't need to visualize."

"Sorry. Did I ruin your appetite for breakfast?"

"No, but we *were* planning to eat before we headed to the morgue this morning. Now I'm not so sure."

"Sorry," she apologized again. Suzanne glanced over the camera. "Ah, there's Dolores. I'd better run."

I blew her a kiss. "Don't work too hard," I cautioned.

"I could say the same," she replied arching an eyebrow. "Call me later?"

"Absolutely."

The screen on my iPhone went dark, plunging the living room back into that weird twilight city dwellers always seemed to have. Dim illumination from the street outside Vasily's condo painted in the contours of the space, allowing me to carefully slip off the mattress and make my way over to the barstool holding the swim gear Vasily had given me the night before. I took a moment to try and release the kink in my neck sleeping on a strange bed had created before giving up and making my way down to the half-bathroom behind the kitchen; shucking out of my boxer briefs, I changed into attire far more appropriate to my best friend's sartorial leanings, put in my contacts and decided there was no point in trying to tame my hair prior to hitting the water.

I happened to be rolling my neck in another futile attempt to release the knot that had taken up residence there when I returned to the living room and found Vasily waiting for me, his swim backpack already slung over a shoulder. His shorter hairstyle continued to feel like a radical departure from the ponytail Vasily had sported for the nearly two decades I had known him; I had to admit, though, his new look suited him far better while emphasizing his roots in the California surfing culture.

Vas caught my neck roll and frowned. "I was worried the mattress might not fit your frame," he said softly. "It's hard to find a sleeper sofa that can accommodate folks like us."

I smiled. "Actually, it was far better than the crappy bed I had in the dorm," I replied. "There was no way for me to fully stretch out on it. I think Residence Life assumed all students topped out at five-eight."

"Maybe back in the 1940s," he laughed quietly. "Clearly, they'd never seen swimmers over six foot. Though if I remember correctly, the basketball players didn't seem to complain."

I rolled my eyes. "*They* were special," I sighed. "And had that new dorm the donor paid for."

"Oh, they were indeed. Too bad they played for shit. Ready?"

"Let me grab the backpack you loaned me," I said as I stepped around him and jammed my feet into my running sneakers. "Are we coming back here to change, or should I assume we're heading directly to the morgue?"

"Actually, I thought we could grab breakfast at the diner right after practice," he replied. "Then we can head directly to the morgue after we've eaten."

I unzipped the backpack and confirmed my more Business Casual khakis and a polo were present. "So shower at the pool then," I sighed.

"Sorry," he apologized. Like me, he wasn't a huge fan of the normally underwhelming locker facilities most pools seemed to offer; for someone over six feet tall like myself, there was always the additional indignity that the flow from the shower heads tended to hit us squarely in the chest. "You'll get to meet Rosie, though, not that it completely offsets."

"I'll take what I can get," I smiled as I zipped the backpack up and hooked it over my shoulder before following my friend out of the condo. The corridor was quiet, but given the hour, I found myself keeping my voice low as we approached the elevators. "So... the two of you were busy last night."

Vasily's head snapped toward me, and I could see a hint of embarrassment on his cheeks. "How much did you hear?"

"Enough to get a sense of what was going down," I replied with a sly smile.

"Interesting choice of words," Vas mumbled as the doors opened to the elevator, his face shading a bit darker as he spoke. "I'm sorry — I tried to fend off Alejandro, given we had a guest, but I've recently realized I can deny him nothing." He looked at me as the carriage descended toward the garage. "That, and I assumed the walls were thicker. I'll have a chat with Alex—"

"Dude, it's fine — I'm just giving you grief. It *does* make me think we may need to set some ground rules when Suzanne gets here," I added thoughtfully. "Like texting me before you come into the living room."

"I can do that," he chuckled as we exited the elevator lobby and walked over to his Camaro. "Especially since there's no place to tie a sock."

"Exactly," I laughed as I slid into the passenger seat.

There was still far more traffic than I would have expected at such an early hour, but based on how unaffected Vasily appeared to be, I presumed for *him* it was reasonably light. We chatted about mundane matters on the drive over to his home pool — the weather, my chances of getting any surfing in before Suzanne arrived; having spent a week out there a year earlier, I recognized the odd landmark or two as they passed outside my window. Much as before, I found the rich mélange of styles that represented Southern California architecture just as enthralling as ever. As we turned off the freeway at the exit for Rancho Linda, the vista became much more familiar, enough that I was struck by inspiration. While we waited for the red light at the base of the offramp, I turned to Vasily.

"Do we have time to swing past the scene?" I asked.

Vasily's eyes darted to the clock on the dashboard. "If you don't mind missing some of the pre-practice warmups," he replied. "What do you expect to see at this time of day?"

"I'm not sure," I said. "You know me. I always like to get a sense of the crime before I start."

He nodded as he turned the Camaro onto the major route through the city. "All right."

We passed the parking lot for the Rancho Linda High School and continued up the street; a weird sense of déjà vu washed over me as Vasily smoothly turned into the Rancho Linda Mall and then deftly made his way around the massive structure toward the rear. Slowing, he flicked on the high beams of the sports car before swinging around to focus them on an unremarkable giant blue dumpster. Several empty parking spots were next to it, and behind it, multiple doors labelled with specific suite numbers for the merchants on that end of the mall. Based on the curve of the building, and my rusty recollection of where we had determined Chase Cromwell had died, I nodded toward a set of parking spots on the far side of the dumpster that were full.

"Our favorite coffee shop is just over there?" I asked.

"Yes," Vasily replied. "Looks like they're already here making up a fresh batch of croissants."

"I didn't know they made everything on site."

"Some items," he continued as he put the Camaro into park. "Did you want to walk it?"

"Yeah," I replied as I opened my door and stepped out into the damp morning.

Evidence of the recent rain permeated everything, from the humid air to the moisture on the pavement sparkling in the brilliant head-lights. It occurred to me that I really missed the anorak I'd left back in Maine — and that the t-shirt and microfiber short combo I was wearing might not have been the best sartorial choice. Ignoring the goosebumps that rippled up each arm, I moved around the hood of the sportscar and took in the scene. My earlier impression was quickly con-firmed, for there wasn't anything unique about the commercial trash receptacle sitting in front of us; it bore the scratches and dents that any long serving — and maybe long suffering — denizen of waste removal would accumulate over a lifetime of use. Stepping toward it, the faint odor of decomposition wafted toward me, and became far stronger as I lifted the lid to peer into the dark depths. Given how full the interior appeared to be, I wondered what the pick-up schedule was for the mall and asked Vasily.

"Weekly on Thursdays," he promptly answered. "The mall uses a single waste hauler for the entire property."

"And the body was found on...?"

"Thursday morning," he replied, nodding. "The driver of the truck called it in when he saw it. In a sense, it confirms my suspicion that whoever dumped the body here intended for it to be found."

"This is fairly full," I observed. "Considering how early we are in the week, it makes me think the shops along this part of the mall are heavy users."

"I agree," Vasily nodded. "From the canvass we did, it's most likely a clerk from the athletic shoe store behind that door—" he pointed to one that had the logo of a chain I'd seen in Portland, "—was the last to put something in the dumpster Wednesday evening close to midnight."

"Clearly they didn't see a body at that point."

"They didn't, no. Or the glass jars full of blood."

"What time does the refuse truck roll through?"

"Between four and six in the morning. The 9-1-1 call actually confirms that, since it came it at four-forty."

"That gives us, what, about a five-hour window for the body to be dumped?"

"Yes."

I stepped back. "Was the truck one of those that lifted the bin up from the front?"

"Yeah," he replied.

I thought about that for a moment. "How did the driver see the body?"

"I'd have to look at the statement, but I'm pretty sure he saw the containers of blood first. They were lined up along the front of the bin and were hard to miss." Vas smiled slightly. "The driver was pissed that someone had left stuff out of the dumpster, forcing him to get out of the cab in order to clear the path."

That made me nod. "Without the jugs of blood, he'd have simply emptied the dumpster, right?"

"And driven away none the wiser," Vasily agreed. "This stop is about halfway along the truck's route, too, so I'd venture a guess the body wouldn't have been obvious once the contents were dumped at the landfill, either." He inclined his head toward the bin. "Instead, when he flipped up the lid to put the jugs into the trash, he saw the body." Vas smiled a bit. "Guy is a twenty-year veteran of the service; it wasn't his first time coming across a victim. He knew the drill and called 9-1-1 right away."

"I'll want to talk to him all the same."

"I figured. He's on the list."

I peered up at the building looming over us in the semi-darkness of the pre-dawn. "Still no exterior cameras, I suppose?"

"None that had a good angle on this location."

Glancing back toward the rear entrance for *The Alternative Way*, I frowned. "This is popular place for dead bodies," I sighed. "What are the odds that you'd have two in the space of a year?"

I caught the shadow of a smile in the semi-darkness before Vasily replied. "I know how you feel about coincidences, and normally I'm on board with you." He turned slightly and pointed in the general direction of the freeway we'd been on. "Except the 57 is less than a mile in that direction, and there's just the single major intersection before hitting the first parking lot entrance for the mall. Honestly, I'm a little surprised there haven't been *more* of these; like I said earlier, anyone wanting to dump a body could be in and out and on their way surprisingly quickly."

While I found myself nodding in agreement, I wasn't quite yet willing to ignore the nagging sensation that there was a significance to the spot. I scanned the pavement one last time and didn't see any wayward clues hiding within the poorly patched cracks or among the dead weeds sprouting up between the joints of the concrete walkway but didn't feel any less inclined to write off my theory. "Is there *any* connection between Don Davies and this location?" I asked as we headed back to the Camaro.

"Other than his body winding up here?" Vasily shook his head. "It was the first thing I thought of. I did a deep dive into the ownership of the property as well as the shops located in this end; nothing's turned up so far." His eyes narrowed. "Although now that I think about it, the Hilton you wanted me to check into is not more than a few blocks from here."

"That's one hell of a coincidence," I said after a moment.

"Does seem to stretch credulity a bit, doesn't it?" Vas nodded slowly. "I wouldn't have made the connection until now. I did manage to score us an appointment with the Conventions Manager for later today; maybe that will shed some light on things."

"I could use a little," I smiled wryly.

"What are you thinking?"

I sighed. "Too much and not enough, I'm afraid. All I've got is a bunch of hunches with absolutely nothing to back them up. Yet." I looked at him for a moment. "What's your read?"

Vasily frowned. "It's hard to ignore the serious serial killer vibes this is giving off," he replied after a moment. "A dead body in a dumpster means one thing; a dead body surrounded by modern canopic jars speaks to something else entirely."

I smiled slightly. "Canopic jars? Really?"

"I'm still finding ways to make that Ancient History general education class we had to take at UEM relevant to my career," he laughed. "I even put the term into my official case notes. Chief Gilbert will love it."

"That I doubt." I glanced back at the dumpster and wondered for a moment what sorts of secrets such an object might harbor; how many times in my career had I wished inanimate objects had been able to talk! "All right," I continued. "While this feels a bit to me like someone attempting to cover their true intentions, until we have more to go on, we'd better assume this *could* be something far worse; I'm guessing you've already done some prelim work to match this scene up with anything similar?"

"I have. Nothing at all in Orange County," he replied. "It's a quite difficult to dig through the data outside of my home turf; honestly, it's another reason I'm glad you're here in California. I need your charm to induce a bit of interagency cooperation."

"My *charm*?" I asked rather incredulously. "I'm a Mainer. By definition, I have no charm."

"Don't sell yourself short," he chuckled. "The Orange County M.E. is a good friend of mine and did some outreach on our behalf to her L.A. County counterpart, but that was the best she could do. Much like the traffic, everything is more difficult up there."

I frowned deeper. "That doesn't sound very appetizing."

"Where's your sense of adventure?"

"Back in Windeport," I groused.

"I highly doubt that. One other thing — while it was news that a body was discovered behind the mall, so far I've managed to keep the specifics out of the press. I'm not sure the driver knew who he'd discovered — at least, based on the interview I conducted with him, I got that impression — so the circle of who aware of the victim's identity is pretty small."

"That will buy us a few more days, maybe."

"Which is why I appreciate you getting here as quickly as you did." He nodded toward the dumpster. "What do *you* think?"

"I think," I replied slowly, "there appears to have been a great deal of premeditation involved. I know I haven't seen all of your records yet, but I already have the feeling every last aspect of this was planned out. Meticulously."

"Yeah," Vasily replied after a long moment. "I agree. And for some reason it terrifies me."

"As well it should," I said softly. "It's a particular level of malice we've rarely come up against." I looked out at the dark, wet street. "Add to that what I think was a mistake of a murder back in Windeport, and we really have quite the situation here, Vas."

"Can I cook, or can't I?" he asked, a wry smile on his face. "At least I'll get to hang with my best friend."

"That, too," I laughed.

Fourteen

"I t's nice to finally meet you in person, Sean."

"The same," I replied, smiling at the older woman sitting across from me in the strangely curved booth at the homage to mid-century modern diners Vasily seemed to favor. If my friend hadn't told me months earlier that the grandmotherly figure appraising me with her striking brown eyes was a bestselling author and a multimillionaire, I could have easily mistaken her as just one more of the senior citizen crowd we'd seen queued up outside, eager to cash in on the early bird breakfast special. "Vas has told me a lot about you, Rosie."

We'd been late enough to swim practice after our detour that my introduction to Dr. Rosalia Frankenhoffer, Ph.D., had taken place as we'd hauled ourselves onto the deck from what had been a surprisingly grueling workout. I suspected Vasily's coach had made some adjustments owing to the fact that a second Olympian had been present; while we'd been huffing and puffing like floundering fish, Rosie had cleverly used our weakened state against us to invite herself to breakfast. Not that I minded; I was actually rather eager to get to know the woman that seemed to have become a significant part of Vasily's new life in California.

Rosie narrowed her eyes in good humor. "All good, I trust," she replied, glancing meaningfully at my friend.

"Along with the bad," Vasily chuckled. "He wouldn't have it any other way."

She turned those deep brown eyes back to me. "I suppose not," she sighed. "Damn but the two of you make a fine, *fine* pair."

I felt my eyes widen and face heat slightly. "We're not a couple," I replied hastily, looking at Vasily. "He's already got someone. And so do I."

Rosie chuckled, a deep, rich sound that seemed vaguely familiar to me. "Oh Lord. No, not that — I meant *physically*."

"Physically?" I repeated blankly, looking back at Vasily again.

Vasily rolled his eyes. "*Seriously*, Rosie. We're not eye candy," he replied with a slight smile. I got the sense this was some sort of ongoing joke between them, confirmed when I saw the devilish glint to Rosie's eyes.

"The *hell* you aren't," she sighed appreciably.

"I'm feeling objectified," I said.

"As well you should," she chuckled again. "Give an old woman her dreams. How long are you staying?"

I set aside the menu I'd been scanning; as with my prior visit, nothing on it appeared to be remotely edible or in the right ZIP code to healthy. "A few weeks, at least," I replied. "Vas and I are working a case that spans the coasts, and then my girlfriend is joining us to attend the comic book convention."

Rosie's eyes widened. "No kidding? You don't strike me as the cosplaying type."

I smiled slightly. "You've not seen me in my Chat Noir costume."

Her eyes raked over me again, and I got the distinct impression she was imagining me in the form-fitting black outfit my cousin had crafted for me by hand a year earlier. I was starting to understand what it must feel like to be mentally undressed by another, and felt my face heat up again. "Not yet," Rosie replied. "Now I have something to look forward to."

My smile faltered. "Sorry?"

"I'll be there," she beamed. "I've got a new book coming out next spring chronicling the shift from hand-drawn to computer-generated animation, and that landed me a featured speaker spot on the second day." Rosie smiled at us. "It's kind of a dream come true, given how long I've been a fan of the art form."

Vasily looked stunned. "You're... you're *speaking*?"

"Yep. They also asked me to help judge the costume contest on Sunday — what fun that will be!" she said, clapping her hands merrily. "I can't believe they're actually *paying* me to geek out on stage. And you wouldn't *believe* the perks they offered! I've got a three-room penthouse suite at the Marriott, for Christ's sake. *Three rooms!* What am I going to do with that much space?"

"That's—" Vasily started, still clearly digesting the info.

"You'll stay with me, of course," Rosie interrupted suddenly.

"We—what?" I stammered.

"Be my guest," she continued. "You won't find a spot any more convenient."

I looked at Vasily. "His condo is just down the street," I started. "I wouldn't want to put you out."

Rosie arched an eyebrow at me. "You aren't *seriously* thinking of cramming four grown adults into that tiny excuse of a condo Vasily owns?"

"Hey!" Vas cried. "It's not *that* small!"

She turned her glare on him.

"It's just... cozy," he added defensively.

"And only has one full bath," she pointed out before turning to me. "Come stay with me. I won't take no for an answer."

I turned to Vas again, who shrugged in defeat. "Once she sets her mind to something, Sean, it's impossible to get her to change it."

"So I'm discovering," I sighed. "Then I guess we have no option but to accept."

"Wise," Rosie chuckled. "When does your girlfriend get in?"

"Two weeks from tomorrow," I answered. "Unless she can find someone to cover for her sooner. She's pretty much the only medical practice for miles back where I live."

"I've never been to that part of Maine," Rosie said. "I've done some events in Portland and Bangor, but never had time to get to the coast."

"If you ever find the time to return, we'd be happy to host you. Windeport isn't the best example of a seaside village, but it's about as close to what it's *truly* like to live along the ocean in Maine as any other place."

"I don't know," Rosie said, a slight trace of teasing to her voice, "from what Vasily tells me, it sounds uncomfortably similar to Cabot Cove."

I frowned. "I'm not sure where that is, honestly," I replied, before catching Vasily's smile. "What did I miss?"

"I'll tell you later," he chuckled.

The waitress happened by at that moment to refresh our coffee, and seemed a bit put out that we'd not yet made any decisions as to what we wanted for breakfast. As she sailed away after promising to return in a few minutes, I was reminded that Vasily had been in something of a relationship with a waiter I had met briefly during my prior visit. At the time, I had assumed it to be another in a long line of one-night stands Vasily was rightly notorious for engaging in, but had later learned that the waiter — his name was Drew, if I recalled correctly — had taken care of Vas in those first few days after the assault. Not one to want to dredge up bad memories, I decided to table asking my friend if he'd stayed in contact and instead focused on trying to locate something on the menu that wouldn't send me to the ER afterward.

Looking at Vasily over the top of my menu, I could see he'd already put his down. "What are you getting?"

"I always get the oatmeal and whatever fresh fruit is on offer," he shrugged. "I'm not one to mess with success. Or any of the deep-fried items on the menu"

"I don't see that on the menu," I said a fraction of a second before smiling. "Ah. That's on the *secret* menu, isn't it?"

"It is."

I nodded as the waitress re-appeared and took our orders; Rosie was the odd person out, getting a stack of pancakes with a side of bacon and scrambled eggs. Taking in her slight form once more, I wondered if she worked out beyond the impressive number of laps we'd all done in the pool that morning; I thought it more likely she might be planning on nibbling slightly and taking the rest home for later.

"So." Rosie lowered her voice conspiratorially after the waitress withdrew once more. "Tell me about this case you're working on."

I glanced uncomfortably at Vasily. "Uh... I don't usually discuss open investigations with outside folks."

"Rosie's something of an old hand at this now," Vasily explained. "Except for the time she *was* the case—"

"Not one of my finer moments," Rosie interjected.

"—she's actually helped me out a time or two during an investigation. She even let me use her mansion as a safe house for a bit once."

"Oh," I replied, not entirely convinced. But the look on Vasily's face said *trust me*; besides, hadn't I leaned on Suzanne more than a few times in a similar vein? It was clear my friend had faith in the multimillionaire sitting across from me. "Well, since I'm on Vasily's turf, I'll let him explain the particulars."

Without giving away too many specifics, Vasily quickly sketched in the general outlines of what we were working on, though he was incredibly careful when it came to the sorts of details we would normally hold back from the public. Still, it seemed to be enough to at least satisfy Rosie's curiosity at what her young friend was going to be working on for the next few days. By the time our food had been delivered from the kitchen and a third round of coffee had been poured, she had a thoughtful look on her face.

"Why fly Sean all the way out here for this?" she asked.

"It's a reasonable question," Vasily replied. "And one that I can't really answer for you quite yet. Suffice it to say he brings some experience to cases such as this one that I don't have."

"Indeed," she replied as she considered me once more. "It's because of who the victim is, I'll bet."

I tried not to let the shock show on my face, for that was *entirely* the reason I was sitting there. That Rosie had managed to zero in on it told me there was sharp intellect hiding behind those gentle eyes; it was no wonder Vasily thought so highly of her. I decided to try some subterfuge with a bit of humor to see if I could throw her off the scent. "Actually, I'm known far and wide for my dumpster diving skills. That, and Vasily is allergic to garbage slime."

"Truth," he nodded solemnly, immediately picking up on my thread.

Rosie looked between us. "You are both so full of *shit*," she sighed. "But I've seen enough of how Vasily works to understand that there are some things he can't divulge due to their sensitivity to the case." She smiled slightly. "I'll get it out of either of you eventually. Don't you worry."

"Thanks for understanding," I said.

She eyed me again. "Two glasses of wine, I'll bet."

"Sorry?"

"Before you spill your guts," she explained. "Maybe three." She looked to Vasily. "He sings like a canary after three."

"*That* is a spurious allegation," Vasily replied.

"Hardly," she chuckled before looking at her watch. "Damn. I've got to run," she said as she flagged down the waitress. "Can I get a to-go container for my breakfast?" she asked before pressing a credit card into the young woman's hands. "And put entire table on this, please?"

I tried not to smile at how I'd correctly deduced why she'd ordered so much. "You don't have to pay for us," I objected, confusing the waitress for a moment.

"Nonsense," she replied as she waved the waitress away. "I invited myself along this morning, it's only fair that I should pick up the tab."

"That's not necessary," I replied.

"Of course it is," she chuckled. "And that's that."

I looked to Vasily again. "Don't fight it," he smiled. "Believe me, it's not worth it."

"Listen to your friend," Rosie added as she accepted the bill from the waitress, signed the paper then started to put the receipt and card back into her rather sizable handbag. "I trust you'll be up tonight per usual?" she asked before sliding out of the booth.

Vasily shot a glance at me, and for a moment I saw a slight smirk, too. "Yes," he replied. "*We* will."

"We?" I repeated.

"Good. And don't forget."

"How could I?" Vasily smiled. "See you this evening."

Rosie leaned down and gave him a quick hug. "Good. Until then. Sean," she nodded before diving into the crowded diner in search of an exit.

As I watched Rosie work her way through the serpentine walkway, I found it hard to believe she was even remotely connected to the senior citizen set; I was certain her fluid movements spoke to how much time she continued to spend in the pool. I wondered briefly if I'd remain as limber when I reached that milestone age myself, then turned to Vasily. "Tonight? What was that all about?"

Vasily chuckled. "Now you have a sense of what I put up with," he sighed. "But Rosie is pretty special, and we've been through quite a bit together in the short time we've known each other. In some ways, I feel like she's adopted me."

"That much was easy to see," I nodded. "And this evening?" I pressed.

"I have dinner with her once or twice a week," he replied. "Part of my attempt to keep tabs on her health. We watch whatever sport is in season on her tiny tube television or play old fashioned board games, depending on what sort of mood we're in. You'll love it."

Rolling my eyes, I sighed. "I'm not sure we'll have the time."

"Think of it as an excuse to take a break," he countered. "Besides, it's one of the few nights Alex doesn't have practice and can hang with us. It'll be fun. Trust me."

I frowned. "She has a tube television?"

"And no cable or internet access," he nodded. "Honestly, I keep going mostly for the conversation, and the indoor pool."

I blinked. "I forgot about that — she's the one with the secret underwater vault, isn't she?"

"One and the same," he said. "Most visits, we wind up in the solarium anyway since Rosie gets chilled, though I think it's just an excuse to ogle me and my boyfriend." He paused before adding with a sly smile: "Yeah, with you in the mix... better keep those Speedos I loaned you a bit longer."

"What I do for my friends," I sighed.

I drained the last of my coffee and slid the empty bowl that had contained reasonably good oatmeal toward the pile of dishes we had on the table, then followed Vasily back out of the diner. The parking lot had been nearly full when we'd arrived, and the situation hadn't changed in the least as we made our way over to the Camaro. "Popular spot," I remarked as I slid into the passenger seat.

"Especially for breakfast," Vasily nodded. "Half of the swim team comes here directly after practice, and as close as it is to the high school, most of the faculty make an appearance, too."

"Well, it can't be for the menu."

"Not everyone treats their body like a temple," he reminded me.

"Good point."

Carefully backing out of his spot, Vasily made his way out to the street and smoothly accelerated into the flow of traffic. I wasn't surprised to see the thoroughfare clogged in both directions as far as the eye could see; we'd left the diner close to seven-thirty, putting us into prime rush hour pandemonium. Once more, Vasily weaved in and out of the lanes of vehicles with a deftness that spoke to his longevity in dealing with such trifles; on my previous trip to California, I'd been quickly disabused of the notion that driving in Boston would have been a suitable training ground. Trying not to look too obvious about gripping the arm of my door, I found myself silently grateful that my friend had taken the wheel as I tried to will my blood pressure down into a more reasonable range.

Dawn — such as it was — revealed another cloudy day, one that looked to be as dreary as its predecessor. Intermittent splotches of raindrops pelted the windshield, not quite enough to force Vasily to switch on the wipers; the Camaro's headlights reflected off the glisten-ing pavement, reinforcing the general feeling of gloom I'd had since arriving. Sometimes, a case will do that to me — connect on a visceral, deeply primal emotional level that leaves an undercurrent of unease running through everything. I'd seen a lot in my time as an investigator, but nothing could compare with what had been done to Don Davies. Our upcoming meeting with the Medical Examiner was guaranteed to exacerbate that sense of unease, and likely with it, further inflame the righteous anger at whomever was responsible that had begun to smolder just after finding Frank in Windeport.

Lost in my thoughts, I didn't realize we'd gotten onto the freeway until I heard Vasily curse under his breath; looking up, I quickly saw why, for all six lanes in front of us had become a massive parking lot. Red taillights stretched for at least a mile or more until they were lost at a curve in the highway, though it seemed a good bet that it likely continued well beyond. My eyes went to the potential salvation of an offramp not far ahead, though given the fact we were stopped completely, it might as well have been lightyears out of reach.

"What time was our appointment?" I asked, glancing at the clock on the dashboard.

"Eight," Vasily sighed as he drummed his fingers against the steering wheel. "I should have been watching the Caltrans website. This looks buggered up pretty badly."

"I don't suppose you have lights and a siren in this thing?" I asked hopefully, eyes going to the emergency lane that seemed to still be clear.

"No, but if I did, you know as well as I do it would be against department policy to use them in this situation. Unless I was responding to whatever accident did this."

"I figured," I smiled slightly. "A guy can hope."

We crawled forward a few feet, enough that Vas was able to start to ease himself into the lane that would align the Camaro for the offramp I'd spied. "If I can make that exit, I can cut across to the 91. It'll add a few minutes to the drive, but we might still make it on time." He scanned his mirrors. "How am I on that side?"

I turned to look into the lane he was attempting to squeeze into and was immediately greeted with an obscene gesture from the driver we were apparently cutting off. "Well, you're not making any friends, that's for sure."

Vas smiled. "Welcome to the dog-eat-dog world of the Southern California commute."

"And you do this *every* day?"

"Pretty much, though I generally miss the morning rush hour. One of the benefits of getting to the pool at such an ungodly hour."

"How are you even *sane*?" I asked incredulously.

"Who says I am?" he replied.

"Good point," I laughed.

Traffic broke up just a bit more, allowing him to completely move into the proper lane; the flow picked up for those of us getting off the freeway, and a few moments later, Vasily was cruising along a tree-lined three lane city street. We appeared to be in a more industrial portion of the county, passing warehouse-like structures intermixed with three- or four-story commercial office buildings. One glass-and-concrete structure sported a set of massive satellite dishes, making me think it was a likely a local television or radio station; that made me turn to Vasily.

"Gennifer told me Don Davies did a few months of his show out here when she lost her husband about a decade ago," I said. "She mentioned something about taking over a conference room at a hotel so he could do it."

"I don't doubt it," Vasily replied. "That sort of tech existed *long* before the internet. What brought that up?"

"That building we just passed. It reminded me Davies had something of a home recording studio at his place in Southern Maine. It was pretty well tricked out, too; now that I think about it, probably not just for the random snow day when he didn't want to drive into Portland."

"Did he do any interviews on his show?"

"I've no idea," I admitted. "I never listened."

"Well, if he *did*, it's possible he may have recorded them outside of his normal broadcast. You know, catching the interview subject when it was convenient for them."

I nodded. "Definitely need another conversation with the General Manager at WWWD."

Vasily sighed as he slowed down once more. "All this rain really makes it a shame we're going to Santa Ana. Had the weather been better, I'd have recommended hitting the beach at lunch time."

I glanced at him. "I can't believe a bit of inclement weather would dissuade you so easily. You're getting soft in your old age."

"Do you hear that?" he asked suddenly.

"No," I replied.

"That's the sound of the trap I laid for you snapping shut. I happened to have stashed two wetsuits and matching knee boards in the trunk." Vasily looked at me devilishly. "If you can handle the cold, old man."

"You're on — though I'm not sure I see how that would enhance our investigation," I observed dryly.

"You'd be surprised."

Fifteen

The Orange County Sheriff's Office of the Coroner was tucked into a modern looking building that appeared to house a number of other departments and had the feel of something built in stages lockstep with the growth in population. Whoever the succession of architects had been, they had managed to blend each addition into the one prior, making the structure a thematically complete whole. My Brutalist concrete abomination back in Windeport couldn't hold a candle to what I was seeing.

Vasily managed to make good time, pulling into one of the massive parking lots ringing the building with more than five minutes to spare. After locking up the Camaro, the two of us hustled through the drizzle that had developed toward the side door he'd identified for me as the entrance for Law Enforcement; the gust of refrigerated air, far cooler than necessary, did more than anything to emphasize we had reached the morgue. The dampness from the drizzle combined with the near-frigid temperature of the space, immediately chilling me to the bone. I was reasonably sure my teeth were chattering while Vasily spoke briefly with the young man behind the glass windows at reception.

Turning back toward me, I saw him smile. "Chuck says Peggy is in her usual haunt of Exam Four. I hate to break it to you, but it's only going to get colder from this point forward."

"I don't know why it's affecting me so," I said as I followed him toward the locker room. "I live in Maine for crying out loud. But, *damn!* What I wouldn't give for a few minutes in a hot tub right now."

"There's one at the condo," Vasily replied. "Though if you can hold out long enough, the solarium at Rosie's will make you all nice and toasty."

"I'll do my best," I said, unable to keep myself from shivering.

I took a set of the brilliant blue scrubs from the shelf, picked an open locker, and quickly changed out of my quasi-uniform of polo and khakis and into the provided scrubs. I couldn't help the odd feeling of déjà vu, considering it hadn't been all that long ago I'd done the exact same thing in order to attend the postmortem for Frank Davies; even the industrial surroundings of the morgue in California felt nearly identical to the one in Augusta. It was yet another subtle reminder the two cases were, in fact, just one. Grabbing gloves, a face mask and a hair cap, I trailed my friend out the rear exit of the locker room and stayed close as he navigated the rabbit warren that was the inner sanctum for his Coroner.

Pushing through the doors of Exam Four, we found Dr. Pembrooke hovering over an unopened body bag that had been placed atop the metal examination table. If it was possible, the temperature in the small room felt like it was twenty degrees colder than the locker room had been, making me wish the scrubs were a bit thicker. Or made from some sort of thermal material.

She turned at our entrance. "Gentlemen, welcome," she said cheerily. "Has it started to rain yet?"

"Not quite," Vasily replied. "Peggy, this is my friend Sean Colbeth. He's working the East Coast angle on this case."

"How do you do?" she asked as she shook my hand. "You're the Olympian from Maine?"

"Yes," I replied. "Thanks for taking the time to do this today."

"Of course." Her eyes flicked to Vasily. "This is quite the case he's caught, but then again, I've found in the short time I've known him, Deputy Chief Korsokovach rarely brings me anything ordinary."

"I like to keep it interesting," he replied.

"If that's what you want to call it," she chuckled before turning her eyes back to me. "I've already spoken to Dr. Hamilton; now that we know these two cases are linked, we've been comparing notes."

"Anything interesting crop up?"

"Maybe," she smiled. "But let's not get ahead ourselves, shall we."

Vasily half covered his mouth as he leaned into me and stage whispered: "Peg has a flair for the dramatic."

"I *heard* that, Deputy Chief."

"Am I wrong?" he chuckled.

Dr. Pembrooke rolled her eyes. "See what I have to deal with?"

"That's why I sent him out here," I deadpanned.

Vasily pantomimed as though I had stabbed him in the heart. "*Et tu*, Sean?"

Rolling her eyes more dramatically, Dr. Pembrooke then shook her head. "You two must have been a nightmare for Lou at her post-mortems."

"We were the perfect gentlemen," Vasily replied defensively.

"Somehow, I doubt that."

Stepping over to the table, she deftly unzipped the bag and carefully pulled it open, then down around the pale body that was all that was left of Don Davies. I was immediately struck by the colorless nature of the cadaver; normally, when a person dies, bodily fluids tended to pool at the lowest point of rest, causing discoloration where they have gathered. Often, it allowed us to confirm the position the body had been in at the time of death — or whether it had been moved. Getting a bit closer myself, I turned slightly to take in the entire tableau; it was hard to shake the feeling I'd *already* seen this body, which in some ways, I had. Much like his twin, Frank, Don Davies had the shape of a man well past middle age, with a roll of fat around the midsection and slight hint of a double chin. Post-mortem stubble had given his cheeks a silvery sheen, the color a match to the thinning hair that had the look of being professionally styled. The lips were the most striking, perhaps, given their bloodless appearance; based on the line of his jaw, I assumed his dental work was normal, but would confirm that with the x-rays Dr. Pembrooke had already likely taken.

Wisps of silvery chest hair were of a darker shade, matching the tufts around what had once been his pubic region. It was quite difficult to take in what had been done to the radio host and not feel some sort of sympathetic pain; still, I forced myself to review the damage, and though it wasn't my specialty, it appeared to my eye that what had been removed had been done with a surgical precision. Looking up, I could see the medical examiner had returned to the computer station that stood just next to the table and had been patiently waiting for me. Catching my eye, she nodded.

"Vasily has already heard all of this, but I promised him I'd go through it again for you."

"I appreciate that."

Pembrooke's eyes began to read her notes from the small screen on the workstation. "Victim was about median for height — converting from metrics, about five-eight or so. As you can tell, he was more than a little overweight; lab results showed that he was a type-two diabetic. Needle marks in all of the usual places make me suspect he was on some sort of insulin regimen, but you'd need to track down his physician to confirm that."

"All right," I said. "Oddly, I didn't find any insulin in either of his homes back in Maine. Would that be normal?"

"Depends on how long he was planning on traveling," Peg replied. "And the dosage he was taking. Given the expense of insulin, my guess would be your victim brought the supplies with him to California, with an eye toward refilling them when he returned home."

"We might find it here, then," Vasily mused. "Assuming we ever discover where he was staying."

"I have a thought about that," I said.

"Why am I not surprised?"

"Aside from the wounds," Dr. Pembrooke continued, "exterior of the body shows significant ligature marks around the wrists and ankles. There was some residual fiber trace in the wounds that came back to a commercially available clothesline, found in just about any hardware or warehouse store."

Vasily shifted on his feet, causing me to turn toward him. "I have some experience with that sort of rope," he said softly. "Insanely cheap and very hard to trace," he added; what I could see of his face had gone a bit ashen, which concerned me greatly. It was a look he generally wore after suffering one of his horrific nightmares spawned from the assault he'd endured, and he confirmed my suspicion a moment later. "It's similar to what Mark used. Intentionally chosen, I think, to make it nearly impossible to connect to our murderer."

"Lovely," I replied, turning back toward Peggy. I wondered if this part of the case was a little too close to home for my friend, and filed it away to ask later. "It's a shift, though. Our killer used duct tape back in Maine; I wonder why the change?"

"Might have been easily available," Vasily offered.

"I suspect it was more practical," Peg interjected. "Lou explained to me how you found the body in Windeport; the purpose of those restraints was to keep the victim from stopping first the slashing of the wrists, and then later, stemming the flow of blood; I think this is similar."

"Was Don bound differently?"

"That gets me to the next part," she nodded. "As you probably have noted from the lack of coloration to the body, all but a half-liter of blood had been drained from the body. My best guess is from these three points," she added, moving back to the body and pointing to gashes at the neck and both arms with gloved finger.

"Was it replaced with anything?" I asked. "My significant other wondered if that was how the body had been drained."

"Like embalming fluid? No," she replied. "These wounds were created with a sharp edge, the only consideration being making an opening sufficient enough to insert a small tube to drain the body." She pointed to the legs, where there were clear ligature marks around the ankles. "My best professional guess is that this poor guy was strung up and slaughtered like cattle in a meat packing plant; gravity is the most effective method for getting it done."

"Tube?" I asked. "What kind of tube?"

"Something flexible, I would think," Peggy replied. "We pulled a little residue from the wound at the neck, flecks of something made primarily of plastic. There wasn't enough to match up to anything in the database, and to be honest, it might not have been a tube. It could have been a shell from a ballpoint pen."

"That's a pretty wide field."

"I'm thinking we might want to focus on something surgical," Vasily mused.

"That assumes whoever did this had access to medical supplies," I pointed out.

"It could be more mundane than that, actually. Even something from the local hardware store's irrigation section might suffice," Peggy noted.

"So much for narrowing down the options," I sighed, then pointed to the wounds. "On the other hand, these *do* look somewhat professional; we found something similar on my victim."

Pembrooke nodded. "You have a good eye, Sean. You're right, the edges are smooth and regular; whoever did this was experienced in one of several areas, the most obvious being surgery. But they could just as easily have been an expert wood carver or a chef, even. Pretty much any occupation that requires a steady hand."

"Again, not really narrowing things down for us, Peg," Vasily sighed.

"Maybe she has," I replied. "What if the tubing in question isn't from either a medical supplies or hardware store? What if it's from food preparation? Like a straw, or one of those things to inject flavoring into a turkey?"

"The rope speaks to the hardware store angle," Vasily replied skeptically; I could see his frown based on how his eyebrows had wrinkled. "I'm not enough of a cook to know what sort of items a chef might have in their kitchen that would be useful for murder — save for the obvious, like a knife."

Feeling like a connection was tingling on the edge of my senses, I nodded slightly. "You know more than you think. But I agree, we need to sketch in more about our killer before making guesses about how they purchased their supplies."

"This might help even more," Peggy said. Reaching to a wrist, she pointed to one of the gashes with a gloved finger. "The angle of these cuts indicate someone who was left-handed."

"Well, *shit*," I breathed.

"What?" Vasily asked. "Clearly you've had an epiphany."

"That's how the killer realized he'd murdered the *wrong* Davies; he must have figured out Frank had everything on the wrong side — wrong wrist, wrong side table. It would have been wrong for *him*, too."

"Oops," Peg said. "Sounds like someone messed up."

"It's my fervent hope he did. We could use a break."

"I might have one more for you," Peggy laughed. "Lou asked me if there were any identifying marks on my victim; since these two were identical twins, it would be exceedingly unusual for them to have any sort of skin deformities that the other didn't already exhibit."

"Makes sense," I said. "So there wouldn't be an unusual mole or birthmark to help shed some light on whether we have Don or Frank here."

"Not normally." Snatching a small flashlight from the equipment tray, Dr. Pembrooke leaned down and carefully rolled Davies onto his side, then snapped on the light to illuminate a small scar along the lower part of the spine. "I found this on my first examination and was able to confirm it with x-rays. The vertebrae in this portion of his back were fused, likely in an effort to relieve chronic back problems." She looked up at me. "Your victim in Maine doesn't have anything like it. If you can track down medical records, you should be able to use those plus the additional lab work to conclusively identify your victim."

"That is *extremely* helpful," I said thankfully.

"All of the test results are done and are slowly being added to the case file; I'm sure Vasily told you about our I.T. problems."

"He did."

"I'm halfway back to using typewriters and carbon paper at this point," Peg continued. "Not that I've ever done that, but the transition to a computerized case system is what led my predecessor to retire."

"Not a fan of change, I take it?"

"Not in the least. I hear he's enjoying the good life from his porch on a beach in Maui."

"There could be worse places to wind up," Vasily chuckled.

"We'll keep Mr. Davies here on ice for a few more days. Now that we know who the next of kin is, we'll be under the gun to get the body over to a mortuary."

"I imagine you've found everything you are going to find," I replied. "Thanks for giving me the overview."

"Of course. Enjoy your time here in California."

"Only if it warms up," I said as we headed for the door.

I'd never been so grateful for a hot shower in my life; despite how tepid the water cascading from what passed for a shower in the morgue locker room was, it went a long way toward thawing me out. Between the cold drizzle and the seemingly subzero temperature of the exam room, I wouldn't have been surprised to see myself blue around the edges when I glanced in the mirror. The less-than-hot water wasn't an inducement for luxuriating in the experience, however, so I quickly tried to scrub away the stench from the morgue before toweling off and changing back into my street clothes.

Vasily had beaten me out by a few minutes and was in front of the mirror, running his hands through his blond hair in an attempt to get it to look mussed up once more. Sighing deeply, he ran one final hand through it before giving up. "I didn't think to bring my gel," he explained at my arched eyebrow inquiry. "Not that it matters; if it continues to rain as forecast for the rest of the day, it'll just become one sticky mess."

"Or if you make good on your threat to take me surfing at noontime," I reminded him.

"That, too." Glancing at his watch, he nodded to the door. "Ready?"

"Sure," I replied. "Where to next?"

"We have time to satiate your caffeine addiction before the appointment I set up at the Hilton," he replied as we moved out into the corridor. Waving to the handsome guy behind the glass at reception, Vas continued. "I did some initial digging before you came out about that convention you think Don Davies attended; it must be pretty boutique, for the internet completely failed me. Even a secondary search at the library came up with nothing."

"Nothing? Like it doesn't exist?"

"I wouldn't go *that* far," Vasily said as we exited the morgue; the drizzle had become a steady downpour, making me realize that toweling off after my shower had been completely unnecessary. "I have a contact who works for the Orange County Visitor Bureau, and she reminded me yesterday that this part of Southern California hosts a gazillion events every year, from small corporate gatherings to huge multi-day conventions like the comic book one coming up in a few weeks. Not all of them are widely recognizable, or notable, for that matter; while she didn't have the National Radio Personality Convention in her database, that doesn't mean it wasn't here — or that it might not have been the annual event in Don Davies' industry WWWD inferred it to be."

I tried to shake off the worst of the rain before sliding into the Camaro. "Maybe our soon-to-be new friend at the Hilton can tell us more; the notepad certainly makes it seem like it might have taken place there at least once."

"Don't hold your breath," Vasily sighed as he started up his car and smoothly backed out of the parking spot. "There's been some turnover, and the new guy in charge has only been there since December. He *thought* he had heard of the event I was asking about, but promised to go through the files before we interviewed him."

"Let's hope his predecessor kept good records," I frowned. "Damn. I just *feel* a thread winding around that location and connecting everything together." I looked out the window. "I can't explain *why* but it feels central to this whole mess."

"You're gut rarely leads us astray," Vasily observed. "Maybe we'll get some answers."

"But not before we get some coffee," I replied.

Vasily chuckled as he changed lanes to align the Camaro with the first Starbucks that came into sight. "That is one bad habit I did pick up from you. Bad enough that I have my own personal Keurig now."

"I'm so proud of you," I laughed.

Parking the Camaro, we dashed through the unbelievably heavy rain and into the lobby for the coffee shop, then patiently worked out way through the queue to place our order; given how many people were ahead of us, it was easy to see we weren't the only people looking for a way to warm up — and that it would be a few minutes before our concoctions came out. Normally I ordered straight up drip coffee, but for some reason, the larger-than-life-size poster hawking a new crème brûlée flavored expresso struck a chord; deciding to be comfortable, Vas and I picked out two lounge seats toward the rear that faced the service window and settled in for the wait.

"Did you catch Suzanne this morning?" Vas asked.

"Yeah," I nodded. "She looked pretty tired."

"Without you there?" he teased. "Sounds like she's got a man on the side."

"Far from it," I snapped, finding myself suddenly irritated at his attempted joke; immediately, I knew why, but not before I saw the look on Vasily's face.

"Sorry," he replied softly. "I didn't think it would strike such a nerve."

I smiled weakly and waved him off. "Nothing like that," I explained. "Though I do worry constantly about forgetting to remind Suzanne how important she is to me. I made that mistake once before and paid for it dearly; now that I've got a true soulmate in my life, I don't want to ever lose her."

Vasily reached for my hand and squeezed it. "You won't," he said with a certainty I desperately needed for some reason. "I've seen how the two of you click together; you're literally made for each other, Sean. I recognize it because that's *exactly* how I feel about Alex." He waited for a beat before adding, softly: "And I worry each and every day about screwing up my best chance at love. I think, honestly, it's the price we pay when we finally hit pay dirt."

I nodded slowly. "You might be right." I watched as the barista finished their work at the complex-looking machine, glanced at the writing on the side of the cup and then called out a name before turning back to the station to start the process all over again. "Did I mention I ran into Deidre?"

"No *shit*," Vasily breathed. "In Windeport?"

"Yeah. I think that's why I'm a little tense about my love life at the moment."

"No *shit*," Vasily repeated. "I totally get it. I mean, truly. You've got to be feeling the same way I did when you popped into my life last year here in Rancho Linda."

"Over it, but somehow, not," I nodded slowly. "Yeah." I blew out a breath. "And... she was pregnant. Very, *very*, pregnant. So much so that Suzanne had to deliver the kidlet early."

"You have *got* to be kidding me," Vasily said. "That's like a plot ripped straight from the telenovela Alex watches. 'Current girlfriend delivers boyfriend's ex-girlfriend's baby.' Shit."

"It gets better," I continued. "When I first ran into her, she used her pregnancy to remind me *why* she left."

Vasily looked at me for a long moment. "I did try to warn you about that," he said softly. "That day we drove up to the Colonial together."

"I remember," I nodded, recalling the initial stages of our investigation into the death of Ingmar Pelletier. "And I heard you, too. The thing is, De and I had something of a disconnect on that point; my concerns all stemmed from whether I'd be a good father, not that I *never* wanted kids."

"That's definitely not how she saw it," Vasily replied.

"I know." I smiled slightly. "I actually ran into her twice; the second time was in her old IGA, of all places. And I was wearing my Chat Noir costume, too."

"You — wait, *what*? Are there photos?"

"Stop with the leer; I had them all destroyed," I chuckled. "Suze and I were babysitting Charlie's twins and I was dressing for the evening, essentially; a last-minute change of dinner plans tossed me into Deidre's path, and, apparently, created something of an epiphany for her."

Vasily started to slowly nod. "The costume."

"Exactly. I won't say we patched up everything completely — I *still* think that new husband of hers is an asshole — but we're in a much better spot."

"Enough you've added her to your Christmas Card list?"

"I wouldn't go *that* far," I replied quickly. "Baby steps."

"Whatever you need to tell yourself," he chuckled. "Come on, looks like our coffee is ready."

Sixteen

Not knowing Rancho Linda half as well as Vasily, I was still pretty sure his definition of *down the block* and mine were a tad different, for while we did indeed passed his office on the way to the Hilton Orange County, by my reckoning, the sprawling resort nestled just at the base of one of the hills surrounding the city felt to be more than a few miles distant from the public safety building. The continuing rain and associated overcast sky diminished somewhat the vacation vibe the tall palm trees lining the long drive to the main entrance were attempting to generate; even with the landscape lighting doing its level best to alleviate the gloom of the storm, the pervasive darkness felt overwhelming in a way that I'd never experienced in Maine. Pulling around the cars huddled beneath the canopy directly outside the lobby, Vasily continued toward a multistory garage that appeared to have green vines clawing their way toward the uppermost levels, another attempt to make the facility seem like it was some sort of tropical getaway, not just another four-star hotel among many in that part of California.

Surprisingly, the first floor of the garage was full; Vasily managed to locate a spot better suited for a small golf cart than his Camaro on the second level, and it appeared his year-plus of practice of parking at his condo had paid off, allowing him to figure out how best to squeeze his vehicle between the thin lines painted on the concrete. Getting out of the Camaro, I was assaulted by the overwhelming scent of dampened asphalt, with a liberal dose of soggy vegetation thrown in for good measure. Wishing once more I'd thought to bring my winter jacket that day, I tried to ignore the chilly air as we made our way to the stairs; somewhat fortunately, there was a covered walkway between the garage and the hotel proper, dumping out into a wide reception space carpeted in soft pastel colors, with walls painted in a complimentary palette. Wall sconces every few feet were at a low level, denoting double doors that presumably led into ballrooms of various sizes; a small alcove to one side appeared to be there to serve as some sort of conference check-in area, replete with a long marble counter and multiple widescreen monitors mounted on the wall behind, likely for displaying conference announcements or changes to the schedule. As empty as the space was that day, though, the deep pile of the carpet muted any sounds, giving it a far more intimate feel that it truly deserved.

Deciphering the understated directional signage, Vasily discovered the whereabouts of the Convention and Catering office, then led me across the space to a cross hall that appeared to bisect two massive ballrooms. Passing a few more sets of double doors had me revising upwards just how many people that particular convention center was able to host comfortably; by the time we reached a clear office door bearing the logo for the resort, I found I had little trouble visualizing multiple different events taking place simultaneously without either having to interact with the other. Pausing at the door, I turned and looked back down the long, empty cross hall and wondered why the space was empty during what seemed to be prime convention season.

I heard the door open behind me and turned to follow Vasily into the office. While I'd not had much occasion to book a conference in the course of my professional career, I had to admit, the area we'd entered fit my idea of what such an office might look like. Essentially a small rectangular reception area, comfortable couches upholstered with fabric that came from the same color palette as the rest of the center had been set along either wall, with potted palms serving as end tables; an oblong coffee table sat in front of each, tastefully displaying brochures which I assumed delineated the various offerings the hotel could provide. Framed photos that I assumed were from scenic landmarks around Orange County had been artfully placed on several walls, save for the one opposite the entrance; that held two additional doors seemingly protected by a small reception desk, which was currently unoccupied. Judging from the cup of coffee sitting beside a phone headset, it seemed likely whoever was staffing the desk had just stepped away; as if to confirm that thought, the sizable phone on the desk started to ring, adding one additional blinking light to the multiple already on display across the phone's surface.

A muted curse from within one of the offices was quickly followed by the appearance of harried looking guy, dressed in a modest grey suit a size too large for his slight frame, hinting that it might have been purchased at a national discount menswear retailer that only provided limited tailoring services. The pocket square would ordinarily have been a nice touch but did little more than draw attention to the poor cut of the suit that didn't compliment the wearer at all. Muttering as he rounded the corner, he came up short after catching sight of the two of us standing in the small aisle that had been created between the couches. Multiple emotions washed across his face, though his glance between us and the flashing bank of lights on the phone underscored what sort of dilemma he was sorting through.

Smiling, I nodded at the phone. "Go ahead. We can wait."

Shaking his head in relief, our presumed host reached down and snagged the headset, careful to place it such that he didn't mess up his carefully done conservative part. Tapping a button, he picked up the call. "That weekend is still open," he said, his voice the picture of calm that didn't match what we were seeing. "I would need a deposit—yes, that includes the cabanas..."

I looked to Vasily and by unspoken agreement we settled on the couch to the left to wait. Fortunately, my coffee was still fairly hot — and far tastier than I'd expected. I realized when more than half of it had disappeared the various concoctions created by Starbucks were designed to go down very easily, and leave behind the desire to try another. As soon as possible. Uncomfortably aware of just how many calories I'd managed to sneak in, I'd just committed myself to sticking with old-fashioned drip from that point forward when I heard our host finish up his last call.

"I am *so* sorry," he said as we stood once more. "I'm Xander Vallejo; you must be Deputy Chief Korsokovach?"

"Actually, I'm Chief Sean Colbeth," I replied before nodding at Vasily. "That's Deputy Chief Korsokovach of Rancho Linda."

"Whoops," Vallejo chuckled. "Well, in fairness, I had a fifty-fifty chance."

"That you did," Vasily said as he shook. "Sean is working this case with me."

Xander eyed me. "Seems odd your superior would be with you," he said.

"We're from different departments," I replied hastily. "I'm actually from the Windeport, Maine, Police Department. This case seems to span a few jurisdictions, so we teamed up."

"Maine? Oh, okay," he nodded, though I wasn't entirely sure he'd caught on yet. Looking at Vasily, he continued. "On the phone, you mentioned wanting to know about any bookings for the National Radio Personality Convention."

"That's right," Vasily said. "We think our victim might have attended it when the convention took place here at the Hilton."

Xander nodded thoughtfully before smiling slightly. "I apologize for not being a ton of help over the phone," he started. "While I'm pretty new to *this* position, I've actually worked for the hotel since I was in high school, long enough to gain a sense of the ebb and flow of conventions we hosted. Several were considered 'all hands on deck' situations when they came to town, though it wasn't until I looked up your specific convention in our CRM that I realized that was always the one where we scored the most overtime."

"CRM?" I asked.

"Customer relationship manager," Xander promptly answered. "It's a software package that allows us to track who we're working with, manage our bookings, and possibly reach out to them again in the future to make another." He shrugged. "At least, in theory. It would probably help if I knew how to work the damn thing effectively — it's insanely complicated to use and I have zero support from our internal I.T. staff for it."

"I feel your pain," Vasily laughed, looking at me. "We're going through some system troubles at the moment back at the station."

"It sucks, doesn't it?"

"In more ways than you can know," I nodded. "You started here in high school?" I asked casually. The longer we talked, the more comfortable the young man seemed to be with us — young, of course, being relative to anyone over thirty-five. I pegged him in his late twenties, and smiled when I backed into confirmation with his answer.

"Yeah," he smiled, showing a wide, white grin. I figured it was likely part of the overall package that came with being in sales and marketing. "I started as a lifeguard at the pool, oh God, I think I was a sophomore in high school at the time; I'd gotten the gig through a friend I had on the swim team." He smiled. "I was young enough to think it would be the best gig in the world: I mean, who wouldn't want to hang out at the pool all day? A few years on the deck, though, convinced me it would be wise to slowly work my way up into the catering side of the business. That's partially how I was able to land my first full-time position here after I graduated from UNLV — the General Manager already knew me."

"They have quite the hospitality program," I remarked.

"One of the best in the business — though thank God I was on scholarship."

"Swimming?" I asked.

"Yeah," he nodded, before frowning. "I wasn't a star, but it got me my degree."

"That's all that matters, right?" Vasily said.

"Totally. Anyway, if you hang on a moment, I printed off everything that matched what you asked about."

"Thanks," Vasily smiled.

We waited for a moment as Xander disappeared through one of

the doors and then reappeared a few moments later holding a sheaf of paper. Setting it down on the desk, he drew us closer before pointing to the paper. "From what I could tell, the National Radio Personality Convention has booked in at the Hilton every year like clockwork since 1986, save for 2002," he explained. "A lot of conventions were cancelled that year after the terrorist attacks in New York, so that doesn't really surprise me."

"Is it held at the same time every year?" Vasily asked.

"Generally," Xander nodded. "Third week of January, usually just after MLK day, though according to my records, it has been as late as Memorial Day or as early as New Year's." Flipping up a few pages, he nodded more to himself than us. "This year was on its normal date; it ended Wednesday." He looked up. "You just missed it."

"How big a convention is it?" I asked.

"Larger than you would think," Xander replied. "We fill most of our ballrooms, along with the majority of our hotel rooms. It's one of the few events on our calendar each year that we count on to keep us in the black."

I noticed that Vasily had brought his notebook out and was reading through something before he asked the next question. "Ever had any issues at the convention?"

"This year? Or in the past?" Xander asked cautiously.

I glanced at Vasily. "At *any* point," I replied, trying to keep my expression neutral; that unusual sense I seemed to get telling me I'd correctly pulled a thread kicked in, causing me to focus like a laser beam on Xander.

Almost as if to confirm my suspicions, Xander shifted on his feet, then glanced to Vasily before returning his eyes to mine. "That's an overly broad question. I'm not certain how I can answer that."

Vasily looked at me, and I could see he was completely in tune with my thoughts. "I think you just might have," Vasily observed.

Xander looked extremely uncomfortable for a moment. "What do you mean?"

"It's been my experience that when someone replies to a question with a question, they are looking for a way to avoid answering," I supplied.

"I'm not trying to avoid answering *anything*," Xander said somewhat defensively. "It's just — I'm pretty new in this position — *hell*, it's only my first senior-level position since college. I'm still figuring out what I can or *can't* do when it comes to talking to people like you."

"Like us?" I asked. "You mean law enforcement?"

"Yeah," he nodded. "Look, I'll be honest. You're not the first person asking about this particular convention — another detective was in here in December, literally a week or so after I started, and I was reprimanded for telling him too much."

That thread started to feel more like a rope. "What did you tell him?" I asked.

"This might have been a bad idea agreeing to speak to you," Xander replied, looking more worried by the minute. His hand edged toward the phone handset. "Maybe I should get the General Manager."

"You could do that," I said with a smile, laying on a thick version of my Downeast accent; often, when interviewing people for a case, I'd found it tended to put them more at ease. "But you've already spoken to the authorities once; I highly doubt simply telling us what you told *them* would get you into any further trouble. What do you think, Vas?" I asked amicably, turning to my friend.

"I can't see the harm in it," he nodded. "It's up to you, though, Xander. If it were me, though, I'm not sure I'd want to bother my boss again."

The young manager looked between us. "Well... I suppose you're right," he laughed nervously.

"So something happened during the National Radio Personality Convention, then?" I asked.

"Yeah," Xander nodded.

"And that's what you told them about?"

"Oddly, this guy knew about it *already*," he nodded. "He pretty much told me I was confirming details for him."

"And?"

"About ten years ago — when my predecessor was here — the conference took place like it normally would," he answered. "I should explain that we offer multiple standard packages depending on how many days a conference books with us. They include things like the number of ballrooms, the sorts of meals we can provide and how large the room block will be at the hotel. The NRPC has always been one of the longer ones, so they generally check all the boxes, including the themed beach party at our outdoor pool."

"Sounds comprehensive," I said, nodding encouragingly.

"Beach night," Xander continued, "from what I understand, became something of an issue. The GM gave me the essentials when I was hired; bottom line was that several of the attendees had, shall we say, made liberal use of the open bar that evening, including the keynote speaker. He was found later that evening in a cabana with one of the pool attendants."

"Was it consensual?" Vasily asked.

"I was led to believe by the GM that there was a... difference of opinion on that," Xander replied. "Officers from Rancho Linda responded to sort the whole thing out."

"How different?" I pressed. "Did anyone press charges?"

"Not that I am aware," Xander said. "You'd probably know better than I would, right? There must be records at your station."

Vasily grimaced, a clear reference to the sad state of affairs for the case system. "Undoubtedly," he answered. "I can look it up if you can provide me with the exact date."

"I'm not sure I have that."

"Then how about the week the conference happened?" I asked. "We can narrow it down from there."

"Yes..." Xander nodded, looking back down at his paperwork. Flipping through a few pages, he paused to grab a pen from a small gaggle sitting in a holder so he could circle something. "I'm certain this was the conference in question, but I can confirm that with my boss."

"I'd appreciate if you would," Vasily said as he took the stack of paper from Xander. Fishing through his pockets, Vas produced his business card, which he handed back. "Call me at this number once you know, all right?"

"I can do that."

"Did the officer you spoke to earlier leave his contact information?" I asked. "If they are looking into this same issue, it would make sense for us to compare notes."

"Yes... yes, he did," Xander replied as he pulled open a desk drawer that was below my line of sight. "I think I left it in here..."

"You seem a little understaffed," I remarked as he pulled out a wad of material and placed it on the surface of the desk. "Are you running the entire department?"

"Pretty much," Xander nodded. "I lost my booking agent last week to the Marriott across town, and my catering manager is on maternity. I've been so busy trying to stay afloat, it's been impossible to even get the job posted."

"That sucks."

"It does indeed. Here it is," he continued, fishing a piece of paper from a stack. Glancing at it, he frowned before handing it to me. "Sorry, I thought I had more than that."

Taking the paper, I felt my eyebrow arch as I read the hand-written note.

Call Detective Houston with more details on NRPC - (626) 555-5555

Showing it to Vasily, I looked back to Xander. "How would you describe this Detective Houston?"

Xander frowned. "I'm not certain I could," he said after a moment.

Pulling his phone from a pocket, Vasily tapped at it for a moment before coming up with the photo of Houston we'd pulled from the DMV. Turning the screen to the Conference Manager, he asked: "Is this the guy?"

Xander looked at it for a brief second. "Yeah, I think so."

"What, specifically, was he asking about?"

"Like I said earlier, same as you," Xander replied. "Details around that one convention and the alleged assault in our cabanas. I told him exactly what I've told you, but come to think of it, he kept pressing me about the names of those involved."

"He did?" I asked. The buzz in the back of my head told me I knew the answer to my next question. "What did you tell him?"

Xander smiled. "I think I joked that his department had to have kept lousy records; while I certainly don't know who was involved — I wasn't here then, after all — I assumed his database probably *did*. I remember now thinking it was kind of odd — I would have expected a detective to know something like that before taking the trouble to drive down here."

"You're not wrong," I replied. "Do you recall what department this detective worked for?"

"What *department*?" Xander echoed blankly. "I assumed he was from Rancho Linda. Why wouldn't he be?"

"Think for a moment, if you could," I pressed. "How did this detective introduce himself?"

He looked back at me. "Now that you mention it, I don't think he said, specifically. Just that he was a detective looking into a cold case; yeah, that was it," Xander started to nod slowly. "Something about new evidence being reviewed."

I looked at Vasily for a long moment before returning to Xander. "Can you put us in contact with the organizers of the convention?" I asked. "I'm sure you don't have the names of the people running the one in question a decade ago, so anything current would be fine."

"Top page of that printout," he replied. "I figured you'd want that. Detective Houston did too."

Shit, I thought. "And you'd be right," I smiled slightly. "Thanks for your time."

"Sure," he said. "Anytime."

I had my doubts about that last sentiment but smiled nonetheless as Vasily and I turned to exit. Just a few steps into the cross corridor —

and certain the door to the Convention and Catering Office had closed — I paused and pulled Vasily sideways. "This Houston person seems to have been conducting the same investigation we've stumbled into," I said softly. "I'm not sure I need to speak to the conference organizers to know who the keynote speaker was that seems to have gotten into a so-called misunderstanding."

"Don Davies," Vasily nodded. "I was thinking the same thing. If Rancho Linda *had* rolled anyone to the call, we should have the record back at the station, assuming the damn database system is back on-line. That would confirm both parties to the assault, as well as who the responding officer was."

I frowned slightly. "I don't think the conference organizers will be too keen to give us the information, but if Houston has already paid them a visit, we need to as well — if for no other reason than to begin to lock down our suspect's movements in the weeks prior to the murders."

Vasily looked at me. "I'm not so sure we need to go to LA any longer."

"It was never a serial murderer," I nodded. "I think we both knew that; poking through similar cases may still be worthwhile, but let's push it to after we contact whoever runs the annual shindig."

"Agreed," Vasily. "Let's head back to the station, then. I can look through the case system — assuming it's available — if you don't mind making some phone calls."

"Not in the least," I said. "Except I want to make one more stop while we're here at the Hilton."

He looked at me again. "You've not solved this yet, have you?"

"No," I shook my head.

"Good, because—"

"But I think I'm close."

Vasily rolled his eyes at the interruption. "I hate you," he sighed as we started to walk again. "And I mean that with love."

"I never doubted it," I laughed.

Pausing a second time as we entered the wider conference corridor, I took a moment to get my bearings before turning away from the parking garage; the open area narrowed a bit as we entered another corridor, this one with windows that faced out onto the main drive for the resort. Despite the ugly weather, it appeared business was brisk, with helpful employees buzzing among the vehicles parked beneath the massive canopy in front of the grand entrance. Carts piled high with shopping bags seemed to vie for supremacy with other carts sporting well-used luggage, making it impossible to tell whether the guest tide was coming in or going out.

The corridor let us out into a large rotunda-type area just inside the rotating door; a sizable fountain was in the exact center, adding gentle sounds of water cascading to the general hubbub of people coming and going. In pride of place directly opposite the rotating door was a modern looking bar, sporting comfortable looking clutches of furniture in pods of two or four either facing the tastefully backlit wall of spirits behind the tender, or floor-to-ceiling plate glass windows looking out onto the pool area. Despite the hour of the day, there were few open spots available; two cocktail waitresses were buzzing among the patrons, removing or replacing glassware depending on the table. Considering how early it was in the morning, I revised my assessment of the flow; I revised it further when I saw the sizable line at the ornate reception counter.

"Flights to catch," Vasily murmured. "Or so I would assume."

"Probably right," I replied as I moved to get into line. "I didn't see any evidence of a conference back there, though – which is odd, if the NRPC just ended."

"These places tend to turn conventions over pretty fast, but it might not be that," Vasily replied. "Many schools across the country have staggered winter vacations this month; could just be tourists. We are, after all, not far from Disneyland."

I rolled my eyes. "There's more to California than Disneyland."

"Really?" Vasily asked innocently. "I wouldn't know. Why are we here?"

"Playing a hunch," I replied.

"Care to clue me in?"

"I don't want to be wrong and disappoint you."

Vasily's eyes narrowed. "Like that would ever happen. On either count."

"I appreciate your faith in me," I smiled as the line snaked forward. "But my theory feels held together by bubble gum and bailing wire," I explained, shaking my head slightly. "And this is just a wild, wild guess."

"If it leads to a clue," Vasily said as the line moved again. "I'm taking you surfing to celebrate."

"I thought we were *already* going surfing."

"Then we'll go twice."

I didn't get a chance to respond, for a clerk behind the desk waved me forward. "Hello," I smiled. "I'm Chief Sean Colbeth and this is Deputy Chief Vasily Korsokovach of the Rancho Linda Police Department. I was wondering if you could tell me whether a guest was staying here at the moment?"

The young woman behind the desk smiled that retail smile all four-star hotels trained their staff to be proficient in. "Is this an official police request?" she asked. "If it is, I'll need to speak with the manager."

"I won't lie," I smiled back, "it's not at the moment, but it could lead to one." I nodded toward the archway behind her that I presumed hid the accounting and management folks. "Maybe you should get the manager just in case."

"Very good, sir," she replied as she stepped away from the desk and disappeared.

"Clever not delineating which department *you* are working for," Vasily said softly.

"I thought it might make them more amenable to answering questions," I replied, "if they think we are working together. Which we are."

"True."

Our clerk returned with an older black woman in tow; dressed in a muted power suit, she had her grey hair teased into an afro, with a pair of reading glasses nestled within it. Wearing that same retail smile, she took the two of us in. "Gentlemen," she said. "I'm Latoya Danvers, the General Manager. What can I do for you?"

"My colleague and I are working a case," I explained. "I can't get into specifics," I said as I pointedly glanced at the line behind us, "but we're trying to locate someone who may have checked into your hotel a few days ago, possibly for the National Radio Personalities Convention that recently ended. Their family reached out to us as they missed a gathering where they were expected."

Danvers looked at me. "So this is a wellness check?"

"Of a sort," I nodded.

"What is the name of the guest?" she asked as she moved to the computer console embedded in the reception desk.

"Davies," I said. "Frank Davies."

I saw Vasily's head snap around to me, but he kept his council as Danvers typed the name into her console. Her eyes flicked across the results before returning to mine. "Yes, we have Frank Davies as a guest," she replied.

I glanced at Vasily. "Could you ring his room for me?" I asked. "We'd like to let his family know he's okay."

"One moment." Picking up a handset from the phone beside her computer, Danvers tapped something into the controls and then waited. I mentally counted the number of rings before she looked to me. "There doesn't appear to be anyone in the room at the moment."

"I really need to ensure he's okay," I pressed; it was hard infusing concern in my voice, considering I *already* knew the status of Frank. And Don, for that matter. "The family is pretty worried since they've not heard from him."

"Let me call again," Danvers said as she redialed. "If there's still no answer, I'd be happy to take you to the room personally."

"Thank you," I replied.

Vasily and I waited patiently as she tried a second time to get someone to pick up at the other end of the line; frowning as she placed the handset back in the cradle, she looked back at us. "Just to set expectations, given the time of day, it's not extraordinarily unusual for a guest to not be in their room."

"Makes sense," I agreed. "Have there been any room charges recently?"

Danvers face briefly looked surprised before she recomposed it back to her professional facade. "No," she replied slowly. "How did you know I checked?"

"Lucky guess," I smiled. "Based a bit on how much typing you did to locate the room."

The General Manager returned my smile with one more on the rueful side. "It's part of the curse of being in this line of work," she explained. "We come to anticipate a guest's every whim. I assumed you'd probably ask about that, too, especially when I saw how long Mr. Davies is booked in with us."

"Three weeks, right?" I guessed.

This time, Danvers *did* look surprised. "What exactly is going on here?" she asked. "And can I see some identification?"

"Nothing beyond what I've already told you," I replied as I pulled my badge from my belt and slid it over to her; Vasily matched my action, and I watched as her eyes immediately picked out the differences between the two.

"Windeport?" she asked as she slid the badges back to us. "That's not here in Southern California."

"It's not," I nodded. "To answer your next question, the case we are working is bicoastal. Vasily is handling the California end, and I was digging into the Maine angle before our leads converged here at the Hilton."

"I see," she replied. "Mr. Davies is a regular guest here, as is his brother."

"Don?" Vasily asked. "The radio personality?"

"Yes," Danvers replied. "We usually host Don Davies while the convention is here, but from time to time he has Frank attend on his behalf, representing the foundation work he does for Don." She smiled slightly. "Although I have to admit, I generally find it hard to tell them apart."

"You know them personally?" I asked.

"Yes," she nodded. "Judging from how old the two of you look, I've likely been the GM here since before either of you were born. The Davies brothers tend to spend the end of January and the first part of February with us each year — though not at the same time, like I said earlier."

"I'm older than I look," I smiled.

"If you are the Olympian my kid looked up to, I'd respectfully disagree."

"Got me there," I laughed.

"As you can imagine, it's rare these days for a guest to remain with us for that length of time. So, we tend to take notice — and do whatever it takes for them to continue to visit." Reaching under the desk, Danvers pulled out an unmarked card from a drawer. "I'll take you to the room now."

Danvers spoke softly to another clerk behind the counter before walking to the end; we met her there and followed her over to the bank of elevators hiding behind several rows of potted dwarf palm trees. Pressing the up button, we stepped into the carriage as soon as it arrived and watched as Danvers swiped the blank card through the reader before pressing the top-most button. "Davies is staying on our concierge level," she explained. "Keycard access only."

"Sounds secure," Vasily replied.

"As it should," Danvers chuckled before looking at Vasily for a long moment. "You were an Olympian, too, weren't you?"

"Yes," he nodded.

"They say you'll meet the most interesting people working in hospitality," she laughed. "But this has to be a first for me."

"Happy to have spiced up your day," I said.

The elevator smoothly decelerated to a stop on the tenth floor of the hotel; with a metallic hiss, the silver doors parted to show a hallway in standard four-star luxury resort styling of walls in tasteful pastel hues and complemented with expensive looking industrial carpet. Wall sconces meant to evoke the old-fashioned elegance of tapered candles were mounted between the tasteful six-panel wooden doors marking off what I presumed were larger-than-normal suites for guests expecting a taste of the better things in life, however briefly. Following Danvers down the hallway, our footsteps were muted by the surprisingly deep pile of the carpet, an unexpected nod to the elegant ambience. I wasn't surprised as our host bypassed all but the final doorway at the end of the hallway; I suspected Davies had booked some version of the corner suite with all the trimmings.

Hanging on the doorknob was one of those standard *do not disturb* placards guests who wanted to sleep off the worst effects of a hangover would often use; that sense I had guessed right got more intense. "How long do you observe that request?" I asked Danvers, nodding toward the sign.

"After that shooting in Las Vegas, Corporate changed our policy to not going more than a day if the sign is out. Except," she added, eyes flicking to the door, "we tend to give guests such as the Davies twins a little more leeway. On this floor, the housekeeping staff would be likely to honor the request indefinitely."

I glanced toward Vasily. "Interesting."

Rapping her knuckles against the door, Danvers called out. "Mr. Davies? It's Latoya Danvers." I strained to hear any sort of noise from inside the suite that might indicate someone had heard us. Danvers waited a few heartbeats before knocking again, and calling out louder. "Mr. Davies?"

Pulling Vasily back a bit, I lowered my voice. "Do we have enough probable cause to enter?" I asked.

My friend thought for a moment, then nodded slowly. "I think we might be on the same wavelength about what is on the other side of that door, so yes," he replied, before turning back to Danvers. "Ms. Danvers, would you open that door for us, please?"

"I'm not sure I can without talking to Legal," Danvers hedged. "Mr. Davies is likely out sightseeing or something; you can't read much into why he's not answering the door."

I looked at Vasily, who nodded. "Ms. Danvers, the key to understanding why Frank Davies hasn't spoken with his family in a week or more could well be inside this room. We'd like to ask for your cooperation, but if you feel we should go through a more formal process of obtaining a warrant, we totally understand." I lowered my voice. "I've been in this business long enough to know that Corporate won't appreciate being served."

Danvers weighed what I was saying; I hated to prey on her desire to remain off the radar of her corporate overlords, especially since I was more and more certain what was in the room beyond the nondescript six-panel door would ultimately draw massive attention to her hotel. In the end, though, Danvers nodded slightly before pressing her unmarked card to the lock. The light flipped from red to green for a moment, and the door clicked open; Danvers pushed the door open further and strode in.

"Mister Davies? Are you—holy mother of *God!*"

Danvers had come to an abrupt halt at the edge of what looked like it would ordinarily be a massive living room; stepping around her, I paused just a step ahead of her as I took in how the space had been transformed. An L-shaped couch had been shoved over to the far wall, though the coffee table remained at the center of the space. There was an elegant chandelier in pieces beside the couch; the anchor point was just above the coffee table, though, and still had the remnants of what looked like standard clothesline hanging from the metal loop. A massive blue plastic tarp was beneath the coffee table, nearly covering the entirety of the industrial carpet, and several sheets of clear plastic had been wrapped around the table and over the couch. Stepping closer, I knelt down to confirm there were a few splotches of blood on the tarp, something of a trail leading toward a doorway that appeared to be the master bedroom.

Standing, I leaned as far as I could around the corner and saw the rumpled sheets of the bed; normally bleached white, the crimson stains made me nod further. Turning back to Vasily, I saw he was already on the phone, quietly making his request to roll whatever crime scene techs he had at his disposal. Danvers was rooted to her original spot, her face as white as her dark complexion could allow. Slowly, she tore her eyes from the coffee table and looked at me.

"Davies isn't missing, is he?" she asked.

"I'm afraid not," I said sadly.

Danvers put a hand to her face and closed her eyes. "I knew I should have retired last year..."

Seventeen

T rue to his word, Vasily set me up in a modestly sized conference room that looked as though it had seen better days; the faux woodgrain surface of the wide table was scuffed with use, and the mismatched set of chairs ringing the perimeter spoke to the space being more of an impromptu storage area than a true meeting location. I wasn't terribly surprised at the air of disuse, given just how empty the cubicle farm outside the room appeared to be; not for the first time did I find myself wondering why the department hadn't downsized into a smaller building. I figured the cost of relocating the underlying infrastructure was far greater than simply shrink-wrapping parts of the office that were no longer needed – or that upper management suffered ongoing delusions of someday restoring the department to its former glory. Still, there were *some* perks to the forgotten corner of the station I'd claimed as my own, not the least of which was the small Keurig that Vasily had transferred from his office to a counter running along the far wall of the room. Leaning against said counter, I watched as the machine cheerfully chugged through my second cup of coffee since returning from the Hilton, blissfully ignoring for a while longer my girlfriend's entreaties that I cut back a bit on the caffeine.

Pulling the RLPD-logoed mug out from beneath the spigot once the cycle had completed, I contemplated the borrowed iPad I was using while sipping on the hot brew and frowned again. Any momentum from our trip to the Hilton had completely evaporated upon our return to the station, for the county-wide network issues hadn't improved in the least, as evidenced by the blank screen I was staring at. It was easy to understand the grim expressions I'd seen on what few personnel I'd encountered in my wanderings about the station; modern policing relied heavily on access to reliable technology. Without it, we might as well turn off the lights, lock the doors and call everything off indefinitely.

Maybe that's a bit too harsh, I thought as I took another sip from the mug and looked over to the stack of three-ring binders Vasily had retrieved from some other part of the building. *Fortunately, modern policing also relies on standards and practices honed over years of effort; for every system, there's a redundant backup. And thank God for that.*

I shifted my eyes to where Vasily had taken up residence beside the stack of binders; while we awaited the results from the techs currently scouring the hotel room back at the Hilton, the two of us had planned on tracking down any information surrounding the possible assault Xander Vallejo had revealed to us. Our hopes to make quick work of it with a simple search of the case system had, of course, been dashed, forcing us to instead pull the manual logs the Chief of the Watch routinely kept. While we knew from the reports Xander had provided what dates to focus on, that had still left us with a sizable number of incidents to review for the week in question. There was no easy way other than slogging through each line in the logbooks, reviewing every entry to determine if it was the one from the Hilton or not. Slowing us down further was the decided lack of specificity in the one-line descriptions attached to each incident; clearly, the Chief of the Watch at that time had subscribed to the notion that brevity was the soul of wit. Despite that, a quick glance at the whiteboard showed we'd already flagged a half-dozen possibilities, and that was only in the first two volumes we'd reviewed.

Vas had his MacBook closed, his attention focused instead on a rather sizable green binder that he'd been perusing for the better part of the last hour. As he ran his finger along whatever page he was reading, my eyes flicked to the companion binder I'd been scanning myself, sitting passively beside the iPad that had been less than helpful. The theory was that between the two of us, we might discover the elusive file number that *should* have been attached to the call from the Hilton; once we had *that*, it was a somewhat simpler search to dive into the physical archives and retrieve whatever paperwork might have been filed away for safe-keeping. By Vasily's reckoning, it was likely the incident predated the case system, but without access to the software, whether or not the case notes had been digitized was beyond irrelevant.

Eyes flicking back to the still-to-be-reviewed stack of binders, I marveled at how different life was in a sizable metropolis like Rancho Linda. Back in Windeport, the pile would represent data going back to the turn of the *last* century; it was difficult for me to wrap my brain around the fact we'd only pulled seven days of records for the city. From what I'd reviewed myself, though, the vast majority of incidents had been of the misdemeanor variety — shoplifting, minor burglaries or other petty thefts. Still, the sheer *quantity* made me thankful Winde-port was as small a village as it was.

Dropping back into my aging chair, I sighed deeply as it squeaked beneath me. "This is almost worse than looking for the proverbial needle in a haystack. Did your I.T. contact have *any* idea when the system might be back online?"

Vasily spoke around the pencil he had in his mouth. "He said something about us having enough time to take in a movie — or three. Or that the arctic ice cap might be fully melted by the time they had everything up and running."

"That doesn't sound hopeful in the least."

"I doubt it was intended to be," Vasily replied, taking the pencil from his mouth and absentmindedly trying to slide it into his hair. It took him a moment to realize that his ponytail didn't exist any longer. "I sometimes forget I can't store anything up there now," he chuckled softly as he tossed the pencil back on the table.

"Old habits can be hard to break," I nodded as I returned to reading the lines on the page in front of me. "I really wish there was someone left here in the department that had been on staff back then," I sighed. "It would be far faster if we could have been looking for whoever the beat officer might have been."

"I agree," Vasily said. "With our budget problems, though, we've had a ton of turnover. I imagine Chief Andrews would have known off the top of his head; he was that kind of boss, able to keep tabs on every-thing nearly effortlessly."

"I was sorry to hear he'd passed," I said softly.

"It was unexpected," Vasily replied. "He'd survived a massive heart attack last year, too," he continued as he flipped a page. "But as they say, those blood thinner medications aren't completely foolproof." Flipping another page, he paused to look up at me. "I'm just glad he didn't linger long after the stroke. It was damn hard seeing him in that hospital bed, knowing he'd been so full of life just a few months earlier."

"I hope I go out differently," I said. "In my sleep, I think. Nice and peaceful."

Vasily smiled crookedly. "Come now. I thought *all* cops wanted to go out in a blaze of glory, taking out a bad guy or two while saving the world as we know it."

"Not *this* cop," I chuckled. "There's far too much paperwork for that scenario."

Vasily arched an eyebrow. "You'd be dead. Why would you care?"

"*Someone* would have to do the investigation," I pointed out. "I'd prefer not to tie up resources quite that way."

"How noble of you," he laughed as he turned back to his page. "And given my budget constraints, a sentiment I can get behind."

Sipping at my coffee, I swiveled my chair to look at the white board again, my eyes moving to where we had taped an enlarged copy of Daniel Houston's photo from his California Driver's License; beside it, we'd jotted down what little we had been able to dig up on our suspect. It wasn't much more than his last known address, another frustrating byproduct of the ongoing system problems we were endur-ing. Just below Houston's photo, we'd taped up photos of the Davies twins that Caitlyn had emailed earlier after pulling them for me from the State of Maine's Motor Vehicle database. Side by side, it was almost impossible to tell the difference between the two head shots, save for a slight variation in hairstyle; even the faint smiles each face sported seemed identical. I imagined it must have been fun being their parents while they were growing up — telling them apart had to have been an extremely difficult task.

Returning to the photo of Houston, I stood from my chair and moved a bit closer to the whiteboard. Sipping my now tepid coffee, I took in the genial expression of the man I suspected was our killer and wondered if my assumptions about his motivations were accurate. Brown hair cut in a professional manner complemented a boyish face that he'd tried unsuccessfully to age behind a layer of stubble; piercing blue eyes seemed to look directly at me in an appraising manner that was somewhat unsettling. I couldn't put my finger on *why* it made me feel that way; most identification photos tended to catch people at their worst, anyway, so there was a good chance it was simply an artifact from that.

And yet, I had the distinct impression I was seeing the essence of Daniel Houston.

Tapping a finger against the side of the mug, I was struck by a thought, albeit an incomplete one. "Vas, what do you think about our suspect being ex-police?"

"If the system were up, it would be a simple enough search to make." I heard him push away from the table behind me and move to my side. He took a moment to look more closely at the photo as I had been doing. "The hair certainly could lean in that direction," he allowed. "And the chiseled jaw doesn't exactly hurt, either. Why?"

"I'm not sure," I replied honestly. "A sense, maybe? Driven by the rather methodical way Houston went about tracking down the Davies twins." I turned to Vasily. "Frank's receptionist felt a bit like Houston was going to grill her boss over something, and if you add to that the way Xander assumed Houston was a cop..." I shrugged again. "If not police...?"

"Private?" Vasily asked, finishing my thought. His eyes flicked back to the photo. "That would be easy enough to find out too, save for the obvious system issue. We might get some joy if we call the State, though. Or the FBI. Either should have his private license on file. I might be able to call in a favor from Sacramento."

"If you don't mind burning one," I cautioned. "As you said, it would be a simple enough search were the system up. You might want that favor later."

Vasily smiled. "Oh, I've got Reuben on a tight leash," he said as he turned to the table to pick up his iPhone. "He owes me more than a single favor."

I felt my eyebrows go up. "We're talking *figuratively*, right?" I asked, knowing a thing or two about Vasily's private life and predilections.

The smile grew wider. "Absolutely," he replied as he scrolled through his contacts. "Alejandro isn't into that scene, anyway."

"Good to know," I said.

Vas looked up at me, pausing in his search for a moment. "How did you know about the hotel room? And the name of the guest?"

I smiled slightly. "It was a hunch," I replied. "I don't quite understand the motivations yet but suspect strongly Don Davies made a point of telling everyone he was heading to Windeport before taking his normal trip to California, then had some sort of arrangement for Frank to stand in for him." I sipped at the now cold coffee. "Don had some reason to want to be here in California earlier than his designated visit with family; the subterfuge would allow him the time for whatever that might have been."

"But he boarded a flight under his own name," Vasily reminded me. "He wasn't exactly covering his tracks."

"Why would he?" I asked. "If he'd appeared on Gennifer's doorstep at the appointed time, she would have been none the wiser. She only knew something was wrong because he *failed* to appear."

"Interesting theory," Vasily allowed. "How does the Hilton figure in?"

"The answer to *that* likely lies in whatever we can dig out of those archives of yours," I said.

Vas frowned. "I'm beginning to suspect you believe that attempted assault Xander revealed might be the root of our troubles."

"I do," I nodded.

My friend ran a hand through his hair, messing it up even more than normal. "A decade is a long time to wait for revenge," he said, frowning deeper. "Why the lag?"

I shook my head. "I don't know," I sighed. "That, too, may be relevant to the case in some way."

Vasily tapped the photo of Houston. "You think he was occupied for some reason?" he asked. "I don't want to make generalizations based on this one snapshot, but he doesn't look the type to have done jail time."

"I think it's more that Houston only recently discovered the assault," I replied. "Or was told about it. Or, if we allow he is just a hired gun, recently got the contract."

Vas shook his head. "Not a hit," he said after a moment's consideration. "The murders — both of them — feel too personal to me. Houston had a stake in their deaths."

"Yeah," I said after a moment. "I agree."

Vasily returned to his phone and tapped the number for his contact, then wandered a few paces away from me to make his call. Unsure of how long he would be tied up, I glanced at my binder once more and decided it was an awesome time to check in with Suzanne back home. Grabbing my own iPhone from the table, I attracted Vasily's attention long enough to pantomime I'd be outside before heading out to the rear parking lot of the station.

Opening the door, though, I quickly found the weather situation hadn't improved much since we'd returned from the Hilton, with a brisk gust of cool air nearly inducing me to do an about-face and return to the relative warmth of the station; I persevered, though, and moved out and over to small picnic table that was just barely covered by the overhang of the building. Judging from the cigarette disposal container beside it — and the sizable quantity of butts scattered around its base — it felt like I was intruding on smoker territory. The terrible weather seemed to be offsetting anyone's urge to ease nicotine cravings, though I figured sooner or later, I'd no longer be alone.

Suzanne picked up on the first ring. "Hey," she said.

I frowned. "You sound exhausted," I said without preamble.

"It has been an exceedingly long day," she replied. "Which followed an exceptionally sleepless night."

"That's not what I was hoping to hear," I said, sure some level of my concern had crept into my voice. "Deidre?"

"Mostly," she sighed. "I've just gotten her off with that jerk she calls a husband; what a piece of work! Absolutely zero empathy for what she is going through at the moment. Zero," she emphasized, her voice growing cold with anger.

"And now you know *why* I feel the way I do about Feldman."

"I think he must have taken a few too many hits to the head," she continued. "I couldn't make him understand that Deidre is in a delicate place; I wouldn't let him leave with her until I forced him to promise that she'd see her primary down in Atlanta as soon as they arrived."

"He may have promised that," I observed, "but the likelihood he'll make good on it is pretty low."

"I know," Suzanne sighed. "I've done what I can; like I said earlier, her personal doctor is expecting her to show up. Maybe, just maybe, that will be enough to make sure *someone* follows up with her."

I watched as a leaf blew across the dull pavement of the parking lot; the way it skittered one way, then the other before floating off in a totally different direction felt a bit like a metaphor for my relationship with Deidre. Still, it wasn't surprising I was concerned about her, given we'd been together for more than a decade before the sudden split. "I don't have any contacts down in Atlanta," I said after mentally sorting through the long list of those I'd worked with over the years. "There is someone in Northern Florida, though. If it would put your mind at ease, I could put a bug in her ear and see if she can scare up someone to keep tabs on De."

"I'd appreciate that," Suzanne replied.

"Otherwise, how are you doing?"

"Awesome," she chuckled. "Five o'clock can't come soon enough."

Glancing at my watch, I smiled slightly. "You know what Jimmy Buffett has to say about that," I reminded her.

"I'd agree, save for the fact I'm doing physicals for the swim team in less than an hour."

"You are?" I asked innocently, well aware of who had accidentally volunteered her.

"Nice try," she teased. "Speaking of favors, you owe me big time for this. I'm going to miss the finale of *The Bachelorette* because of you."

"There are such things as DVRs these days, Milady," I replied.

"It's not the same as seeing the big reveal live," she countered. "Don't worry," she added with just a hint of glee, "I've been considering just how you can make it up to me. I won't lie: most of my plotting centers on ways to get you undressed, slowly." Suzanne paused for a beat. "*Excruciatingly* slowly."

"I'm... not entirely sure I like the sound of that," I replied, though it was clear at least one part of me might.

"Good," she chuckled. "Now that you know what to look forward to, tell me how the case is going."

"Slowly," I laughed, unintentionally echoing her. "The damn computer system is fried, so we've been reduced to going through paper logs and calling in favors from other departments. Vasily's on the phone as we speak, actually. Despite that, though, we've managed to pick up a few more leads."

"That sounds promising."

"Here's hoping."

There was a chiming at the other end of the line. "Oh, crap. I've got to go — call me later if you can?"

"I will, my love."

We blew each other virtual kisses over the open line as we ended the call; I took a long moment to let my somewhat aroused libido cool off in the wintry breeze before sliding off the picnic table and heading for the door to the station. *Damn,* I thought as I pulled the door open. *How on earth can Suzanne so easily turn me from a calm, cool and collected professional into a randy teenager? Dear Lord. She's* totally *got my number...*

Thoughts of what Suzanne had in store for me were distracting enough that I managed to make a wrong turn in the cubicle farm, forcing me to take the long way around to the conference room I'd been using. I found Vasily still on the phone, scribbling on his notepad, when I entered; looking up, he flashed a thumbs-up before going back to jotting down whatever information he'd miraculously managed to dig up. Grabbing my empty coffee mug, I squelched the tiny voice in the back of my head telling me I'd already had plenty of caffeine and instead plugged yet another K-cup into the Keurig. By the time the device had chugged to completion, Vasily had wrapped his conversation.

Tossing the used K-cup into the trash, I pulled my mug out and turned toward him expectantly. "That went longer than I anticipated."

"There's always a bit of give-and-take when I call Reuben," Vasily smiled.

"Do I want to know what you had to *give*?" I asked, eyes narrowing.

"Two leather dog collars and—"

I held up my hand. "I'll stipulate that a transaction took place," I chuckled. "I'm not sure I want to know more than that."

Vasily eyed me wickedly. "They're for a puppy of his," he explained.

"TMI," I groaned, pressing my hands to my ears. "*God almighty,* TMI."

"You had such a sheltered life up there in Windeport," Vasily clucked. "I wish I'd been able to broaden your horizons more while I'd been there."

"Vas."

"You'd be surprised what kind of subculture exists in that county—"

"*Vas!*"

"Anyway," he laughed as he looked down at his notebook, clearly pleased he'd managed to get a slight flame to my cheeks. "Turns out, both of your hunches were right on the money. For the past seven years, Daniel Houston has been a licensed Private Investigator operating from an address in Pasadena; prior to that, he was a detective with the San

Diego Police Department." Looking back up, he continued. "He's not a whole heck of a lot older than we are, so I have to imagine something came up for him to abandon a life as a police officer well before he was eligible to draw his pension."

"Something worth checking into," I agreed. "Know anyone down in SDPD?"

"No," he sighed. "I've not had a chance to go south for any reason since returning to California."

"Damn," I said. "Well, we can always dial for dollars."

"I can ask Chief Gilbert to reach out," Vasily said thoughtfully. "He might know his counterpart down there."

"Can't hurt."

"One other thing," Vas continued. "The address on the PI License doesn't match the Driver's License."

"Really?" I swung around to the whiteboard. "Yeah, you're right," I murmured. "This says he lives in Santa Ana."

"Which would be ridiculous," Vasily observed. "The commute from there to Pasadena could easily stretch to an hour or more during rush hour."

I sighed. "We're going to have to check them both out, aren't we?"

"Yep," Vas said. "My vote is Pasadena first; then we can surf after hitting the address in Santa Ana."

"It's still raining out there," I pointed out.

"Your point is?" he laughed. "Besides, Suzanne texted me after you spoke with her. Said you sounded tense and could use a break."

"Did she, now," I rolled my eyes. "I suppose she also told you to take away the Keurig."

"I value my life quite highly," he chuckled. "I texted back I'd do no such thing."

"Good boy." Looking down at the three-ring binder, I groaned slightly. "I suppose we should finish what we started here before beginning to gallivant around greater Los Angeles."

"Sounds like a plan," Vas replied.

Settling back into my chair, I reluctantly went back to reading through the log entries I'd been avoiding. After a few moments, I fell into a kind of rhythm: read an entry, take a sip of coffee, move to the next line. That managed to sustain me through four additional pages before I ran out of coffee and stood to make another cup. Vasily pointedly kept his eyes on his own binder, but I could still feel his judgement radiating off him in waves; obstinately, I ignored him and popped in a fresh K-cup.

Freshly topped off with more caffeine, I managed to make it through the rest of that binder and halfway through the next one before my eyes began to cross. Leaning back in my chair, I reached over to my backpack and retrieved some eyedrops to try and relieve the worst of the grainy feeling from my contacts; given how blurred my vision was becoming — and the slight headache that had begun to form — I reluctantly retrieved the pair of cheaters I kept with me for reading. Once I'd found myself the wrong side of thirty-five, my near vision had begun to go, which my optometrist informed me was not all that unusual. I may have accelerated the process slightly with sheer quantity of reading I had to do in my position; it didn't help that I also seemed to spend endless hours in front of a laptop monitor as well.

"You ever thought about getting LASIK surgery?" I asked as I decanted a drop into one eye, and then the other.

"No," Vasily said absently. "But I don't need it, anyway. My vision is perfect compared to yours."

"That's not true," I accused. "I've seen you borrow my cheaters a time or two."

"Only in low light situations," he replied. "No contact lens works perfectly in darkness."

"All right, then. *Hypothetically* speaking, if your vision were similar to mine, would you do it?"

"I think I would..." he trailed off.

I turned toward him. "Would what?"

"Holy hell," he breathed before he slid across to me, binder in hand. "Look at this entry."

Looking down at the line he had indicated with a finger, I felt my pulse quicken.

Hilton Orange County — attempted assault. Victim: Houston, Isabella. Suspect: Davies, Donald

"Wow," was all I could think to say. "That's pretty damn specific compared to the vast majority of entries I've been reviewing." Turning back to Vasily, I smiled slightly. "I guess it was about time for a clue to dump itself into our lap."

Glancing to the clock on the wall, Vasily chuckled. "Too bad it couldn't have happened two hours earlier," he said as he grabbed his pencil and scribbled the file number down on the small pad beside his computer. "We might have actually been able to eat lunch."

"We *still* can," I replied.

"Are you kidding?" he asked as he ripped the page from the pad and stood. "I don't know about you, but I want to see what's in that file. Like, *now.*"

"Lead on, then."

Setting my eyedrops down on the table, I followed Vasily out of the conference room and fell in beside him as he crossed the cubicle farm. Unsurprisingly, we didn't run into more than one other person as we made our way toward the far end of the space; the noise-dampening fabric on the sides of the cubicles was entirely unnecessary, doing little more than make the area feel all the emptier and consequently far more depressing than it already was. At the opposite end of the massive squad room, the cubicles gave way to a wide corridor that I'd not been down yet; our footsteps echoed as we walked across the industrial lino-leum to a set of double doors painted a light gray. Vasily fished out his identification badge and tapped it against the reader off to one side of the portal; the red light flashed for a moment before turning green in synch with the loud *clunk* of the lock being released.

Pulling a handle, Vas held the door for me as I entered the space beyond. A small, brilliantly lit anteroom fronted a glass service window, beyond which was an empty desk; two small tables on either side of the room were present, presumably for reviewing whatever item had been removed from the archive without having to completely exit the area. My own evidence space back in Windeport wasn't much more than an oversized storage closet that would have quite easily fit inside the footprint of just the anteroom, though my space jealousy was somewhat tempered by the overall air of disuse. While there wasn't dust on either of the countertops, it was clear that much like the conference room I was camping out in, this area didn't see much love.

A more robust set of double doors were set into the wall beside the service window; Vasily first went to a small console that appeared to have been recently added to the transaction counter and tried to swipe his ID in the card reader bolted to the side of the monitor. The small device beeped rather lethargically, which was followed quickly by a short but rather colorful curse from my friend.

"That can't be good," I observed as I came to stand beside him.

"We had to let the archivist go earlier in the year," Vasily explained. "So now we rely heavily on the computer logs of entry to this place, and matching transactional notes entered into the case system when people like myself retrieve or deposit items."

"You mean that *same* system that is offline currently?"

Jabbing at the screen with his ID, he sighed. "Yes, dammit." He looked up at me. "The hell with it, I'll scribble a notation into my notebook and digitize it later."

Vasily moved over to the double doors and began to hover his ID over another of the seemingly ubiquitous RFID readers the station seemed to have sprouted like mushrooms. The fact that the underlying tech running the electronic locks hadn't been affected by the system outage seemed ironic, to say the least. My friend turned toward me, ID still in his hand.

"Strictly speaking, I shouldn't have you follow me in," he said. "You're not a member of the department."

"I'm your consultant," I corrected. "While I'm happy to hang here and wait, technically that makes me more or less an employee."

Vasily considered me for a moment, then nodded before tapping his badge to the reader. There was a muted buzzing sound, followed by the loud *click* of the lock snapping open; Vasily pushed through one half, and held the door long enough for me to enter behind him before allowing the pneumatic hinge to close the portal with something of a *thunk* behind us. Almost immediately I was hit with the pungent odor of decaying paper and moldering cardboard, telltale signs we had entered the massive archive for the department — if the rows and rows of industrial shelving hadn't already made it clear. Rising the full two stories of the station, I could see portable staircases positioned in more than a few places to allow access to the upper shelves. Florescent lights hung from the open ceiling at regular intervals, throwing the space into harsh, white-tinged relief.

Checking his notepad, Vasily began walking along the main aisle before locating the right row; turning, he led me more than three-quarters of the way down the row before pausing in front of one section. "Should be about here," he murmured as he compared the case number on his pad to the boxes. "Got it!" he said, handing me his note-pad before reaching up to retrieve the box.

I watched as he carefully removed a standard cardboard evidence box from the fourth shelf; it slid out fairly easily, telegraphing perhaps just how empty it might be. My suspicion was quickly confirmed when Vasily placed the box on the polished concrete floor, ran his finger through the tape holding the cover on and revealed a small bundle of paperwork huddled at the bottom of the container somewhat hidden by a clear plastic bag holding what looked to be some sort of garment. Reaching in, Vas pulled out the handful of pages first, then the bag before frowning.

"This might not be as helpful as I was hoping," he sighed.

"What on earth is that?" I asked, pointing to the bag. "It looks like a towel."

"I think it is," he replied, putting the paper back into the box for the moment. Holding it out, he scanned the handwritten note on the exterior. "'Cabana towel, possible trace' it says."

"Trace?" I asked as I took the bag from him. Turning it over in my hands, I could see it was a pretty standard high-end beach towel commonly used at resorts such as the Hilton; stripes of green and blue differentiated it from the all-white version patrons had in their rooms, making them easy to spot. Squinting, I *thought* I could see a stain of some kind on a portion of the green. "They would have run DNA swabs ten years ago," I mused.

"If they did, it didn't match either Davies brothers," Vasily replied thoughtfully. "Peg would have gotten a hit when she ran the samples from the body. Same for Lou back in Maine."

"Curious," I murmured before handing it back to Vasily. "I'm having a hard time seeing *anyone* getting it on inside a semi-private cabana, though. You?"

"Not as much," he grinned. "You clearly ignored the rumors about the equipment closet at the UEM aquatics center."

I stared at Vasily. "I thought it was all hyperbole."

"You really can be rather blind to what's going on around you." Vasily's grin went wider. "Happy to have finally corrected you on that."

"Dear *Lord*," I breathed.

Vas started to put the cover back on the box. "Let's take this back to the conference room—hang on," he paused, mid-sentence. "There's something else here..."

"What?"

Fishing around in the depths, he came up with several small manilla envelopes. "Fibers, by the look of it," he said after reading the labels. "For a crime that was never reported, they seemed to have done a pretty thorough job collecting evidence."

"Curious," I said again, but I felt a smile playing at my lips.

Vasily caught the expression and immediately rolled his eyes. "You've gone and solved it, haven't you?

"Maybe," I smiled wider.

Vas stood and put his hands on his hips, clearly annoyed. "How the *hell* can you do that from a moldering cardboard box and a few envelopes of fibers?"

"Watch and learn, grasshopper," I chuckled.

Eighteen

T he cold water of the Pacific Ocean seemed far more frigid than
normal beneath the overcast late afternoon sky. While the rain had
finally stopped, it didn't appear that the golden orb was slated to make
an appearance of any kind that day; given how we'd slogged through
just about all of it in pursuit of the truth, seeing even a tiny amount
of sunshine would have been enough validation for me that we were
on the right path. Sadly, it looked as though I'd have to settle instead
for what felt like two late inning rallies by the home team: first, quite
suddenly, the case system spontaneously came back to life not long after
we toted the evidence box back to the conference room. That welcome
surprise allowed us to quickly review the alleged assault without pawing
through the decaying paperwork and led to another discovery: while
Isabella Houston had been the alleged victim, she'd been unwilling to
press formal charges against her alleged attacker, none other than one
Don Davies.

My call to the contact listed for the National Radio Personality As-
sociation — the group sponsoring the conference Don Davies attended
annually — led me down a rabbit hole that netted me, after much
transferring, our second victory: an appointment with the current head
of the group. I'd chafed a bit that the soonest I could speak with them
was the following morning, especially given the increasing sense I had
that there was, finally, a light at the end of our investigative tunnel. I
felt confident enough that said light wasn't a locomotive bearing down
on us and had consequently given in to Vasily's entreaties that we blow

off some steam before heading to his friend Rosie's home for dinner later that evening. It hadn't hurt that we were also awaiting results from the Crime Lab; Vasily's main contact there had told him it that though they were willing to expedite testing the evidence we'd found in the archives, they were backed up enough that it would still be a few hours before they could get to us. So off to the beach we had gone.

Vas had loaned me one of his neoprene wetsuits, and though it had been a bit too snug for my tastes, I found myself thankful for the thin layer of warmth it was providing as we bobbed among the swells awaiting the next candidate we might tackle. While I wasn't as accomplished as Vasily — who had more or less grown up along that portion of the sandy Southern California coastline — I'd spent a fair amount of time refining my technique under his patient tutelage during college and in the years after; our portion of the Maine coast had its share of decent waves, but the rocky shores required a bit of deliberateness in choosing when to get on your board — and when to sit it out.

Onshore winds were gusting briskly; between that and the low rumble of the crashing surf, I had to raise my voice considerably just to be heard, despite Vasily being less than a few feet away. "You carved up that last wave amazingly well," I said over the wind.

Vasily smiled. "I am one with the ocean," he laughed. "Have been for as long as I can remember."

"I'm a little out of practice," I groaned, still smarting from going headfirst into the roiling water on my first attempt. Nothing more than pride had been damaged, but I had to admit, it had held me back from trying again.

"Don't sell yourself short," Vas replied. "You were doing good until you clipped the edge of the curl. It happens to the best of us."

I shrugged as much as I could in the restrictively tight wetsuit. "I confess to being far more comfortable in the pool. Besides," I continued with a knowing smile as I tried to roll my shoulder, "this suit is far too tight."

"Is it?" Vasily replied innocently. "I hadn't noticed."

"The *hell* you hadn't."

"Maybe I did," he laughed harder. "I might be in a relationship, but that doesn't mean I can't appreciate—"

"*Seriously?*" I said, eyes widening. "You gave me this suit on purpose, didn't you?"

"I believe," he said with mock seriousness, "I have the right to remain silent."

"Wise."

We floated there for a few minutes, paddling every so often to avoid getting caught up in a less desirable wave as it rushed beneath us and then onward toward shore; despite the cacophony, being out there provided a sense of peace I hadn't felt since beginning the case days earlier in Windeport. It struck me that true to form, I'd been full steam ahead, taking little more than a coffee break here or there while trying to get by on just enough sleep to remain sharp. Old habits were hard to break, and in truth, I *had* nearly passed on Vasily's repeated suggestion that we catch a few waves before we headed to Rosie's.

We'd pretty much skipped even a late lunch in our effort to corroborate what Xander had told us at the Hilton. Though he'd been just as anxious to see how the pieces were beginning to fit together — and how that fed the narrative of what we suspected — I knew Vasily had skipped his normal noon hour ten kilometer run in order to keep digging; agreeing to an hour or two of ocean therapy was my way to make up for skipping the earlier workout. Still, as peaceful as it was to be out there in the surf, I found it hard to keep from thinking about the case.

We had created a conundrum as we'd planned out our movements for the following day. The corporate offices for the NRPA were in downtown Los Angeles, less than a block from the *Times* building; the addresses for Houston in Pasadena and Santa Ana were essentially in polar opposite directions from that spot, and when we added in the beachfront complex in Santa Monica where Isabella Houston appeared to be living, even the best logistical software would have been hard pressed to figure out the best routing minimizing travel time among them. I wasn't looking forward to what was quickly shaping up to be a

rather long road trip through the lousy traffic of Southern California —
even if I wasn't the one to be driving.

Vasily caught me shaking my head and called over from his surf-
board. "What are you thinking?"

"That our suspect is probably in the wind at this point," I replied.

Running a hand through his short hair, he smiled slightly. "This guy
hasn't been exactly *hiding* his activities," he pointed out. "I think he
wants us to find him. It'll close whatever sick circle he's started."

I cocked my head slightly. "That certainly fits my hunch that this is
some sort of personal retribution," I said. "We don't have enough yet to
understand the reason underlying it yet. I'd like to know that before we
confront him."

"I'm sure he'll be at one of the addresses when we go," Vasily said.
"I'm not as certain we'll have a sense of the *why*, even if we uncover a
juicy tidbit tomorrow morning."

"Maybe." Paddling my board around so I could face him, I continued. "How late do you think we'll be at Rosie's? I'd kind of like to take
another run at everything we have, now that the case system is back up
and running."

Vas nodded slightly. "Preparation for our interviews tomorrow," he
replied. "I was thinking the same thing, actually. It depends entirely on
Rosie's mood. Some weeks, we're out of there by ten; others, well, let's
just say I'm no stranger to the guest suite she seems to keep ready for
me." He smiled crookedly. "Maybe this is the wrong time to tell you
that I keep a complete set of swim gear at her place so I can use her
Olympic-sized pool for workouts the morning after."

I shook my head. "So, we should bring our tablets with us, then?"
I asked.

"And the 5G hotspot from the station," he added. "She doesn't have
internet up there and the cell service is terrible."

"Lovely," I sighed.

"Don't worry," Vasily added. "We might have to stay over, but I'll see
if Alex is willing to distract Rosie long enough for us to slip away and
look over the files one more time."

"Will he mind running interference?"

"No," Vasily smiled. "But if he does, I'll make it up to him later this evening."

"I'm not sure I want to know more than that."

"Probably not," Vasily laughed.

I looked over his shoulder at the darkening sky. "What time were we supposed to pick up Alejandro, anyway?" I asked.

Vasily rolled up the arm of his neoprene suit and swore when he saw the time. "*Shiiiiiit.* We'd better get going," he said as he began to paddle toward shore. "Alex is likely to have beat us back to the condo at this point and may well be cooling his heels wondering where the *hell* we are."

"Isn't it rush hour at this point?" I asked as I followed his lead and turned for the sand.

"*Shit shit shit!*" he exclaimed as we both flattened ourselves against our respective boards and began to stroke in earnest for the sandy shoreline.

Though it went against my better judgement — I wasn't a fan of how itchy the salt water made my skin when I didn't rinse it off properly — I nonetheless continued to follow Vasily's lead and stripped off the wet-suit once we hit the shore, then wrapped the towel he loaned me about my waist, covering the excruciatingly vivid purple Speedos he'd let me borrow to wear beneath the neoprene. Hiking our gear back to his Camaro in the gathering darkness, I helped him wedge our equipment into his trunk — thankfully, we were using his shorter knee boards — before pulling on the t-shirt and shorts I had also borrowed from my friend. As only a native Californian could do, Vasily managed to deftly navigate around the insane rush hour traffic, pulling into his condo's parking garage less than thirty minutes later. We passed Alejandro standing on the raised concrete walkway by the elevator lobby; dressed in a light-colored button down, dark slacks and a perfectly coordinated tie, it looked as though we'd managed to catch him just as he'd returned from his job as a Career Counselor at Cal State Irvine. Alex waved before following us down to where Vasily parked his Camaro behind a brilliantly yellow New Beetle and stood just at the rear bumper as we exited the car.

Vasily didn't waste any time moving directly to his partner, then pulled him into a quick hug before leaning into a kiss that seemed to be promising something far, far steamier later; it was such a personal moment between two people who clearly loved each other, I felt a bit awkward standing there just a few feet away. Feeling the heat of my embarrassment on my face, I decided the drawstring on my shorts needed adjustment, and managed to fuss with it long enough to allow the two of them to finish saying hello to each other.

"Hey there," I heard Vasily say. The delight in seeing his partner was clear in his voice. "How was your day?"

"Meh," Alex said. "I had a slew of undecided students today; directionless spirits always take a lot out of me. Better now that I'm with you."

"I think I could say the same," Vasily smiled.

"I'm not sure if I should be offended," I laughed, causing both to turn toward me.

Vasily looked sheepish. "That's not what I meant."

"I know," I replied, putting a gentle hand on his shoulder. "Believe me. Alex," I nodded.

"Sean." Alejandro made a show of sniffing. "You've been surfing," he observed, folding his arms against his chest while simultaneously arching one of his perfectly sculpted eyebrows beneath the mountain of dark curly hair he had pulled away from his face with some sort of band. "I had no idea the Pacific Ocean would be the cornerstone to solving your case."

Alex's eyes danced with merriment as he looked me over; when I'd first met him back in December, he'd been quite literally terrified our Christmas get-together would rekindle Vasily's feelings about me, sinking Alex's nascent relationship with my best friend. I'd had my own worries about the former diver, for the two had met not long after the assault that had landed Vas back in Windeport for his summer of recovery. The last thing I'd wanted was someone taking advantage of my wounded friend, but fortunately, neither of us wound up being what the other had expected. Suzanne and I had quickly adopted Alejandro into our rather unusual extended family dynamic that had long included Vasily; from the warm greeting I'd received upon my unexpected arrival a day earlier, it was clear Alex had happily accepted the arrangement as well.

"Absolutely," I replied with a chuckle. "Honestly, the Zen-like state you can get out there in the surf can lead to a clarity of mind that shakes something loose," I continued, seeing Vasily nod in agreement. "Often I've seen the answer to a case without realizing it. Unplugging for a bit lets the subconscious mind get to work sorting out the wheat from the chaff — and presenting the answer you were looking for all along."

"I night have to recommend that to my directionless students, then," Alex smiled before looking to Vas. "Is that your excuse, too?"

"Oh no," Vasily replied. "I was just there to ogle Sean in his wetsuit. He's pretty sexy when he's thinking."

Alejandro rolled his eyes before looking at me. "Now you know what I have to put up with."

"I've known him for nearly two decades," I reminded him.

"Ah," he laughed. "Need some help?"

"Thanks," Vasily said as he popped open the Camaro's trunk. "And I have a slight favor to ask, too."

"If it's about wearing that skintight costume at the convention," Alejandro said immediately, "I'm not entirely sure I'm ready for that. I mean, the privacy of our bedroom is one thing, but walking around downtown Anaheim with literally next to nothing on—"

"It's not," Vasily interrupted hastily, "though you're a diver. I'm surprised you're so self-conscious, given how little you wear up there on the platform."

"That's different," Alex insisted before glancing at me. "We'll discuss that later, *mi amor*. Name your favor."

"After we get these upstairs — and you change into something more appropriate for Rosie's pool — I've got to swing by the office to grab an internet hotspot."

"That's not much of a favor," Alejandro laughed. "You know I'd follow you just about anywhere on the slightest pretense. Save for the morgue, of course."

"Well... the favor part is distracting Rosie later this evening so Sean and I can review the case files tonight. We've got some interviews planned and need to be ready."

Alex paused. "'Distract' Rosie? In what way?"

Vasily grinned wickedly. "Wear those briefs you bought me. The ones from Australia."

Despite his dark tones, it was remarkably easy to see the flush on Alejandro's face. "Vas... those are rather... sheer... when they are wet..."

"Exactly." We started toward the elevator lobby doors once more as Vasily continued his sales pitch. "Just jump in with us when we get to the pool party portion of the evening, then maybe pop out long enough to take a sip of whatever beverage she's serving tonight. Then hop right back in until I come rescue you."

"I might need more than a sip, *mi amor*," Alejandro sighed. "How long do you expect me to keep up this distraction?"

Vas looked at me. "Two hours, max," Vas said as he stabbed the button for the elevator with his elbow. "After that, we're probably going to start seeing double anyway, given how long we've been at this today."

"You sure know how to sweet talk a fella," Alex laughed. "So, the big favor is for me to give Rosie a bit of a show, then cool my heels in the pool for an hour or two?"

"Have I mentioned just how sexy those heels are?" Vas asked.

"*Dios mío*," Alejandro breathed as we crammed everything into the elevator. "The things I do for love. So much for critiquing resumes tonight," he added with a meaningful glance over his shoulder to the backpack he was wearing.

Vas leaned over and kissed Alex on his nose. "I promise to make it worth your while."

"You'd better," Alejandro whispered quietly as he leaned over and nibbled at Vasily's ear.

"Do you two want me to get off at the next floor?" I asked diplomatically. "'Cause I'm starting to feel like a fifth wheel here."

The two lovers parted hastily.

"We're good," Alex said, his eyes dancing merrily once more.

I'll bet, I thought.

I made the assumption that we'd be spending the night at Rosie's mansion and packed up what little I had brought with me from Maine; based on what Vasily had told me on the drive to the condo, I didn't bother to change out of what I'd worn to the beach, though I was already feeling guilty about not having showered off the worst of the salt from the Pacific before diving into her pool. While we waited in the small living room for Alejandro to change, I shot off a text message to Suzanne reminding her how much I loved her — and that it might be a bit later than normal before I'd be able to call her.

My iPhone immediately rang. "Suze?" I asked when I answered. "Everything okay?"

"It was easier to call than text," she chuckled. "Yes, everything is fine; I just wanted to remind you that I'm actually on call tonight."

I snapped my fingers. "This is part of your swapping with Yasmine, right?"

"Exactly. So feel free to call whenever you can. I'll be up."

"I thought you stopped pulling those twenty-four-hour shifts when you finished your residency?"

"That was before I moved to a veritable healthcare desert," she laughed. "I'm expecting it to be quiet, though. Your midnight call would likely do quite a bit to alleviate the boredom, kitty."

"As you wish, Milady," I replied without thinking.

Vasily's head snapped in my direction. "'Milady?'"

Feeling my face flame slightly, I turned away from my friend. "Uh, I'd better go," I said hastily. "Love you."

"I love you more," she said softly before hanging up.

Sliding the phone back into the shorts I was wearing, I turned to see an impish grin on Vasily's face. "Just how often do you use that Chat Noir costume, Chief?" he asked innocently.

"As often as you wear your favorite Spider-Man one, I'll wager," Alejandro said as he rounded the corner. Attired in a tight compression muscle t-shirt and contrasting shorts, he had a windbreaker tied around his waist and a knowing grin on his face.

Vasily coughed slightly, which in no way hid the brilliant red tint on his cheeks. "Let's see if we can beat the worst of rush hour," he mumbled as he slid his own backpack over a shoulder and led us back down to the parking garage.

Since the Camaro was truly a two-person vehicle, Vas and Alejandro rearranged their cars in the parking garage so we could take the slightly roomier New Beetle; I managed to slide my six-foot-plus frame behind the passenger seat and find at least one position on the rear bench that didn't cut circulation off for one part of my body or another. Alejandro handed the keys over to Vasily for the drive to the mansion, freely admitting his boyfriend was far better at navigating the nightmare of Southern California traffic than he was; I found myself agreeing — and also silently thankful Vas would have the same duties ferrying me around on the morrow.

Our conversation was light as the city streets slipped by in the gathering darkness; I faded into the background intentionally, allowing the couple in the seats ahead of me to decompress together as I assumed was their normal nightly pattern. Watching the two of them interact filled me with immense joy, underscoring yet again that they were perfectly matched; the way Alex looked at Vas — and how my friend reciprocated — reminded me of what I saw in Suzanne's eyes each time we had a private moment together. After a while, I tuned out of the conversation and instead found myself watching the strangeness that was California as it moved past the small rear window.

I remembered thinking on my first visit to Rancho Linda the prior year how eclectic the architectural styles were; from what I could see in the semi-darkness, that didn't appear to have changed much in the twelve months I'd been gone. Vasily deftly wove his way through the traffic around the fantastical architecture of Disneyland, which quickly gave way to the standard concrete corridors just about every freeway seemed to have. Just above what I assumed were meant to be sound-dampening walls, hints of rooflines came and went at regular intervals, interspersed with billboards advertising local news stations or the best deal on car insurance. Every so often, the walls would fall away to reveal a massive mall, the parking lot surrounding it every bit as clogged as the six lanes we were traveling — even on a weeknight. The obsession with shopping seemed to be baked into living in that part of the state, a passion other parts of the country had seen cool significantly over time. I knew the mall back in Portland was struggling to retain some sort of consumer base after losing both anchor stores; from what I could see, that didn't appear to be a problem out West.

Vasily changed lanes and made for the exit I now recognized as leading into the main portion of Rancho Linda; after making a quick stop at the station to pick up his hotspot, he turned back out into traffic, taking us past a portion of the city I'd not yet seen. To my surprise, there was a general consistency in the homes and businesses we were passing, speaking to some level of zoning ordinances that had been designed to give Rancho Linda a particular look and feel. I wondered if that part of the city had been developed later, for the section around the high school where we had been swimming had seemed less coherent and far more ambivalent about blending into the overall cohesive whole.

Slowing down once more, Vas turned up an inclined street, and within moments the density of houses began to decrease, indicating another shift in the demographics. Thick hedges began to appear, hiding what I assumed were larger, more luxurious homes for the well-heeled; every so often, a gate would appear, flanked by lamps with enough patina designed to make you assume they were far older than they actually were. As we climbed higher, even those began to become sparse, underscoring a sense that we had entered the rarified air people of our pay scale could only dream of attaining.

Massive lions in gold or bronze appeared in the headlights of the Beetle, and Vasily slowed further; turning one last time, I felt (and heard) cobblestones beneath the wheels of the car, an unusual throwback to a time when something other than a sedan trundled toward what I could now see in the distance was a rather massive mansion. Smiling slightly, it occurred to me the approach had been designed almost as if we were looking through the widescreen viewfinder of a motion picture camera; every angle emphasized just how perfectly the mansion had been perched against the hill. Rounding some sort of working fountain, Vasily parked the Beetle just a few yards from an oversized portico that sported two smaller versions of the lions I had seen earlier; after sliding out of the back seat, I could easily see that the front of the mansion commanded amazing views of the valley below. It had to have been stunning in the daylight, but even in the dark, seeing the twinkling of the lights of Rancho Linda beneath us still managed to have a certain peacefulness of spirit descend upon me.

"Wow," was about all I could manage.

"Isn't it stunning?" I heard from behind me.

Turning, I found our host standing just outside of the massive wooden front doors for the mansion. "It certainly is," I replied as we moved to the steps. "You have to be at the very edge of the city out here."

"I am," she nodded. "The line is on the ridge just above us; as I understand it, the original owner, the film producer Thomas Andrews, wanted to build something that was still *in* Rancho Linda, but far enough *outside* of it to maintain some sort of privacy."

"He seems to have succeeded," I said, turning back toward the magnificent view.

"I can't argue that it's an amazing place to write," Rosie continued as she came down to stand beside us. "My writing room almost has *too* good of an angle; I can get lost in watching the way the colors change across the valley on a cloudy day."

"Sounds like a serious job hazard," I smiled.

"It can be." She looked to Vas. "Please tell me you plan to stay over? Chef made us something of a banquet, and I've paired it with wine I had sent down from Santa Barbara."

The gentle light from the carriage lamps on either side of the door caught Vasily's expression. "Did you get that Pinot Noir we like?"

Rosie looked a little smug. "Two cases. And I expect us to make a serious dent in at least one of them while you fill me in on this murder you're investigating."

"Rosie—" Vasily started.

"I won't take no for an answer," she replied as she turned back toward the door. "Get your gear from the trunk of whatever car that is and hike it to the guest rooms upstairs. Dinner will be out in the solarium in fifteen minutes."

And with that, the slight form of the millionaire author disappeared into the mansion, leaving the three of us staring at her receding form. I turned to Vasily. "Is she like that all the time?"

Alejandro was the one to answer as he popped the trunk. "You have no idea," he chuckled.

Nineteen

The "guest room" Rosie had set aside for me felt like a two-room suite at the swankiest hotel I could have ever stayed at; while the furniture appeared to be rather sparse, the space itself had an understated elegance, with pristine period-perfect wallpaper, thick-piled carpet and massive windows that had to have provided views to die for. It also had its very own bathroom featuring a generously sized walk-in shower *and* a jacuzzi; a rather ornate mirror had been hung above the vanity, with delightfully whimsical sconces mounted to either side. Even the bathroom had a massive window, making me wonder for a moment if a tub might have once been perched just in front, allowing the weekending guest an ability to soak in the view while taking a bath.

Locating the towels where Vasily had told me I would find them, I met him and Alejandro at the edge of a balcony that looked down into an entrance foyer that wouldn't have been out of place on a Hollywood set; a massive chandelier hung between two staircases that curved down from the second floor along opposite sides of the space. I had no doubt the flooring was actual terrazzo tile, likely imported; what did strike me as unusual was the absolute lack of any of the usual accouterments I was used to seeing in a house as grand as Rosie's. While Vasily had warned me in advance that our host had donated nearly everything that had come with the mansion — including a couple of rare paintings — actually *seeing* the space empty made it difficult not to assume the millionaire was actually down on her luck. Significantly.

I frowned when I saw the duo had already stripped down to their swimsuits, though; Vasily was still wearing his deep blue Speedo I'd seen at the beach, for like me, he'd not changed after our return from the beach. Alejandro, on the other hand, appeared to have donned a brief from a manufacturer I didn't recognize. Cut a bit more severely than I would have been comfortable with, the suit barely covered the basics; the light-blue fabric shimmered slightly as Alex moved, telling me it was likely not made from the traditional Spandex I was used to wearing. Two yellow swatches at either hip accentuated how insanely low the suit sat on his hips; given his well-muscled diver's physique, Alejandro was probably the only one of the three of us who could pull off wearing the brief without embarrassment. It was more than clear how the distraction portion of our evening would proceed, though.

"Did I miss a memo?" I asked. "For I'm suddenly feeling a bit over-dressed for dinner."

Tapping the thick towel he had draped over his shoulder, Vasily smiled a bit wickedly. "I suppose I should have warned you that the towel won't really be all that useful."

"It won't?" I asked, confused. "What do you mean?"

"You'll see," Alejandro chuckled before carefully wrapped his towel around his waist. "Though I need to hide this a bit longer, I think."

"See what—" I started to ask.

"Come one, let's not keep our host waiting," Vasily interrupted. His knowing smile was a clear warning I was on the wrong side of an inside joke, but I let it go for the moment.

I trailed Vasily and Alejandro as they trotted down one of the staircases, then turned to head down the central hallway I'd seen from the main entrance. We passed a number of doors though all were closed, thwarting any chance of my investigator brain getting a better sense of our host. At an intersection of the hallway, Vasily appeared to be in familiar territory and easily continued along a different direction, coming to a stop at the end of the corridor in front of a glass door that had been completely fogged over.

Looking back at me, Vasily smiled a bit wider. "Once more unto the breach," he said before pushing open the door.

A blast of tropical air, heavily laden with moisture, gusted down the hallway and washed over us; the effect made it feel as though I'd stepped into the middle of an Amazonian rain forest, despite remaining on the other side of the door. Vas disappeared into what appeared to quite literally be a jungle, followed closely by Alejandro; not wanting to risk getting lost and possibly eaten by some sort of predator Rosie had stashed in her solarium, I hurried to catch up to the duo, carefully picking my way along a rather overgrown path of flagstone. Not apparently interested in straight lines, the landscaper had crafted the most serpentine route possible, one that wended its way this way and that beneath the towering palms and around dew-laden succulents. Less than a handful of steps beyond the glass door, though, my t-shirt began to stick to my skin in the most uncomfortable manner possible; wiping at my brow with the back of my hand did little to keep the sweat out of my eyes. By the time we reached a massive clearing, multiple curls of my hair had cemented themselves to my forehead despite my best efforts, and a veritable river of sweat was running down along my spine. Through some wild stroke of luck — or smart planning on the part of my friend — the microfiber shorts Vasily had loaned me managed to not show any moisture, despite how they felt as though I could wring a gallon or two out of them. All at once I understood what the joke had been, and resolved to get out of the uncomfortably clingy fabric at my first opportunity.

The centerpiece of the solarium made the temporary discomfort worthwhile, however.

Pausing at the edge of the clearing, I was blown away by the hand-tiled Olympic pool and its waterfall at the far end; I was well aware of what secrets the water feature had protected for more than five decades, but also had to admit that while it was an odd addition to the space, the magical sound of the water cascading over the rocks created a merry atmosphere and a light mood. The water itself was the typical shimmering blue of any swimming pool; I watched, transfixed, as the underwater lighting accentuated the ripples from the cascading waterfall as they expanded outward. Ringing the pool was a deck also comprised of tile, with small tables set for two every few feet; I thought the vase holding a small orchid on each was a little extravagant, but again, seemed thematically well suited.

Rosie was sitting in a wicker chair that was part of a small conversation area: two loveseats and an additional single chair surrounded a low coffee table from the same material that appeared to be loaded down with enough food to last an entire swim team a few days. Despite the overwhelmingly oppressive heat, though, our host appeared to have bundled herself up in thick sweats and was holding, of all things, a steaming mug of something in her hands. Smiling at our entrance, she put the mug down on the arm of her chair and stood, then beckoned us over.

"Excellent timing, gentlemen," she said. "Chef just put out our spread and has, unfortunately, retired for the evening. I hope there's enough here for everyone."

"Are you kidding?" I found myself saying, all traces of my normally reserved personality washed away by the humidity. "We could hunker down here for a week with what you've provided."

"Good," she laughed. "Now, sit down, dig in and tell me your tale..."

I decided to let Vasily lead the conversation and was rewarded with a master class in how to tell a story without revealing any pertinent details; as I loaded up the plate of white china I presumed was worth more than my MacBook and all of its expensive accessories, I realized it was something of an old game the two of them appeared to play. To my surprise, for someone I had pegged as the stereotypical writer — one withdrawn from society in order to ply their craft — Rosie appeared to be up on nearly *everything* that went on in Rancho Linda, including some key aspects of our very case. When Vasily mentioned a possible tie in with an assault at the Hilton a decade earlier, Rosie frowned slightly.

"I think I remember that," she said after a moment. "I don't recall it being in the papers, but I was on one committee or another with someone who'd been at the pool the day it happened."

"Really?" I asked, my forkful of the best Spanish rice I'd ever had paused in midair. "Any chance we could talk to them? We're still struggling to get specifics for what happened."

"No," Rosie said after glancing meaningfully at Vasily. "Amanda passed away last spring in a rather tragic house fire. Huge loss to the Rancho Linda community. Huge."

"I'm sorry to hear that," I replied. "Sounds like they were a close friend."

"She and her husband both," Rosie replied. "If it helps, I still recall what the gossip was."

"I'll take innuendo at this point," Vasily laughed. "Out with it."

Rosie took a sip from the excellent Pinot she'd provided, and looked thoughtful. "Had it come from anyone other than Amanda, I would have written it off, but she was never one for hyperbole." Taking another sip, she continued. "You already know the basic plot — the keynote speaker was caught with his hand in the cookie jar, so to speak, in one of the cabanas at that beautiful pool. The young woman in question was one of the pool attendants who initially claimed she'd been surprised while getting the area prepped for some sort of party that was part of the convention."

"Probably the tropical luau," Vasily said as he polished off the last of his enchilada. Wiping his hands on a napkin, he smiled slightly. "I've never understood the fascination with staging such things outside of Hawai'i."

"Tourists are easily impressed," Alejandro replied with a smile; of the three of us, he'd chosen to remain standing and had taken up position at the arm of the chair where Vasily had sat. It wasn't lost on me that his towel had somehow disappeared, though I wasn't sure Rosie had noticed. Yet. "I feel the same way whenever I see one of those overly produced *Dios de Las Muertes* specials on TV." He got a faraway look in his eyes for a moment. "My opinion is probably biased, for I was able to attend the celebration in Mexico City growing up. There isn't anything quite like it."

"Sounds a bit like trusting lobster outside of Maine," I chuckled.

"Exactly," Alex replied. I caught him exchanging a look with Vasily, and smiled slightly; it appeared that Operation Distraction was about to begin. Alejandro set his empty plate down on the table before turning to Rosie. "Mind if I dive in?" he asked.

"Have at it," she said.

"*Gracías,*" he smiled. "The food was amazing as always."

"I'll tell Chef."

Alejandro padded toward the pool and then made his way down the steps at what I assumed was the shallower of the two ends; I couldn't be sure, but he *seemed* to be moving with the exaggerated emphasis you'd see from a supermodel, slowly, nearly seductively, allowing the water to creep up his sculpted body. Glancing at Rosie, I could see it had caught her attention and hid my smile; not surprisingly, Vasily also appeared rather entranced. I tried not to roll my eyes and decided to prod the conversation forward.

"We gathered from the police report we were able to dig up that the victim didn't want to press charges," I said. Rosie reluctantly turned her eyes toward me as I continued. "The way you characterized what Amanda told you — she didn't think the attendant had been surprised?"

"Hardly," Rosie laughed, a deep resonant affair that unfortunately made it seem like she smoked two packs of cigarettes a day. It was also oddly enthralling. As the evening had progressed, I begun to understand why she was such an interesting part of Vasily's new life in California. "Quite the opposite, actually. No one truly believed that radio guy had raped the young woman, nor was he on the pool deck when the alleged rape happened. Amanda told me the entire area had been closed in preparation for the party; only staff had been on the deck."

"How did she know that?" Vasily asked.

"About the pool?"

"Yeah."

"Easy," she smiled. "Amanda was hosting a meet-and-greet with that speaker at the lobby bar; the group she represented at the time was trying to get him to sponsor something, I think. Don't quite remember that part. I do remember her clearly telling me that they had been slotted in to speak with him just ahead of that pool party — and, as it happens, the lobby bar looks out onto the pool."

"So it does," I nodded, recalling our recent visit.

"Anyway, she had a clear view of what was going on out there, especially when the speaker had to excuse himself to get to the party; he was late enough that quite a crowd was already there when he left the bar. It wasn't long after that she saw the cops out on the deck; only later she found out about the allegation of assault."

"Wild," I said before looking at Vasily. "How on earth did our victim get accused, then?"

"That's an excellent question," he replied. "One that we might get answered tomorrow."

I nodded. "I don't think walking the space will tell us much. After nearly a decade, I imagine a few things have changed or been rearranged on that deck."

"Your victim," Rosie said slowly, "was the keynote speaker, wasn't he? The one accused by the young woman?"

Vasily and I both looked at her. "You know the rules," Vasily replied carefully. "I can't confirm or deny anything at this point. Even if you might be, hypothetically speaking, in the ballpark."

I picked up on the thread. "Did you know the speaker yourself?" I asked. "Hypothetically."

"Not personally," Rosie replied. "I *was* scheduled to be interviewed by him on his program for one of my books, oh God, must have been more than fifteen years ago?"

"Hypothetically?" I prompted.

"Might as well have been," she sighed. "Guy cancelled on me at the last minute and never rescheduled."

"You know you need to keep this close to the vest, right?" Vasily reminded her.

"I promise not to spill my guts to the local paper, if that's what you're asking," Rosie chuckled before looking to me. "You're not here for dumpster diving at all, are you?"

I smiled slightly. "Not entirely, no," I replied.

"Hypothetical my ass," she said softly before directing her attention back to the table still brimming with food. "Please, take a second helping or more. Otherwise, I have to cart this back to the fridge."

"Is there still guacamole over there?"

The three of us turned and watched as Alejandro deliberately made his way back up the steps; the water cascaded from his body as he rose from the surface, abetted slightly by how he ran his hands along first his hair and then the sides of his body in an attempt to get the worst of it off him. Out of the corner of my eye, I could see a wolfish grin on Vasily's face; Rosie, for her part, let out a startled gasp. I could understand the sentiment, for as Alex stepped onto the tile of the pool deck, I found myself a bit shocked at just how transparent the lighter fabric of his suit had become — enough that the modesty panel sewn into the front was clearly visible and about the only thing preventing a somewhat more scandalous exposure.

For his part, Alejandro was acting as if nothing was going on, easily moving back to our little grouping before kneeling beside the table to begin filling another plate. Rosie had followed him all the way in, her eyes never leaving his form; looking back to Alex, I realized he knew *exactly* what he was doing, for the way he'd sat had essentially placed the table between him and our host, giving her little more than an unobstructed view of his torso. It appeared to be enough, though, to thoroughly fluster Rosie, who seemed to have lost the thread of our conversation.

I thought perhaps it was a good moment for Vasily and me to make our escape, despite my desire to take a dunk in the cool water of the pool myself; peeling my t-shirt off earlier had helped immensely, but a quick swim wouldn't have hurt, either. Before I had a chance to make the suggestion, though, Vasily's phone went off.

Digging through the towel he'd left folded on the tile beside his chair, Vas retrieved his phone and tapped at it. "Korsokovach," he said, his eyes going distant for a moment as he listened to whomever had called. His eyes then snapped to mine as he stood from his wicker chair. "Hang on just a second," he said before muting his phone and turning toward Rosie. "My apologies, Rosie, but work is intruding on our social time. I'm afraid Sean and I need to take this call."

"I understand," our host smiled. "I'll be out here for a bit longer if you still fancy a swim later."

"I'd like nothing more than that," I replied.

"I'll keep my fingers crossed," she chuckled before turning back to Alejandro. "Are you hanging around?"

"If you don't mind the company," Alex said.

"Then let me pour you some more wine," she replied.

"*Señora*," Alejandro said with a trace of laughter in his voice, "are you trying to get me drunk?"

"Maybe," Rosie chuckled. "How are things at Cal State Irvine?"

"*Dios mío*," Alex breathed. "These kids, they don't know which way is up..."

Leaving the two of them to their conversation, I stood and grabbed my t-shirt and towel from where I'd stashed them on the couch and followed Vasily back through the jungle. The shirt was a total loss, heavy with the combination of my sweat and the dense humidity from the solarium; as Vas had predicted, the towel wasn't a whole lot better. I threw it over my bare shoulder, shuddering slightly at its clamminess before hurrying to catch up to my friend.

Vasily quickly led us through the forest and out the fogged over door; pausing in the hallway just beyond, he held up his phone. "Gina, from the Crime Lab," he said, before glancing over his shoulder at the solarium. "It might be best to take this upstairs."

I nodded and fell into step beside him, trying to ignore how I'd begun to shiver in the relative cold of the hallway. By the time we'd climbed the steps to the second floor, my body had acclimated enough that the desperate urge to return to the warm embrace of the solarium had passed. Vasily preceded me into the room he was sharing with Alejandro, then closed the door behind us; the space was nearly identical to mine, though it did seem to have the added bonus of a small table with two chairs over by the window. Vasily quickly made his way over to it and put his phone down on the surface.

"You're on speaker, Gina," he said as he leaned his hands on the back of a chair.

"I'll try to be good, then," came a very feminine chuckle. "I presume you have Sean with you?"

"I'm here," I replied. "Nice to finally meet you."

"It's a pleasure to get a chance to work with you," she said. "Vasily has told me all about you."

I caught the grin from my friend. "The good *and* the bad, I'm sure."

"Totally," she chuckled. "We managed to squeeze in your testing this evening, so I wanted to update you on the lab results. I know the case system is back up and running, but frankly none of us thinks it will last. I figured you'd want to hear it directly from me anyway."

"I appreciate that," Vasily said looking up at me.

"I'll start with the mundane," she began. "Well, I guess that's not entirely accurate, for your first evidence envelope had an interesting mixture of fibers that took a bit to unravel. They appear to be from a garment of some type that was crafted with a nylon/polyester blend; a rather shocking color of red pigment was in there, too. Based on the condition of the fibers, I'm going to go out on a limb and say they were abraded off the original garment."

I nodded to Vasily. "Red? Interesting."

"It gets better," she continued. "The second envelope held a slightly better sample, with fabric from what we think was a swimsuit made of a spandex/polyester blend. It was also showing the same sort of abrasion as the first sample, which leads us to speculate that it might have been worn beneath the first garment and was damaged at the same time."

"Velcro," Vasily said thoughtfully. "Would Velcro damage fabric in the way you're seeing?"

There was a long pause from Gina. "Maybe," she said after a moment. "If the fabric was caught up in those little hooks as it was being opened or closed. What are you thinking?"

Vasily looked at me. "It's par for the course when you are a life-guard," he replied. "When I was working the beach, I used to wear briefs beneath the official board shorts I'd been issued since they didn't come with any sort of liner; it was, uh, far more comfortable than the alternative." Vas smiled slightly. "I lost more than a few briefs to inadvertent snags in the Velcro fly closure."

"I can run some other tests," Gina replied. "But sounds like you might be on to something."

I nodded at Vasily. "If you would, that could confirm our thinking," I said.

"Will do, should have it for you tomorrow. Now, on to the towel. As you probably saw, there was residue in quite a few places; we've taken samples of all of it and have quite the buffet of evidence. We have condom lubricant, sunscreen, and two distinct DNA samples from, shall we say, separate pools of bodily fluids."

"Condoms *and* semen," Vasily observed. "Something went wrong, do you suppose?" he asked. "A break?"

"Or an interruption," I mused. "Maybe our passionate couple was surprised at just the wrong moment."

"Either way," Gina said, "the semen samples were taken from several spots on the towel — possibly where something was wiped, would be my guess. But the bulk was in one spot, commingled with the other donor."

Vasily nodded. "The towel must have been beneath them," he said. "If they were in the cabana, it might have been a half-assed attempt to protect the expensive chaise lounge chairs there."

"That's my guess," Gina replied.

"Any hits on the DNA?" I asked.

"None," she answered. "Which only means this couple had never had a reason to be in the system."

"Which *also* means you've just ruled out Don Davies as being the sperm donor," Vasily added, smiling at me. "Or his brother. But you already knew it wasn't going to be either of them, didn't you?"

"I did," I nodded.

Vasily looked at me for a long moment. "You think we've met the actual sperm donor, don't you?" he asked, a half-smile on his lips.

"Maybe."

Gina groaned audibly. "Is he always like this, Vas?"

"Sometimes worse," he deadpanned. I rolled my eyes.

"Now I know where you got it from."

"I learned from the best," he laughed. "Thanks, Gina."

"My pleasure," she replied. "Like I said, I'll touch base tomorrow after we re-test that sample. Until then, have a pleasant evening, gentlemen."

"Same," Vas said as the line went dead. He turned toward me, hands on his waist and a look of exasperation on his face. It would have come across better had he not been standing there in his Speedos. "Out with it. Who's our donor?"

"I'm not sure," I replied honestly.

Vasily folded his arms against his chest. "But you have a hunch."

"Maybe," I smiled slightly. "Like everything else, I want to be cautious with the accusation until we get a bit more information."

"And where, exactly, are you planning on finding it?" he asked.

I smiled wider. "I think our interviews tomorrow are going to be *very* interesting."

Twenty

We didn't get a ton of sleep that night.

Partly it was due to the fact that my search warrant for the Davies brothers had finally come through; not long after we got off the phone with Gina, my iPhone pinged with an email from Caitlyn that she was forwarding everything we'd received to Vasily's case system. As the California end of the investigation had begun to heat up, I'd completely forgotten about my conversation with Judge Rayo less than three days earlier. Or was it four? Shaking my head as I'd re-read the message, I'd realized I was at the stage in every case where it began to feel like I was caught up in the cascade of a waterfall, simply going where the flow of evidence directed me.

The receipt of new data pretty much torpedoed the original plan of reviewing the case file prior to our interviews the following morning; after a hurried discussion about the pros and cons of trying to access said data over the underwhelming 5G hotspot Vasily had brought, we decided to make our apologies to Rosie and return to the condo and its fiberoptic gigabit connection. I was a bit sad to not have had a chance to take a dip in the pool before we left, but Vasily assured me we'd likely have the opportunity to visit with Rosie in the coming days.

We returned to the condo close to ten; while Vasily and I set up shop with our respective MacBooks along the breakfast counter and got logged into our various systems, Alejandro mixed up another pitcher of his unique margarita blend; after pouring out two healthy portions, he came around the counter and leaned in to kiss Vasily. Although it was brief, I could easily feel the sizzle between them.

Pulling away, Alex rubbed a bit at the dark smudges that had taken up residence beneath Vasily's eyes. "Don't stay up too late," he said softly. "You could use some rest."

Vasily smiled tiredly. "I'll try."

"Good," Alex replied before turning toward me. "Same goes for you," he added. "The two of you look like you've been mainlining caffeine. It's not a good look."

"The price of being an investigator," I replied.

"One of many," Alejandro replied, nodding slowly before turning back to Vas. "Speaking of prices, I'm going to shower and turn in."

He didn't have to say *alone*; I could see it in his eyes, and in the way Vasily reacted. I wondered if this was something of a sore spot for the two and filed it away for a later private conversation with my friend.

"My loss," Vasily smiled sadly as he slipped off the barstool and pulled Alejandro into a hug. "Good night."

"'Nite."

I watched as Alex disappeared into the master bedroom and closed the door behind him. Looking at Vasily, I could easily see he was torn between what he presumed his duty to the case was and wanting to follow his partner into the bedroom. When Vasily had reached out to me initially, he'd mentioned juggling multiple cases; looking back at the closed door, I started to suspect it had begun to put a significant strain on his personal life. That led to the other reason I didn't get any sleep that evening.

Reaching over, I put a hand on his shoulder. "Go. I've got this."

Vasily eyed me. "Sean—"

"I'm just going to quickly scan through what Caitlyn sent," I continued with a smile. "And then turn in myself. If there's anything significant, I'll let you know in the morning." I nodded toward the door. "You deserve a few hours of bliss."

"But what about going through the case files before the interviews?" he asked.

"That's pretty much what we did all day," I reminded him. "I think just this once we can skip the belt-and-suspenders part of our investigative technique. Besides," I smiled a bit wider, "you'll be more effective to me tomorrow if you are relaxed and well rested."

The slight shading to my friend's cheeks told me he understood the innuendo. "Are you sure?" he asked.

"The other night?" I asked in return. "When you were quote-unquote 'unable to fend off Alejandro' — how long had it been?"

Vasily's face flamed dark red, and he looked away quickly. "A... while..." he replied at length.

I turned him toward me. "This work will eat you alive," I said softly. "You and I know that better than most. I lost a relationship over it, and I damn well won't let you do the same thing." I nodded back at the door. "You've got a keeper in there. Now go to him. I'll see you in the morning."

Vasily stared at me for a moment, then unexpectedly smiled slightly. "Promise me you'll call Suzanne?"

"I will," I said.

"We are likely to be noisy," he warned me as he moved toward the bedroom.

"I used to live in a dorm," I reminded him, "one that was full of athletes with raging hormones. I'll survive."

Vasily chuckled softly as he entered the room and then shut the door behind him.

Eying my friend's untouched margarita, I slid back onto the barstool and began to pour through the financial records for both Don and Frank Davies. All of the usual suspects were there, from bank accounts to investments to tax records stretching back ten years; it wasn't until Vasily had left for California that I realized how much I had relied on him to dig though balance sheets, property tax records or the other hundreds of ways a life was recorded as it moved through our economic systems. I'd gotten pretty decent at it since his departure, but knew I would never attain his ability to read a spreadsheet and intuitively understand that a number looked wrong in some way.

By the time I realized it was close to three a.m., I had drained both margarita glasses and crafted a tidy list of transactions that I thought needed more follow-up. For a long moment, I considered seeing how much mix was left in the refrigerator, but realized I would need my own wits about me in the coming hours. Sighing, I shot off a quick email to Caitlyn with my questions, then closed up my laptop. As I shut off the lights in the kitchen and padded across the rug of the living room to my pullout bed, I realized I'd been so engrossed in the files I'd never heard anything from the master bedroom. I hoped that meant Vasily had gotten some rest — at least, more than appeared to be in my future.

The set of streetlights just outside the condo provided enough ambient light for me to kneel beside my duffel bag; rooting around in its depths, I came up with my final pair of clean boxer briefs and sighed. Considering I'd originally planned on spending just one night in Portland, I'd nonetheless taken a page from my days as a competitive swimmer on the national team and overpacked by a factor of three. You never knew as an athlete whether your flights would get changed or cancelled in some far-off land — or if you'd be summoned to join a relay at the last minute, extending your stay in a distant city by a few days. Still, as I sat back on my heels, I added the need to do a load or two of laundry to my burgeoning to-do list for the day.

I wasn't one to sleep in the nude save for when Suzanne shared my bed; smiling slightly, I realized that was actually just about every night now, other than the weekends she had to do her rotation at Maine Medical Center. Glancing at the master bedroom, I decided it would be wise to stay on the conservative end of the scale and stripped off the t-shirt that still had the faint odor of salt water on it from our surfing expedition before slipping between the sheets of the spare bed. Closing my eyes, I made a good attempt to try and catch some shuteye, but as often happens, my brain instead insisted on mulling over what I had found.

Sighing, I fluffed up my pillow a bit and turned to my side so I could watch the way the lights from the cars passing by on the street below moved across the glass of the sliding doors; squinting slightly, I was able to catch the shifting spectrum of spots as they danced along the silhouette of Space Mountain in the distance and tried not to think too hard about the fact I was still wearing my contact lenses. I sighed again, and decided it wasn't worth the effort to get back up and take them out, especially since we were likely off to swim practice in less than ninety minutes anyway. Flipping onto my back, I angled my head slightly against the pillow and gave in to my investigator's brain and its need to make sense of everything.

Staring at the ceiling, I realized I'd not been surprised that either Davies brother had been wealthy; what *had* shocked me a little was the disparity between Don and Frank. For whatever reason, I had expected that the radio personality would be the better off of the two, but from my cursory review, it appeared that the investment business had been very good to Frank. Don wasn't hurting, to be sure; the number of digits in his checking account balance alone looked close to the weekly Megabucks jackpot the Maine State Lottery offered, with far more sizable numbers in multiple savings accounts and certificates of deposit. The latter had surprised me, given how little interest the bank appeared to be paying on them, especially considering how the returns on his mutual funds were several magnitudes higher. I'd not looked over the taxes but presumed the reason he still had so much money on hand was likely attributable to a solid accountant capable of shielding him from the revenue service — legally, I hoped.

Don also appeared to own the two homes in Maine free and clear, and had a condo in Old Orchard in escrow, aligning nicely with what I'd discovered from the real estate agent in South Windham; Frank had a small condo in a suburb of Portland and, interestingly, owned a sizable amount of real estate in Florida, Texas and California through a separate entity he'd cleverly named Frankly Holdings, LLC. Glancing through the list had told me they were rental properties; some were multi-unit, but the vast majority were single-family homes, generally in places where people would either be vacationing or escaping cold weather. The rental income from the properties alone would have been enough for someone to live comfortably, but when combined with the bottom lines I'd seen on the profit-and-loss statements from his invest-ment business, it was clear Frank was exceptionally good at managing assets.

Thinking about the financials from Frank's business returned my thoughts to Don's checkbook. While he didn't appear to have much more than a courtesy balance on his credit cards, there were regular deductions of around $5,000 on the fifteenth each month. What little digging I'd been able to do hadn't turned up a fourth property or another car other than the one we'd found in Windeport, nor had I located some sort of investment he'd been making, through Frank or anyone else for that matter. There was little to go on with the bank notation on the transaction other than knowing it was a recurring elec-tronic funds transfer. It was one of the anomalies I had jotted down to run past Vasily.

Another anomaly that continued to bother me was Frank Davies deciding to take a long weekend in Windeport; with all the properties he owned, some in rather desirable destinations, spending time snow-bound in Downeast Maine felt more and more like it was what I'd initially assumed: some form of misdirection to give Don cover for his trip to California. I'd also found the gas station transactions on one of Frank's credit cards, backhandedly confirming both his identity and itinerary a few days before his untimely demise.

All of it was by design, I mused as I shifted the pillow beneath my head. *Until it wasn't. I'm certain now that Don was coming here to visit with someone before meeting his grandkids; my gut tells me it was one of the people associated with that attempted assault ten years ago. But* which *person was it?* I wondered as I gave up and pushed the sheets back to sit on the edge of the mattress. *I know at least one person he met with that he wasn't planning on, too.*

Picking up my phone from where I had it charging on the carpet, I did some mental calculations and decided I could risk calling Suzanne; despite knowing she'd be on duty all night and her open invitation for me to call her, I'd been loath to, fearful I might wake her should she manage to catch a quick nap in between patients. With the three-hour time difference, though, I presumed she was likely by now up for the day. Unplugging my iPhone, I quietly moved to the sliding glass door and gently slid it open; the cold air of the early morning was more refreshing than I expected but standing on the tile of the balcony in bare feet might not have been the wisest move. Tapping her icon, I waited for her to answer my FaceTime request. Her beautiful — albeit tired — face appeared before the second ring.

"Kitty," she smiled. "It must have been a long night for you to have not called."

I returned her smile. "I'll be honest, while it continues to be a late night here, I was worried about interrupting what little downtime you might have gotten overnight."

She sighed. "You must have been on my wavelength, then," she said. "It was far busier than I expected. I quite literally just returned from the Colonial; one of the landscapers cut himself badly while pruning those potted whatever-they-are in the atrium."

My eyes widened. "Why were you there? The EMTs—"

"They were *already* on a call," she explained. "Logging truck took out a moose about a mile from UEM; driver went into that same ditch where Vasily found that developer last summer."

"Shit," I breathed. "Busy night indeed."

"Yeah," she yawned. "I managed to stitch the wound closed on site; he'll need to see a specialist, of course, but shouldn't lose a digit at this point. And that was *after* three house calls."

"Wow."

"Yeah. And in just a few hours, I get to see a full slate of patients. I'm living the life," she chuckled before yawning again. "So, tell me what kept you up all night?"

"Research," I replied. "The warrants I requested before leaving Maine came through, so I've been chugging through the finer points of the lives Don and Frank Davies lived. That, and we managed to get some intriguing results back from the lab on a decade-old, attempted rape that seems to be at the center of this whole mess."

Suzanne's eyes widened. "There's a cold case connection?"

"Yes," I nodded. "One of the pool attendants alleged that Don assaulted her while he was attending a conference at that hotel, but I have somewhat reliable evidence that it wouldn't have been possible for him to have done it. Not unless he could have been in two places at once."

"Seems unlikely."

"That was my thought too," I smiled.

"Are you outside?" Suzanne asked. "That doesn't look like the living room in the condo."

"I'm on Vasily's balcony," I replied. "I didn't want to wake my host when I called you, though I have to admit, it's a bit colder than I expected."

"Not as cold as it is here," she chuckled. "Pipes are freezing all over the village."

"Then I'll quit complaining," I laughed before getting a thought. "Mind if I ask your opinion on something?"

"Of course not."

"How rare is it for a condom to fail during intercourse?"

Suzanne looked at me. "Sean, are you worried about the other night? I've already told you—"

"No," I hurriedly said, flushing slightly at the uncomfortable memory. It had been my fault entirely — I'd been so caught up in the moment, I'd rolled it on wrong and it had slipped off at the worst possible moment. Suzanne had repeatedly told me that she was taking her own precautions, but some level of male chivalry required me to continue to do my own part regardless. "I was thinking more in general. My sex ed teacher back in high school put the fear of God into us with respect to their proper usage, and repeatedly warned us that the slightest deviation could lead to a rip or a tear. And," I smiled slightly, "a new baby."

"Ah," she laughed. "Well, the tech isn't foolproof, of course, but you have to work pretty hard to damage them. I'm not up on my literature, but the last thing I read indicated that the primary reason for failure tends to, ah, be around inappropriate application, so to speak."

My face flamed again. "I'll have to make sure I get professional assistance next time."

"Sounds like a plan to me," she chuckled. "The second most common failure is the stupidest, in my opinion; that's when teeth are used to tear open the foil packet and wind up poking a hole in the latex in the process. Rounding out the top three is when the wrong size is used."

I nodded. "Not everyone is, uh, well endowed," I said. "I have to admit, I was surprised to see there were variations in shapes and sizes the first time I bought condoms."

"Most kids think they need the largest size imaginable," she continued. "Those slip right off, of course. Paradoxically, some men will purchase the smallest version in a misguided thought it will be more sensitive. If they don't split during intercourse, they are more likely to at least tear slightly. Either case is not good if you are trying to prevent, well, anything."

I smiled slyly. "How did you know what I was thinking as a kid?" I asked.

Suzanne shrugged. "Most teenage boys at least want to try on one when they find out about them," she said. "Regardless of whether they are sexually active at that point or not. I presume that was your situation."

"Something like that," I allowed. "Let's just say that having a parent as a pharmacist led to some uncomfortable moments when I turned sixteen."

"I suppose it could," she replied. "Why do you ask?"

"We found both condom lubricant *and* semen on evidence from the assault," I explained. "I'm casting about for a reasonable explanation for how that could have happened; some sort of issue with the condom was the first thing I thought of."

"Well," Suzanne said, "if things were getting hot and heavy, it's possible the condom came out and just never went on. But that doesn't jive with an assault, does it?"

"No," I replied. "It does, however, align with something more consensual; given the location *where* this might have taken place, I have a sense that there was a level of illicitness underpinning the act. Enough that my couple in question might have been interrupted unexpectedly."

"Hooking up where they weren't supposed to be," Suzanne said. "Sounds a bit like that equipment closet at the UEM pool."

I shook my head. "I can't believe even *you* have heard about it."

"I'm a doctor," she laughed. "I talk to everyone. I know everything."

"Don't I know it."

"Which reminds me... were you ever in the closet? So to speak?"

I felt my face begin to burn. Despite my professed ignorance to Vasily, Deidre and I may or may not have had one of our first encounters in that very space while we were both competing for the UEM team. "I... think I hear Vasily getting up," I managed to choke out. "I'd better run."

"All right," Suzanne laughed, but her eyes told me she'd seen the answer on my face. "Go get the bad guy."

"I think we might just do that," I replied. "Vas is going to be annoyed that I'm changing our plans slightly for today, but I think we will finally be getting to the bottom of everything."

"That sounds like good news," she said. "Now get inside before you turn completely blue."

"As you wish, Milady," I intoned.

"Good kitty," she chuckled as her image faded out.

Twenty-One

Vasily had been waiting for me when I returned to the living room; I hurriedly stuffed my last set of clean *everything* into my borrowed swim backpack before slipping my t-shirt back on. It took another moment to pack up our laptops before we were on our way to practice at the Rancho Linda High School. I could tell on the ride over Vasily was eager to hear what I had discovered in the files I had reviewed, but reluctant to ask; I shamelessly used it against him and instead leaned my head against the window of his Camaro, somehow managing to squeeze in a quick catnap on the drive to the pool. Practice itself was just as difficult as the morning before; when we regrouped back at his car, freshly showered and ready for the day, every muscle in my body felt like I'd done back-to-back events with no warm-down between them.

Starting up the Camaro, Vasily paused before putting it into gear. "Breakfast at the diner?" he asked, before casually adding: "We can talk about the files and plot out the day over coffee."

"I have a better idea," I said. "Didn't the Hilton have an all-day restaurant?"

Vasily looked at me. "Yes," he replied. "It's in the lobby, right across from the convention center entrance. I imagine it would be a bit more expensive than the diner, though."

"Don't worry," I smiled. "This one is on me."

"Which means you're going to back charge it to me once you do your itemized expenses for this trip," he chuckled as he reversed out of his spot and then pulled to the street.

"Something like that."

"Then I hope they have Eggs Benedict," he replied. "Seeing as though you're paying."

It didn't take long for us to reach the Hilton; a tad after six, we were pleasantly ensconced in a booth that had a nice view of the massive fountain in the main rotunda. As with most four-star hotels, breakfast appeared to be a massive buffet affair, with items ranging from pastries on one end to a chef making omelets to order at the other. I waited until we'd both made substantial inroads on the plates we'd filled from our first foray before starting the conversation.

"I have a few items I want you to double check for me, but on the whole, there wasn't anything extraordinary in the financials for either Frank or Don," I said before taking my first bite of fresh watermelon. The flavor exploded across my tongue, reminding me that it was insanely hard to get such exotic fruit in Maine at that time of year. "Don seems to have been paying someone about five grand a month, but I wasn't able to determine who it was — or, I suppose, what it might have been, for that matter."

"Could be a mortgage," Vasily said as he broke the yolk on his Eggs Benedict with an edge of his white toast. "Or a lease on something. Does he have a yacht?"

"Not that was part of the data we received," I replied. "We'll need to do a title search to rule it out, I suppose."

"Now that the system is back up, shouldn't take too long," he said, "but the look on your face tells me you think that would be a dead end."

"I do," I nodded. "I've been thinking about it all night, and honestly, I couldn't come up with an explanation until we did that final fifteen-hundred at the pool. What if he *was* paying someone?"

"Like a salary?" Vas asked. "Did he have personal staff at his place back in Maine?"

"No," I replied. "There's not enough metadata in what I received to know for sure, but it's a recurring electronic funds withdrawal. I think he's doing a bank-to-bank transfer."

Vasily put his fork down. "Blackmail?" he asked.

I nodded slowly. "That's what came to me at the pool. The transactions ran back as far as the date range I'd requested; I'm willing to bet they started around the time of the assault."

"We already ruled out Don was at the pool, remember? The DNA didn't match."

"I don't think he raped Isabella that day, no," I agreed. "That doesn't mean he didn't know her."

Vasily slowly nodded. "That's why he came here, isn't it? To this hotel?"

"I don't have all of it worked out yet," I replied, "but that is where I'm going."

"If he was paying her off electronically, why come in person?" Vas asked. "And what would she be blackmailing him over?"

"Both good questions," I replied. "I think Xander Vallejo might be able to provide a partial answer."

"The convention guy?" Vas asked. "He was less than helpful the first time we spoke to him."

"I'm not so sure about that," I countered. "There was at least one important nugget he let slip."

Vas arched an eyebrow. "Which was?"

I flagged down our waiter as I answered. "Do you want your coffee to go?" I asked Vasily as I handed the server my credit card.

"If it's going to be that kind of day, then most definitely," he sighed.

Though I could feel Vasily brimming with questions, he kept his own council as we made the walk from the lobby of the Hilton down to the convention center; unlike our visit the prior day, the space had been transformed completely, with clutches of business professionals milling about several portable carts that were loaded with coffee and pastries. The long marble registration desk now had a half-dozen people behind it, with lines of patrons patiently queuing to presumably check in for whatever conference was clearly now underway. We made the turn down the side hallway and had to navigate both people and tall signs denoting what breakout sessions were in which ballroom; while I didn't recognize the name of the particular group that had rented out the space, the vaguely technical sounding nature of some of the sessions made it seem like some sort of software development conference. Vasily had to drag me away from what looked like a vendor room when I spied the giant lit Apple logo just inside the door.

The clear glass door to the Convention Manager's office was propped open; as before, the space was quiet and empty when we entered. I thought it was at odds with the hubbub going on out on the convention floor, but then again, maybe it was a sign that all was running smoothly. My first sign that might not be the case came when Xander Vallejo dashed out of one office and into the other, panicked expression on his face as he nearly shouted into the cell phone smashed to his ear.

"—two hundred *pounds* of bananas? What the *fuck* am I going to do with that many—no, *fuck* no, we didn't order that for the luau! We've never served—"

I glanced to Vasily. "I'm not sure his day is starting as nicely as ours."

"That's my sense of it," Vasily deadpanned.

We watched as the young Convention Manager buzzed between the two offices for a few minutes, apparently trying to locate some paperwork to confirm (or deny) what the disputed order in question had been. On one of his passes, he noticed us and did the whole retail smile thing; we pretty much remained standing just in front of the reception desk, a gentle but obvious statement that we weren't going anywhere anytime soon. Ultimately, he wrapped up the call, but not before letting out a string of curses while simultaneously tossing his cell phone across the reception desk.

I waited a heartbeat before speaking. "Have we come at a bad time?" I asked, trying hard to remove the sarcasm from my voice.

"No," Xander replied. He ran a hand through his hair, tousling it out of the perfection we'd seen earlier. "No, not at all. What can I do for you, Chief Colbeth?"

"I just wanted to follow up on a few things we'd spoken about yesterday," I replied pleasantly.

"Okay," he said, eyes warily looking from me to Vasily and then back again.

"You mentioned you used to work here as a lifeguard," I said, noting as I did so that Vasily shot me a look.

"That's right," he replied cautiously. "I started when I was sixteen."

"And then transitioned into catering, if I recall correctly."

"Yes."

"When was that, exactly?"

"The summer after my first year at UNLV," he replied.

I pulled my iPhone from my pocket and brought up website I'd bookmarked last night. "You said you were at UNLV?" I asked.

"The swim team? Yes," he replied.

"You must have hated leaving the lifeguard duty, then," Vasily said, picking up on my thread. "Most swimmers we know tend to try and find a way to stay connected to the water, even in the off season."

Xander shrugged, but his face had flamed slightly. "Like I told you before, I was ready for a change. Catering gave me a leg up on everyone else when I went for the full-time job."

"I'm sure," I nodded, before looking at Vasily. "Did you swim with Isabella Houston?"

Xander's face faltered. "Isabella?" he replied. "Uh, you know, that name sounds familiar, but I don't think she was on the UNLV team."

"No," I agreed as I held out my iPhone. "But she *was* on the Gregory Preparatory High School team with you. Seems you won a state title in division three together."

The color drained out of his face. "Ah... yes, that's right," he said. "I'd forgotten."

"You won a state title," I said again, looking to Vasily. "That feels like a memorable experience to me."

"It was a long time ago now," Xander replied. "A lifetime ago."

"Had you also forgotten that the two of you worked together here at the Hilton?" Vasily asked. I kept my face passive, for while we'd not asked for employment records from the hotel as yet, the fact that Isabella had been listed as an employee of the Hilton in the file we'd dug up seemed sufficient.

"She might have," Xander allowed.

I slid my iPhone back into my pocket. "How long were the two of you a couple?"

Xander blanched. "I have no idea what you mean," he said. "I mean, yes, I knew her—"

"Xander," I said, teeing up my best — and only — shot. "We have the DNA from the assault."

I didn't think it was possible for the young man's face to get any whiter, but it did; he sagged into the chair behind the reception desk and put his hands into his face. "Shit," he said softly. "I always knew that morning would catch up to me."

"And so it has," Vasily said before looking at me. I nodded slightly. "We think we have a pretty good idea of what happened; Isabella wasn't raped by Don Davies — or anyone else for that matter — was she?"

"How much trouble am I in?" Xander asked through his fingers.

I leaned toward him. "That's to be determined," I said quietly. "However, we are both certain that whatever went on between you and Isabella led to the death of two men."

Xander's head snapped up. "What?"

"Tell us what happened that morning," I said.

The former swimmer looked between us, then slowly got up and came around the reception desk; taking the door stop out, he closed the door to the office and locked it, then collapsed onto one of the couches. "This stays between us?" he asked quietly.

"I doubt it very much," I replied. I leaned my back against the reception desk and folded my arms to my chest. "But if you don't want to tell us here, we can go down to the station—"

"No, no, fine," he sighed. "*Fine.*" Xander looked up at me. "Isabella was the one who told me about the lifeguard job when I was sixteen; because we were teammates, we worked pretty well together and wound up scheduled for the same shifts."

I nodded.

"We were already friends, but that last year before college, something... changed." He sighed again. "Our birthdays are just a few days apart in November; as it happened, we were working the late shift together during Thanksgiving that year, and I mentioned we'd both turned eighteen. She asked me how I was going to celebrate, and I laughingly told her I wanted to get... laid." Xander looked up. "I mean, I was *fucking* eighteen and a virgin. The definition of raging hormones."

Standing, he started to aimlessly wander the room. "To my surprise, she thought it was an excellent idea; before I understood entirely what was going on, Isabella had pulled me into one of the high-priced cabanas the hotel offered and pulled the flaps closed." His eyes took on a distant look. "I will never forget that first time she pulled my board shorts down; the briefs I'd worn beneath them had a knot that we couldn't get undone in the dark."

"Must have been frustrating," Vasily observed.

"It was," Xander replied with no trace of irony before looking at us. "But it worked out, actually. Neither of us had planned on—well, I guess what I'm trying to say is that we didn't have any protection," he said, though a faint trace of a smile appeared. "She managed to get me off anyway, though, sealing the promise we'd try again. A week later, she was on the pill and I had a supply of condoms in my first aid kit."

"Clever," I said under my breath.

Xander continued without hearing me. "From that point forward, whenever we closed, we snuck back into the same cabana. The thrill of doing her there, with the possible chance of discovery—it was intoxicating."

"Then your shifts changed," I observed.

Xander nodded. "Yeah. We flipped to opening the pool in February."

"And yet you continued," Vasily said. "Right up to the day of the alleged assault."

Xander nodded again. "When we opened, we kinda reversed the process and *started* in the cabana before getting the pool ready for guests; by that point, we were the two most senior lifeguards, working with minimal supervision."

"Which you used to your advantage," I said.

"Yeah. *That* morning is still seared into my memory. It wasn't just us that day; the luau was an all-hands affair, so the entire pool staff was on deck setting up. Even with all of that help, it took far longer than we thought it would; still, Isabella figured we had enough time before the pool opened, so we ducked into our usual cabana, using the larger-than-normal crowd to cover our departure." Twisting his hands, his eyes took on a faraway look again. "I'd looked up a new position on the internet, one that promised orgasms that would blow our minds, and had wanted to try it out; that morning, we were so horny from having to wait so long, we were kind of frantic once we were alone."

"Did it?" I asked.

"The position? *Fuck* yes, but Isabella twisted the wrong way just as we were—" he choked for a moment, flushing deeply at his frank discussion of what had transpired. Taking a deep breath, he continued. "Let's just say I realized too late that the condom had ripped, but before we could deal with *that*, we heard the PA announce the pool had opened for the event. Isabella had me slip through the rear of the cabana; I raced out and made it to my stand just a minute before the first swimmers hit the water."

"And Isabella?" I asked.

Xander frowned at the memory. "I'd assumed she'd made it to her stand — she had been assigned to the wading pool that morning, for some strange reason — but the angle from where I was working prevented me from seeing her." He looked at me. "Then the police arrived and all *hell* broke loose."

"In what way?" I asked.

Xander frowned deeper. "All I know is the cops arrived and the party pretty much stopped. They escorted Isabella off the deck — she looked pretty upset when she went by my stand — but I didn't start to freak out until they strung fucking crime scene tape around the cabana."

"Why?"

"Why *wouldn't* I freak out?" he countered. "Given what the two of us had been doing on company time — in a public place — I figured I was five minutes from becoming some sort of registered sex offender."

"You were both above the age of consent," Vasily observed. "Other than a possible charge of indecent exposure, I don't see what you had to worry about."

"I had a fucking *scholarship*," Xander breathed. "Just an arrest could have torched my chance of going to college."

"You thought she was going to accuse you of something?" I asked.

"It was hard not to," he replied. "Especially when I heard one of the cops say they were investigating an assault. And I wasn't wrong — I found out later Isabella accused some older dude of raping her."

"You said they escorted her off the grounds?" Vasily asked. "Was she alone?"

"Yeah," Xander replied. "I never saw the guy she accused."

"Did you find that odd?" I asked.

"Yeah," Xander nodded. "I mean, I was literally *with* her right up until the cops appeared. I have no idea how someone else would have been able to get into that cabana so quickly."

"Which is why you thought she might be pointing the finger at you," I mused.

"Exactly," he sighed, running another hand through his hair. The expensive styling had been completely obliterated, underscoring his discomfort. "Honestly, it kinda put the breaks on our relationship. I made sure I was never scheduled with her again, and as I said, transferred to Catering as soon as I could. In the end, it didn't matter; Isabella quit a few weeks later."

"You never talked to her again after that? Never had sex with her again?"

"Never."

"Even at school?"

"Even at school," Xander said firmly. "The whole thing scared the shit out of me. Enough that it was years before I had the courage to ask another girl out."

"You must have heard that the assault was never investigated," I said.

"Yeah. It was all anyone wanted to talk about. I was so relieved not to get caught up in it I put it aside and focused on getting to college; honestly, until the General Manager brought it up when I was hired, I'd more or less forgotten about it."

I looked at him. "You broke up with Isabella after the incident?"

Xander looked away. "Not exactly. She sorta told me it was over, and I had to admit I wasn't willing to fight it. I mean, how could I? I felt like she could haul out that assault allegation any time she wanted and I'd have no way to explain it. So I walked."

"After all of that passion, I'm surprised either of you could turn it off so quickly," Vasily said dryly.

"It was over," Xander replied. "And that was that."

"So it would seem," I said, looking at Vasily. He pulled out the DNA sampling kit from his backpack. "I'd like to ask you to give us a sample of your DNA, if you wouldn't mind."

"Why?" Xander asked, immediately on guard.

"We're looking into that assault from ten years ago," Vasily said as he stepped forward with the swab. "New evidence has been analyzed, including semen that was found at the scene. We'd like to rule you out."

Xander's eyes went wide. "Stuff was collected?" he asked quietly.

"Quite a bit, actually." I smiled slightly. "You don't have to provide a sample here, of course. We can get a warrant and bring you back to the station... but I'm not sure how your employer would feel about that."

"It was on the towel, wasn't it?" Xander asked. "Shit. We always had a towel down on the bed, just in case, but that morning I didn't have time to grab it before she pushed me out the back of the cabana." He looked up at me. "The condom broke," he added helplessly. "It's probably going to match me."

"Probably," Vasily nodded as he held out the swab.

Xander looked between us for a moment, then snatched the swab out of Vasily's hand. "Shit. Just, shit."

Twenty-Two

"A re you sure it was wise to cancel our appointment with the head of NRPA?" Vasily asked.

Sipping my third cup of coffee for the day — but first Starbucks, as if that made a difference — I nodded. "I think we know all we need to know about the convention and what happened there; the most we'd get now would be additional confirmation that Don Davies was the keynote speaker that year. I don't think it makes a difference to our case at this point."

We were once more in his Camaro, slowly moving along the 57 freeway toward Los Angeles; after swinging by the station to drop off the DNA swab from Xander, we'd hit the road once more with the hope of speaking directly with Isabella Houston. While we were well outside of the rush hour at that point, what passed for normal traffic in Southern California was snaking its way around a disabled vehicle that had effectively closed down the rightmost lane. Despite the fact that the 57 was five lanes, to me, it felt as though we were back in Maine on the two lane stretch of Interstate 95 with each car jockeying for prime position in an attempt to get around the stoppage. I was glad Vasily was behind the wheel, as just watching what was going on around us had begun to increase my blood pressure.

"Well, makes sense, I guess," he replied before glancing down to his iPhone.

Vasily had warned me it was likely close to an hour just getting to Los Angeles, and probably another twenty minutes or so to reach the address we had for Isabella Houston in Santa Monica; that was *before* we'd become ensnared in the slowdown. I didn't need his dramatic sigh to know our estimated arrival time had slipped further toward the afternoon; it was also a tiny indicator that even my born-and-bred native Californian had his limits when it came to slogging through clogged freeways.

Sipping my coffee, I smiled slightly. "Bet you miss Maine traffic now."

"Hardly," he replied. "I miss the fresh seafood, for sure, but the number of times I got stuck behind a slow-moving tourist on Route One? I'll take the California freeway life any day." He chuckled. "Just maybe not *this* day."

"Understandable," I laughed.

"What are you hoping we'll get from Isabella?" he asked.

"The truth," I replied. "I think we've heard bits and pieces of it from a number of sources. My sense is that much like the Hilton, she's at the center of everything that happened."

"You think she'll actually be home?" he asked. "At this time of day?"

"I do."

Vasily shook his head. "May fortune favor the bold."

A comfortable silence settled on us as we continued to slowly move past the disabled vehicle; at such a deliberate speed, I found myself taking in details that would ordinarily zip by in a blur. I'd never noticed the decorative tiling that had been applied to the top of the noise-dampening wall running alongside the freeway, nor the bas-relief sculptures that seemed to grace just about every overpass we went beneath. Though nice touches, neither could completely remove the far more noticeable aspects of disrepair, underscoring that aside from a few potholes patched here or there, the visibly crumbling freeway as a whole appeared to not have received much love in years. Weeds were everywhere, of course, sprouting up between the expansion joints of the concrete; they seemed only slightly less prevalent than the discarded fast-food wrappers and soda cans that littered both sides of the freeway.

Erase the cars and you'd have the desolate wasteland of any post-apocalyptic movie, wouldn't you? I thought. *Even the overcast sky seems to be playing a role in making everything seem far more depressing than it actually is.*

My eyes caught a recognizable foil packet caught in the grasp of a weed that swayed slightly as each car passed by; I put aside what it meant that someone had been using a condom on the freeway (it *was* California, after all), and turned to look at Vasily. "The teenage hijinks in the cabana have me thinking of UEM," I started as I shot a glance at him. "I... might need to make a confession."

I saw a smirk on my friend's face. "We all knew, Sean. You've never been very good about hiding *anything*. Not then, and certainly not now."

I felt my jaw drop. "*Everyone* knew?"

"Well," Vasily smiled wider. "Maybe Coach didn't."

I slowly banged the back of my head against the headrest of my seat. "I am *so* clueless sometimes."

"It's one of your most endearing qualities," Vasily laughed.

"If you say so," I sighed. "What do you think about Xander's relationship ending so abruptly?"

"I think he was full of shit," Vasily replied. "But at this point we're probably not going to have a way to confirm it. You?"

"I suspect there was a nugget of truth there," I said. "The look in his face spoke to remembered pain; young love often creates the worst heartbreaks. I do believe he wasn't the one to end it, but I don't think it happened right after the assault."

"Even if it *was* the final weeks of their senior year, I can't believe he'd be able to completely avoid his girlfriend – especially in high school."

"Yeah. Ex or otherwise."

The traffic began to clear up, allowing Vasily to return to something close to normal highway speeds; I found myself unusually drawn to the view outside the window as it shifted more and more toward the urban. Elements of the big city began to pop into view shortly after we merged onto Interstate 10; soon, the very visible skyscrapers that had come to dominate the skyline of the city appeared. Vasily's phone began spitting out staccato course corrections with an increasing cadence, making me feel compelled to stay silent; the last thing I wanted was to talk over some critical instruction, especially given how the highway now seemed to be ten lanes wide.

I'd looked at the map before we'd begun, so I knew that the interstate quite literally terminated at the ocean that was growing in size ahead of us. Isabella's address had put her into what Vasily had called a "somewhat" rarefied section of beachfront real estate; the satellite photo had made it appear it was possible to walk from her back patio directly onto the wide sandy beach of Santa Monica. We'd not had time to dig into Isabella's background at all, but as we exited I-10 and turned north on the Pacific Coast Highway, I began to suspect she was either a multimillionaire like Rosie Frankenhoffer or had married one. The homes perched along the edge of the beach all looked like they were well out of reach for anyone with a normal, middle-class income.

"I think that's it," Vasily said as we slowly passed a clutch of houses. "I don't see any parking, though. If you don't mind a walk, there's a lot just a bit further ahead that I've used when I've surfed here. We can grab a spot there and then take a leisurely stroll along the beach promenade."

"I'm up for it," I said.

Vasily switched into the next left-turn lane that appeared, then waited for a break in the traffic to pull into a rather full surface lot. Despite it being a weekday — and overcast, on top of that — I could see there were hundreds of people on the sand, and a number more out in the surf proper; the froth suggested that the onshore wind was favorable, something that was quickly confirmed when a gaggle of black neoprene-clad forms suddenly stood and worked their way across a crashing wave. Only one or two managed to ride the length of the curl successfully; the rest went into the water in every ungainly manner possible, resurfacing a moment later to resolutely paddle back out beyond the breakers for another try.

As we got out of the Camaro, I looked across to my friend. "Busy day."

"There tend to be few down days along the shore," he said. "Die hard surfers will come for the waves regardless of the weather. This part of the shoreline also creates some of the better conditions than on the other side of the pier; it's one of the more desirable places to hang out."

"It's a bit of a drive from Anaheim," I observed. "But you sound like you know the spot well."

Vasily smiled. "Any surfer worth their salt knows the prime real estate along the coast. I've surfed here a few times over the years, but I don't come up very often; I prefer the beaches in the OC instead."

"Snob," I chuckled.

"I own it," he laughed. "Come on, the path is over this way."

I followed Vasily across the lot and past what looked like a small café complex, then turned in a southerly direction to follow a paved walking path that acted as a de facto demarcation between the sand of the beach and the homes facing it. It took me a minute to realize that most of the houses had been oriented such that the *front* was toward the ocean; given how tiny the driveways we'd seen from the PCH were, I wondered if visitors to any of the beach homes along this stretch were forced to do as we had and park in the public lot. The houses themselves were an eclectic microcosm of California itself, with designs as varied as the decades from which they had been constructed. Their only commonality — if you could call it that — was the fact that they managed to somehow fill every square inch of the lot they occupied; the tiny alleyways between them were hardly big enough for a feral cat to use, let alone a human.

Scuffing away some of the windblown sand on the walking path revealed markings indicating walkers were to keep to one side; it wasn't hard to picture how clogged it was likely to be with people on rollerblades, cyclists and pedestrians on a typically sunny Southern Californian weekend. The open-air fitness pavilion we passed was something of a surprise; the sand volleyball courts, not so much. As the numbers on the various houses began to move into the range of the particular one I was searching for, I realized the sounds of the crashing surf did an admirable job of eliminating any traffic noise from the Pacific Coast Highway. Had we not actually just been on it, I could have easily assumed we were miles away from civilization.

A grand, three-story modern glass-and-steel structure turned out to be our destination, protected by a picturesque picket fence about five feet in height. Given the size of the lot — and how much of it was taken up by the home — the small yard just inside the fence was barely large enough to hold three potted dwarf date palms and the handful of flagstone pavers leading to the main door. Two bikes were leaning against the rear of the house; one was a typical adult size, while the other more appropriate to a child. Overhanging the entrance and the yard was a porch just slightly larger than the one Vasily had at his condo, rimmed with glass half-walls designed, presumably, to allow unobstructed ocean views while still providing some measure of safety. The architectural signature of the house appeared to be a slightly smaller version of the porch attached to the third story, accessible via a tightly twisted spiral staircase artfully connecting both to the ground level. Save for the exposed beams holding everything together, the entire structure came off like one giant window looking out across the ocean.

Set into the picket fence was a quaint-looking gate with a small flower box, filled to overflowing with artificial petunias and ivy; a small mailbox had been mounted just above a modern smart doorbell similar to the model that had helped me crack a murder back in Windeport almost two years earlier. I glanced at Vasily before pressing the button; while I waited for a response, my eyes happened to notice a small placard that had been tastefully attached below the street number for the house.

Managed by Frankly Holdings, LLC. Rental Inquiries: (207) 555-9011

And just like that, another piece of the puzzle clicked into place. "Hot damn," I said softly.

Vasily moved to my side. "What?"

I pointed to the sign.

His eyes narrowed. "Not a coincidence," Vas said.

"Hardly," I nodded.

Above us, I heard a door slide open on the patio and looked up. A striking woman wearing a bikini that subtly enhanced her beauty was leaning over the glass railing. Large sunglasses from Hollywood's golden age were nestled against her dark hair, helping somewhat to hold the mass away from her face. "Can I help you, gentlemen?"

"Isabella Houston?" Vasily asked.

"Who's asking?"

"I'm Deputy Chief Vasily Korsokovach, Rancho Linda Police Department. This is my colleague, Sean Colbeth. Do you have a few moments to talk?"

"About what?"

"It might be better if we were to come in," I said. "Would you mind?"

Isabella looked at us for a long moment, then nodded. "One sec."

She disappeared back into the house, then reappeared when she opened the door on the first floor. Somewhere between the second and first floors, she'd found some sort of wrap that she'd tied around her waist, and a pair of flip-flops that made rubbery squeaks as she came across the flagstone to the gate. Unlatching the gate, she pulled it open and stood to the side to allow us entrance. Carefully locking it up behind us, she put out a hand toward the house. "This way."

We followed her through the door and into a small galley kitchen, then immediately up a steep stairway to a wider living room space. One of those plastic commercial doll houses in vibrant pink had been pushed up against the rear wall, with scale debris surrounding it; clearly, someone was in the middle of a bout of interior decorating, right down to tiny rolls of wallpaper. In the living room proper, several couches had been arranged facing the massive windows looking at the beach, with a separate chaise lounge just off to the corner. A towel was down on the chaise, rumpled slightly from Isabella having gotten up to see who was at the door; a fistful of tabloid magazines were splayed on the ground beside the chair, some open to full-page photos of celebrities I didn't recognize. A tall glass containing a deep green liquid was perched on a side table between one couch and the chaise; Isabella went to pick it up before settling back down on the lounge.

"What can I do for you?" she asked.

I tried not to think about how odd it was for her to be attired in a bikini; the weather certainly wasn't conducive to sunbathing, and there were no obvious tanning lights in the room we were sitting in. I wondered if living on the beach significantly altered your perception of what passed for comfortable loungewear. As Isabella sipped her drink, I could see her nail polish had been expertly applied — to both her fingers *and* toes.

"Thank you for letting us drop by unannounced," I said, glancing at Vas. "Look, there's no easy way to say this. We're working a case that connects to the assault you suffered ten years ago at the Hilton Orange County."

Isabella's face shifted slightly. "You are?"

"Yes," I nodded. "At the risk of opening old wounds, we'd like to ask you a few questions."

"I never pressed charges," Isabella said. "I'm not sure there's much to talk about."

Interesting, I thought. *Most victims wouldn't lead with that.*

"We understand that," Vasily said. I noticed he had his notebook out already. "At this point, we're pretty much just trying to tie up some loose ends. Even though – as you say – no charges were filed, there was evidence collected at the scene and some preliminary work done by our officers."

"Is that standard practice?" she asked. "Reviewing a case that's not a case?"

I smiled warmly. "Not really, no, but as we said, there might a connection to a current case we're working."

"How could there be?" Isabella asked. "It was ten years ago."

"True," I agreed before looking at Vasily. "Honestly, there are times when our job comes down to asking questions that either connect the dots or erase them completely. This could be one of them, but I hope you can humor us."

"All right," she said after a long, pensive moment.

"You were a lifeguard at the Hilton Orange County?" I asked.

"Yes," she nodded. "It was a part-time job I worked while I was in high school."

"You didn't continue it during college?" Vasily asked. "During breaks?"

"No," she replied. "I didn't."

"Why not?" I asked.

"I didn't go to college," she replied simply.

That answer, combined with the one ahead of it, threw me completely; from the way Xander had described Isabella, I had made the cardinal sin of assuming she, too, had scored a swimming scholarship. Quickly regrouping, I decided to follow up on her answer. "Really?" I asked. "Weren't you a swimmer at Gregory Prep?"

"I was," she nodded.

I tried to recall what I'd read on their website; despite the coffee, my thoughts were more sluggish than normal. "My impression was that most student-athletes who attended that school went on to full-rides in their respective sport."

"The best of the best went to Gregory," she said. "That tends to make it hard for anyone slightly *less* than the best to make an impression on recruiters."

Something tickled at the back of my brain; the longer we sat there with Isabella, the more I had the sense that I'd seen her before — despite the rational part of my brain reminding me this was our first visit. "Ah. My apologies."

Isabella shrugged. "Life interrupted, anyway," she smiled.

I'll bet, I thought as I looked around at the room we were in. "You appear to have been successful in whatever endeavor you went into," I observed. "This home can't have been cheap."

For the first time since we arrived, she smiled. "It's a rental," she confirmed. "There's no way I could afford a property this grand or this close to the beach."

"Who could?" I smiled. The only way I'd managed to snap up my bungalow along the seashore back in Windeport had been the fact I was the only person willing to live in a place where someone had been murdered. As much as I wanted to dig deeper into how she was able to afford even the *rent* on her place, I set it aside for the moment. "Do you know a man named Don Davies?" I asked.

"Yeah," she nodded. "That's the guy who assaulted me."

"At the Hilton?" Vasily added.

"Yeah," she nodded again. "He was one of the attendees for that massive conference that was there every year."

"We only know what was in the file," I said. "Would you be willing to walk us through what happened to you that day? It would help us fill in the blanks."

She looked over her shoulder and out one of the large windows. "I've tried to block it," she said softly before turning back toward us. "I'm sure you can understand."

I looked at Vasily, intending on having him continue from that point; we'd tossed around a few scenarios on how the questioning would go, and assumed when we got to the assault Isabella might be uncomfortable discussing aspects of it. My friend had volunteered to lean on his own experience as a way to gain her trust, but as I started to nod at him to begin, another puzzle piece snapped into place and I instead held my hand to him.

My eyes went back to Isabella, though I saw not the woman in front of us; instead, in my mind's eye, I recalled the small, framed photo that had been on Don Davies desk at his home in South Windham. "How long have you known Mr. Davies?" I asked.

Isabella blinked. "I... I hadn't met him before that morning in the cabana," she answered carefully.

"Allow me to ask it slightly differently," I continued. "Did you stay in touch with Mr. Davies *after* you decided not to press charges?"

"No," she replied quickly. "Why would I?"

"That's an excellent question," I replied. "I was hoping you'd be able to tell me why he had a framed photo of you on his desk."

"I wouldn't know," Isabella said just a bit too quickly.

"Really?" I asked, not all that amazed that she'd not replied with something closer to shock. Most people would be a little uptight that someone they didn't know had something so personal close at hand.

Most *innocent* people.

Deciding to change the direction of the conversation a bit, I nodded toward the dollhouse. "That looks like quite the project."

"It is," Isabella replied. "My daughter decided the bedrooms needed new wallpaper. We've spent more than a week on it so far."

"I wasn't aware you *could* wallpaper a dollhouse," I smiled. "Do you have to use scale tools to put it up?"

"Probably," she replied. "But I don't have the patience for that level of purity."

"I don't blame you. How old is your child?"

"She turns ten in October."

"Is she a swimmer, too?" Vasily asked.

"You'd think she would be," Isabella laughed. "I can't even get her to surf."

Vas groaned. "Sounds like a parent's worst nightmare."

Isabella shrugged. "I've gotten past it. She has other interests."

That sense I always had when I knew I was tugging the right thread in a case almost became overwhelming. Certain I was on to something, though, I nonetheless found myself torn on the best way to proceed; while Isabella had relaxed slightly as our conversation had turned away from the alleged assault a decade ago, I had done the job long enough to know that the *wrong* approach would likely land us on the other side of an interview table at the station, staring down Isabella and her lawyer.

And yet...

I stood up and walked to the massive glass sliding door to the patio; the surf had picked up somewhat, with long, winding waves crashing along the shoreline at regular intervals. The darkening sky portended worse weather to come, or conversely, better waves. Going with my gut, I watched my reflection in the mirror as I asked: "Isabella, have you told Xander Vallejo he's the father of your daughter?"

The crashing of the glass against the tile of the living room had me spinning on my heel; Isabella's face had gone white, and her eyes, wide. She swallowed a few times before finally managing to speak. "I... I don't know what you mean."

"I think you do," I replied softly. "And I'm willing to bet you've never told him."

Isabella looked away.

"That evidence we mentioned earlier?" Vasily said. "It included a towel stained with bodily fluids, including semen."

"A towel we think you and Xander used while you were in the cabana that morning," I added. "Xander consented to us taking a DNA sample, and we're running it now."

"Based on what Xander told us, we have little doubt he'll match. I'm not great at math, but if your daughter is as old as you claim her to be..." Vasily let his conclusion hang in the air.

Watching Isabella carefully, I decided to unspool more of my thread. "You've never told him."

Isabella continued to stare out of the balcony windows. "No," she said after a long moment.

"Why?"

She slipped off the chaise lounge and carefully stepped around the broken glass and spreading puddle of green ooze; kneeling in front of the dollhouse, Isabella began to methodically start putting the small pieces of furniture that had been scattered around in their appointed locations. Feeling like she was deliberating whether to tell us more, I let the silence linger, knowing it would ultimately become oppressive. It was a technique I had long used when interviewing suspects; sooner or later, the desire to clear the air would become too much to ignore.

As she placed a tiny rocking chair inside the house, she sighed deeply. "I was eighteen," she said softly. "I was on the pill and didn't think it was possible to get pregnant."

"No form of birth control is one hundred percent," I said.

"I found that out the hard way," she replied as she stood up and walked back to stand beside me at the sliding door. "In retrospect, I *should* have been worried given how Xander's condom split. I suppose it was a sign, one that I ignored."

"When did you find out?"

"Too late to change our trajectories in life," she smiled wryly.

"Xander freaked out after what happened on deck; we split up almost immediately and avoided each other until graduation."

"Your classmates must have noticed something," Vasily said. "Xander couldn't have been *that* blind."

"They would have, had I stayed in school," she sighed. "The assault gave me cover in more ways than one; my family used it as the excuse for me to drop out so I could 'recover' from the trauma."

"Xander has no idea of his responsibility to you," Vasily observed.

"It's as much my fault as his," Isabella replied. "He owes me nothing. I've managed to get by on my own."

"I can see that," I said, waving a hand at the room we were in. "This seems a bit grand, though, even if you are getting a great deal on the rent. Is your family supporting you, then?"

"Not entirely. My grandmother bequeathed me some investments when she passed away. It's allowed us to live comfortably."

I nodded. "Your family assumes Don Davies raped you."

She nodded.

"Why'd you accuse him in the first place?" I asked. "Our evidence indicates he would have been incapable of being on the pool deck when you said he'd raped you."

Isabella shrugged. "He was the keynote speaker," she replied. "I'd seen his name on the displays in the lobby." Her eyes went a bit soft. "I wanted to protect Xander and, frankly, I panicked when our supervisor caught me in the cabana trying to pull my suit back on. Don's name was the first one I could think of."

"That's insane."

"It was," she nodded. "I never expected it to go as far as it did. I figured the hotel would quietly deal with it like we always did when the heavy hitters misbehaved, but for some reason they called the cops." Isabella began to twist the shift in her hands. "The best I could do was decline to press charges."

"You've never told your family your daughter is not his, have you?" I asked.

Isabella blanched. "I've never revealed the truth to anyone, no," she said. "They took the assault pretty seriously; especially my older brother. He was *pissed* that I wouldn't go forward with a criminal complaint, but I just couldn't do that to Don."

I felt myself getting a little angry at how long she had maintained the fiction. "If you *did*, the money would quit coming, wouldn't it?"

She nodded.

"But not all of it," Vasily said, looking at me.

Isabella looked at him. "I'm not sure what you mean."

"We have Don Davies' finances," I said softly. "We know about the payments."

She looked out the window again.

"The part I'm having trouble with is that he would consent to paying you five grand a month *after* you accused him of assault. He didn't rape you, did he?" Vasily asked.

"No."

"And he could have requested a simple paternity test to confirm the child wasn't his."

She nodded. "Don would never ask for that. He's the most honorable, gentle soul I know." Isabella looked between us. "In many ways, he's become a second grandfather to me."

"How did the payments begin?"

Isabella twisted the wrap in her hands. "It was a chance conversation at the Hilton's pool about a month after the convention," she said. "I was working the late afternoon shift — Xander and I had intentionally begun working opposite shifts to avoid each other at that point — and Don was wandering around the edge of the pool with one of those umbrella drinks. He looked so distraught that despite what had happened between us a few weeks earlier, I went to see what was wrong."

I felt myself nodding, another piece of the puzzle clicking home. "Gennifer's husband had died."

"Yes," she replied. "He'd booked a few months at the hotel to help her get through the worst of it, so I saw quite a bit of him." Isabella smiled at a memory. "I got to know him pretty well. Enough that he came to one of my last swim meets."

I nodded; the framed photo explained. "When did he realize you were pregnant?"

Isabella smiled a bit sadly. "The week I shifted from the bikini life-guard outfit to a more traditional swimsuit," she replied. "I'd begun to show and wanted to try and hide it a bit longer."

"Was that when you dropped out of school?"

"It wasn't long after," she said. "Don figured out pretty quickly what had *actually* happened in the cabana; he also understood how my family would react. Before I knew what was going on, he'd arranged everything." She looked around the beach house. "His brother made this property available to Don, so after I had Nathalie, I moved in here. The rent is covered, and the monthly stipend allows me to be a mom without having to work."

"Nice arrangement," Vasily said.

"Yeah."

"So why is Don Davies dead?" I asked.

"Dead?" Isabella's eyes went wide. "He can't be! I just talked to him a few days ago. Don's staying at the Hilton."

"He's *quite* dead," I assured her. "And your brother seems to be the person most likely to have killed him. Tell me, Isabella, just how angry *was* Daniel over your rape?"

What little color had been left in her face drained away. "My god. He always said he'd find a way to make Don pay. I... I've told him repeatedly I was over it, that it was behind me; I thought he had accepted it."

"We don't think he did," Vasily said. "And from what you've just told us, he appears to have had plenty of motive, however false the accusations might have been."

Isabella put a hand to her mouth. "Don came out early to see us," she whispered. "He loves my daughter and treats her like family."

"I'm sure he did," I replied. "Did Daniel know he was here?"

"Oh my *god*," she whispered as her eyes darted to the ceiling of the living room. "That's why he wanted to stay here..."

Twenty-Three

S *hit.*
Vasily already had his Glock in one hand, and his iPhone in the other; as he crouched beside the couch and called for backup from the local law enforcement, I reached for my own sidearm and moved quickly to Isabella. "Is he upstairs?" I asked softly.

"Yes," she whispered.

"Is your daughter at school?"

Isabella nodded. "She won't be back until three."

I glanced at Vasily. "How far out?"

"Five minutes," he replied as he slid his iPhone back into a pocket.

"What's upstairs?" I asked Isabella.

"Master bedroom and bath," she replied in hushed tones. "Some storage under the eaves."

"And this floor?"

"One small bedroom, a bath, and this space. Kitchen and laundry are below, plus the garage."

Eyeing the spiral staircase out on the balcony, I realized there were only two ways out of the level above us; that presented a conundrum, though, for we needed to get Isabella to safety. Having either of us take the time to escort her out of the house would leave a possible escape path open. Sorting through the best of the worst possible options, I pulled Isabella close to me.

"Listen to me very carefully," I whispered as I watched Vasily take up position at the edge of the interior staircase that led upward. "I want you to go downstairs and lock yourself in the laundry room. Stay there until one of us comes for you. Can you do that for me?"

Isabella nodded.

"Go," I urged.

Taking off her flip-flops, she quickly dashed past Vasily and disappeared down the steps. Turning toward the sliding glass door, I flipped the lock open as quietly as I could and gently began to slide the door open; a rush of salty air blew in immediately. Turning, I went down into a crouch and backed through the door sideways, my gun trained on the spiral staircase; once I reached the base, I nodded to Vasily and watched him creep up a step, then another. I waited until he was no longer visible before I started up the metal staircase, cringing slightly at how it creaked and groaned under my weight. Pausing just low enough to keep my head below the level of the deck above, I took a deep breath and passionately sent up a prayer that Vasily was on the same page.

"Daniel Houston! Come out with your hands—"

A staccato burst of gunfire was enough of a warning for me to throw my hands protectively over my head a fraction of a second before the glass half-wall of the porch above me shattered, showering me with shards sharp enough to easily slice and dice exposed skin. A thousand tiny pinpricks made themselves known along my arms, and I could feel a sharp sting on the cheek below my left eye. The sudden burst of pain forced a grimace; wearing a short-sleeve polo had clearly been a mistake. Another round sailed over me as I crouched against the stairs, followed by a third; when the pause extended for more than a few heartbeats, I crept upward again, my shoes crunching on broken glass as I moved. The fourth round had me pulling back so quickly I stumbled against the treads and unceremoniously fell onto the steps, driving shards through the thin fabric of my khakis.

Trying to ignore the pain, I was well aware that our suspect was a former police officer, reminding me most of our standard tactics would be utterly useless. Given the level of anger we had seen in the murders of the Davies brothers, I similarly suspected that simply trying to *talk* him out of the house wouldn't get us very far, either. Glancing below me, I could see a small crowd of onlookers had gathered, attracted to the noise of gunfire; more than a few had their smartphones out, documenting what was taking place in real time.

Lovely.

"Houston!" I called out again. "There's nowhere to go! We just want to talk!"

Another fusillade of bullets burst from the space above me; given their trajectory, I realized he was essentially laying down fire to prevent me from getting to the next level. That also told me he was probably trying to keep an eye on *both* staircases; closing my eyes, I tried to visualize the floorplan of the home and figured there was only one angle in the room that would allow for that.

If I can draw his attention, I thought, *Vasily will have a chance to get to him.*

Looking at what was left of the patio above me, I groaned inwardly when I realized far more than my pants would soon have holes. Steeling myself, I re-gripped my gun, took a deep breath, and then bolted up the remaining steps to the porch. As I exited the stairs, I went into a baseball slide toward the far side of the porch while twisting in the direction I thought Daniel would be in; as the shards of glass shredded what was left of my khakis and began to do a number on my thigh, I was rewarded by seeing a figure crouched against a wall of the bedroom. It appeared his first shots had taken out the glass of the slider, allowing the curtain to flap wildly in the sea breeze. Flipping to my knees, I squeezed off a shot aimed for a point just above his left shoulder and was surprised at the sudden recoil from my gun; I was thrown back against the lone remaining glass half-wall protecting the porch, hard enough that the wind was knocked out of me.

Sagging to the tile of the porch, I felt the unwelcome sensation of something warm trickling down my arm; it took a moment for me to realize my gun was no longer in my hand. Instinct took over and I dragged myself behind yet another lounge chair, which I tipped over in front of me. It wasn't likely to provide a whole heck of a lot of protection, but at the very least it would temporarily shield me from view.

Crammed between the chair and the remaining glass half-wall facing the ocean, I felt for the wound I knew was on my bicep; a gentle probe by my index finger confirmed I'd been shot, with the warm stickiness of the blood warning me it was serious.

Fuck. Suzanne is going to kill me...

Figuring I'd rather it be her than Daniel, I flexed my hand enough to know I'd be able to use my gun, then quickly scanned the tile of the porch for my weapon. The Glock was sitting a few feet from me, just beyond the relative protection of the upended lounge chair; the barrel had come to rest a few inches over the edge of the porch. While it didn't appear to be in danger of going over, it also seemed plausible that my lunge for it could put it beyond reach for good. That was, of course, if Daniel didn't nail me before I got to it.

The wound at my bicep began to throb, and I pressed my hand against it, trying hard to ignore the blood that managed to flow around it. I didn't think a major artery had been hit given I was still relatively alert but harbored no illusions that I was likely to slip into shock before I realized what was happening. I figured I had two moves at most and sent up another prayer to whatever gods looked out for police officers that Vasily was where I needed him to be.

Taking a deep breath, I plunged ahead. "Daniel! I know you killed both Don and Frank Davies — I've got the evidence and it's pretty solid. Don't make it worse by killing a member of law enforcement!"

There was no response from inside the room, but I thought it was positive he'd not tried to take me out as I spoke. I carefully flipped around to creep down to the edge of the lounge chair and nearly yelped at the pain the movement produced; gritting my teeth, I pulled myself toward my gun.

"You want to know what is worse?" I called out, risking a quick look over the chair. Daniel was still crouched in the bedroom, a semi-automatic gun of some type pointed directly at me. I ducked back behind the chair. "You killed the wrong person! Davies wasn't the father. Davies didn't rape your sister!"

A bullet sailed over my head. "Stay where you are," Houston called out, "and don't try to stop me as I leave, or you will regret it."

"Where are you going to run?" I called back, sliding closer to my gun. "We know who you are. You won't be able to leave the country."

"I'm less than two hours from Mexico," Houston called back, his voice growing louder as he moved toward the stairs. "Or maybe I have a boat in the marina down the street. I've had time to plan this, detective. You won't be able to find me."

The edge of the chair was just in front of my face; as I glanced across to my gun, I heard Houston step on some glass as he moved through the destroyed sliding doors. "You won't make it that far," I said, unintentionally accentuating the noise of approaching sirens. "We've got the angles covered."

"I doubt that," Houston said quietly.

I looked up and into the cold eyes of a murderer, his gun pointed directly at me. It was odd that in that moment before I was to die, my only thought was Houston's DMV photo had done a damn good job capturing his very essence. He'd carefully grown a full beard in an attempt to make visual identification more difficult, but it couldn't hide the pure malice beneath it. I took a breath and lunged for my gun.

The shot rang out just as I grabbed my Glock and twisted it toward Houston; I originally assumed the reason I didn't feel the bullet meant I had lost a critical amount of blood, but immediately corrected that assessment when the second bullet burst out of Houston's chest, spraying me with blood as it sailed over me. Houston staggered toward me just as a third bullet hit him center mass, propelling him forward and through the gap of the missing glass-half wall behind me. A sickeningly sodden *thump* from below a moment later confirmed that Houston would never make good on his escape – at least, not in the way he'd originally intended.

Whatever last vestiges of strength the adrenaline had been providing to me quickly faded, and I slumped back to the cold tile; it was hard to fight the overwhelming desire to close my eyes and just drift away, but the sound of footsteps crunching across the shattered glass caught my attention. Looking up, I watched as Vasily dropped to his knees at my side, his eyes quickly roving over me. From the concerned frown on his face, it wasn't hard to deduce I was in worse shape than I thought.

"Jesus, Sean," he breathed as he ripped off his polo in a smooth motion. "Jesus *fucking* Christ."

"Nice shot," I managed to smile as he quickly tore his shirt in half, then tightly wrapped it around the wound on my upper arm before tying the ends off. "Who taught you how to shoot like that?"

Tearing another section from his polo, he kept his eyes on his work as he lifted my thigh; a shard of glass a few inches tall was protruding through what was left of my pants. I thought it was funny I'd not seen it earlier and wondered briefly why it didn't hurt more.

Wrapping the torn shirt around his hand, he looked at me. "This will hurt."

"I can't feel anything at the moment," I replied, my eyes feeling leaden. "Tug away."

In a quick movement, he yanked out the glass and tossed it away; I watched with detached amazement as blood started to bubble through the wound. Unwrapping the shirt from his hand, he pressed it against the wound hard enough that I actually gasped. Keeping pressure on the wound with one hand, he managed to somehow get his belt off with the other; in what felt like super slow motion, he slid it under my leg and then over the now soaked shirt, then cinched it tight enough to elicit another gasp.

The world faded for a moment before I saw Vasily in my face again. "Stay with me, dammit," he practically yelled. "God-*fucking*-dammit! Stay with me...!"

I smiled and tried to tell him I had no intention of leaving, but my body seemed to have other plans. Closing my eyes, I finally gave myself over to the peace of oblivion.

Twenty-Four

What felt like just a moment later, my eyes fluttered open to reveal a bright, but blurry world.

Blinking a few times didn't clear up matters much, nor did it alleviate the fuzziness around the edges of my thoughts. It took a long, long moment for me realize my contact lenses had been removed, and even *longer* to begin to consider how that might've happened without my knowledge or consent. Some tiny part of my brain seemed to understand that my inability to think straight was the result of having been sedated, but that led to other questions I couldn't seem to answer, the most important one being *why* I'd been put under. Closing my eyes, I tried to use my other senses to scope out the world around me.

It felt like I was lying on a bed, with my head slightly elevated; between that and the gentle beeping coming from behind me that appeared to be in synch with my heartbeat, I suspected I was in a hospital. The tug of adhesive tape across the back of my left hand as I flexed it, and the cool touch of plastic just above it told me I had an IV inserted; shifting slightly, I realized the other unpleasant sensation was a catheter pushed way, *way* deeper than I thought was physically possible. My right arm appeared to be in some sort of sling that had been cinched tightly to my chest, holding it in place. I started to wonder *why* before remembering I'd been shot; flexing my fingers, it was reassuring to know that my hand still worked.

My mouth felt like cotton, but at the same time, I was suddenly insanely thirsty. I'd never been a patient in a hospital myself, but knew from my volunteering with Suzanne that a call button of some sort should be close to my hand. Re-opening my eyes, I started to squint around my left hand for the device in question when I realized I could see the rough outline of a figure curled up in a chair next to the bed. While the finer details were hard to make out, the mountain of dark curls was very familiar.

Swallowing hard, I managed to rasp out one word: "Alex?"

The figure started and immediately came to my side, close enough I could see Vasily's boyfriend clearly. "Sean? You're awake!" he said as he reached down to squeeze my hand. "Welcome back."

"How long...?" I croaked.

"A while," he smiled gently. "Vasily had to go back to the station to close out the case, but he's been by your side since they brought you in."

"Where...?"

"You're at UCLA Medical. It was the closest trauma center to the firefight. How are you feeling?"

"Woozy," I answered. "And... thirsty."

"Give me a minute," he said before disappearing. A moment later, he returned, accompanied by another figure in blue scrubs.

"I'm Betty," she said as she slid a table over me and then placed a small cup in front of my chest. "You've been asleep for a while, so sip on this very slowly. Are you hungry?"

I shook my head as I pulled the cup toward me.

"Okay. That might change in a bit. I'm going to let the doctor know you're awake," she said before disappearing.

Getting the straw to my lips turned out to be harder than I expected; Alex wound up gently lifting the cup for me. The cool water tasted amazing, but that likely had more to do with just how thirsty I was. Trying to be a model patient meant taking more than five minutes to drink what had to have been just a few ounces of water; even so, as Alex pulled the straw away from me, I felt a bit more like myself. "Thank you."

"Sure." He rustled around what sounded like a backpack and then returned to my side. "This might make things better," he said as he gently placed my glasses on my face.

The world immediately resolved itself, and I found that I was in a small hospital room with a tall window; the darkness outside it matched the clock over the whiteboard on the wall which claimed it was one in the morning. Looking down, I confirmed the sling before turning back to Alex. "Holy *shit*. How long was I out?"

"You came in unconscious," Alex said. "And went straight into surgery for your arm. I don't have all the details but from what Vas was able to tell me, the bullet nicked something important which is why you lost so much blood. You also had a rather nice slice taken from your thigh, too. I'm sure the doctor will give you all of the gory details."

I did the math and realized I'd been unconscious for close to fourteen hours. "Damn."

"Vas will be back as soon as he can," Alejandro continued. "I'll be here until then. We don't want you to be alone."

As I looked into Alex's tired face, it dawned on me he was wearing his poolside gear, telling me he'd come straight to the hospital after diving practice; the shading of stubble against his toffee skin underscored just how long he'd been by my side. Maybe it was the drugs they had me on, but I suddenly felt overwhelmed by the generosity of my best friend and his partner. "Alex," I said as my eyes watered. "I... I'm so sorry to put you both through this..."

"Hush." Alejandro leaned over and hugged me as best as he could considering I had cords running all over my body, then kissed me gently on the cheek. "You told me a short while ago that we're family," he said softly. "This is what family does."

All I could do was nod.

As he pulled back, there was a knock at the door; we both turned to see an older gentleman in dark blue scrubs standing at the door. "Sean Colbeth? I'm Dr. Rivers."

"Nice to meet you, Doctor," I smiled.

"I'm glad to see you awake and smiling," he said as he stepped over to the side of the bed. "How do you feel?"

"Tired," I replied. "Thirsty." I looked down at the sling. "Restricted."

Dr. Rivers chuckled at that. "As lucky as you were that the bullet didn't shatter any bones, it *did* do a number on the muscular tissue in your right bicep. I was able to repair most of it, but you have a bit of a road ahead of you in order to regain full range of motion."

Thoughts of not being able to swim must have been visible on my face, for the doctor continued before I could open my mouth.

"Your friends filled me in on who you are," he said. "With appropriate physical therapy, I don't see a lasting impact to your ability to continue to swim, competitively or otherwise. You did loose a lot of blood, though; we did a number of transfusions to get you back where you need to be, but we might need to top you off, so to speak. Regardless, you'll be taking it easy for the next week to fourteen days." He pointed to one of several red welts on my arm. "Most of the lacerations you received are minor and will heal on their own, save for two. The one on your thigh required six stitches to close, and the one under your eye required three. I've already booked you a consultation with a plastic surgeon for your face so as to minimize the scar, but I have to warn you, you're likely to retain some sort of memento of this experience for the rest of your life."

"I understand," I said. "Honestly, it's better than the alternative."

"Indeed," he chuckled.

"Thank you for patching me back up."

"My pleasure," he smiled. "Now, get some rest. If you behave, we'll get you out of here in a day or so."

"I'm dating a doctor, Doctor," I smiled. "I know how to follow orders."

"Good," he laughed before nodding to Alex and then withdrawing.

Once he left the room, I turned back to Alejandro. "Do you have my phone?" I asked. "I should call Suzanne—"

"I do," he smiled, "but there's no need. Vas called her right away and she booked the first flight she could to LAX. Suzanne will be here in a few hours."

I sank back into my pillow. "You might need to protect me," I said softly. "She's likely going to be a little upset."

"*More* than a little," Alex laughed, "if what I overheard was accurate in any way."

"Yikes."

"Don't worry," he said. "I have some experience in this area. She helped me with Vasily when he took that little swim in Windeport Harbor, remember? Maybe I can return the favor."

"Thank you," I smiled.

"Now," he said, "close your eyes and get some sleep."

"I've *been* sleeping," I protested.

"Sean," Alejandro said, putting a hand on his hip. "Don't make me call the nurse for a sedative."

"All right, all *right*," I huffed good naturedly.

Despite my best efforts to resist, once I closed my eyes it didn't take long for me to drift off into a deep, dreamless sleep. Considering how *little* rest I'd had during the course of the investigation, it made sense that my body had already been primed to try and catch up. Still, I could have done without landing myself in the hospital in order to accomplish the task. I could think of more than a few better places to relax — and one person in particular to do it with — that would have been far nicer.

The warmth of the sunshine streaming through the window of my room ultimately roused me; blinking away the sleep from my eyes, I saw that Vasily had replaced Alejandro in the chair by the side of the bed. His hair was sticking up in all of the wrong places, confirming he'd been snoozing at some point himself against an arm or the wall behind him. At the sound of my movement, Vasily's head came up; the tired smile and dark streaks below his eyes told me he'd not gotten much rest at all.

Standing, he came to the side of the bed. "Hey."

I reached for his hand. "Thank you," I said simply.

He leaned closer to me. "If you *ever* do something that *fucking* stupid again—"

"I feel like I said something similar to you back in December," I interrupted, "but point taken. I'll do my best not to get shot the next time I'm working a case with you."

Vas squeezed my hand, and I could see real fear in his eyes. "I thought I'd lost you," he said quietly. "It's not an experience I want to repeat anytime soon."

"Me either," I replied softly before nodding at the sling. "This is going to put a crimp in wearing my Chat Noir outfit at the convention, though."

"It might," Vasily smiled. "I have a hunch, though, that between Suzanne and I, we'll figure out something."

My eyes widened. "Why does that concern me?"

"You have a rather healthy sense of self preservation, I think," he laughed before getting serious again. "Which failed you miserably up there on that porch. What we you *thinking*?"

I tried to shrug, but with the sling, it came off half-baked. "I thought I could talk him down," I replied after a moment. "That's my style and it normally works. I didn't count on Daniel Houston being a cold-blooded son of a bitch."

"You've worked in Windeport too long," Vasily said. "I've run into that far more often out here."

"Maybe I have," I nodded before looking at my arm. "Or maybe I'm not as good as I thought I was."

"Don't be having a crisis of conscience on me," Vasily said. "Mine was bad enough; I'm not sure I could handle *yours*."

"I'm not," I replied. "What I *am* is pissed off I misread the situation so badly. I'll learn from it and adjust, though heaven help me if I have another case like this one."

"Amen to that," he breathed.

"Alejandro said you were wrapping up the case earlier," I said. "Want to fill me in?"

Vas smiled slightly. "There's not much to tell that you don't already know — or suspected," he began. "It's a bit of a jurisdictional mess at the moment, but I think Chief Gilbert has managed to keep me the lead on the case. Crime techs are going over Houston's place in Santa Ana and his office in Pasadena as we speak, but the early returns aren't favorable."

I smiled wryly. "I take it Houston didn't leave a manifesto on his coffee table for us to find?"

"No such luck," Vasily replied. "Gina's team is scouring the computers we located in both places, and I woke up my favorite judge to get a warrant for Houston's detailed finances. There's still a lot of digging through data left to do; I'm confident we'll have the breadcrumbs we need to close out the file." He smiled slightly. "Well, I guess technically *two* files, since we more-or-less solved the non-assault from ten years ago, too."

"Solving *another* cold case, Vas? You're going to get a reputation."

"Seems that way." He yawned and stretched his arms for a moment. "Speaking of, the last thing I did before coming back here was the formal interview for Isabella Houston."

I nodded. "Her life is about to change, isn't it?"

"Not as much as you would think," Vasily replied. "I had a hunch on that and — I hope you don't mind — I called back East and had Caitlyn pull the probate for Don Davies; we had to do some finagling with the lawyer for the estate — they hate being woken up at midnight, it seems — but I managed to get a peek at the will. The five grand Isabella has been receiving will continue until her daughter turns eighteen."

"Wow. Davies was in for the long haul."

"So was his brother," Vas yawned again. "That sweet beach house is *managed* by Frankly Holdings, but the *deed* was changed to Isabella Houston four years ago. It's been hers all along, though I suspect she was unaware of that."

I felt an eyebrow rise. "I missed that on the listings I reviewed. Then again, I didn't pay attention to the addresses enough to notice that she was living in one of Frank's rentals, either."

"There was a lot of data to go through and little time to do it," Vas said. "You would have caught it."

"Probably."

"For the record, Isabella doesn't seem to have been part of the scheme to kill Don Davies. The interview fleshed out more of her story; it's clear she had a vested interest in keeping the lie going with her family."

"Maybe," I mused. "But that lie led her brother into premeditated murder."

Vasily nodded. "I know she feels responsible; I'm also somewhat torn over whether to charge her as an accessory." He looked at me for a moment.

"Except for the kid," I said.

"Except for the kid."

I looked out the window and was a bit sad that all I could see was the other side of the building; I'd hoped for some sort of view of the Los Angeles skyline. Gunshot victims couldn't be choosers, it seemed. "You have to charge her," I said softly. "And the kid has a *true* father, too, doesn't she?"

"Looks that way," Vasily replied. "Xander's DNA matched the sample taken from the towel; I was already considering compelling a paternity test for Isabella's daughter as part of closing the case." He sighed. "California law is pretty clear in these situations, too. Xander's life is about to take a hard left turn."

I could see Vasily was on the fence about pushing forward on both of those fronts and couldn't blame him, but the actions of Isabella and Xander from a decade earlier had consequences that they both needed to deal with. It was part of the social contract each of us made with society; I had to admit, our need to enforce such norms was sometimes the crappiest part of our job.

"Vas," I said after a moment. "You've got to do it."

"I know," he sighed before smiling a bit tiredly. "What's a little more paperwork, right?"

A different nurse than the one I'd met overnight took that moment to breeze into the room; for the next few minutes, I was poked and prodded and measured in ways that didn't allow you to be self-conscious. As I sat there in the very drafty gown I had been dressed in, I realized at the end of the day, the hospital experience appeared to me to be the great equalizer. After taking my breakfast order — yay, Jell-O — she breezed right back out again only to be replaced by the amazingly gorgeous figure of my girlfriend, standing at the edge of the doorway. Alejandro was just behind her, indirectly confirming he'd made the run to the airport.

Suzanne took a tentative step into the room; despite knowing she had left Windeport in the middle of the night to catch her flight, she appeared to be perfectly put together. If I'd not seen the way her one hand was twisting the leather strap of her purse, I would have assumed she was just another attending physician meeting a patient. Taking another step, she paused at the end of the bed before looking to Vasily.

"Out."

Vasily nodded and silently withdrew, closing the door to the room behind him as he left.

We looked at each other in silence, the hums and beeps of the equipment adding punctuation to the tension. Suzanne was the first to break eye contact when she turned toward the window; still, the silence lasted another few moments before she turned back to me.

"What the *fuck* were you thinking?"

A million half-assed jokes flew through my mind, but I knew none of them would be as good as the honest truth. "I wasn't," I replied simply.

"Clearly." She moved to my side, and I reached for her hand.

"We talked about this," I continued softly. "People in my line of work *can* get hurt."

"I know we did," she replied curtly. "I have to admit, it seemed academic at the time. Now, having flown across the *fucking* country in the *fucking* middle of the night, it now feels all too real a possibility."

"I'm sorry to have done this to you," I said softly. "I truly am."

"Promise me you won't do something this *stupid* again?"

"I can't and you know it," I replied quietly. "What I *can* promise is that I'll be more careful moving forward."

"Shit," she sighed. "It's a damned good thing I love you, Sean Colbeth."

"I've never taken it for granted," I said with a soft smile. "Not for one minute. And if it helps me get out of the doghouse, I love you *more*, Milady."

A trace of a smile appeared. "You are more like Chat Noir than you realize," she replied. "Throwing yourself into dire circumstances with no trace of self-doubt."

"I wouldn't go quite that far," I replied.

Suzanne looked at me, the tears barely held back. "This is the *last* time you go to California — or go *anywhere* — without me, you hear?"

I smiled slightly as I pulled her toward me. "No arguments here."

Twenty-Five

Epilogue

There had never been a time when the Fourth of July had been a holiday for me, save for those few years when I'd been a toddler and hadn't quite yet discovered my talents in the pool. All through elementary and high school, major meets had tended to be scheduled around the holiday, forcing swimmers and their families to crisscross the country during one of the busiest travel periods on the summer calendar; it wasn't much better in college, either, especially once I'd become a fixture on the Olympic training circuit. Any thoughts that I'd finally be able to sit back, relax, and grill some hamburgers in peace and quiet once I exited the world stage and became a private citizen had been dashed the moment I joined the police force; if anything, the demands on my free time had become even *more* severe, forcing me to become extremely selective about what national competitions I'd be able to attend each year.

Being Chief of Police had, naturally, taken that madness and bumped it to an entirely new level. Mix in Windeport's surprising success as a cruise ship destination and it wasn't hard to understand the foul mood I found myself in three days before the next national celebration of the country's date of birth. Ensconced behind my battleship of a desk, I frowned at my laptop sitting off to one side of the empty space, then frowned deeper at the empty mug of coffee beside it. That the desk was devoid of anything other than my tech and omnipresent caffeine fix wasn't overly unusual; unlike the current iteration of our town manager, I had long ago given up tactile files and paperwork for the more efficient computerized systems we used in modern police work. No, what was really bugging me that overly warm July morning was the rather plump woman sitting in one of the guest chairs just across the expanse of my desk who had been talking my ear off for the past half hour. To hear her telling of it, she had suffered a major indignity after receiving a parking ticket from Officer Smart for, of all things, sneaking her late model Mercedes into the no parking zone just in front of Calista's Bakery.

Oh, the humanity! I groaned inwardly, trying hard not to roll my eyes as the tourist launched her third attempt to convince me she had been unfairly singled out. *Why does everyone think asking for a supervisor will get them what they want?*

I tried to ignore the deep ache in my bicep from where I'd been shot months earlier. While it had healed up nicely, there were still days when I felt it more than others; given the pressure I was under to keep the Village humming smoothly during the long weekend for the Fourth, I'd ramped up my workouts to try and take the edge off and had clearly irritated the injury. Looking back at my verbally rambling guest, I figured she had done a pretty good job on that front, too. It seemed best to ignore Suzanne's gentle (and repeated) reminders I wasn't as young as I thought I was any longer and therefore prone to needing longer recovery periods between sessions.

As if, I nearly snorted.

Glancing at poor Lydia, I caught her blanching at the rather salty language now issuing forth from our guest and decided the exercise had finally gone on long enough. Trying hard to hold onto what was left of my fraying temper – this happened to be the fifth such meeting I'd been subjected to that morning, and it wasn't even ten yet – I pushed my chair back from the desk and stood up. Given my over six-foot frame, the action had the desired effect, with the woman lapsing into something of a stunned silence.

"Madam," I said calmly, "you may pay the fine at the front desk on your way out."

"I will do no such thing!" the woman cried. "This officer---"

"Was doing her duty pursuant to Windeport ordinances and in accordance with the laws of the state," I interrupted. "You are welcome to protest the ticket, of course," I added.

"What the *hell* do you think I've been doing?" she asked.

Annoying me was the answer I wanted to give. Instead, I tried my best to don my retail smile. "Should you wish to officially dispute the ticket, we'd be forced to take this to traffic court and have a judge make a final determination."

"That's exactly what I want—"

"All right," I sighed. "Officer Smart, please take our guest into custody."

"Yes, Chief," Lydia said, catching the drift of where I was going. She stood from her chair and pulled her handcuffs from her belt. "Ma'am, if you could turn around---"

"What the *hell* is this?" the woman fairly screamed. "I demand you take me to see the judge!"

"And I am happy to do that," I replied. "Unfortunately, the court is in recess until after the holiday. Until then, you'll be our guest in one of the comfortable holding cells we have here at the station." I smiled slightly. "You might be able to see the fireworks from the window. I think."

I watched as the wheels began to turn for our guest. It took longer than I expected, but in the end, she seemed to decide spending several nights in jail over a thirty-dollar ticket wasn't worth the effort. "And if I pay the fine?"

"You'll be able to enjoy the rest of your vacation here in Windeport," I assured her.

She thought for another long moment. "Do you take Visa?"

"Yes," I nodded, "we most certainly do."

Without saying another word, the woman stood, turned on her heel and stormed back out of my office, with Officer Smart a reluctant few steps behind her. Sighing, I dropped into my chair, closed my eyes and started to rub my temple, wondering how early was *too* early for taking another Aleve for my headache. It would normally be a question for my girlfriend, but I figured the doctor in Suzanne would be alarmed that I'd already taken a dose that morning and opted to will the throbbing pain away.

Cracking an eye open, I caught the screen on my laptop and the email I'd been reading from Vasily; I frowned again, thinking that justice moved at its own pace out in California, and not always at the speed I'd have preferred. Still, six months on from the showdown at Isabella Houston's seaside retreat it seemed that things were *finally* being resolved, including the disposition of the Davies estate; despite Gennifer Davies-Benson being less than thrilled to discover what her father had done with respect to Isabella, she'd not fought his final wishes. And while Xander Vallejo had initially been rather shocked to discover he had a ten-year-old daughter, he'd nonetheless quickly taken up his mantle as the birth father, supporting Isabella and her child – *their* child – in any way he could. Vasily's parenthetical observation that the couple seemed to have rekindled their romance from a decade earlier was an unexpected but albeit welcome outcome. It was rare that happy endings came out of such tragedy, but when they did, I always felt a bit like they meant even *more* than usual.

"Sean?"

Looking up, I saw the figure of my cousin hovering at the open door to my office. Despite the Windeport Public Library being just next door to the Public Safety Building, it was rare for Charlie to make a personal appearance; more often than not, I was the one looking to escape from rigors of my position, and the beautiful facility that was her domain tended to be a perfect getaway. It didn't hurt that my cousin kept a flavorful blend of Kona coffee on hand in her breakroom. The look of concern on her face underscored whatever urgency had spurred her to walk up the street.

"Charlie?" I asked. "What's wrong?"

"You've got to do something," she replied breathlessly as she crossed to my desk and leaned toward me. "She's gone missing. I've looked everywhere – absolutely everywhere!"

A bolt of adrenaline chased away the headache and I immediately reached for the phone on my desk. "Caitlyn," I said brusquely when my ace intake officer picked up the phone. "One of Charlie's kids has disappeared. I want you to pull Lydia and---"

"No – the kids are fine," Charlie interrupted.

I felt myself blinking. "They are?" I asked blankly.

"Yes."

Feeling like I was in some sort of strange reality show, I waited foolishly for something further before finally asking what had to have been the expected punchline: "Then who is missing?"

"Whisker," Charlie said promptly. "The girls are frantic! We've looked everywhere---"

Carefully, I replaced the handset of the phone, inadvertently cutting off Caitlyn's queries. "Whisker," I repeated. "Your cat. Your *cat* is missing."

"Yes—"

Wondering just how much *worse* that day could get, I slowly began to bang my head against the surface of my desk.

Notes

^ Author's Note: As I get this question quite a bit, a quick primer – these pool dimensions are pretty typical at the college level as collegiate swimmers tend to compete in both short course (the 25-yard side) and long course (the 50-meter side). All Olympic competitions are done using long course (50-meters). I have a longer explanation on my website at https://chrisjansmann.com/pools-and-sizes/.

Acknowledgements

As I wrapped work on the second of two Vasily Korsokovach books, I felt the strangest sense of guilt over having left my original main character on the sidelines for so long. It didn't help that Sean Colbeth is more or less omnipresent in the back of my writer brain, constantly observing the world through that particularly unique perspective of a Downeaster who has seen it all. I decided I needed to make it up to him and wound up writing two books for *him* back-to-back, although it wasn't without a bit of pain on his part. (Honestly, it's not really my fault that Sean stepped into that gunfight at the end of this book, but to make it up to him, I figured out a way for him to spend a few extra weeks in California helping Vasily out with another case.)

For those of you keeping track, this book (*Duality*) feeds directly into *Bewitched*, but if you want to follow the entire character throughline, you'll probably want to read *Focus* in between the two. I've intentionally crafted each of the novels to stand on their own, so you aren't missing anything from the overarching plot if you happen to skip around.

I continue to be blessed by my dedicated core of beta readers who once more kept me on the straight and narrow. Eight books in and I am *still* finding ways to try and circumvent the rules I have established for my universe, and these trusty folks continue to step up and ensure that I remain consistent to these characters that we have all come to love:

Charlotte, Tristan and Lisa, aka the **Writing (S)quad of Doom**: As always, my ability to send out an SOS to the group at any hour, day or night and receive a number of thoughtful responses is more precious to me than I you can know. Thank you for continuing to be there for me.

Kristen: I know you have your hands full now with your growing family; that you nonetheless continue to lend an eye to my writing is something I truly treasure.

My wife, **Paula**: where do I start? As I write this, I've just finished work on my eleventh book – which is eleven *more* than I thought I would ever get done. Your quiet, calm, thoughtful support as I've worked through ever thornier plot issues continues to ground me and help me to move forward. With you by my side, I feel capable of sailing out into the uncharted waters of my next ten books. You remain my muse and my biggest fan, and there is absolutely no way I could have done this without you. My love is yours, always and forever.

-- C

October 31, 2022

About The Author

Born and raised in Maine, Chris has spent nearly three decades as an IT nerd, writing just about everything other than a novel in the process. That changed in early 2019 when he was advised to find a way to wind down from his day job; sifting through his options, he recalled a childhood ambition to become a writer and quickly found himself weaving an entirely new world from the comfort of his laptop. *Duality* is the fourth book in the *Sean Colbeth Investigates* series and the eighth overall featuring Sean and his best friend, Vasily Korsokovach.

Despite his love for the Northeast, the author escaped the cold for Arizona, where he currently resides with his beautiful wife and a Shar-Pei mix that insists on being walked regularly.

For all of the latest information, including hints about upcoming books in both series, please visit the author's website at https://chrisjansmann.com

CPSIA information can be obtained
at www.ICGtesting.com
Printed in the USA
BVHW030810271122
652760BV00045B/556/J